THE ACCIDENTAL GROOM

Book Two in the
Mad Matchmaking Men of Waterloo

By Barbara Devlin

#ownvoices

#ownvoices

ARE YOU SIGNED UP FOR DRAGONBLADE'S BLOG?

You'll get the latest news and information on exclusive giveaways, exclusive excerpts, coming releases, sales, free books, cover reveals and more.

Check out our complete list of authors, too!

No spam, no junk. That's a promise!

Sign Up Here

www.dragonbladepublishing.com

Dearest Reader;

Thank you for your support of a small press. At Dragonblade Publishing, we strive to bring you the highest quality Historical Romance from some of the best authors in the business. Without your support, there is no 'us', so we sincerely hope you adore these stories and find some new favorite authors along the way.

Happy Reading!

CEO, Dragonblade Publishing

Additional Dragonblade books by Author Barbara Devlin

Mad Matchmaking Men of Waterloo Series
The Accidental Duke (Book 1)
The Accidental Groom (Book 2)

Pirates of Britannia Series
The Blood Reaver

De Wolfe Pack: The Series
The Big, Bad De Wolfe
Tall, Dark & De Wolfe
Lone Wolfe

Dedication

For everyone suffering in silence. Know you're not alone.
I'm with you.

For Tanya Hix Lukas, a talented and amazing author, I miss our
girls' lunches in Weatherford. Thank you for sharing your
equestrian knowledge, which has been indispensable in this series.
You are a great friend.

Finally, as always, for Mike.

Author's Note

Dear Reader,

Survivor's guilt can be lethal to someone already suffering the trauma associated with PTSD. I speak from firsthand experience. It crept into my world in slow and steady waves, a festering wound that never healed, wearing me down like the evening tide, and I was powerless to fight it. The overwhelming impression that I would have been better off dead, as opposed to confronting the new future, so far removed from everything I knew, that condemned me to years of painful physical therapy, was almost seductive in its lure.

In the years following the accident that left me with a permanent disability and ended my law enforcement career, I struggled with the dark, persistent presence of guilt. The toll my accident took on those I loved almost killed me. Being forced into retirement by the department I served remains the worst betrayal of my life. A retirement plaque with the wrong initials hangs on a wall in my office as a stark reminder of what my sacrifice meant to my department. Whereas before I had always been fiercely independent, I began to see myself as a burden. Anger was eating me alive, and I was searching for an escape.

It was my husband Mike who intervened on my behalf, and he saved me. It's as simple as that. We entered therapy together, because I didn't have the courage to face it alone. I was terrified. I was drowning in misery that distorted my reality. I thought seeking help made me crazy. I believed the social stigma associated with mental health. Together, we embarked on a journey almost as excruciating as my injuries, sometimes engaging in sessions jointly and at other times individually. While I never directly thought about suicide, I'm convinced I wouldn't be here today if not for therapy and the support I received from those closest to me.

In this series, I never portray my wounded warriors as healed in the end, because that's not possible. PTSD cannot be cured. It can only be managed. Over the years, I've learned to cope—I'm still learning to cope. Every December 23, the anniversary of the accident that turned my world upside down, I allow myself to look back to the past, at the former version of myself, and remember what I was then. I mourn. But only on that day. To do more would send me into a downward spiral from which I doubt I would recover.

If you or someone you know is experiencing PTSD, I urge you to seek help. Don't spend your days suffering in silence. Reach out to someone. Anyone. Use the myriad services that exist solely to offer support. While the situation may appear a lost cause, I promise, there is a better way. You just have to take the first step, but you don't have to take it alone.

CHAPTER ONE

London
April, 1817

T HE PATH TO ruin often diverged from the garden of good intentions. Indeed, as a fanciful young girl, Patience Rosamund Wallace regularly donated her monthly allowance to charities in service to the less fortunate, because she always had plenty on her dinner table. While starry-eyed dreams of a home in Mayfair, filled with children, a loving husband, and laughter seemed certain in those days, she felt honor-bound to support the indigent who, by no fault of their own, had been born into tragic circumstances. Unlike most in the *ton*, she never scorned the lower classes, because they were people, no more or less. At the time, she never thought she would experience the pain and humiliation of poverty and hunger, firsthand.

The daughter of a decorated general who served Wellington at Waterloo, her life was supposed to be marked by invitations to the best balls, summer house parties, and at-home musicales, in search of a well-heeled, proper suitor. All that changed after her mother died of a fever while her father fought on the Continent, and the military denied the tributes owed him. Devastated by the slight, he spent his days drowning his misery in a bottle of brandy, subsisting on a meager pension intended to support the lone recipient, not an entire household.

Waiting in line at the grocery, a weekly ritual in misery and humiliation, she sifted through the items she hoped to trade for food and ignored the stares and whispers her presence always provoked. The customer in front of her collected her parcel and rotated on a heel.

"Lady Seton." Patience curtseyed as she was taught. "How are you this fine day?"

"Humph." Lady Seton lifted her chin and sidestepped Patience.

Her composed façade fractured, but Patience ignored the slight, even as the merchant, Mr. Ellis, cast a sad smile, and she summoned the courage to muster an amiable demeanor. Never would she let them see her cry.

"Good morning, Miss Wallace." The grocer, always cheerful, nodded an acknowledgment. "What can I do for you, today?"

"Hello, Mr. Ellis. I would like to procure some beef filets, potatoes, and any other bruised vegetable seconds you thought to discard, along with a sack of flour and a small tin of the jasmine tea." From her reticule, she produced a worn and tattered, lace-edged handkerchief, which she unfolded to reveal a delicate, gold filigree bracelet. "In exchange for this lovely bauble, if you are amenable."

"Hmm. Let me have a look at it." From his pocket, he pulled a monocle, which he positioned over his left eye. "Nice. Very nice. But the clasp is broken. I will have to pay to have it repaired before I can sell it, so I must deduct the expense from my price." He narrowed his stare. "This link is bent. I could offer five pounds."

"I see." She bit her bottom lip. "Will that cover the cost of the items I require?"

"It is possible, if you are willing to accept third quality cuts of meat." He frowned. "But I am afraid the jasmine tea is too expensive for your budget. You must economize. What about my proprietary blend?"

"Oh." She hesitated, because the local tea, a bitter brew, often incorporated untaxed hedge rows and other unpalatable bramble.

"Perhaps you could put the balance on account?"

"I'm sorry, Miss Wallace." Mr. Ellis shook his head and averted his gaze. "The last time I allowed General Wallace to buy on credit, it took me months to collect the sum."

"I understand." Crestfallen, she bowed her head. "I suppose—"

"Permit me to settle the debt." How well she knew that voice, given it often dominated her nightmares. From over her shoulder, the Earl of Beaulieu extended a card to the grocer. "Miss Wallace will take only the best filets and first quality items. And she will have the largest tin of jasmine tea, which she will take now. The remainder of her order is to be delivered."

"Yes, Lord Beaulieu." The merchant returned the gold bracelet, which she tucked in her reticule, and scribbled notes on a piece of parchment. After thrusting an oversized container of tea at her, he checked and rechecked the list and clapped his hands. A young assistant scurried from a back room. "Gather the following inventory and see that it is dispatched, at once, to Miss Wallace's residence on Gower Street, in Bloomsbury."

"Aye, sir." The stock boy nodded.

A chorus of whispers filled the establishment, and several patrons cast disapproving stares and pointed at Patience. Her ears rang and tears welled, but she refused to let them celebrate her defeat. Swallowing her pride and her shame, she rotated to face her nemesis.

"Lord Beaulieu, what a lovely surprise." She lied. Patience wanted to shrivel up and die on the spot. Bile rose in the back of her throat, and she feared she might be ill, as she tried but failed to ignore the critical audience to their exchange. "While I commend your generosity, I cannot accept such a gift. It isn't proper, and I am quite content with the purchases I requested."

"Indeed?" The insufferable soldier, with the guise of a fallen angel, too beautiful to be real, had the audacity to arch a brow and fold his arms, as though she acted out of turn. "All right. Then refuse my benevolent offer. Make a fuss and attract even more unwanted attention to your person."

With a huff of impatience, she grabbed him by the elbow and led him outside, to the pavement.

"You did that on purpose." She checked her tone and lowered her voice. "Why do you torment me? What have I done to you that you should embarrass me in public? You know what people will think."

"Do tell." The tall, blond earl, who bore more than a passing resemblance to the mythological Apollo, sported his customary patch, having suffered an injury to his left eye in battle. Dressed in black breeches, a pair of polished Hessians, a dark green waistcoat trimmed in old gold, a coat of grey Bath superfine, and a crisp cravat tied in a perfect mathematical, with a diamond twinkling at center, the hero of Quatre Bras captured the heightened regard of many a society lady, and more than one debutante swooned whenever he entered a room. Clothed in the garb of a gentleman of means, with an undercurrent of a dangerous predator, he reminded Patience of a pirate, and she suspected he was no less lethal. "What will they think?"

"Must I explain it to you?" How she longed to slap the smirk from his patrician face. Or engage in some other shocking behavior. "They will think we are...we are—"

"We are—what, Miss Wallace?" Now he favored her with a lazy grin, which harkened to his boyish streak, which she could never resist, and she wanted to scream. Or kiss him.

"That I am beholden to you." She shuffled her feet and tugged on her frayed poke bonnet, ruing her less than elegant attire. "That I am your special friend."

"Well, well. This is a welcome surprise." He chuckled, betraying not the slightest bit of contrition. "What a naughty mind you have, Miss Wallace. I should dearly love to exercise it, further."

"Lord Beaulieu—"

"Miss Wallace." He mocked her.

"Are you always so insistent?" She squared her shoulders.

"Yes."

"Haven't you the good sense to recognize that, after this

morning, we will be the subject of the latest *on-dit*?" It was bad enough the *ton* already thought the worst of her. Given her father's fall from grace, the only proposals she received were those she would never consider, those of an indelicate nature, because all involved physical intimacy while none included marriage. "People will whisper of inappropriate liaisons."

"So."

"Is that all you have to say for yourself?" She stomped a foot.

"Aye."

"You are incorrigible, and I will not encourage you. Were your best friend not married to my best friend, I should never presume to associate with someone so far above my social status. And it is doubtful our paths would have ever crossed but for our mutual acquaintance with Lord and Lady Rockingham." Patience tugged on her aged kidskin gloves, almost a size too small, as her flustered mind fought to compose a suitable rebuke. "Be that as it may, I thank you, very much, Lord Beaulieu, for the provisions, and I will see to it you are repaid in full no matter how long it takes. Now, I shall infringe on your hospitality no longer and bid you good day."

Dignity intact, she held her head high and made for home, until a vise-like grip locked about her arm.

"Hold hard, Miss Wallace. Infringe on my hospitality, indeed." Beaulieu tugged her to stand toe-to-toe with him, and she refused to look him in the eye. But the smell of sandalwood teased her nose, and she inhaled the intoxicating scent. Telltale warmth pervaded her flesh, and her heartbeat quickened. What was the strange sensation that swept over her whenever he was near, and why could she not quash it? "Where is your rig?"

"I have none." She wrenched free. It was too late when she realized what she said, and her thoughts raced in search of a clarification, one that would salvage the final shred of her pride. "That is to say, I prefer to walk."

"You prefer to walk, from Bond Street to Bedford Square, in a threadbare pelisse that affords no serviceable protection from the elements? You will catch your death in that rag." His mouth fell agape and he blinked, as if something occurred to him. Then he inclined his head and narrowed his stare. "And pull my other leg, Miss Wallace. You wish to avoid me for reasons I am eager to explore, at leisure."

"I will have Your Lordship know this pelisse belonged to my mother, and it is a treasured keepsake that I will thank you not to criticize. As for the distance, it is but a good stretch of the legs, and I am stronger than I look," she said primly. Of course, she would never admit her father sold the last of their carriages, along with the horses, to pay the note on the house. In truth, he bartered most of their belongings to dispatch his obligations and gambling markers, leaving her to scrape by on what remained. "I rather enjoy the time to myself, really I do."

His expression of incredulity declared he did not believe her. With nary a word, Lord Beaulieu dragged her toward the street corner and snapped his fingers. A resplendent coach, with an impressive coat of arms emblazoned on the door, pulled to the curb. Liveried footmen scrambled to place a small stool and stood at attention, as the temperamental earl unceremoniously tossed her into the pale blue damask-covered squabs. Padded velvet blanketed the interior walls of the sumptuous compartment, and a tin foot stove provided delicious warmth. Never had she enjoyed such opulence.

"What is your address?" Beaulieu asked. When she didn't immediately reply, he compressed his lips. "We can stand here all day, if you wish. I am in no hurry. But if you do not answer I shall dance a jig and sing a rousing rendition of my favorite regimental march, 'Hot Stuff,' attracting more societal notice, if you do not cooperate. I could remove some of my clothing to sweeten the deal."

"Gower Street, number ten," she blurted, because she doubted him not for an instant. Yet, pain nestled in the pit of her belly as she voiced the words, because she didn't want him to see where she lived. While the surrounding community posed a tidy collection of modest homes, her father had been unable to maintain their property, and she rued a broken windowpane and chipped paint. "But you may drop me in Bedford Square."

"Ten Gower Street," he shouted at the coachman and then climbed in beside her. "I will deliver you to your front stoop, Miss Wallace, safe and sound."

"Are you sure about that?" When she tried to move to the opposite bench, he grabbed a fistful of her skirts, as was his most annoying habit. "Unhand me, sir. I have no chaperone, and we are not related, so polite decorum, not to mention common sense, forbids us from sharing a seat."

"I care not for polite decorum and even less so for common sense, given both are designed to inhibit conventional male urges." He snorted and draped an arm about her shoulders, and she dared not venture a guess at what he meant by conventional male urges. "Besides, is this not more comfortable?"

"No." She stiffened her spine, ignoring the strange tickling in her belly that occurred only in his company. "Nothing about this situation is remotely agreeable. Are you determined to destroy what remains of my reputation? Will you not be happy until I am cast out from all good society?"

"What do you want, Miss Wallace?" She quieted and glanced at him, given his odd query. To her dismay, when she scooted toward the door, he stretched his legs and rested his booted feet on the opposite bench. "Are you like the *ton*'s plethora of blushing debutantes, in search of a wealthy husband, a healthy bank account, a set of chatelaine's keys, and a house filled with screaming brats?"

"Not that it is any of your affair, but I want to be loved, and I care not for a well-heeled man unless he loves me." She folded her arms. "I should rather be loved and poor in Cheapside than barely tolerated and in clover in Mayfair."

"Would you not prefer a life of comfort and luxury?" The coach slowed to a halt before her residence. A footman opened the door, and Lord Beaulieu leaped to the ground. Then he turned and lifted her to the pavement. "I know you have had offers."

"It is true." She turned to face him. "I have had more than my fair share of propositions, none of which involved marriage."

"And you will settle for nothing less." He rested fists on thighs. "You cannot be persuaded?"

"No, Lord Beaulieu." Patience shook her head. "There are some things money cannot buy, and I must preserve my family's good name. What remains of it, in any case."

"Well said, Miss Wallace." Beaulieu scrutinized her home, and he softened. "Reminds me of my quarters in Brussels, during the war. I was happy there."

"Would you like to come inside for tea?" She hugged the heavy tin to her bosom and prayed he would decline, because she had no furniture. "It is the least I can do to thank you for your kindness."

"Never touch the stuff." He wrinkled his nose, giving him an almost childlike appearance, and she laughed. It was the first time in their brief acquaintance when he didn't intimidate her. "But I shall accept your invitation, at a later date, if you will receive me."

"I can hardly decline, given your goodwill." Well, it was a reprieve, and she would find a way to avoid the meeting, because she couldn't bear him to discover the house had little in the way of furnishings. She sold anything of value to pay the servants and keep a roof over their heads. "Of course, I shall accommodate you, Lord Beaulieu."

"I look forward to it." In a single fluid movement, he grabbed her hand and flipped her wrist. With his thumb, he adjusted her glove and pressed his lips to her bare flesh, and she shivered. His sly smile declared he noticed her reaction. "Until then, lady mine."

Unusually heated, she stood on the top step of the entrance stairs and waved, as his resplendent equipage continued down the road and out of sight. With a sigh, she turned and opened the door, the hinges creaking as she pushed the heavy oak panel. In the foyer, a single wooden chair sat, and she draped her pelisse over the back and dropped her reticule on the seat.

"Hello." She walked past the closed entry to the drawing room. It hadn't been used in years. A clean spot on the rug marked the previous location of the antique long case clock that belonged to her grandparents. In the hall, she collected a candlestick, which held a single taper, and strolled to her father's study.

Once festooned with hand-tooled mahogany bookcases, rich tapestries, two Hepplewhite chairs, and his military regalia and medals, his domain now boasted naught but an old desk and a single overstuffed chair, with moth-eaten velvet cushions.

The drawn drapes closeted the chamber in darkness, and she squinted to survey the area. Slumped in the chair, her father slept. An empty bottle of brandy, toppled on its side, rested on the floor at his feet.

Patience retreated from the study and closed the door. Gazing at the worn rug and otherwise empty corridor, she inhaled a deep breath and leaned against the wall. "Oh, Papa. I must marry, or we will perish."

WHEN, AS A young boy, Rawden Philip Carmichael Durrant, sixth Earl of Beaulieu, planned his future, it never included a barbarous war with France, inexpressible violence, countless dead, and unimaginable loss. Oh, no. His aspirations tended toward the fantastical, positing a beautiful blushing bride, six children, no more or less, summers in the country, and evenings spent gathered in a back parlor as he read from the latest sensational novel. Yes, prior to serving in the British Army, Rawden had been a dreamer.

All those juvenile, unabashed hopes came crashing down on a

bloody battlefield at the crossroads of Quatre Bras. A captain in the British Fifth Division, he led the Thirty-Second Regiment of Foot in the First Battalion, of the Eighth British Brigade, under the command of Lieutenant General Sir Thomas Picton. The notorious leader at once venerated for his incomparable bravery and feared for his unpredictable bouts of uncontrollable rage often inflicted on friend and foe.

Fanciful visions of grandeur, including majestic regimentals with a chest covered in glistening commendations, drove Rawden's impetuous decision to purchase a commission in the infantry, against his father's expressed wishes, and resulted in the fateful charge that forever scarred him. In hindsight, he rued his rash choice to enlist, because war was no fickle amusement. The reality bore no resemblance to the diverting games he played with tin soldiers as an impressionable lad.

"My lord, I beg your pardon." Mills, the butler, stood at attention and rapped on the study door, which sat ajar. "I called to you several times, Lord Beaulieu. Are you unwell, my lord?"

"I'm fine." Rawden shifted in his comfortable, Seddon armchair and dropped the book he hadn't been reading. "What is it, Mills?"

"Lord Rockingham is just arrived." The butler clasped his hands behind his back. "Shall I install His Lordship in the drawing room?"

"No." Rawden stretched his legs and noted the afternoon sun reflected on the toe of his polished Hessian. "Bring him here."

"Yes, my lord." Mills bowed.

For a pregnant moment, Rawden returned his thoughts to his morning interaction with Miss Wallace. Patience. He adored the name, given the contradiction in her temperament, as there was naught about the woman that seemed indicative of that particular trait. Indeed, she moved with grace and purpose, an exhilarating combination, and he could not get her out of his mind. For whatever reason, she fascinated him.

"Beaulieu, my old friend." Major Anthony Bartlett, Marquess

of Rockingham, strolled into the study and straight to the opposite chair, whereupon he plopped to the cushions. "So, how are you? When did you journey to London?"

"A sennight ago, and I am in good health." Rawden neglected to mention the boredom and loneliness that blanketed his existence. The terminal ennui broken only by his stubborn attachment to a particular blonde-haired woman. "And you? How is your charming bride and your heir?"

"My son grows with each passing day, and he has quite overtaken the entire household." Rockingham's expression softened as he spoke of his firstborn, and a small part of Rawden envied his lifelong friend, more a brother than a close acquaintance. "And Arabella remains as handsome and feisty as the day I married her, but that is an observation, not a complaint."

"That is no surprise, because I should sooner see a leopard change its spots than Lady Rockingham alter her personality." He chuckled. "Care for a brandy?"

"When have I not?" Rockingham snickered. "Must confess I am curious about your summons and have awaited our appointment with interest and trepidation. While I was glad to receive your letter, the contents intrigued me. What troubles you?"

At a side table, Rawden lifted a crystal decanter. After removing the stopper, he filled two brandy balloons, one of which he offered to the man he had known since they were in short coats.

"Have you heard any rumors regarding my charge at Quatre Bras?" He reclaimed his seat and took a healthy gulp of liquid courage. "Have you come across any suspicious accounts, or exaggerated gossip, of my actions that fateful day?"

"Are we back to this tired song, again?" Rockingham rolled his eyes, because Rawden belabored the legitimacy of his citation from the moment it was awarded. "How many times must I assure you that whether or not you want to admit it, you are a hero. You singlehandedly dispatched more than fifteen enemy soldiers, saving countless comrades in arms, and bought Wellington the opportunity to retrench and hold the line. For your bravery, you were rightfully decorated, and no one can take that from you."

"You know that is not an accurate report of what occurred."

It began as any other day in the camp. The sun shone bright. The excitement of battle loomed. The men prepared their weapons for the upcoming skirmish. When the drums sounded, he advanced, leading his men into the fray, as he had on many previous occasions. But something happened in the midst of the gun smoke and cannon fire. Everything yielded to a haze of terror and confusion. When the fighting ended, Picton lauded Rawden a hero, but the truth lingered deep in his bones. Gnawing at his conscience. Tearing at his insides. Leaving him trapped in an invisible prison marked by guilt and remorse and living a lie he could never escape.

"And it appears someone knows my secret and my shame, just as I dreaded."

"What do you mean?" Rockingham furrowed his brow and accepted the letter Rawden pulled from his coat pocket. As the marquess scrutinized the envelope, he asked, "What is this? There is no sender address or identifiable franking."

"I received it a fortnight ago, before I left the country." Rawden recited the simple message, in silence, from memory. "Am I to be blackmailed? Am I to be disgraced? If I am to be punished, and I welcome it, I would know my accuser."

"But this is so vague." Rockingham studied the missive. "Some mysterious person with naught better to do with their time writes, '*I know the truth of Quatre Bras,*' and you panic? Are you sure it isn't just a poor excuse for a joke?"

"Who would write that to me?" Rawden shook his head and considered the possibilities. Of his close associates, none would exhibit such poor judgement in humor. "Would you? What of the other Mad Matchmakers? Can you fathom any of them pouring salt in my open wound, when they know how I feel?"

"No." Rockingham frowned. "It is in questionable taste, I will give you that, and I must admit there is a sinister undertone to the correspondence. Someone wants your attention. However, what have you to fear? You did your duty, and much was done in service to the Crown that I wager many regret. You answered the call and survived. No one could ask more of you. Whatever you consider the truth, it will change nothing. Men are alive, today, because of your courage."

"I'm not so sure about that." Rawden folded and unfolded his arms, refusing to believe his exploits merited glory and sought to change the subject. "By the by, what did you want to discuss? Your reply mentioned a rather odd and embarrassing request but didn't elaborate."

"I need your assistance in a delicate matter, and discretion is an absolute necessity." Rockingham crossed and uncrossed his legs. He perched on the edge of the seat. He rested his elbow to his knee and huffed a breath. "Can't believe it has come to this, but my wife wants me to act as matchmaker for her friend, Miss Wallace, and if you laugh, I shall gouge your other eye, because this is, in some respects, your fault. Must confess I am at a loss to identify a single viable candidate."

"Indeed?" Rawden's ears perked up at the mere mention of her name, more ethereal goddess than human, even as he ignored his friend's jabs. After all, it was his idea to form the Mad Matchmakers, the group of Waterloo veterans who came together to bring Rockingham and his bride to the altar. But surrender his Patience? When pigs flew. "Must she wed? I mean, is there some urgency?"

"Unfortunately, I concur with Arabella's assessment that Miss Wallace's situation is grievous, and marriage is her only viable solution." Rockingham rubbed his chin. "Are you aware of General Wallace's circumstances?"

"No, I am not privy to such intimate information." Rawden shrugged and fought to appear nonchalant, as he pretended to inspect his fingernails. Strange and utterly foreign emotions surfaced at the suggestion that his Patience was somehow in jeopardy. "Although I suspect there are financial difficulties."

"It is far worse than that, I am afraid." At Rockingham's statement, Rawden came alert. "General Wallace has a problem. At my bride's request, I made inquiries, and the talk among the ranks is that Wallace often got deep in his cups. That is why his cavalry mistakenly pulled back at Talavera, which cost us the victory."

"Bloody hell." No wonder Wellington withheld the erstwhile respected general's tribute. Now Rawden understood the extent of Miss Wallace's peril. It was clear he would have to act. "I gather that is why she receives naught but offers of an indelicate nature."

"How do you know that?" Rockingham narrowed his stare. "Do you enjoy Miss Wallace's confidence?"

"No." With a hand pressed to his chest, Rawden affected an offense. "I am much too engaged with the merry widows of the *ton* to shackle myself to one particular lady."

"Too true." Rockingham chuckled, yet did not appear convinced. "Then again, who is willing to commit themselves to a woman with such low connections?"

"Patience is not low." Rawden gripped the armrest of his chair, digging his nails into the thick fabric. Indeed, over many sleepless nights in contemplation of the delectable Miss Wallace, he could not identify even the slightest imperfection in her. "Her position is a consequence of her father's excess. Such shortcomings are not hers to own."

"Oh?" Rockingham cast a sly smile. "Miss Wallace has made you free with her name?"

"Patience—that is to say, Miss Wallace and I were quite thrown together during Lady Rockingham's efforts to free you from Little Bethlem, and I would have you know I observed the proprieties, in every exchange." All right, Rawden lied, but he would not allow anyone, not even a revered friend, to besmirch her character, because she was too fine a creature. "I will concede she presents an exemplar for the female sex, in much the same fashion as does Lady Rockingham, but I have no use for a wife. I would argue I was not meant for that sort of happiness, and I am content in my status. Never once have I had to exercise myself to fill my bed."

"Yet it is not the same, is it?" Rockingham sighed. "I will not pretend to understand why you continue to punish yourself for simply being human. If there is anything I have learned in the last year, it is that there is no real rhyme or reason to life. I will never comprehend how my father could have imprisoned me in that heinous asylum or entrusted my care into the hands of that evil Dr. Shaw, because I lack an arm, which he equated with insanity. But one thing saved me, and that was my wife's love. I endured because I knew, without a doubt, Arabella would rescue me, and she has, in every way possible. I would have the same devotion for you, my friend."

"Therein lies your problem. You found a rare gift, and you think everyone is owed the same prize." Rawden recalled that night in Weybridge, when his friend sacrificed himself, so Lady Rockingham could flee. Later, in London, after searching for more than a fortnight, she did the same for him, to gain his father's cooperation and Rockingham's freedom. It was humbling to witness, and he never forgot it. "Were I to wed, what would come of it? While I agree I could provide a comfortable living and a title, with all the benefits, I would end my unfortunate wife by taking everything she has to offer and leaving her with naught of myself."

"You might find love." Rockingham inclined his head. "Which is why you must choose wisely."

"What does that mean?" In that moment, Rawden imagined Patience by his side, making her declaration in much the same fashion as had Lady Rockingham. "Love is but a poet's muse, unattainable, impossible to define in the real world, while leading sane men in a fruitless endeavor they can never win."

"In truth, love is but a word. You must give it meaning." Rockingham averted his stare. After downing the last of his brandy, he stood. "Now then, I require your assistance in finding

Miss Wallace a suitable husband, and Arabella insists he must be a gentleman. Will you or will you not help me?"

"In the spirit of comradery, of course, I will do it." When hell froze. If Miss Wallace married anyone, she would marry Rawden. The instant he formed the thought, he dismissed it. Then he considered it again—and quashed it just as fast. "Besides, how do we know the lady is amenable?"

"She has no real choice in the matter." Rockingham tugged at his cravat. "My wife proposed a few prospective candidates."

"Oh?" Rawden fought to remain calm, because Patience had no equal, and she deserved none the less. "Anyone we know?"

"A few." The marquess adjusted the empty sleeve pinned to his lapel. He lost his limb from the elbow down, at Waterloo, after a mortar blast blew his horse from beneath him. "Wycliff, Rutledge, Audley, Lymington, and Sedgewick."

"That motley band of fools?" Rawden humphed in disgust. He would seize her before he allowed any one of them to have her. "Squeeze waxes, the lot of them, not to mention they are all second sons. Miss Wallace deserves a titled husband, a chap who can match wits with her, not some sixpence with little if any sign of intelligence who will stifle her spirited nature."

"I agree, but we must accept that any viable choice must be willing to wed what the *ton* has already declared, however unfairly, a toad eater." Rockingham jutted his hip and gave his weight to one leg. "Given I am fond of Miss Wallace, and she is my wife's best friend, I am duty-bound to be of service to her."

"Patience is no toad eater, and you may rely on me." Rawden ignored Rockingham's sly smile. For the second time, he considered making an offer for the fair angel. She would do well as his countess, and he could not avoid the marriage trap, forever. Still, a woman of her attributes merited only the best, and that fact disqualified him. "But she will have a gentleman of rank with an estimable fortune who would appreciate her unique gifts."

"Fascinating." Rockingham cast a lopsided grin. "One might think you describe yourself, and you could do worse. Miss

Wallace is strong. Indeed, she could be the making of you. Daresay, she could engage your heart, if you give her a chance."

"She is too wise to waste her time on me," replied Rawden. "And I have no capacity for such sentiments."

"Neither did I, when I met my bride." Rockingham turned and strode to the door. "Now, if you will excuse me, I must away. Promised Arabella I would take her for a drive in the park and to Gunter's for ices. But you give Miss Wallace some thought and compose a list of names, and we shall see who wins the lady."

"Aye." Rawden waved farewell to his friend. After Rockingham exited the study, Rawden lowered his chin and considered his prey. In silence, he allowed himself to consider a possibility. An exercise rooted in sheer madness. "We shall see."

CHAPTER TWO

A SINGLE STRAND dangled from the lace edged sleeve of the dated muslin gown sprigged in green floss silk and couched gold thread. With care, Patience tried to hide the pesky string, but it resurfaced like a bad penny. Frustrated, she yanked hard and opened a large tear in the material. Such was her life.

"Oh, no." Arabella set her cup of tea on the table and stood. "Allow me to ring for my lady's maid. Emily is a wonder with a needle, and she can mend your charming frock, in no time." She averted her stare and scooted to the edge of the *chaise*. "Of course, I would love to take you shopping and perhaps purchase new items, in fashion, for the Season. Will you not let me help you, dear friend? After all, you are like a sister to me. Indeed, we are family, so it is not exactly charity. Rather, I consider it a duty."

"You are blessed with a sly tongue, Lady Rockingham." Patience assessed the ruined fabric to stall for time, because Arabella could charm a sweetmeat from a babe when she wanted something. "Regardless of our longstanding association, for which I am eternally grateful, I cannot, in good conscience, allow you to undertake such an expense on my behalf. It wouldn't be proper."

"I will tell you what is not proper." With an upraised chin, Arabella folded her arms, and Patience steeled herself against an ensuing lecture from her stubborn but well-intentioned childhood chum. "It is neither proper nor fair that you should be forced to live in poverty, when your mother brought a sizable dowry to your father, and he squandered the lot of it on brandy and gambling. Daresay Lady Elizabeth must be rolling in her grave, to see the circumstances to which the general has reduced you. It is not proper for you to eke out a living on substandard fare I wouldn't feed to Anthony's hounds.

It is not proper for you to traipse about London in naught but secondhand clothing, announcing to all that you are brought to ruin, when you were meant for so much more. It is not proper for you to suffer the consequences of actions for which you are blameless. It is most certainly not proper for me, a titled noblewoman of means, to sit idly while you sink lower still, when I might prevent it. And stop calling me Lady Rockingham. I am Arabella, as I have been and always shall be to you."

"As you point out, I was afforded an excellent education, and I was raised to respect my betters. Whether or not you acknowledge it, you outrank me, and the dictates that govern our set require I show deference, Lady Rockingham." Patience stood and walked to the *chaise*, whereupon she eased beside Arabella. "It is true. This is not what I planned for myself, when I considered my future, but it is the reality I must endure, and I intend to make the best of it. Thank you for caring, but I shall find my own way."

"Regardless of what you say, I will not let you starve." Arabella clasped Patience's hand. "If it comes to that, you will move into the cottage at Glendenning. But I vow to find you a suitable husband, this Season, if it is the last thing I do."

"Promise me something." Patience wound her fingers in Arabella's. "You will not undertake any extraordinary measures on my behalf. Further, you will offer no monetary incentives to any prospective candidates. If I am to marry, I prefer a willing husband, not one motivated by profit."

"Extending financial support would preclude the need for a spouse, given you refuse to accept any assistance from me, so that makes no sense." Compressing her lips, Arabella pretended an offense, but she could never fool Patience. "Still, I should remind you that my marriage represented the culmination of a protracted negotiation that commenced before I was born, yet I secured a love match. Take heart, because all we require is a gullible man with deep pockets, and nature will do the rest."

"You truly have your head in the clouds." Patience laughed. "So, knowing you as I do, I'm certain you have composed a list of potential targets. What names do you put forth for my inspection?"

"Well, to be honest, I have not drafted a tally of possible suitors." Arabella tugged on her earlobe, a habit that always marked her reluctance to discuss the respective topic. "I had thought to first inquire after your predilections. Do you prefer tall or short? Dark or fair? Blue, green, or brown eyes?"

"I have no particular preference." Patience blinked, as an image of Lord Beaulieu, cocky smile and all, formed in her brain. His broad shoulders...his beautiful mouth...his arresting smile...just as fast, she quashed the unnerving visions. "But I half expected you to recommend the Mad Matchmakers. Are you not determined to secure wives for them?"

"Perhaps, for Lord Michael, because he fancies a bride and has been most vocal about it, but he looks upon you much like a sister, and that would not work." Arabella frowned. "As you know, Lord Warrington's affections are already engaged, but he steadfastly refuses to act on his desires, due to his diminished sight. The bloody fool believes his lady is better off without him, despite the fact she loves him. Lord Greyson is afraid of his own shadow, owing to his extended solitary confinement during the war. We must ease him into the idea of marriage, and I fear it would take too long to keep you from the workhouses. As for Lord Beaulieu. Well, Beaulieu is...Beaulieu."

Patience tried not to seem too interested.

"He is troubled," Arabella continued. "But I do not know the source of his agitation, and if Anthony knows anything, he has remained silent on the subject. However, it is common knowledge the wayward earl is a favorite among the widows, and I would never saddle you with that sort of embarrassment. So, as much as I adore the Mad Matchmakers, and you could not do better, excepting Beaulieu, we must set your cap elsewhere."

"As usual, you could strategize and orchestrate a troop movement for Wellington." Still, Patience clung to her girlish fantasy. Yes, Beaulieu traveled in circles beyond her reach, but that did not mean she couldn't dream. And what a dream he manifested. For a moment, Patience contemplated apprising her friend about her impromptu meeting with the brash earl. "And I should be satisfied with a second son, as long as he loves me, but I cannot be too choosy, given my situation is dire."

"Then we stay the course." Arabella tapped her chin and narrowed her gaze. "The Season commences with the popular Northcote ball. We should consider what you will wear. I had thought to loan you my blue gown, the one trimmed in seed pearls, because it would bring out your eyes. But we would have to ask Emily to add a ruffle, or some such, to the hem, because it will be far too short for you."

"Your blue gown?" Patience searched her memory and could recall no such garment. "Is this a repeat of the Little Season, when you commissioned a new wardrobe, for my benefit, and tried to pass it off as your used attire?"

"No, it is not." Arabella humphed. "I can assure you, with sincerity, the stunning creation was purchased for me, to my specifications. And I should love to know what gave me away, last autumn. I swore the modiste to secrecy."

"You are shameless." Patience laughed, and it felt so good, as she revisited fonder times. Carefree mirth was a luxury then. "But I know your objective was true. However, I have my mother's trousseau, and I shall make do, as must needs." When Arabella made to protest, Patience quieted her friend with an upraised hand. "Pray, I have naught left but my dignity, and I cannot sell it for something so frivolous as a new frock. I hope you understand."

"As much as I would love to claim otherwise, I cannot, because were I in your position, I should do the same. Still, I wish you would reconsider the blue gown. It gathers dust for want of use." The mantel clock chimed, and Arabella yawned. "Oh, dear. I beg your pardon, and I promise mine is not a reaction indicative of boredom."

"My friend, you just gave birth, and you appear in dire need of a nap." With a smile, Patience stood and turned to help Arabella to her feet. "I am afraid I have overtired you, and I should depart. Besides, I must supervise dinner preparations, else Papa will sup at his club, and that is an expense we really cannot afford. Since you ask nicely, I shall take you up on your most generous offer."

"Wonderful. I shall have the garment sent, posthaste, once Emily adds to the length of the skirt." Arabella rubbed the small of her back. "And you are right. I am spent. Now, I shall summon Merriweather to have the coach brought to the front door, and I warn you I shall brook no refusal. No matter what you submit, and I know you are made of sterner stuff, I will not have you walking about town, as if you wear the willow."

"All right." Arm in arm, Patience strolled with her friend into the oval shaped foyer. "Must admit no one spurns me when I ride in your rig."

"My lady." After hanging a coat and a hat on the hall tree, Merriweather bowed. "How may I be of service?"

"Where is his lordship?" Arabella inquired.

"In his study, with Lord Michael and Lord Warrington, my lady," the butler replied. "Lord Greyson is just arrived."

"Ah, yes. The Mad Matchmakers gather to strategize for the Season." Arabella patted Patience's hand. "Merriweather, have the coach hitched to take Miss Wallace home."

"Yes—er, my apologies, Your Ladyship." The butler appeared out of sorts. "Just this afternoon, the stablemaster informed me that one of the horses threw a shoe. Should I summon a hack?"

"Oh, no." Patience shrugged free and waved dismissively. "It is a lovely day, and I am quite fond of walking."

A knock at the door interrupted her grand show of independence.

"I beg your pardon, Your Ladyship. Miss Wallace." Quick as a wink, Merriweather opened the heavy oak panel and bowed, as he granted entry to none other than her nemesis. "Lord Beaulieu."

"Hello, ladies." Scrutinizing Patience, from top to toe, Beaulieu surveyed her like he knew how she looked in her chemise, and she shuffled her feet. "Lady Rockingham." The insufferable peacock clicked his heels. Then he gave Patience his attention, and she almost swallowed her tongue, given his smoldering stare. "Miss Wallace, always a pleasure."

"Lord B-Beaulieu." She sucked in a breath when he pressed his lips to the bare flesh on the underside of her wrist, and admired his thick blond hair. How unfair it seemed that a veritable devil traveled with his own halo.

"Well, this is a stroke of good fortune, and right on time." Arabella snapped her fingers, and Merriweather fetched Patience's worn pelisse. "Beaulieu, Miss Wallace requires a gallant savior to share a rig, because one of our horses has thrown a shoe. Would you be kind enough to permit my dear friend the use of your graceful equipage, else she is stranded?"

"I can do more than that." The audacious rake offered his escort. "It would be my honor to see your charge to her residence."

"That is not necessary." Even as Patience protested, Beaulieu dragged her across the threshold. In a painfully familiar scene, his footman placed a small stool, and the bawdy lord tossed her into the squabs, before anchoring himself beside her. "Lord Beaulieu, I must object to—"

"Ten Gower Street." After saluting Arabella, which struck Patience as rather odd, Beaulieu propped a booted foot on the opposite bench. When she tried to reposition herself, he grabbed a fistful of her skirt and rudely returned her to her seat. "Why do you always try to run away from me, when you know you will not succeed?"

"Lord Beaulieu, this is most improper." Of course, it was difficult to argue anything when he draped his arm about her shoulders. Whether or not she wanted to admit it, her day had just improved. But she could never let him know that. "I am not your—"

"You are not my—what, Miss Wallace?" With a most inappropriate wink, he gave her a gentle nudge. "My ladybird? My mistress? My courtesan? A man can dream."

So that was how he saw her.

"How dare you," she replied in a bare whisper. Were she a woman of quality, he would never speak to her thus. The simple truth hurt the most, and the shattered fragments of her former life came crashing down about her. His words cut like the sharpest dagger, and she realized he would never see her as anything more than a whore. A plaything to be passed about for his amusement, given her social standing. The girlish fantasy died in that moment, and she ached to cry. To mourn what might have been had fate taken a different turn. "Lord Beaulieu, I would ask you to maintain your distance, or stop this coach and let me walk home."

"I have offended you." His tone changed, as did his demeanor. To her surprise, he stretched tall and took her hand in his. "I enjoy your company, my dear Miss Wallace. It was never my intent to cause you even the smallest measure of distress, and I apologize. Let me assure you, those words do not come easily for me, and it is a rare occasion that I extend an expression of regret, yet I do so for your benefit."

"Thank you, Lord Beaulieu." The coach rolled to a halt in front of her house, and she accepted his assistance, as he handed her to the pavement. When she skipped up the entrance stairs, she started when he followed in her wake. After she pushed open the door, she rotated. "Again, I offer my thanks, your lordship."

"Where is your butler?" He inclined his head and pushed past her. In the empty hallway, he glanced left and then right. Before she could stop him, he peered into the vacant drawing room, and she wanted to die. When he pinned her with his stare, she gulped. "Why have you no furniture?"

"There is an explanation." She fumbled with the chipped mother of pearl button at her throat. "We just sent everything out to be cleaned."

Even she did not believe her paltry excuse.

"I understand." She feared he did, but he said naught more on the subject. "Well, I should return to Grosvenor Square, for my appointment with Lord Rockingham, so I will leave you to it." He bowed with a flourish. When he studied her face, he frowned. "I am not forgiven, and why should I be, when I have behaved like the worst of libertines."

"Pray, Lord Beaulieu, think nothing of it." For a long while, he stared at her, and something within her fractured. With his thumb, he caressed her cheek. "I assure you I am fine."

"Despite evidence to the contrary." He chucked her chin. "But I shall set it to rights." Then he narrowed his stare. "Why don't you call me Rawden?"

"Because it would breach the limits of polite decorum in a most grievous manner, and I was raised better than that." Mortified. Humiliated that he should learn the extent of her desperate circumstances, she needed to cry, but she would perish before doing so in front of him. "And I do not make you free with my name, because such conduct would imply an understanding of an intimate nature, which is not mine to own."

"And you are so very polite, are you not?" To her dismay, he grabbed her hand, pushed aside the cuff of her kidskin glove, and pressed his lips to the underside of her wrist, in a decidedly indelicate manner, as was his habit. A delicious chill coursed her spine, and she tried but failed to suppress a shiver, and he smirked. "But you betray your true self and give me hope, and that is something, Miss Wallace. I bid you a good day."

After sketching a mock salute, he strutted down the steps and leaped into his coach. As the rig pulled from the curb, the rogue blew her a kiss and waved.

Patience slammed the door shut and threw the bolt.

THE FOOTPATHS OF Mayfair were alive with activity, as the fashionable set made the rounds, to see and be seen. For Rawden, the *haut ton* manifested naught but deuced hypocrites, frowning on Patience because she had been reduced to poverty, through no fault of her own, after her father squandered his fortune, while the elitists inherited their wealth. Somehow, he had to help her, but he would go to the devil before finding her a husband. There had to be another solution, one he could endure.

"Beaulieu, do you hear me?" Rockingham cleared his throat, and Rawden shook himself alert. "Are you all right?"

"Er—yes." He took his seat amid the Mad Matchmakers, as Rockingham's marchioness referred to the group of Waterloo veterans, and crossed his legs. "So, what is the problem?"

"We were discussing Miss Wallace." Rockingham inclined his head. "You took her home, today, and my wife said you appeared quite familiar with the lady. What can you tell us of her situation?"

"I beg your pardon, but Lady Rockingham possesses an overactive imagination." Rawden cursed in silence, because he had only himself to blame. Earlier, he shouted Patience's address, unprompted, to his coachman, and he perched beside her in the squabs, for all to see. Although his actions were meant to ruffle the adorably imperturbable Miss Wallace, he garnered unwanted attention, and that must have set Lady Rockingham's tongue wagging. "Miss Wallace required assistance, and I provided it at Lady Rockingham's request. What is remarkable about that?"

"How did you know where she lives?" Greyson smirked, and Rawden's goose was well and truly cooked. "I am just as acquainted with Miss Wallace as you, yet I could not begin to fathom where she resides."

"I thought it common knowledge that General Wallace maintains a house in Bedford Square." With a shrug, Rawden mustered an air of calm confidence, until he noted Rockingham's cocky expression. "And you may wipe that smug smile off your face, else it could cost you a few teeth."

"*A-ha.*" Rockingham pointed for emphasis. "I knew it. You *are* interested in Miss Wallace."

"I most certainly am not," Beaulieu insisted, however half-hearted. Of course, he was interested in her. He wanted her. Ached to have her naked and splayed beneath him. Or bent over the side of his mattress and calling his name. Better yet, spread across the desk in his study. Oh, his mind supplied a host of lurid encounters. "I'll be hanged if I am."

"And you deny it." Lord Michael slapped his thighs. "Well, I am convinced."

"As am I." Lord Warrington laughed. "I may be half blind, but the intensity in his voice rings clear. Our usually stalwart Lord Beaulieu is smitten with Miss Wallace."

"I am not." Beaulieu checked his tone and folded his arms. "I merely provided aid to a woman in need, and Lady Rockingham asked me to escort Miss Wallace to her door. Who am I to refuse a simple charge that was well within my ability to fulfill? Any one of you would have done the same, or is chivalry dead?"

"You make yourself sound quite noble." Lord Greyson grinned the sort of grin that gave Rawden collywobbles. "But I have seen you expend half as much effort pursuing Lady Howard, and you wanted her, last year, so give over. Tell us about the increasingly intriguing Miss Wallace and how she captured your special attention."

"My friends, hear me when I say it is not like that." Beaulieu leaned forward and rested elbows to knees. He could see her standing on her doorstep, gowned in her frayed cloak, welcoming him with a warm smile that touched every part of him. "Patience—Miss Wallace is a very fine lady, but the general is another story, and she requires our support if she is to survive."

"She made you free with her name?" Lord Michael waggled his brows. "Now that is remarkable."

"No, she did not." Rawden tugged at his cravat and shifted his weight. "I misspoke."

"Sure, you did. Be that as it may, how bad is it?" Rockingham asked. "What do you know?"

"Dire, I am afraid. A sennight ago, I chanced upon her at the grocer, and she was trying to barter a bracelet for low quality food." Frustrated, Beaulieu stood and paced before the window.

As long as he lived, he would never admit he happened to overhear Lady Rockingham detailing Miss Wallace's usual schedule, on a previous visit, and their meeting was no accident. He could not explain what drew him to the oh-so-charming general's daughter, so he kept his attraction to himself. In time, he would grow tired of her.

"The house is empty. I wager they have sold everything, just to keep their home. And I suspect they have no rig, because Miss Wallace walks everywhere. While she claims it is merely her preference, I believe it is a matter of necessity."

"Bloody hell." Greyson huffed a breath. "It is worse than I thought."

"Indeed." Rockingham scratched his cheek. "I had my man make inquiries. Wallace defaults on debts from London to Waterloo, and his daughter pays the price. Arabella tried to pass off a new wardrobe as used clothing, last year, and Miss Wallace refused the items. Our every attempt to be of service is met with staunch resistance, so we must approach her predicament from a different angle, else she will fall."

"Then she is a fool." Warrington compressed his lips.

"Why?" Rawden fisted his hands. He would brook no criticism of Patience, because she was everything good and noble. "Because she prefers to earn her way? Because she is too proud to accept charity? I find her actions commendable."

"Then what do you suggest?" Lord Michael arched a brow. "Given such behavior, however estimable, will not fill her belly. We must identify a solution that satisfies Miss Wallace and saves her from a fate worse than death. The work houses are no place for a gently bred woman."

"You need not worry on that account." Rawden squared his shoulders. "I placed a standing order to be delivered every fortnight, so Miss Wallace will not go hungry. And I shall settle the general's debts."

"S-she agreed to that?" With a sputter, Rockingham blinked like an owl. "She offered no protest?"

"No, she did not, because I gave her no opportunity to object." Rawden lifted his chin. "I did what any reasonable man would do and simply commanded it to be so. What choice does she have but to acquiesce? After all, she is but a woman, and she will do as she is told."

"You can't be serious." Rockingham burst into laughter. "My friend, you may be a past master with the merry widows, who have naught to recommend them but cheap brandy, decent cigars, and easy friendships, but you know nothing about the sort of adversary Miss Wallace presents. I suspect there will be hell to pay for your good intentions when she discovers what you've done."

"What do you mean?" Rawden rested fists on hips and shrugged. "What can she do? I am the Earl of Beaulieu, and what I say goes."

Rockingham glanced at Greyson, who peered at Lord Michael. In unison, they collapsed into unhinged mirth. Even Warrington shook his head and chuckled. Just as they appeared to quiet down, they exploded in mass hilarity. When Rockingham looked at Rawden, the marquess sobered and elbowed Greyson, who nudged Lord Michael, who poked Warrington, and the group fell silent.

"While I am uncontrollably excited to provide sport for your amusement, I believe Miss Wallace takes precedence." Rawden clenched his jaw and tamped his temper. "If we could return our attention to the matter at hand, instead of wasting precious time, her cause would be better served."

"Ah, yes." Duly chastised, Greyson wiped a stray tear from his eye and smoothed the lapels of his coat. "Well, then. How are we to compensate for Beaulieu's lunacy and convince Miss Wallace to accept our assistance in finding a match?"

"Very funny." Beaulieu returned to his chair. "I see nothing wrong with extending my hospitality. And if I am able to keep Miss Wallace fed and clothed, why does she require a groom?"

"An excellent point, except one thing." Lord Michael narrowed his stare. "Only a husband can provide such support without damaging the lady's reputation, or are you planning to install her as your mistress?"

"Indeed." Warrington nodded. "Were you to continue in your charitable endeavors, society would presume a connection, and that would not bode well for Miss Wallace. Her family name would be forever ruined."

"My friends, I am nothing if not discreet." Rawden snorted. "Considering Miss Wallace's financial position, from what sort of man would she garner interest? Some addlepated, simple-minded fool with more money than sense."

"Sounds familiar," Greyson replied in a low voice and snickered.

"I resent that, Greyson. Really, I do." Rawden pounded his fist on the armrest of his chair. "Miss Wallace is a woman of uncommon intelligence. She deserves a mate every bit her equal."

"I took the liberty of composing a list of possible candidates." Greyson pulled a note from his coat pocket and smoothed the corners. "Of course, we cannot be too choosy, but I believe—"

"Let me see that." Rawden leaned forward and snatched the missive from his friend. As he perused the odd cast of contenders, he checked off each prospective groom. "No. No. No. Absolutely not. Strange? The name, alone, is sufficient reason to disqualify him." He shuddered at the mere thought of Patience in that oaf's embrace. "And Chudleigh?"

"Now, what is wrong with him?" Rockingham asked. "He may be a second son, but he made a devil of a fortune in the tobacco trade."

"She would have to live in the Peak District." Although Rawden posed perfectly acceptable objections, he feared his fellow veterans were willing to surrender Patience to anyone who could support her, and she deserved so much more. She merited a husband who would appreciate her. Who would indulge her every independent whim. "And it is likely their children would inherit his nose."

"All right." Rockingham inclined his head and pinned Rawden with a lethal stare. "Why don't you offer for her?"

"Don't be ridiculous." He huffed a breath and adopted an air of indignity, even as he savored the prospect of finding Patience in his bed every night for the rest of his life. But he destroyed any hope of happiness, on the battlefield at Quatre Bras. In a sense, he died that day. "She is too wise to fall for my charm, and I have no intention of marrying anyone. I am far too entertained by the merry widows."

"If you keep telling yourself that, you just might believe it by the end of the Season." Warrington closed his eyes and smiled. "Of course, Miss Wallace may be someone else's wife by then."

"Go to the devil." The Mad Matchmakers studied him to an uncomfortable degree, and he fidgeted beneath their scrutiny. The persistent *tick-tock* of the mantel clock echoed in his ears, driving him to the edge of some imaginary precipice. Rawden swallowed hard and rolled his shoulders. "Look, I know you mean well, but my soul is far too damaged for a gentle spirit like Miss Wallace. Were the situation otherwise, I might consider it. But all things being as they are, I cannot begin to contemplate imposing my shame upon her. However, we were quite thrown together during Rockingham's ordeal, so it is only natural that I care for her welfare. Do not mistake that concern for something more significant."

"What a curious account you provide." Rockingham compressed his lips. "Arabella says you tormented Miss Wallace, without mercy, and behaved in an ungentlemanly fashion in my absence."

"I can't help what Lady Rockingham claims. Perhaps she mistook harmless play between two individuals for something more momentous."

Still, her assessment stung, however true, because Rawden prided himself on maintaining a ruthlessly detached persona. It was the key to his success with the ladies. The longer he denied them, the more they chased him. By the time he yielded, which was really a trap, the women would do anything to please him. But Patience was another story altogether. Because he pursued her.

"I admit Miss Wallace possesses incomparable beauty. Indeed, she is one of the handsomest creatures of my acquaintance. I have already remarked on her unrivaled perspicacity. But it is not a simple matter of attraction. Unlike the rest of you, my wounds are self-inflicted. I owe a debt I can never repay."

"Are we back to Quatre Bras?" Lord Michael glanced toward the heavens. "I read Wellington's report, and regardless of your assertions, you are a hero."

"Don't call me that." Rawden flew from the chair and smacked a fist to a palm. "I, alone, know what happened, and I deserve no accolades."

"Do you imply Wellington lied?" Rockingham inquired.

"Who am I to account for Wellington's words?" In the blink of an eye, Rawden drifted from the secure room in Grosvenor Square, traveling the distance and time, journeying back to the battlefield. To that singular day when he yielded to the horrors of war. When he let go the reins and charged without mercy, leading his troops into the fray. When he faltered. When the dust settled, all that remained was immeasurable grief. He mourned the loss of those who died around him and suffered immense guilt and mortification that he outlived far better men. "I only know what I did and what happened as a consequence of my actions. I repeat, I am no hero."

"All right. You are no hero." Rockingham splayed his arm. "Will you at least stop torturing yourself for things that were beyond your control? We none of us here escaped unscathed, so you are not alone in your pain. What you must learn is how to move past your personal history and start anew. I, for one, can attest to the possibility of life after war. Trust me, it is there for the taking."

"Indeed." Lord Michael nodded. "I may have lost part of a leg, but I can still function as a man. Somewhere out there is a woman willing to overlook what I lack and marry me. When I find her, I will move heaven and earth to make her happy. On that you can wager your firstborn."

"You are so certain you will find what you seek." Discouraged, Rawden gazed at the oriental rug. "I know no such confidence. When my dishonor is revealed, no one will want me."

"Why don't you share your sad tale with us, and permit us to offer our perspective?" asked Warrington in a soft voice. "Many dubious deeds were committed in the name of King and Country. I doubt it is as serious as you claim."

"I don't possess the spine necessary to cross my Rubicon." And the motley band of wounded veterans were Rawden's only friends, so he wasn't about to risk losing them. "Rest assured, my ignominy is of my own making, and the resulting scandal, were my humiliation known, would forever stain my family name. Were I free of such encumbrance, I would take a wife, and Miss Wallace would be my first choice."

"So you have thought of her?" Rockingham inquired with unimpaired aplomb. "The lady piques your notoriously fickle interest?"

"I am damned, not dead." Although Rawden often found it difficult to tell the difference. "Make of that what you will."

"Believe me, we will." Lord Michael lowered his chin. "And we shall see what happens."

CHAPTER THREE

T HE GRACEFUL EQUIPAGE bobbled along the lane, and Patience relaxed and settled into the squabs for the ride home. It was a weekly luxury she savored after spending two hours at the Blue Coat Girls' School in Greenwich, where she volunteered as a teacher, instructing children marked by poverty in the finer techniques of embroidery.

"How far did you get today?" Sitting on the other side of the coach, Arabella rubbed the back of her neck and sighed. "My class presented unique problems. Little Alice Ann sewed her silks to her shirt again. And Penelope pierced her finger three times."

"I fared a tad better." Patience chuckled. "My students mastered the running stitch and the French knot. Although, sometimes I wonder how much use our instruction offers, given our pupils teeter on the brink of financial ruin and utter devastation. What good are decorative pillows and crocheted doilies when you are hungry and homeless?"

"It may not sound like much, but when you have nothing, it is something to master a trade. It is a means to survive. It is self-reliance." Arabella smiled. "Such skills may help them find gainful employment, enabling them to put food in their bellies and a roof over their heads."

"You are right." Patience gazed at the world beyond the window and pondered her own perilous predicament. As was the case with her young charges, she did naught to reduce herself to her hand-to-mouth existence. While her father had an unhealthy predilection for brandy and gambling, her mother indulged him to the point of penury. Yet it was her responsibility to either solve their problems or yield to receivership. "At least they are afforded the opportunity to make a living. It is moments like this I wish I hadn't been born into society. Had we been poor from the start, I should have gone into service. Although I once enjoyed the privilege of rank, I would rather I had never tasted the advantages of the upper class. Now I am penalized because we were once wealthy, and my only hope of salvation is to land an affluent husband."

"Life is not fair." Arabella lowered her stare. "Consider what happened to Anthony. His father had him imprisoned and tortured because he lacks an arm. As with the poor, my husband is often looked upon as lesser than others because of his war injury. We all have our struggles, my friend. It is important that we do what we can to assist those who cannot help themselves. And you are not alone. As I have told you on occasions too numerous to count, you have me, and I will go to my grave before I allow you to end up in a workhouse. And you have the full support of the Mad Matchmakers. How can you fail?"

"Including Lord Beaulieu?" Patience bit her tongue, because she never intended to ask that aloud. But all her thoughts seemed to circle back to him. "I mean, if he is as fickle as you say, I would not expect him to participate in the marriage mart."

"According to Anthony, Beaulieu wholeheartedly endorsed your campaign, which will commence with the Season." Momentarily distracted, Arabella picked a speck of lint from her ermine-trimmed pelisse and did not notice when Patience slumped her shoulders. "By the by, I secured vouchers for Almack's. Between that, the Northcote invitation, a concert at Vauxhall, a couple of nights at the theatre, and our event, we will find you a worthy suitor. And I am not done trying to negotiate additional invites."

"That is enough." Patience ignored the imaginary punch to

the gut in the wake of Arabella's pronouncement and considered her wardrobe, which would be stretched to the limit with that meager schedule, and bit her lip. She would have to wear more than one dress twice. Perhaps it was good that she didn't have to worry about Beaulieu. But she wanted to worry about Beaulieu. He made her feel naughty, and naughty never felt so nice. "Oh, if you are still willing to loan me your blue gown, I will take you up on your generous offer."

"Of course, we already agreed on that." Arabella tapped her cheek and then snapped her fingers. "What about the burgundy satin trimmed in old gold and pink rosettes? To be honest, I have never favored that frock, but I think it would look stunning with your hair."

"I don't remember that one." Patience probed her memory and shook her head. "Have I seen it?"

"I'm not sure." Arabella narrowed her stare and wrinkled her nose. "It has always been too long on me, and the last time I wore it, to the Howards' *fête champêtre* last year, I tripped on the hem. I should have had it altered, but I fear it would have destroyed the intricate embroidery that extends to the demi-train. It is so pretty, and you would be doing me a favor if you take it."

"Well, I am so inclined, if you insist." If Patience availed herself of her friend's generosity, she would only have to remake two of her mother's garments. "But I will return them as soon as the Season ends."

"I will make you a bargain." Arabella leaned forward. "You take the gowns, and in future if I have need of them, I shall ask for them."

"Agreed." Patience nodded once.

The coach pulled to the curb and slowed to a stop. A footman opened the door and stood at attention.

"Wonderful." Arabella cocked her head and grinned. "I shall have them delivered, posthaste."

"Thank you." Patience scooted to the edge of the bench, and the footman handed her to the pavement. "I will see you on

Friday."

"As always, I look forward to it." Arabella yawned and covered her mouth. "Oh. Naptime for me."

"Get some rest." Patience retreated to the top step of the entrance stairs and waved as the Rockingham coach pulled into the road. She turned on a heel and opened the door. As she crossed the threshold, she noticed an expensive crystal vase filled to overflow with lush red roses.

"Good afternoon, Miss Wallace." Abigail, the housekeeper, dipped her chin. "How was your visit to the school?"

"As well as can be expected." Patience shrugged free of her pelisse and draped it on the back of the chair, which functioned as a hall tree. Then she removed her gloves. "Pray, tell me my father did not purchase the flowers."

"No, ma'am. They are for you." Abigail handed Patience an envelope. "And there is a card."

"Indeed?" Patience flinched when she noted the waxed seal and a telltale letter B. "Thank you, Abigail. That will be all."

"Shall I put the bouquet on your bedside table?" The housekeeper toyed with a velvety petal. "They are lovely, Miss Wallace. Whoever sent them must be quite fond of you."

"Please, do so, although I believe it is a simple misunderstanding." Patience unfolded the missive and read the contents.

My Dear Miss Wallace,

Please accept this humble token, which pales in comparison to your beauty, as an apology, given my unforgiveable behavior. Know that I never meant to insult you. While I have no excuse, suffice it to say I enjoy your company. You remind me of my old self, before I went to war. In future, I shall try to contain such youthful expressions.

Faithfully Yours,
Beaulieu

For a while, she simply stood there and reread the dispatch, wondering what to make of the curious correspondence. A sharp knock interrupted her thoughts, and she glanced at Abigail.

"I will get it, ma'am." The housekeeper turned the bolt and opened the heavy oak panel. "Yes, sir?"

"A delivery for Miss Patience Wallace." A messenger handed Abigail a beribboned tin, which she passed to Patience. When she tried to offer the lad a few pence, he shook his head. "I have been compensated for my services. Good day."

"What now?" Patience tugged on the emerald strip of satin, which loosened a familiar looking card nestled beneath, as Abigail closed the door.

"How fancy, ma'am." The housekeeper peered at the parcel. "*Billets-doux*, I daresay."

"It is no such thing." At least, Patience prayed Lord Beaulieu would not tempt her so cruelly. She lifted the lid and discovered beautiful strawberries, lush and ripe, almost too perfect to be real, nestled in a bed of white cotton. "Oh, my."

"Miss Wallace, you have an admirer." The bespectacled, grey-haired woman chuckled. "And it is about time, if I do say so, myself."

"Will you have one?" Patience offered a tempting treat.

"No, thank you, ma'am." Abigail winked. "Too sweet for my blood, but I should love to know what is in the card."

"Ah, yes." Dreading what she might find, Patience broke the wax seal, which clearly identified the sender.

A sweet for a sweet.

~Beaulieu

"Well?" Abigail rocked on her heels. "Do tell, ma'am."

"It is from a friend." Patience inhaled the decadent fruity aroma, and her mouth watered. She sampled a juicy morsel, savoring the delectable tangy flavor, as it harkened to fond memories of summers past, and hummed her appreciation. Then she gave the tin to the housekeeper. "These are heavenly, and I would have you see to it that the cook and the footman get one."

"You are too generous, Miss Wallace." Abigail smiled. "Then again, you always were as a child."

"It is the least I can do, given you and the other staff have been so understanding about the back wages." Patience swallowed hard, because she hadn't been able to pay the domestics in three months, due to her father's excess spending. "I promise, I have economized enough to fulfill some of what we owe you, in a fortnight."

"I beg your pardon, ma'am, but there must be some mistake." Abigail furrowed her brow. "Miss Wallace, we received the sum of our salaries, along with a substantial advance, with the most recent delivery from the grocer."

"What?" The walls seemed to collapse on her from every angle, and Patience swayed. "And to what order do you refer?"

"The one we received on Monday." Abigail closed her eyes. "Oh, it was so nice to enjoy a decent roast for dinner, ma'am. Thank you, for thinking of us."

"Of course." Patience set the tin of strawberries on the chair and donned her pelisse and gloves. She knew, without doubt, who sent the food and made the payment. "Abigail, I am going out, but I shall return in time to help prepare the evening meal."

"All right, ma'am." The housekeeper hefted the vase of roses. "Mind the hour, though. I do not like you walking the streets of London after dark."

Riding a crest of high dudgeon, Patience skipped down the entrance steps and crossed Gower Street. After traversing Store Street, she dodged a few hacks and sucked in a breath, as she rushed along Tottenham Court Road. Furious by the time she reached Goodge Street, she hurried to Mortimer.

As she approached Four Cavendish Square, with its red-bricked façade, urn-topped rails, and Portland stone tapered columns framing the grand entrance, the front door opened, and a well-dressed lady emerged. Patience halted in her tracks, when Lord Beaulieu bent his head and kissed the woman's cheek. He escorted the interloper to a resplendent coach and waved a farewell as the equipage pulled from the curb.

Her ears rang, and the earth seemed to pitch and roll beneath her feet, as she came face to face with the reality of her circumstances. He would never be hers. She feared she might swoon, as her lungs seemed to deflate in her chest, and she rotated and retraced her steps. She made it to the corner when her tormentor called her name.

"Miss Wallace?"

She pretended not to hear him, as she neared Mortimer Street and quickened her pace.

"Miss Wallace, wait." Beaulieu caught her as traffic stopped her flight. "Miss Wallace?" Beaulieu twirled her about, and he searched her eyes as a single traitorous tear betrayed her heartbreak. With his thumb he caressed the curve of her jaw. "Patience, what is wrong?"

"Nothing." She hiccupped and tried to free herself, but he tightened his grip and steered her toward his home. "Please, let me go."

"Why?" He dragged her up the steps. "You came to see me, did you not?"

"Yes—no." She wrenched hard, and he shoved her across the threshold. In the stately foyer, he collected her pelisse. "Oh, I don't know."

"Liar." To the butler, Beaulieu said, "We will be two in the drawing room. Jasmine tea for the lady, and I will take a brandy. Have the coach hitched, and when next I ring, have it brought forth."

"Very good, your lordship." The manservant bowed.

The rake ushered her into a stunning chamber, the *pièce de resistance* of which sat at the center of the rear wall. A magnificent fireplace featured an over-mantel comprised of tiles embossed with cinquefoils in the Tyrolean tradition. The surrounding décor boasted pale blue damask and velvet textiles, with the five-petalled alpine flower motif continued throughout, and matching wall coverings accented with mahogany paneling. The impressive residence served to contrast with and draw attention to her pitiful attire, reminding her that she did not belong in his world.

"Really, Lord Beaulieu, I should depart." When she attempted a grand exit, she caught the toe of her worn kidskin slipper on the thick Aubusson rug and landed in his ready embrace.

Their noses mere inches apart, he met and held her stare. The warmth of his breath teased her flesh, and he licked his beautiful lips. The subtle scent of sandalwood mixed with a hint of bergamot teased her senses, and she inhaled deeply. For a moment, she thought he might kiss her. Prayed he would kiss her.

Instead, much to her disappointment, he retreated and set her at arm's length.

"Now, have a seat and tell me why you are here." He led her to the sofa and eased beside her. "Has it something to do with the gifts I sent?"

"The gifts?" She blinked and organized her thoughts. "Ah, yes. The roses and the strawberries. They are too much."

"Tsk, tsk, Miss Wallace. Where are your manners?" He sniffed. "I believe it is customary to extend an expression of gratitude in such circumstances."

"Gratitude?" She folded her arms and humphed. "You paid our servants' wages and sent groceries. You deliberately put me in your debt, when I have naught to offer in return."

"In that I am guilty." He grinned unabashedly. "And *you* owe me nothing. Your father is obligated to me, and I shall collect when I am ready."

"My father?" She snorted. "You should sooner draw blood from a turnip. It is no secret he possesses little of any value. Why, we scarcely manage to survive on his military pension. How do you expect him to repay you?"

"As I already said, he has something I want." Beaulieu signaled the butler, who carried a tray laden with a teapot, a cup and saucer, a plate of shortbread, and a crystal balloon of brandy, which he placed on a table. To her surprise, the wayward earl dismissed the servant with a wave and poured her a decent portion of the steaming brew, which he held for her. "My dear Miss Wallace, I believe you prefer the jasmine."

"I suppose it is no coincidence you just happen to have my favored blend?" She inhaled the intoxicating aroma and took a sip.

"I am nothing if not prepared." He reclined against a plush pillow, like a great lion surveying its next meal. "Now then, perhaps you will tell me why you were crying when I found you?"

To her infinite embarrassment, Patience choked on her tea.

The scoundrel had the nerve to provide assistance, when he patted her back.

"I was *not* crying." Again, she collapsed in a coughing fit.

"All right." He smirked as she continued to hack. "But tell me why you were, all the same."

"I will do no such thing." She wiped her brow and composed herself. "The wind blew something in my eye. And I was on my way home and did not wish to intrude on your visit with your guest."

"My guest? You mean my sister?" He frowned and then leaned close and smiled his wolfish smile. Gooseflesh covered her from top to toe. "You are jealous, Miss Wallace."

"Sister?" She shook herself. "And I am not."

"Yes, you are, and I find it an unutterably arresting development. What a delight you are, but I am not too surprised, given women find me irresistible." He winked, and she gave vent to an unladylike groan of frustration. "However, you may put your mind at ease, because she is, indeed, my younger sibling, just arrived in London for the Season. It might interest you to know she is quite anxious to make your acquaintance."

"You spoke to your sister about me?" Patience inquired in a high-pitched tone that conveyed far too much excitement, and she gathered her wits. "That is to say, I am surprised you bothered to mention me, given I do not signify."

"I beg to differ." He stretched his arm along the back of the sofa and toyed with a curl that dangled at the nape of her neck. "Are you feeling better?"

"I am fine." The fire in the hearth cast shadows on the rug, and she noted the time as she drained her cup. "But the hour grows late, and I am expected at home. I really should go."

"Then I shall ring for the coach." Her devastatingly handsome antagonist stood and strolled to the bellpull. Oh, to have such charisma. "And before you protest, I will escort you to your door, so you may spare me your complaints."

"Does anyone ever say no to you?" she inquired, with hands on hips. How she would love to argue with the arrogant nobleman, but that would be an egregious breach in decorum.

"No." With care, he drew her to stand and then steered her into the foyer, where she remained consciously aware of his palm pressed to the small of her back. "But I give you leave to try, if it will preserve your sense of independence."

"Why bother with pretense?" To her dismay, he draped her pelisse about her shoulders and secured the chipped button at her throat. At the moment, pride was an emotion she could ill afford, so she would allow him a victory, however small and misplaced. "And I care not for the ruse, when I am my own person, regardless of what you do for my father. You would do well to remember that. Now, shall we go?"

THE DISCONCERTING LETTER arrived shortly before noon. It bore four pedestrian words when considered on their own.

You are no hero.

Taken as a whole, the sentence posed a malevolent warning Rawden would do well not to ignore. Still, the nondescript stationery, identical to the first note, offered no clue as to the sender. He had no idea who threatened to expose him as a fraud and, therefore, could not guard against a surprise attack. He knew not where danger lurked, and it was eating him alive.

"Beaulieu, you look as if you have seen a ghost." Rockingham plopped in the leather high back chair perched opposite Rawden, in a private room at White's. "Or your last importuning mistress."

"Must you make sport of everything?" Rawden shook himself alert and signaled to the waitstaff, who nodded. "I know you don't take my mysterious adversary seriously, but I do."

"If I am not concerned, it is because I know what happened that day." Rockingham shifted in his seat and crossed his legs. Then he met Rawden's stare. "I spoke with Kempt's *aide de camp*, the night before Waterloo. He told me everything."

"Then you know my shame." In some ways, it was a relief that his friend knew the truth. Still, he suffered the poignant sting of ignominy. The servant arrived and handed Rawden and Rockingham a balloon of brandy. "I am no hero, and I deserve to be humiliated for my dishonorable actions at war."

"Quite the opposite." The marquess took a healthy draw of the amber intoxicant and compressed his lips. "Tell me, in which skirmishes did the Thirty-Second see action?"

"Well, we first deployed to Denmark and fought at Copenhagen. Then we landed in Portugal, under Wellington's command, when he was still known as General Wellesley. There, we clashed at Roliça and Vimeiro, where I promoted to second lieutenant." Rawden sifted through the fragments of his memory and cringed at some of the more brutal reflections. As he recalled his military history, in sharp detail, he flinched. "Under the direction of Moore, the regiment participated in the retreat to Corunna, after which we returned to England, where we were promptly assigned to the Walcheren Campaign, and I made lieutenant."

"But you didn't stop there." Rockingham arched a brow. "You could have gone home, which your parents would have preferred, but you did not surrender the cause."

"No. And my parents never supported my commission, so

their wishes never factored in my decision to fight." Rawden rubbed his chin. The mere suggestion that he quit the field inspired naught but disgust. "We were the Thirty-Second, and I had to lead my men. After malaria cut down a number of our troops, we were supplied reinforcements and sent back to Spain, where we prevailed at Salamanca and pursued Napoleon's army into France, confronting the enemy at the Pyrenees, Nivelle, Nive, and Orthez. During that time, I received a battlefield commission to captain. The regiment was reassigned to Major General Kempt and dispatched to Quatre Bras, where we arrived late in the afternoon, just in time to halt Boney's advance, at great cost. We counted but five-hundred-and-three survivors, two days later when we charged at Waterloo."

"Taking into account all that, and the fact that you led your men while freshly wounded, do you still wish to argue whether or not you are a hero?" Rockingham snorted. "If so, pull my other leg, friend. And, to borrow from my bride, I am rather more than seven."

"How can you say that, given you are aware of the facts?" Rawden replayed the sad events in his mind and closed his one good eye. "I should have been branded a coward and shipped back to London, in disgrace, to be court-martialed."

"A *coward*?" Rockingham scoffed and slapped his thigh. "That is quite enough, brother. While we all tell ourselves lies to survive, in this matter you do yourself a grave disservice, and you have spun me to the length with your gross exaggerations. Stop wallowing in self-pity and take life by the reins. As you once said to me, when I resisted marriage to Arabella, you have a devilishly handsome woman in need of a husband, and you are interested—don't try to deny it. Why have you not offered for her?"

"Perhaps I would have, had not some random villain inserted himself into my world." Yes, Rawden knew it was a pitiful excuse, but the truth was he was frightened. Terrified of what Patience made him feel. As if he could conquer the world. As if he might actually gain the future he desperately desired. As if anything were possible. But he never planned to be a groom. He knew not if he possessed the courage to move forward like Rockingham had with his bride. "Yes, I want her. There. I said it. Are you happy now?"

"I am." Rockingham chuckled but sobered. "Now, if you would only avail yourself of the Mad Matchmakers, the very group you formed to bring me to the altar, you might find the same happiness I enjoy, especially in light of recent revelations."

"What revelations?" Rawden pretended indifference.

"Beaulieu, my man has heard reports of an alarming nature, the grievousness of which I have not shared with Lady Rocking-ham for fear it would break her. It seems General Wallace got deep in his cups at Lady Dutton's evening entertainment. Heavily in debt after one too many games at the hazard table, he did something unforgiveable." Rockingham's throat worked almost violently, and Rawden failed to suppress a soupçon of dread. "I can scarcely bring myself to say it, but...he attempted to barter Miss Wallace's...that is, he tried to wager her...bride's prize."

"He *what*?" Enraged, he slammed a fist to the armrest.

Trembling with unspent fury, everything inside Rawden railed against the implication that his lady, his salvation, his own private angel could be reduced to prostitution by the man charged with guarding her. He tried to compose a calm rebuke, but he struggled to draw breath. He would never allow it. He would fight for her. Would defend her to his death. Anything was preferable to Patience working as a doxy.

Even if it meant marriage to an emotionally wounded soldier.

"The situation is intolerable, and we are running out of time if we wish to save Miss Wallace." Rockingham huffed in unveiled frustration, and Rawden had more than a sneaking suspicion he knew what his friend was about to suggest. "Unless you can recommend another course of action? One that would spare Miss Wallace a life of humiliation, despair, and utter ruin?"

At last, Rawden gave himself permission to think the un-thinkable.

"Suppose—just suppose I put forth an alternative? What if the lady is not amenable?" Rawden had yet to extend a proposal, but he suspected Patience would not cooperate, and he knew not how he would handle her rejection. Actually, that wasn't true. Her refusal would kill him. "If she will not have me, what then?"

"You underestimate Miss Wallace's regard." That caught Rawden's consideration, and he scooted forward, resting elbows to knees. Rockingham smiled his cat-that-ate-the-canary smile. "Given I have snared your attention, my wife tells me Miss Wallace inquired after your potential as a prospective suitor."

"She didn't." Rawden checked his tone and his stance. Inhaling a calming breath, as he teetered on the brink of claiming something he desperately wanted, he eased back in his chair. Adopting an air of nonchalance, if that were actually possible, he shrugged and haphazardly asked, "So, what did she say?"

"Oh, give over." Rockingham burst into laughter, and Rawden wanted to throttle his friend. "Are you aware Miss Wallace accepted the gowns you commissioned at Arabella's direction?"

"Indeed?" What a glorious prospect. The knowledge worked on him in ways he could not have anticipated, and he was instantly aroused. If only Patience were conscious of the fact that he paid for every stitch of clothing that garbed her enchanting figure, that rested next to her sumptuous skin, when she attended the Season's galas. "How did Lady Rockingham fool Miss Wallace, in light of last autumn's debacle?"

"Well, Arabella explained that she did not purchase the frocks. Rather, they were made to her specifications, which is true." Rockingham snorted. "My wife cannot lie with any semblance of self-possession, and that is why Miss Wallace discovered the first ruse. However, I am not so convinced she would object, given her attachment to you."

"Again, you reference a devotion I am not half so certain exists, and I have spent time alone in her company." But Rawden coveted the possibility. He was imbued with hope. Drenched in it. He needed someone to believe in, and Miss Wallace suited his purpose. One way or another, he had to have her, and he was rapidly beginning to accustom himself to that certainty, given her father's reprehensible betrayal. But in what capacity, because he never planned to wed, in light of his dubious past? How could he reconcile his personal history with his future? That depended on Patience. "On what do you base your assertions?"

"I have seen how she looks at you when she thinks you unaware." Rockingham averted his stare and adopted a wistful expression, oblivious to the seemingly innocuous statement's effect on Rawden. "It is how my devoted bride gazes at me in tender moments upon which I cannot elaborate, as a gentleman and a husband, because they are too intimate for public consumption. Believe me, Miss Wallace is not so immune as you argue. She wants you."

"Assuming you are correct, and I have my doubts, where do I begin? Because if what you claim is true, General Wallace poses a unique threat, and I must work fast. Yet, I suspect the usual inducements will not succeed with Miss Wallace." Despite his lack of experience in genuine courtship Rawden knew that a blushing debutante presented an altogether different capricious prey than a potential mistress or a merry widow. "How do you woo a virgin?"

"With great care, because in that I claim no expertise, given Arabella and I were betrothed from the first." Rockingham whistled in monotone. "Brother, had I been required to give chase, I am not so sure we would have made it to the altar, because I was out of my element in the particular shark-infested waters polite society has the unmitigated audacity to call the marriage mart. However, unlike the hunt for a doxy, proper engagement happens out in the open, in full view of the *ton*."

"All of it?" Rawden swallowed hard and tugged at his cravat. "I mean, what of private interludes in dark corners, ravishments in the library or the study, and moonlit garden trysts? Am I not to be rewarded for my honorable intentions?"

"Have you been reading novels, because there is naught much honorable about such intentions?" Wrinkling his nose, Rockingham looked like he'd just walked into the room and smelled boiling cabbage. "Much to my dismay, that sort of behavior is not appropriate, except in women's literature. At least, not unless you plan to play fast and loose with Miss Wallace's reputation. And there are those who already think her low, due to her financial situation and her father's disgrace. Would you add to her hardship?"

And therein resided the primary issue.

The general's behavior grew ever more desperate, and Rawden feared for Patience's safety. Had he time, he would have devised a suitable solution. One that spared her marriage to a wreck of a man. But reports of Wallace's recklessness forced Rawden to ponder the implausible. He refused to risk Patience's welfare. He simply could not wait.

So he would take her.

"Oh, this is going to be painful." Rawden downed the last of his brandy and grimaced. "Am I to suppress all my natural instincts, in order to gain a wife? And how am I to discern whether or not we are compatible in the particular arena of utmost concern to every man considering the connubial plunge into uncharted territory?"

"Are you honestly telling me you, the supreme seducer, have not already assessed that aspect of her character?" Rockingham cast an expression of unadulterated skepticism. "I had not spent five minutes in Arabella's company when I realized she had been blessed with the sort of innate fire most husbands would kill to possess and society mamas work to suppress if not outright eradicate. Given your experience, how do you appraise Miss Wallace?"

"Unbridled, in every sense of the word," Rawden replied without hesitation. Yes, he wanted her. Would have her. "Although she tries to pretend she is something she is not."

"There you have it." With that, Rockingham stood and

checked his timepiece. "Now then, why don't you accompany me to the Temple of the Muses, where I am to retrieve my marchioness and her friend. It would give you an opportunity to form an impression in regard to Miss Wallace. Although I suspect you will find I am right."

"I suppose there is no time like the present." Could he not simply spend the rest of his life coveting his illusions? Was it not enough to pretend Patience desired him as he ached for her? Dreading the worst, and despite his better instincts, Rawden jumped to his feet and followed his friend to the foyer, whereupon he gave his card to an attendant. "Tell my driver I shall journey with Lord Rockingham, and have my coach dispatched to the mews."

"Right away, Lord Beaulieu." The manservant dipped his chin.

On the pavement, Rawden waited. The Rockingham rig pulled to the curb, and footmen scrambled to open the door. After climbing aboard, he reclined in the squabs and peered at passersby. He sighed in resignation and gazed, unseeing, at the cityscape.

Part of him didn't want to know the truth.

Part of him wanted to savor the fantasy, because it was the smallest measure of hope that kept him going, and if he lost that, he would cease to exist. However, alone and unprotected, Patience was especially vulnerable to attack from unsavory characters. Men like him. That knowledge tormented him to his marrow, and he arrived at an incontrovertible fact.

There were some things worth fighting for, and his something was Patience.

"You really are in a sad state." Rockingham shook with half-stifled mirth. "I've handed you tempting fare on a proverbial silver platter. I expected you to gloat. To celebrate fortuitous events that have miraculously landed in your lap. You are anything if not smug."

"I am no such thing." Of course, that was a lie. Rawden folded his arms and strategized his attack. "I am merely focused on the wooing of one Miss Patience Wallace."

"May I make a suggestion?" When Rawden inclined his head, Rockingham clucked his tongue. "Have your servants put away your most prized possessions until the battle is won."

"When have I ever been given to dramatics?" Rawden scoffed at the insinuation and pretended to find the street life infinitely fascinating. "I resent that, brother. Really, I do. I thought you knew me better than that."

"Glass presents a particularly messy hazard." Rockingham appeared indefatigably unperturbed as he overruled Rawden's protest. "Trust me, you don't want anything breakable within reach when you realize you are, indeed, vulnerable to histrionics driven by a healthy desire for your better half."

"I have never in my life lost my head over a woman, and I have no intention of starting now." Rawden brushed aside the idea with a wave of his hand. "You act as if I—" He sat upright and came to attention. "You?"

"Aye. It occurred after Arabella and I quarreled over the prominent placement of my antique, erotic chess set, which I situated in the drawing room of our new home." Rockingham lowered his gaze. "The one with the queen bent forward, on her knees, in a questionable pose."

"I remember that collection." If memory served, the king boasted an impressive erection and fit perfectly behind his mate, to complete the bawdy image. Rawden guffawed and scratched his chin. "What happened to it?"

"I reduced it to rubble, after a wicked row, when she banished me to the daybed in my study." Rockingham smoothed the lapel of his coat and cleared his throat. "But I haven't the faintest notion of the instance. All I remember is my darling bride morphing into an uncontrollable termagant and slamming the door to our bedchamber in my face, and the rest is hazy. When I came to my senses, there was destruction everywhere."

The coach slowed and pulled from the lane, and Rockingham

pressed a finger to his lips. He scooted to one side, as a footman handed Lady Rockingham into the cabin. She quickly eased next her husband. Then Patience followed.

"Lord Beaulieu." Her charming face flushed beetroot red, and she immediately dropped her stare to his lips. *Oh, yes.* She couldn't have declared her interest more had she shouted from the rooftops of Parliament. "I didn't know you were joining us."

"Neither did I, until just recently." Of course, she couldn't know to what he referred, and she didn't need to know of his plans to make her his wife, yet. "I trust you had an enjoyable afternoon?"

"I d-did." She blinked when he took her hand in his and pressed a rather inappropriate, lengthy kiss to the underside of her wrist. Again, she studied his mouth, and he would've made improper advances on her were they alone. "And you? Did you have a pleasant visit with Lord Rockingham?"

"More than I anticipated." Heaven help him if she ever discovered the power she wielded over him. He settled her palm to the crook of his elbow, because he preferred to maintain a connection however innocent. "And I am uncontrollably excited to proceed with my grand design."

Perhaps, if he could rescue her, he just might save himself.

"Sounds rather mysterious." She directed her gaze toward the window, in an attempt to portray an air of calm, but the pulse beating at the base of her swanlike throat declared otherwise, and his confidence surged. "And intriguing."

"It is, my dear Miss Wallace." Satisfied he found his mark, and his course was set, Rawden eased into the squabs and chuckled. "It is."

Let the games begin.

Chapter Four

T HE SEASON COMMENCED with the annual Northcote ball, and it was the first time Patience had been invited to the gala event, due in no small part to her friendship with a certain marchioness. Given the estimable connection, she chose the burgundy satin trimmed in pink rosettes and French leavers lace, which she borrowed from Arabella for the special occasion. She did so want to look her best.

Sitting at her modest vanity, a sad excuse for the furnishing composed of two wooden crates perched on their sides with a board stretched across the top and a chipped mirror resting against the wall, she pinned the last of her blonde curls and assessed her handiwork. She once had a stunning, bespoke Schlichtig transitional dressing table made of rosewood, rosewood veneer, stained wood, and geometric decoration of braces and cubes in *trompe-l'oeil* frames. It held pride of place in her bedchamber. She thought it would kill her to sell it, given she inherited it from her grandmother, but she never regretted the decision, because the money fed the household for almost three months.

As she studied her reflection, she noticed the bodice of the gown fit as if it were made for her, baring just enough decolletage to border on scandalous, and she twirled once to check her appearance in the small square mirror. Against her better judgement, she accepted a pair of new white gloves from her interminable tormentor, Lord Beaulieu. The gift arrived just after the noon hour, and she had not the strength to protest.

"Miss Wallace, you are a vision." Abigail wiped a tear from her eye. "If only your mother could see you. She would be so proud."

"Thank you, Abigail." Patience turned and hugged her friend. "Dear mama, how I miss her."

"We have one more addition, which a messenger delivered after I brought in the wash." Abigail retrieved a small, beribboned box that bore a single, telltale wax seal. "I was instructed not to give you this until you were dressed for the ball."

"Oh, no. What now?" Patience steeled herself for another surprise. She lifted the lid and gasped. "It is a come-out posy."

"How lovely and thoughtful." Abigail lifted the delicate blooms from their nest of cotton and stared at Patience. "Where shall I pin it?"

"But this is not my first Season, although it certainly promises to be the most interesting." Patience bit her bottom lip as she pondered her predicament. To refuse the generous offering would be unforgivably rude, but she was no naïve debutante. "While I have never been invited to so many social events, I do not think it would be appropriate for me to wear a come-out posy, given I have been out for three years."

"What if we arrange it in your hair?" Abigail held the tiny bouquet, comprised of three pink roses, near Patience's crown. "Does this not work? It looks like a floral tiara."

"You are a genius." Patience tilted her head forward. "And it is the perfect solution, because I cannot risk offending Lord Beaulieu."

"*Lord Beaulieu?*" Abigail wrinkled her nose as she situated the last pin and inspected her design. "Is *he* our magnanimous but mysterious benefactor?"

"Indeed." Patience nodded. "To be specific, he is an earl."

"Is he planning to make a decent proposal to you?" Abigail made a couple of adjustments to Patience's coif. "Or is he another of *those* gentlemen?"

"In all honesty, I am not sure. When he is not tormenting me about something, he is impossible to understand. Despite his upbringing, he is pretentious, overbearing, and a veritable scamp. He is handsome, and he knows it, and he flouts all social conventions. And those are his good qualities." That kept Patience from finding any real joy in her admirer's largesse. While part of her coveted a shred of her childhood dream, however absurd in the cold light of day, the realist knew there was little chance a titled suitor would consider marrying a woman with naught to recommend her, except her father's mounting debt. "Still, I cannot risk alienating him. He is too powerful."

"And you fancy him." Abigail smiled and cupped Patience's chin. "Don't try to deny it, ma'am. I know you too well."

"Am I that obvious?" She recalled his boyish grin and huffed a breath. "He is not like anyone I know. Lord Beaulieu lives to the fullest. He knows no bounds, and he cares not for the opinion of others. He says and does as he wishes, without regard for the consequences."

"What consequences would he suffer? He holds rank." Abigail retrieved a modest hairbrush, fashioned of boar bristles and a rudimentary wooden handle, because the silver-backed accoutrements had been sold, and gave Patience's thick locks a final touch. "That can be dangerous, but it can also be exciting."

"Therein lies the problem." Patience stood and eased into a worn pair of kidskin slippers, the toes of which were stuffed with cotton because her mother had bigger feet. "I am the moth drawn to his flame."

"If you are not careful, you will get burned." Abigail patted Patience's chin and sniffed. "But you are smart, and you will find your way. I believe in you."

"Thank you, dear friend. That makes one of us." Patience gathered her reticule and strode into the hall, with Abigail in tow. She wished she shared her servant's confidence, but polite society could be anything but polite. If only she had an escort, she would feel better. After descending the stairs, she paused in the foyer and donned her pelisse. Right on time, a resounding knock signaled the Rockinghams had arrived. "Please, don't wait up for me. I may be late, and I can undress myself."

"All right." Abigail unlocked the door and swung wide the heavy oak panel. "But you must promise to tell me everything, tomorrow."

"Of course." Patience chuckled and then flinched and almost swallowed her tongue when she spied the impressive figure looming at the front step. "Lord Beaulieu." She gulped. "What are *you* doing here?"

"Good evening, Miss Wallace. Apologies, if I startled you." The rake hadn't the decency to appear contrite. Instead, he bowed with exaggerated flourish. He gazed on her as a child with its favorite toy and then studied her from top to toe and back again. When he met her stare, she feared her knees might buckle. "You are stunning, my dear. That color suits you."

"It is Lady Rockingham's gown." She stubbed her toe as she crossed the threshold, and he settled his hands at her hips. Almost as quick, he steadied her and offered his escort, which she accepted. "I merely borrowed it."

"I beg your pardon, but she did naught but put a frame on a masterpiece." Beaulieu winked, and Patience lamented the burn of a blush but rejoiced when she noticed the Rockingham coat of arms on the coach and the liveried footman standing at attention. In a shocking display of familiarity, the errant earl took her about the waist and lifted her into the cabin. Lord and Lady Rocking-ham shared a bench, and to her dismay Beaulieu plopped beside Patience. "Now, let us away."

"Hello, and how lovely you look." Arabella inclined her head and smiled. "I knew that dress would fit you, and you do it far more justice than I ever could."

"Now, I have something to say about that." Lord Rocking-ham pouted. "No offense, Miss Wallace."

"None taken." Patience scooted to her left, and the blackguard shuffled closer. "But I thought the three of us would journey to the Northcotes'."

"Beaulieu didn't want to arrive alone, a perilous hazard for a titled bachelor, so I invited him to join us. I hope you don't mind." With the innocence of one of Raphael's cherubs, Lord Rockingham glanced at the earl. "Is this not cozy? Boy, girl. Boy, girl."

"It is more than adequate." Beaulieu glowered, and Patience stifled a snort of laughter. She suspected there were games afoot, but she was hardly in a position to protest, so she remained silent. "Had I known certain individuals would be so chatty, I should have taken my own rig." Then he turned to Patience, and his demeanor altered in the blink of an eye. "But then I should have missed the pleasure of your company, Miss Wallace."

"You are too kind, Lord Beaulieu." And he was up to something. She would bet her life on it. "Still, I am sure you would have survived my absence, given I do not signify. And as I recall, you never lack for companionship during the Season."

"Ouch." With an upraised hand, he feigned a wound to the chest. "That smarts."

"You two grouse like a married couple." Lord Rockingham stuck his tongue in his cheek and waggled his brows, and Patience shifted. "Practicing for the real thing?"

"Of course not." Mortified by the suggestion, she bowed her head and fumbled with the lace-trimmed edge of her glove. "I would never presume to suggest a liaison between myself and a man of Lord Beaulieu's estimation."

"Let us not entirely abandon the idea." Beaulieu snickered, and she cringed. Did he make sport of her? "Given you brought it up, I should at least consider your most gracious offer."

For a pregnant moment, the coach remained quiet save the steady *clip-clop* of horse hooves against the cobblestones.

"Forgive me, my lord." With an unconvincing laugh, Patience fought to maintain an air of calm and poise, even though her belly twisted into a tight knot. "I am unfamiliar with your particular brand of humor."

"What if I am serious?" Beaulieu inquired with a straight face.

Lord Rockingham suffered a violent coughing fit, and Arabella patted his back, although it sounded as if he said, *Too soon.*

"Lord Beaulieu, while I am certain such jests must garner riotous hilarity with your friends, I am not in the habit of entertaining false promises from men who do not love me, and I would rather be poor but loved in Cheapside than wealthy but scorned in Mayfair. Now, I bid you cease your mock pursuits, which could expose me to society's censure for foolish ambition, and I am already subject to scrutiny owing to my father's situation."

"Be that as it may, you are assuming I am in—"

"Ah, we have arrived, and not a moment too soon." Lord Rockingham didn't wait for the footman. To her surprise, he thrust open the door and leaped from the coach. Then he turned to hand Arabella to the pavement. "Let us go inside, my dear."

Left to Beaulieu's care, Patience breathed a sigh of relief when the earl exited the cramped confines with nary a glance in her direction. The respite proved brief when the rogue gripped her hips and drew her from the squabs. When her feet connected with solid ground, she slapped away his hands.

"I beg your pardon." After righting her gown and smoothing her skirt, she lifted her chin and took a step forward. To her dismay, Beaulieu positioned himself at her side and extended his right arm in escort. When she ignored him, he grasped her wrist and pressed her palm into the crook of his elbow. Gritting her teeth, she ascended the stairs to the grand residence. "Lord Beaulieu, we are not together. I know not what you are about, but your behavior is most discomfiting."

"Really?" At the entrance, he steered her across the threshold and to the receiving line. "I am delighted to know I effect you thus. Tell me more."

"Insufferable peacock." Yes, it was bad form to insult a member of the peerage, but she couldn't contain herself. Of course, it didn't help that he grinned in response.

Unusually warm, Patience smiled and greeted her hosts. While navigating the procession, she became aware of the inordinate glances and copious whispers directed at her. Notoriety was the last thing she needed as she embarked on her quest for a husband. Steeling her spine, she approached the butler and handed him her card. Once she stood at center, alone, she would escape the odious Lord Beaulieu.

To her unqualified horror, Beaulieu resumed his place to her left.

The butler cleared his throat and made the announcement. "The Right Honorable. The Earl of Beaulieu and Miss Patience Wallace."

Patience feared she would swoon.

A swell of murmurs, low at first, built and swept across the cavernous ballroom. Her heart pounded in her chest, and her ears pealed like the bells in a Hawksmoor steeple. Everything seemed to spin out of control, but a pillar of strength provided unshakeable support. At her left, the Lord of Fire and Brimstone chuckled and led her into the fray.

"What have you done?" Conscious of the multitude of stares, she forced a countenance of ennui. Inside, she fractured. "Will you not be satisfied until I am in tatters and begging for a crust of bread on a street corner like a Fielding foundling?"

"I told you I want you," he replied with vehemence that jolted her.

"Oh, my." She clutched her throat and rolled her shoulders. "I have been propositioned by many men in the *ton*, but no one has been so direct."

"I find candor far more successful in getting what I want." He shrugged. "It ensures there are no misunderstandings, although you mistake my offer."

"I am not sure what you mean, but allow me to be equally frank." She checked herself before she brought further shame on herself. "I cannot give you what you want."

"Why not?" He canted his head and frowned. "I will treat you like a queen. You will live in a comfortable home in Mayfair, you will wear the finest clothes, and you will dine on the best fare, with servants aplenty and nary a care in the world."

"And a reputation in ruins and a family name irreparably besmirched." In that moment, her heart fractured. Was money the only inducement a man would extend to wed her? Could no one love her for herself? "I could never do that to my father or to my mother's memory, regardless of my current status. But I thank you for the overture. That you consider me worthy of the position as your mistress is, I suppose, an honor of sorts."

"Bloody hell." Beaulieu compressed his lips and dragged her near the rear wall. He peered left and then right. At last, he leaned close. "My dear Miss Wallace, I am proposing marriage."

Her knees buckled.

"Easy, Patience." Her tormentor drew her to a dark corner where they sheltered behind a large bust of Sir Isaac Newton. He wrapped an arm about her waist and tucked her to his side. For a while, he simply held her, and it was so nice to lean on him. To drink in his strength. Then he pressed his lips, warm and firm, to her temple and whispered, "I thought you understood my intentions."

"No, I did not." Dazed and confused, she wrenched free. With a few gulps of air, she ordered her senses. "Lord Beaulieu, tell me the truth. Do you love me?"

"What is love?" His pedestrian reply, haphazardly uttered, slew her.

"A requirement, if you wish to claim me as your wife." The little girl with childish hopes and dreams died in that brief moment in time. In her place, the woman hardened by inconsolable loss and financial hardship emerged ready for battle. While she would be willing to settle for less with another man, for her, with him, it was all or nothing. "Lord Beaulieu, I am grateful for your friendship, and I hold you in the highest esteem. For that reason, I cannot permit you to marry what you do not love."

Before he could stop her, Patience spun about and pushed through the ocean of ladies and gentlemen, conscious that Beaulieu gave chase. To her good fortune, his bevy of admirers forestalled his pursuit. She didn't stop until she reached the foyer, and she continued out the front door and down the steps. On the pavement, she hiked her skirts and sprinted for home.

As a soldier, when Rawden prepared for battle, he always surveyed the prevailing landscape to anticipate possible flanking maneuvers and vulnerabilities that could imperil his men. He attended briefings and took copious notes. He adjusted his tactics to the overall plan. He was methodical, cautious, and disciplined. He never charged blindly into the fray without considering various outcomes, always driven by the safety of the men under his command and his end goal—victory.

So why had he forced Patience's hand in their first skirmish?

The miscalculation, a monumental blunder, reflected a change in his character that he did not appreciate and left him befuddled by his own actions. Had he bent his will to satisfy a woman? Had he become so entrenched in her position that he forgot to assess his needs? Answers eluded him. No, they mocked him.

As he stood at the entrance to Rockingham House, he pondered his motives and stared at the brass knocker. He had no desire to participate in a postmortem of the previous evening's events, given his unintended oversight. Of course, he could depart with none the wiser, and he considered it. But just as he turned to leave, the heavy oak panel swung open, revealing a smiling Lord Rockingham.

"Ready to face the firing squad?" the marquess inquired with a smirk. Oh, it was going to be painful. "Believe me, we are quite anxious to know what you did to send Miss Wallace running from the Northcote's, last night."

"I knew I shouldn't have come." Flexing his fists, Rawden crossed the threshold and doffed his hat, coat, and gloves. "I should have made for my country estate and spared myself the interrogation."

"Aw, it will not be that bad, and we are all friends here." Which meant the experience would be wretched. Downright agonizing. Rockingham snorted, as they strolled down the side hall that led to his study. "Besides, we gather in full support of your campaign and have much to learn from your humiliation."

And so Rockingham fired the first shot.

"Very funny." As Rawden walked into the man's domain, the faint aroma of cigar smoke teased his nose, and he paused before the large, hand-tooled desk. The Mad Matchmakers were in full attendance, and he garnered their attention, unreservedly. "I make a little miscalculation, and I am the village idiot."

"I would argue you suffered that condition long before you met Miss Wallace." Greyson snickered. "Only now you seem to be playing the fool, as well."

Tension weighed heavy in the room, and Rawden braced.

The collective of wounded warriors burst into uncontained mirth paired with hearty back slaps. Indeed, they found sport in his uncharacteristic fiasco. Given his gaffe, what could he do but stand there and take his punishment?

"All right, all right." Rockingham wiped a stray tear and cleared his throat. "Settle down, men. One of our own is in dire need of our advice and direction, and at some point you will each confront that particular brand of ruthless misery polite society has the unqualified nerve to call courtship. Let us find out what Beaulieu did to terrorize Miss Wallace."

"Oh, this I've got to hear." Lord Michael rolled his eyes. "For a Romeo who has docked his vessel in more honey harbors than Lord Nelson, and has declared as much more times than I can count, I want to know how a gently-reared virgin bested Beaulieu."

"She didn't best me." Rawden pounded his fist on the desk and then plopped in an overstuffed chair. "Things were going swimmingly, in my estimation, but I misjudged her acumen. It could happen to anyone, and I will get her back."

"What, precisely, did you do?" Greyson asked as he leaned forward and narrowed his stare. "Did you regale her with your heroics?"

"That is enough to send any woman screaming for the country," quipped Lord Michael.

"It is a simple misunderstanding, and I will set it to rights at the first opportunity." Beaulieu stalled. He searched for something—anything to avoid the truth. He replayed the disaster a thousand times in his mind, and he still could not fathom what possessed him to force Patience into a corner. Perhaps the Matchmakers could provide answers that thus far eluded him. Finally, he relented. "Suffice it to say I rushed my fences and offered for her."

"Offered what? Greyson asked.

"What do you think?" Rawden tensed. "I proposed."

"You did *what?*" Rockingham appeared on the verge of an apoplectic fit.

"Are you out of your mind?" Warrington pressed his thumbs to his temples.

"Bloody hell." Lord Michael lifted the brandy decanter from the side table and yanked on the crystal stopper. Then he drank a healthy portion straight from the container.

"Were you not telling me this in your own words I would not believe it." Greyson opened and then closed his mouth. "I have nothing. I am at a total loss."

"Are you mad?" Rockingham shook himself and averted his stare. "I mean, beyond your usual level of insanity."

"When have I ever exhibited even a remote interest in sound mental acuity when unrestrained derangement is so much more enjoyable? But I am glad you find this amusing, given courtship was your idea." Balanced on tenterhooks, Rawden raked his fingers through his hair. "I come to you for guidance, and you laugh at me."

"It is our duty to humble you, is it not?" Greyson chortled. "And you are nothing if not diverting."

"But we will offer our sage counsel, given the past master is now the pupil." Warrington slapped his thigh and devolved into another fit of hysterics. "You must admit the situation is entertaining in your gross ineptitude, when we all wagered you would find the least trouble securing a wife."

"Perhaps you should explain your logic, because I can discern no strategy to your actions." Rockingham leaned back in his chair and inclined his head. "What on earth possessed you to cast your lot with Miss Wallace at the first ball of the Season?"

"Indeed." Greyson propped his elbow on the armrest. "Could you not have waited? Could you not have seduced her in the rose garden, debauched her, and then made your declaration, like a gentleman?"

"No, no, no." Lord Michael shook his head and scrunched his face. "You do not woo your prospective bride amid the thorny hedgerows. You must coax her with flowers, embroidered handkerchiefs, and useless trinkets that serve no other purpose than to attract dust and burn money."

"And you are an expert even though you remain blissfully unattached?" Rawden scoffed at the inference, because the only leg-shackled Matchmaker was Rockingham. As long as he lived, he would never forget that awful night in Weybridge when his friend delivered himself into the hands of a madman to save the woman he loved. "I would hear from the lone married member of our set." To the marquess, Rawden asked, "Just how did you win your lady's heart?"

"Well—" Rockingham paused and narrowed his stare. Then he pressed a finger to his mouth. He jumped from his seat and ran to the door. In a single swift move, he turned the knob and wrenched open the oak panel.

Lady Rockingham fell to the floor.

"Arabella, what pray tell are you doing?" Rockingham perched hands on hips and compressed his lips. "Are you eavesdropping on our conversation?"

"Yes." She nodded once, and Rawden had to respect her unflinching honesty. "And you should thank me, because you are all wrong in your guidance. What you fail to recognize is you do not know your quarry."

"What is there to know? Miss Wallace is a woman." Lord Warrington inquired as he scratched his cheek. "Do you argue she cannot be seduced?"

"Therein lies your mistake." Lady Rockingham folded her arms. To Beaulieu, she said, "Do you want to seduce Patience or win her heart?"

"There is a difference?" Beaulieu queried and then faltered beneath her caustic expression. "I was just wondering."

"There most certainly is a difference." Lady Rockingham looked on him with pity. "You are doomed if you do not recognize the distinction."

"That may be, but who knows the fairer sex better than men?" Greyson asked and jutted his chin in a defensive manner. "Do you assert a superior intellect in the matrimonial realm?"

"That is your second miscalculation, Lord Greyson." Lady Rockingham backed her husband to his chair, whereupon he eased to the leather cushions, and she installed herself in his lap. It was not an altogether unfamiliar sight, but that didn't temper Rawden's reaction to the shocking display of intimacy from a highborn bride of character. "Superior intellect is not necessary to win Miss Wallace's heart. What Lord Beaulieu requires is pedestrian knowledge of her passions and pursuits." Then she caught Rawden in a steely gaze. "That is, if he truly wishes to wed Miss Wallace."

The collective focused on him, and he fidgeted and tugged at his cravat.

"Aye, I want her," he mumbled.

"I beg your pardon?" Lady Rockingham arched a brow. "Can

you speak up, Lord Beaulieu?"

"I said I want her." Rawden pushed from his chair and paced before the window. "I want to marry her. I want to partner her in all enterprises. I want her to bear my children. I want her at my side for the rest of my days. Is that what you want me to say?"

"What of love?" He could have wagered the nosy marchioness would pose that pesky question, and she struck him as rather full of herself as she did so. "Or have you no interest in claiming her heart?"

"Is this a trick question?" Rawden suspected as much and resented the assembly of grins his friends cast in his direction. "Because I have no tolerance for games and those who play them."

"This is not a game, Lord Beaulieu. This is life. If you have no intention of committing to Patience, in every way, I can no longer support your campaign." Lady Rockingham lowered her chin. "Indeed, I should have denied your request for assistance, from the first."

"I know not what I can say to convince you I am in earnest." He crossed and uncrossed his legs. How could he explain what even he didn't understand? How could he put a name to what he felt? Or the miracle that he harbored? "All I can give you is my word, on my honor, that I will try to be a good and faithful husband."

"You are afraid." It was a statement, not an inquiry from the prying noblewoman.

"Of course, I am afraid." Rawden shrugged, in an effort to convey detachment. Despite his outward demeanor, inside he waged war with himself. He harbored an awkward companionship with misery. It was easy. It made no demands. He had only to let it run amok. Panic ravaged his gut every time he reflected on whether or not Patience could love him. If he could return the sentiment. If Lord and Lady Beaulieu could foster a deep and abiding attachment to rival what he witnessed that dreadful night in Weybridge. "Never have I embarked on anything so in opposition to my natural instincts."

"You act as if such fidelity requires drastic change on your part." Lord Rockingham furrowed his brow and kissed his bride's temple. In turn, she rested her head to his chest. They made connubial bliss look so simple. Like breathing. "You couldn't be more wrong, because you need only let it happen. And it will not reshape you. Rather, the affection you share will enhance your life, and you will wonder how you ever survived without your better half."

"Darling." Lady Rockingham stretched upright and kissed her husband's cheek. "I should check on our son. Join me in our chamber after your meeting adjourns."

"My lady wife, you may depend upon it." The unequivocal pride in Lord Rockingham's heated stare gave Rawden pause.

The epitome of grace and elegance, Lady Rockingham crossed the study and opened the door. Then she peered over her shoulder, a wealth of meaning in her stance. "Do not make me wait too long, my lord."

Greyson choked.

Warrington shifted his weight.

Lord Michael cleared his throat and appeared to find the buttons of his waistcoat infinitely fascinating.

"Gentlemen, let us conclude our business for today." Rockingham stood and grinned. "It appears I have a very important appointment to keep, and I dare not tarry."

"Uh—I believe we understand." Rawden pushed from his chair and followed the Mad Matchmakers into the hall. In the foyer, he lingered until the other wounded warriors departed. "Will we see you at White's?"

"I wouldn't count on it." Rockingham waggled his brows. "I expect to be otherwise engaged for some time."

"You really are happy," Rawden stated with equal parts awe and bewilderment. "Disgustingly, sickeningly in love."

"Brother, it truly is good to be a husband." Rockingham patted Rawden on the back. "And I hope you find the satisfaction with Miss Wallace as my Arabella has brought me."

"I beg your pardon, my lord." Merriweather bowed and handed Rawden an envelope. "A messenger delivered a note for Lord Beaulieu while you were in your meeting, and I did not want to disturb you."

"Thank you, Merriweather. That will be all." Rockingham inclined his head and loomed at Rawden's side. "I hope it is not urgent."

Rawden didn't believe it was pressing in the manner his friend meant. He recognized the nondescript stationary and wax seal that bore no hint of the sender's identity. When he unfolded the missive, he scanned the now familiar words that haunted his sleep.

You are no hero, and soon London society will know the truth.

"Bloody hell, another one." Rawden clenched his jaw and emitted a groan of frustration. "Well, that settles it. I am doomed. And Patience will never wed a coward."

"No, you are not doomed." Rockingham chucked Rawden's shoulder. "And I am growing weary of reminding you that you are no coward. How you seized on such a point of absurdity escapes me, but you cannot let the past dictate your future. However, it is evident you are being watched, given whoever threatens you knew enough of your whereabouts to strike while you were in my home, and that concerns me."

"You think my mysterious adversary intends to cause me physical harm?" Rawden hadn't even considered the possibility. Then another more sinister prospect occurred to him. "What of Patience? If she were assaulted because of my actions in battle, I could never live with myself. Whoever this person is, they can do as they wish with me, but they better not so much as harm a hair on her head."

"Actually, I am not convinced the villain means to hurt you, Pace." Rockingham rubbed his chin. "Rather, I wager he wants to embarrass you. Why your unknown tormentor wants to cause you me is the operative question. Are you sure you have no idea who could be behind the nefarious scheme? Anyone from Quatre Bras?"

"Out of more than thirty thousand Allied soldiers?" Rawden huffed a breath. "It is anyone's guess."

"Then I suggest you go home and make a list of prospective candidates, especially those who move in polite society, because someone wants to cause you trouble." Rockingham walked Rawden to the door. "It would help if you could find them before they launch an attack against which you cannot defend your lady or yourself."

CHAPTER FIVE

O N AN UNSEASONABLY cool but brilliant afternoon, Patience stood on the pavement, waiting for Arabella to arrive. A gentle breeze whispered and thrummed through the curls that peeked beyond the lace edge of her poke bonnet, and she shivered and drew the folds of her worn pelisse together. Nagging doubt nestled deep in her thoughts, and she had just decided to forgo the Promenade when the Rockingham landau, with the top down, turned the corner.

"Blast." She mustered a smile and waved to her friend. When the rig halted at the curb, she strode forward and accepted the footman's assistance. To Arabella, Patience said, "I had thought you would have kept the top up today."

"I was going to, but it is sunny, and the sky is clear." Arabella handed Patience a blanket. "I wish you would let me purchase a new pelisse for you. I know yours is a treasured keepsake, but it cannot afford much warmth."

"It is adequate." Of course, Patience lied, as she huddled beneath the quilt. Yes, the garment had sentimental value, given it belonged to her mother, but it was also the only outerwear she owned. "While I appreciate your offer, and your generosity knows no bounds, I cannot accept charity." Then she noted the empty seat beside Arabella. "Where is Lord Rockingham?"

"Anthony decided to ride his horse, and I encouraged him, because he has just returned to the sport." Arabella sniffed and daubed the corners of her eyes. "It does my heart good to see him atop Aeolus, given all Anthony endured at the hands of his father."

"What news of His Grace these days?" Patience recalled the details of Lord Rockingham's confinement in an asylum, after he sacrificed himself to save Arabella. It was that devotion that drove Patience in her quest to find a love match. Regardless of wealth or title, she wanted a man to love her the way Lord Rockingham desperately loved Arabella. "I gather there has been a reconciliation?"

"Anthony is the best of men. I knew that when I married him." Arabella shook her head. "He forgave his father, but I never shall. I cannot abide the mere sight of him." Then she pinned Patience with an unflinching stare. "So, do tell, what happened between you and Lord Beaulieu at the Northcotes'? The whole of London is whispering about it."

"I'm sure you exaggerate." Patience recalled the exchange with Lord Beaulieu in vivid detail and shuddered. "I am sure I do not signify."

"You ran from the opening event of the Season, in full view of the *ton*. Trust me, everyone noticed your exit, especially when Beaulieu gave chase." Arabella arched a brow and compressed her lips. "He is the hero of Quatre Bras. What did you think would happen?"

"Oh, I don't know." Patience reflected on the moment. Her nemesis knew precisely where to strike a blow, and she panicked. "What do you know of the situation?"

"Only that he offered for you." Arabella wagged a finger. "And before you protest, I would have you know I had to eavesdrop on the Mad Matchmakers to learn that little tidbit, because my oldest and dearest friend did not share the news with me."

"He didn't." Patience shook her head and hugged herself. "He would not have divulged such personal information to the Mad Matchmakers."

"Of course, he would and he did. They are like brothers." Arabella shrugged. "While I thought he had no interest in taking a bride, it appears Beaulieu's suit is in earnest. He made it clear during a gathering, yesterday. Anthony is certain Beaulieu intends to wed you, and he declared as much in my presence, so you had better decide what you plan to do when he asks again—and he will ask again."

"But—why?" Stunned, Patience envisioned the cocky earl and gooseflesh covered her from top to toe. "I am a pauper compared to him, with nothing to offer but limited connections he shares. I bring nothing but myself to any union. And I have done naught to encourage him."

"Perhaps that is why he pursues you." Arabella waved a greeting to a passing scion of society, and Patience nodded an acknowledgement. "Because he could have his pick of wealthy debutantes, yet he chooses you. Does that not do him credit?"

"He only wants the woman he has not had." The Grosvenor gate of the Park came into view, and Patience gazed at the well-dressed ladies and gentlemen. "That is not the same as wanting me."

"All right." Arabella shed her lap blanket as the rig neared the curb. "Then tell him so. Explain you do not wish to marry him, and ask him to cease his campaign to win your heart."

A strange sensation, fierce rebellion, nestled in her chest as Patience considered doing just that.

"I seriously doubt Lord Beaulieu has any plans to win my heart." Confused by her mutinous emotions, Patience descended to the pavement, and Arabella followed in her wake. "I am a game to him. A challenge."

"I do not agree." Arabella adjusted her elegant ermine trimmed pelisse and took Patience by the arm. "Let us enter the rotation and discuss it further."

When they found an opening, they sidled into the throng. Well-heeled gentlemen turned out in trim and ladies of wealth and influence, some making note of the new arrivals, strolled the path in Hyde Park. It was another gross ritual of opulence during which debutantes vied for husbands, while rakes searched for their latest mark. Patience considered it a necessary evil.

"Why do you believe Lord Beaulieu's intentions are honorable?" Patience recalled Abigail's comment. Yes, she liked the irascible earl. Despite his numerous shortcomings, he stirred something inside her. Something powerful. Something enticing. "What has he done to secure your good opinion?"

"Do you remember the dinner party my parents gave to announce my betrothal?" When Patience nodded the affirmative, Arabella smiled. "I had so many doubts about Anthony, and I never wanted to marry anyone. You pointed out that Anthony already relied on me, thus shifting the balance of power in our marriage. While most conventional unions position the husband as lord and master, my relationship with Anthony is based on shared authority. We govern our household as a couple. A true partnership."

"That is obvious." And Patience would have the same felicitous collaboration with her future spouse. "But how does that relate to Lord Beaulieu?"

"Inasmuch as I could not accurately assess my predicament with Anthony, because I was too close to the situation and blinded by my emotions, you ignore the advantage of accepting Beaulieu." Arabella shook her head. "I resisted my betrothal, because I did not want to be ruled by a man. I was wrong, and you were the one who helped me see that. Will you not trust my judgement when it comes to Beaulieu? Can you not give him a chance to prove himself?"

"I suppose I could." Just then, Patience glimpsed the blond Adonis, garbed in a stunning many-caped great coat, riding alongside Lord Rockingham, perched high atop an impressive black stallion. She dug in her heels so abruptly, an innocent passerby bumped into her. "Arabella, tell me you did not lure me here on false pretenses."

"I didn't, but it appears my husband has ideas of his own.

They don't call themselves the Mad Matchmakers for nothing." Arabella smiled and waved. "I will deal with him later, at home. Right now, you must gather your wits, because I wager Beaulieu expects an audience."

"What should I say?" Patience wrung her fingers and shuffled her feet. She was not prepared to discuss such a personal topic in the middle of the Park, during the Promenade, with untold members of society in attendance. "What do I tell him?"

"What else?" Arabella shrugged. "The truth. But you had better think fast, because they are here."

"Lord Rockingham. Lord Beaulieu." Bolstering her nerves, Patience forced a smile and curtseyed. Whatever happened, she promised to accept it with grace. "What a delightful surprise."

"Is it?" She would have taken exception to his remark had Beaulieu not cast a mischievous grin. He dismounted and bowed with a flourish. Then he took her hand in his and, as usual, kissed the underside of her wrist. "My friends, may I have a word with Miss Wallace, in private?"

"Of course." Lord Rockingham slid from the saddle. "I shall accompany my charming marchioness on a stroll along the Serpentine, so take your time."

With Lord Beaulieu leading his horse, Patience positioned herself to his immediate right and accepted his proffered escort. Together, they navigated the path in silence. Various comments danced on her tongue, but she said naught. Beaulieu sighed and drew her closer.

"Miss Wallace, I wanted to—"

"Lord Beaulieu, I wanted to—" She stumbled but maintained her footing. "After you, my lord."

"No, no." He cleared his throat. "Ladies first, I insist."

"All right." Conscious of her surroundings, she bent her head in his direction and in a low voice said, "I wanted to apologize for my unforgivable behavior at the Northcotes' ball. In my defense, I never anticipated an offer of marriage, and I panicked. Still, that is no real excuse, and I am sorry, Lord Beaulieu."

"Now I feel quite the villain." He peered at her and winked. "My dear Miss Wallace, you did nothing wrong. And if anyone is owed an apology, it is you. I should have made my intentions clear, and I should have secured your permission, and that of your father, to pay court. Instead, I played my hand and frightened you, and I regret that."

"But I should have had the presence of mind to remain at the event." And the more she thought of her behavior, the more she cringed. "Instead, I am ashamed to admit I ran home like a scared little girl, and I am no child."

"A perfectly acceptable response, since I gave you no warning of my proclivities." He paused and pulled her beneath the canopy of a large oak tree. "Miss Wallace—Patience, if I may. Would you be willing to entertain an overture of a different sort?"

"Lord Beaulieu—"

"Rawden." He flexed his jaw. "I make you free with my name and ask the same of you."

"Lord Beaulieu, you may call me what you will, because I am of no consequence in society. However, you are a man of rank and privilege, and I am honor-bound to respect your position, regardless of our acquaintance." Patience considered her words, because she refused to make another mistake. Again and again, Arabella's advice echoed in her ears, and she reflected on the question foremost in her mind. "I am willing to contemplate advancing our relationship, but there is something I must know, and I must know it now. Why do you want me, when you could have your pick of any woman in the *ton*? What makes me special that a man of your importance would consider me worthy as a mate?"

"When the war broke out, I was so naïve and eager to purchase a commission, which angered my parents to the extent we still have not spoken, but I was unprepared for reality, as my sire warned." He nodded in the direction of a bench, and together they sat in the shade. "The military makes demands. You make sacrifices, surrendering your freedom to become part of something larger than yourself, to serve the greater good. In the process, you compromise your integrity. Then your honor. Then your beliefs. You abandon all that is familiar and adopt a new persona to match your regimentals, such that you no longer recognize yourself when you spy your reflection in a mirror."

"I admire your courage and dedication to duty." She fought the urge to take his hand, but she desperately ached to touch him. "Regardless of what happened in battle, you are strong, Lord Beaulieu."

"Not strong enough." So much pain invested his handsome face, and she yearned to comfort him. To extend support and encouragement. "I always thought I wore the uniform. It was too late when I realized the uniform wore me. Even the brutality becomes normal after a while."

"But you did what you had to, in order to persist. To fight another day and defend our country. Even your parents must respect that." Patience suspected that, in that moment, she glimpsed Lord Beaulieu, the very real and vulnerable man, inexpressibly appealing in his sorrow, beneath the haughty exterior and audacious bravado. "Do you blame yourself for living?"

"In some ways, aye. I never imagined a world beyond the war. I never imagined life beyond the carnage, because I never expected to survive. As for my parents, they travel the world. I have had no word from them, other than recriminations uttered in anger upon my return to England." When he turned to her, she started, given the powerful emotions swirling in his turbulent gaze. The black patch that covered his wounded eye contrasted with the chiseled features and patrician beauty that could rival Michelangelo's *David*. "But you give me hope for something more. Something beautiful. I don't know why or how I feel this way, but I believe, beyond all doubt, you are my one chance at salvation."

For a while, she simply stared at him. Never had anyone made a lovelier or more enticing declaration, and only a fool would reject such a noble suit. How had she so grossly misjudged him?

"You do me a great honor, Lord Beaulieu." Nearby, members of the privileged classes loomed and gawked, and she became increasingly aware of the attention the blond earl attracted. As she contemplated their courtship, she realized such scrutiny would befall her. And there would be gossip. Ugly, cruel aspersions cast on her character. "May I make a suggestion?"

"Of course." He smiled. "I am yours, unreservedly."

"Thank you." She could have melted in a puddle on the ground. "I propose we embark on a proper courtship, which would give us time to become more acquainted. You could get to know me and decide you can't stand to be alone in a room with me for more than five minutes."

"I doubt that." Now he appeared wolfish, the look to which she was accustomed. "Because I can think of many things I could achieve in five minutes, especially if I were alone in a room with you."

"Uh—all right." Blinking, Patience opened and closed her mouth. She had no intention of asking him to clarify his statement. "Be that as it may, I am amenable to such a proposition, insofar as you understand you are under no obligation to marry me at the end of the Season. And I would have your word as a gentleman you will observe all proprieties."

"Done." Beaulieu stood and drew her from the bench. "But I have a few conditions of my own I should like to add, if we are to strike a fair bargain."

"I am listening." And she braced, because she knew him too well.

"Forthwith, I shall escort you to the various events of the Season, and I would claim your waltzes, exclusively. I will not tolerate another man holding you in his arms." He tapped his cheek. "You may dance with the Mad Matchmakers but no one else. And we are to court in full view of the *ton*. I will not hide from society. And I will speak with your father, posthaste, to settle our arrangement."

"Agreed." She had no desire to dance with anyone else, anyway. "So, you are courting me."

"My dear Miss Wallace, I most certainly am wooing you." Then, to her shock and amazement, and under the watch of an interloping audience, the scoundrel slipped off her glove and kissed her bare knuckles. "But you should know, I never play fair. I play to win."

And so Patience made a bargain with the Devil.

THE TOWN COACH bobbled along the lane, and Rawden glanced down and checked his appearance. He tugged on his cravat and pulled a speck of lint from his navy-blue coat. Stretching out his booted feet, he scrutinized the polished shine on the toes of his Hessians. From his pocket he retrieved the tiny turtle charm he often fiddled with to maintain calm and then returned it to its place. When the rig drew to a halt before number ten Gower Street, he rolled his shoulders.

As he waited for his footman, Rawden collected the gifts he had fashioned expressly for his future wife and hoped they would meet with her approval. First, he had to secure her father's permission to court and marry her. Of course, he didn't doubt his ability to persuade the general.

In some ways, he had waited his whole life for that moment.

While he was happy to portray the roving rake, the truth was he wanted a family. He longed for a loving wife. Someone who accepted him, warts and all. And he wanted children. Lots of children. But society tended to ridicule men who spoke openly of such dreams. Any bachelor insane enough to announce his search for a bride soon found himself under attack by the marriage-minded mamas. Unlike Lord Michael, who proudly proclaimed his desire to wed, Rawden had no intention of letting the *ton* choose his countess.

As he descended the rig to the pavement, he uttered a silent prayer for calm. Bearing his parcels, he skipped up the entrance stairs and knocked on the door. The rasp of the lock signaled the battle for Miss Wallace commenced.

"Yes, sir." Abigail, the grumpy housekeeper, wrinkled her nose. "How can I be of service?"

"The Earl of Beaulieu to see General Wallace." Rawden stood tall. "I believe he is expecting me."

"Well, don't dawdle on the stoop like a street peddler." After collecting his hat, coat, and gloves, Abigail stepped aside. "Come in, but wipe your feet. I just mopped, and even if you were the King of England, I'd not have you tracking dirt across my clean floor."

"Yes, ma'am." He sketched a mock salute and did as she bade, because she could strike fear in the minds of an entire regiment. "These gifts are for Miss Wallace."

"You may put them on the chair, and I will see to it she gets them when she returns home." The housekeeper wiped her hands on her apron. "General Wallace is in his study. It is down the hall and the last door on the right."

"Oh." Rawden lingered. "Am I to announce myself?"

"Lord Beaulieu, this is not a palace, and you are no royal." Did he think her grumpy? She was downright surly. "I expect you can manage on your own, being an earl and all."

"You don't like me, do you, Abigail?" He folded his arms and narrowed his stare, more facetious than serious. "Come now. Tell me the truth."

"It is Ms. Crow to you." She thrust her nose in the air in a fit of high dudgeon, and he stifled laughter. "And what is there to like?"

"Well, that is strangely appropriate," he mumbled.

She came alert. "What did you say?"

"Nothing." He rocked on his heels and bit his tongue. "If you will excuse me, the general awaits."

"You are excused," she muttered under her breath, "Lord Fussy Breeches."

"I beg your pardon?" Now Rawden rested fists on hips. "What did you just say?"

"Nothing." The old crow smirked, as she turned his words on him. "Now, run along. I have work to do, and I cannot waste my day with you."

He wanted to argue, because he enjoyed her feisty spirit, but he suspected he'd lose, so he ignored the insult. Swallowing a large portion of his pride, he strolled down the dark corridor until he reached the study. The door sat ajar, and inside the general reclined in a chair and drank brandy directly from a bottle. It was awfully early in the day to be imbibing.

"Hello." Rawden rapped his knuckles against the oak panel. "General Wallace, may I join you?"

"Ah, Lord Beaulieu." The once respected military man known for his fastidiousness, now bedraggled and reeking of spirits and sweat, stood and waved a welcome. "Come in, come in and have a seat."

"Thank you, sir." Rawden noted a small wooden stool had been placed near the window. Moth-eaten drapes remained closed, with the barest hint of sunlight peeking through various holes. Walls marked by torn coverings bereft of paintings or plaques framed the worn rug, and a decrepit desk that looked on the verge of collapse held pride of place. With care, he perched on the modest piece of furniture he feared might crumble beneath his weight. "I appreciate your taking this meeting on such short notice."

"Must say I was surprised but glad to receive your missive." The general retrieved a chipped crystal balloon and filled it with the amber intoxicant. "Brandy?"

"Uh—no." Rawden chuckled. "I rarely indulge before noon."

"Well, to each his own." General Wallace downed the contents of the glass in a single gulp. "Now then, I gather you seek to engage my daughter's services, and I am inclined to entertain your patronage, given you are a titled gentleman. However, you must know, and this is a point on which I will not yield, that because Patience remains unspoiled and intact, I am honor-bound to seek a higher price for her maidenhead. And I expect you will be generous in your terms. Of course, if you wish me to auction her woman's prize, I would be willing to accept reduced compensation. And then there is the question of the duration of your sponsorship."

For a moment, Rawden sat in stupefied silence, incapable of forming a coherent thought. Until that instant. Until that very second, he doubted the reliability of Rockingham's reports. Not that he didn't believe his friend, but he had trouble comprehending how any man could abandon his daughter so completely. Uncontrollable rage charged hard in the wake of his confused state. He wanted to hurt someone. To kill. Inhaling a deep breath, he summoned composure.

"Sir, you seem to be laboring under a misunderstanding." Again, he checked his ire. "I did not come here to retain your daughter as a courtesan. I seek permission to marry her, after an appropriate period of courtship."

"Are you out of your mind?" The general sputtered and took another healthy draw from the bottle of brandy. "Why on earth would a man of your estimation wish to wed Patience? She has no money. No connections. Indeed, I resorted to spending her dowry to maintain my household. Her only value is in her ability to satisfy a wealthy benefactor."

"You can't be serious." Rawden's ears rang in horror, and he clenched his fists.

"Oh, but I am." The general cast a lascivious smile that made Rawden's skin crawl. He needed to get out of there. Had to escape before he acted in haste, and his prospective father-in-law met an untimely demise. "Patience is my most precious asset. Indeed, she is the last of my holdings, and I cannot let her go for a mere pittance."

"How much?" Rawden asked, because he would spend no

more time than necessary in the general's company.

"Well, if you prefer a more permanent arrangement, I must factor lost wages into the price." The general tapped his chin. "Patience is young, and she could serve at least three, if not four, patrons, before she is too old for such work."

"Name your price." Simmering with fury, Rawden gritted his teeth. "Give me a number, and you shall have it."

"I should tell you I have entertained an offer from a particular nobleman willing to pay three hundred pounds for the pleasure of my daughter's company." The general smiled, and Rawden's stomach rebelled. "What say you, Lord Beaulieu?"

"I will give you four hundred pounds, and—"

"Papa?" Looming in the doorway, Patience hugged herself. "You are charging money for the privilege of courtship? Is this a new tradition with which I am unfamiliar?"

"Young lady, this negotiation is none of your affair." The general stood and stomped a foot. "You will go to your room, at once."

"I will not." She marched into the study, and Rawden caught her about the waist, but she wrenched free. "You bargain for my betrothal, so this concerns me. What of my dowry? What of Mama's trousseau? The family tiara? Her brooches and rings? Are those not my inheritance?"

"Hold hard, and do as I ask." Rawden backed her into the hall and signaled the housekeeper who lingered, suspiciously, in the immediate vicinity. He bent his head and whispered, "Miss Wallace, I would have you pack your belongings for an extended stay with Lord and Lady Rockingham, because you cannot remain here during our courtship." To Abigail, he said, "Please, see to it Miss Wallace has everything she needs, and prepare yourself, because I would ask you to serve as lady's maid."

"Of course, Lord Beaulieu." Gone was the sarcasm and cocky expression, as the housekeeper ushered Patience down the corridor. "Come along, Miss Wallace."

For as long as he lived, Rawden would never forget the pain

etched in Patience's heart-shaped face. How her peridot eyes, always dancing with fire, welled with unshed tears. Whether or not she realized it, the courtship was but a mere formality. She would be his wife, because he would go to his grave before he let her blackguard of a father sell her like a mare at Tattersall's.

"As you were saying, Beaulieu." The general took another gulp of brandy and dragged his tattered coat sleeve across his mouth. Belching loudly, he doddered to the desk and pulled a piece of parchment from the top drawer. "I believe the amount you mentioned was four hundred pounds. A generous sum I accept and grant permission for you to wed my daughter. As it happens, I have a standard contract drawn up by my solicitor. You need but add any amendments and sign, and Patience is yours."

"You are prepared." Rawden squared his shoulders and trod forward. After scanning the legal document, he made several notations intended to protect Patience from her father's schemes, given the original indenture referred to her as a doxy. Then he affixed his signature. In that instant, by law, Patience belonged to Rawden. "There. We have a bargain, General Wallace. I will arrange for the funds to be transferred into your possession this afternoon, once you provide a copy of the agreement to my solicitor."

"It shall be done, posthaste." The general smiled, baring teeth yellowed from decay, and Rawden almost vomited. "While I am happy with the terms, you should know I would have settled for two hundred pounds."

"How shrewd of you, sir." Rawden snickered and then sobered. "I would have paid a thousand."

The general choked, and Rawden strode from the study. In the foyer, he halted and was about to climb the stairs when Abigail whistled. The housekeeper opened what he surmised was the door to the drawing room.

"Miss Wallace is beside herself, but she wishes to speak to you." Abigail scurried to the chair and collected the gifts he purchased. "Please, follow me."

Inside the empty chamber, Patience perched on a window seat, staring at the world beyond the glass. Her gentle profile, graceful in repose, conveyed an air of quiet serenity. Rawden knew better.

"He *sold* me to you." A tear streamed down her cheek, and he cursed beneath his breath. "I belong to you, by law. I am your property to do with as you see fit."

"In a manner of speaking, aye." Rawden nodded once. "But the agreement I signed does not define you as such, and never would I consider you my property."

"General Wallace planned to barter her as a rich man's mistress." Abigail narrowed her stare. "Is that the arrangement you made?"

"No." Rawden shook his head. "I negotiated a betrothal."

"Saints be praised." Abigail wiped her brow. "You aren't so bad after all, Lord Beaulieu."

"You should know the bargain I struck includes you, Ms. Crow." He couldn't help but grin in the face of the housekeeper's astonishment. "From now on, you answer to me."

"You can dream, Lord Fancy Breeches." Abigail arched a brow. "But that is not likely."

"Are you finished?" Patience wrung her fingers. "I would know in what capacity I am to serve Lord Beaulieu."

"My dear, you are not to serve me." He eased beside her. "You are to be my countess. Of course, after an acceptable period of time, we will marry, if that is your choice."

"And what if I decide otherwise?" She appeared so fragile as she avoided his stare. "What do we tell the *ton*? We enacted a ruse? A pretend courtship?"

"Pretend courtships are for children or amateurs." With a finger, he tipped her chin, bringing her gaze to his. "I am neither."

"What is to become of me?" she asked in a small voice. "Am I to live with you?"

"Not yet." He traced the gentle curve of her cheek. "Until we take our vows, you will reside with Lord and Lady Rockingham. It has already been arranged. I apologize, but I do not trust your father with your safekeeping."

"That makes two of us." Abigail humphed. "Miss Wallace, I need to finish packing your trunk. Will you be all right with Lord Beaulieu?"

"Aye, Abigail." Patience nodded. "I will be fine."

The housekeeper handed Rawden the parcels and departed.

"You never answered my question." Patience shifted her weight. "What if we discover we do not suit?"

"Then we will announce that you called off the engagement." He would never let that happen, but she didn't need to know that. "Give whatever reason you prefer. It matters not to me. And I shall purchase a home, fully staffed, and provide an annual stipend to ensure your comfort."

"You would do that for me?" She pressed a fist to her bosom. "You would bear the embarrassment?"

"My dear, I am Beaulieu. I do as I please, and I am never embarrassed." He clucked his tongue and passed her the items he had made expressly for her. "Now, I would have you enjoy my modest offerings to your beauty and a sign of good faith."

Without a word, she studied the small package. With care, she opened his surprise. Inside, nestled on a bed of pristine white cotton, sat a brooch fashioned of gold, faceted diamonds, and emeralds, in the Sévigné tradition, with two pearls dangling in the girandole style.

"Oh, my lord. Never have I seen anything so lovely." She toyed with the priceless bauble and favored him with a brilliant smile he felt all the way down to his toes. A mistress would've spent the better part of a night demonstrating her gratitude. Yet, Patience's effortless joy, artless and pure, moved him far more than the most skilled doxy. "Thank you. I will treasure it always."

"You are most welcome." He held the larger box between them. "I hope this meets with your approval, as well, because I went to great lengths to procure it."

"How mysterious." Again, she worked free the lid and then parted the paper. The moment she glimpsed the contents, she gasped. *"Rawden."*

The breathy way she uttered his name set his senses alight.

Patience pulled free the pelisse, an exact replica of her mother's garment, for which he paid a modiste twice her regular fee to create, and leapt to her feet. After draping the expensive accoutrement about her shoulders, she fumbled with the mother-of-pearl button. Made of pale pink wool and trimmed in exquisite ermine, with a white satin lining, he captured the original down to the smallest detail. Giggling, she twirled like a young girl wearing a new dress. When she tripped, he moved into place.

His lady fell right into his arms.

"I like it when you call me by my given name." He rubbed his nose to hers. "Have I made you happy?"

"Indeed, I am euphoric, busy fingers." Abigail stood in the doorway, with a forbidding posture that might have succeeded were he not more than twice her size. "Miss Wallace is not your countess, yet. Until then, I will thank you to keep your hands to yourself and maintain a proper distance."

"Oh, Abigail, look what Lord Beaulieu bought me." Shimmering, Patience rotated. "It is just like Mama's. Is it not wonderful?"

Of course, she made no mention of the expensive jewelry. It sat, untouched, where she left it. No, she fussed over a piece of outerwear, the price of which wouldn't have paid for a single gemstone on the brooch. For some absurd reason, that appealed to him.

"Well, then." He stood and collected the jewels. "Shall we depart for Rockingham House?"

"Aye." Abigail arched a brow. "I instructed your footman to load our trunks, so we are ready."

"By all means, let us away." Rawden extended his arm, and Patience accepted his escort. Together, they crossed the threshold and skipped down the steps. On the pavement, she halted and peered over her shoulder. For a few minutes, she simply stood there and stared at her home, and he spied fresh tears. Then she turned and stepped forward. After handing her into the coach, he turned to Ms. Crow. "You know, I had a thought."

"Really?" Abigail pushed him aside. "It must have been very lonely."

To his dismay, the crochety lady's maid occupied his seat beside Patience. "Well, this is going to be fun."

CHAPTER SIX

A SENNIGHT PASSED since Patience moved to Rockingham House, and she still made her bed every morning before dressing. She tidied her room and put away her clothes. She styled her own hair, despite Arabella's gracious overture to share her personal coiffeur. And twice she collected the dirty dishes after dinner. Regardless of the plush surroundings and army of servants, some habits were hard to break.

Standing in the gallery, she gazed at a sea of portraits of Rockinghams past. She glanced left and then right. After a minute, she strolled toward the rear and discovered another maze of hallways. Returning to the gallery, she sighed and told herself she was not adrift again.

"Beg your pardon, Miss Wallace." Emily, Arabella's lady's maid, curtseyed. "If you don't mind my saying, it took me months to find my way in this huge home, and even now I find myself getting lost on occasion."

"I am looking for Lady Rockingham." Patience shuffled her feet. "And I fear I will never become accustomed to such a large residence."

"Don't trouble yourself." Emily smiled. "I am here to help, and Lady Rockingham is in the back parlor. If you will follow me, I will take you to her."

"Thank you, Emily." Patience traced the maid's steps, although she would have preferred to walk beside the domestic. But rank reigned supreme in the marquessate, and she had to abide the unwritten rules that governed their set. While she hadn't accepted Lord Beaulieu's proposal, she agreed to a courtship, but everyone acted as though she were a countess. "How is Abigail faring these days? Is she fitting in with the staff?"

Emily said naught. She merely laughed as she led Patience to the grand staircase.

"Oh, dear." Patience worried her bottom lip. "Did she try to supervise the footmen?"

"That is the least of it." Emily chuckled, and her mirth grew into full blown guffaws. "Aw, don't mind me, Miss Wallace. I find Abigail quite entertaining, as do most of the maids, especially when she tells the butler how the wind blows."

"I will speak with her." Patience shook her head. She wasn't the only one chaffing in her new surroundings. "I cannot have her disrupting the protocols when we are guests of Lord and Lady Rockingham."

"I believe Lord Rockingham favors Abigail." Patience snickered, as they strolled along a side hall. "And His Lordship teases Lord Beaulieu every time she bests him."

"That is unacceptable." Patience made a mental note to talk with Abigail about proper etiquette at the first opportunity, before she upended the entire household. "And I think I know my way from here. I turn left at the end of the hall, and it is the last room on the right."

"Yes, ma'am." Emily curtseyed. "If you would, please tell Lady Rockingham the modiste will be here at any moment, and remind her that Lord Beaulieu will be present for your fitting."

"I will, and thank you for your assistance." Alone, Patience continued down the corridor and wondered what Emily meant. As she neared the back parlor, she noticed the door sat ajar. Peering into the room, she spied Lord and Lady Rockingham sharing an impressively thorough kiss. She retreated and cleared her throat. Humming a little ditty, she knocked on the oak panel and entered the back parlor. "Hello. Am I interrupting anything of importance?"

"No." Newly perched near the hearth, Lord Rockingham peered at Arabella and smiled. "We were just talking about you. Do come in and have a seat."

"What news from my father?" Patience eased beside Arabella on the sofa. "I dispatched a missive four days ago, and I am anxious to settle the unfortunate business regarding my dowry. My mother left money intended for my future husband, and I will not allow him to purloin my inheritance."

"Er—well, that may not be possible." Lord Rockingham glanced at Arabella and then back to Patience. From a pocket he drew her correspondence. "Miss Wallace, the messenger returned your letter, unopened. It appears your father is no longer in residence, and the property is posted for sale."

"*What?*" She traced the edge of the unbroken seal, and it seemed as if the weight of the world rested on her shoulders. "And he cannot auction our home, because it belonged to my mother's family. It is part of her jointure, which was supposed to pass to my spouse."

"Apparently, the general believes otherwise." Arabella reached for Patience's hand. "Worry not. Anthony will investigate the matter and locate your father. However, I think it most propitious that you came to stay with us."

"Indeed, you are safe here." Lord Rockingham frowned. "I know not what the general is about, but I will discover his plot. And I will ensure you are not involved in his questionable dealings."

"This is terrible." Patience considered the circumstances and could discern naught in her favor. But her reputation was not the only one in peril. "And I do not see how I can continue with a courtship. Surely my father's nefarious machinations will out, and I cannot in good conscience embroil Lord Beaulieu in a scandal."

"But I love nothing better than a delicious scandal, especially when it involves me." The scamp strolled into the back parlor and bowed with his customary overzealous flair. "So, what have I done now, and what will it require to make amends?"

"We were just discussing the recent revelations surrounding General Wallace." Lord Rockingham extended his arm and flicked his fingers. "Come, darling. Let us give them some privacy to examine the situation and determine their next steps."

"But I want to stay and hear their conversation." With reluctance, Arabella stood. "I only want to help."

"I know, but this is their predicament, and they should decide on a solution." Lord Rockingham cupped her chin. "What say we adjourn to my study and put that inquisitive spirit of yours to good use?"

"My naughty lord, I like the way you think." Over her shoulder, Arabella waved to Patience. "Call out if you need us."

"Believe me, I will." Patience thought of mentioning propriety and decorum and the fact that she wasn't actually betrothed to Lord Beaulieu. Given her father's scheme, and the theft of her dowry, she could not hold Beaulieu to their agreement. To the errant earl, she said, "Join me, my lord."

"That is an offer I dare not refuse." He waggled his brows. "Perhaps, we will uncover your inquisitive spirit."

"I will have Merriweather send in the modiste when she arrives." To Rawden, Arabella said, "Behave, my lord."

"I always behave—badly, that is," he proclaimed with unabashed pride.

"Heaven help me," Patience said. As Arabella exited and closed the door, Patience faced Beaulieu. Rebukes and admonishments came to mind, because they were unchaperoned, but she had not the energy for that fight. And decorum notwithstanding, she adored him. "Perhaps you can explain who summoned a modiste? I cannot afford new gowns, and I have what I need for the few events to which I have been invited."

"Not quite." From his coat pocket he pulled a stack of envelopes, her name written on the front. "You are to attend every ball of the Season, and you must dress the part of my future countess, so I will purchase a new wardrobe befitting a lady of your station."

"You cannot be serious." Panic tied her belly in knots as she flipped through the summons. "How is this possible? Why, Lady Seton refuses to acknowledge my presence in public, and now I am to be a guest in her home?"

"My dear, your fortune has changed." Cupping her chin, he brought her gaze to his. "I signed the marriage contract and settled my account with your father, prior to his departure from London."

"Then I am yours, regardless of whether or not you want me." It was her worst nightmare come true. It was not Beaulieu she found untenable. Rather, it was the law that defined her as property to be sold to the highest bidder. "What if you decide you no longer want me?"

"Is that your concern?" With a finger, he traced the curve of her ear, and gooseflesh covered her from top to toe. When she nodded, he smiled. "I would have you know that I have no intention of letting you go, now that you are mine."

That was supposed to reassure her?

"But I am only thinking of you." What if he threw her over for another lady? One with impeccable breeding and connections. What would happen to Patience? "I want you to be happy. You are an earl. You deserve a countess with flawless manners."

"I am happy when I'm with you." He caressed her bottom lip with his thumb. "And I prefer a countess with a few imperfections, to balance mine. Does that put you at ease?"

"Not really." Dispirited, she slumped forward. She had so many misgivings, like the fact that he didn't love her, but she still wanted him. "Have you any news of my father's whereabouts or the status of the house?"

"No." He shook his head. "The general appears to have fled his creditors. It is doubtful he will see any of the money from the sale of your family home, and even that will not satisfy his debts."

"I suppose that means I should give up all hope of securing my dowry?" How could her father have stolen her marriage

ıs it not enough he had sold her precious belongings
ıf her mother's heirlooms? "So, I come to you with
the clothes on my back, and this does not bother you
"

ıld prefer you without clothes, but you would set off
ıproar in the all-together." Without doubt, he wasn't
ınd I have no need of the money."

: is not the point." She pressed a fist to her bosom. "Can
ıee? Until you receive my dowry, you lack a part of me.
ıritage. It is not just money. It is my gift to you. Instead, I
ınd empty-handed at the altar?"

ould give you something to hold, but the archbishop
ıbject, and the ladies would swoon." He winked, and the
ıible rake resurfaced with a vengeance. She scooted to the
ıs she expected, he drew near. When she tried to stand, he
d a handful of her skirt and yanked her back to the sofa.
ıt run from me."

knock at the door offered sanctuary.

ıome." She smoothed the folds of her tattered yellow,
ıed muslin morning dress and ignored his crude curse under
ıeath.

ıI am sorry to intrude, but the modiste is just arrived." Ara-
ı waved to a portly woman. "This way, Madame Clothilde.
ı may set up a temporary salon."

"We will continue our discussion at another time." Patience
ıdered her unanswered questions. What most troubled her
ıut the handsome but wounded earl was what he hid from her.
ıgardless of whether or not he admitted it, he coveted secrets,
ıd she could not trust him with her future until she knew what
ııe concealed about his past. "And don't presume I will forget,
because I am not finished with you."

"Sounds delicious." He cast a lopsided grin. "You should
threaten me more often."

"What am I to do with you?" She gained her feet.

"You want suggestions?" He stuck his tongue in his cheek,

but she ignored his innuendo. "Believe me, I am happy to oblige."

"And that is part of the problem." She gave her attention to the modiste. "Hello, Madame Clothilde. It is a pleasure to make your acquaintance."

"*Enchantée*, Mademoiselle Wallace." The modiste curtseyed. "The pleasure is mine." To the footmen, she said, "You may set the screen in the corner, and I would have my fabrics draped on the *chaise*."

A small army of servants constructed a makeshift boutique in the back parlor. Madame Clothilde sifted through what appeared to be various ready-made garments. One, in particular, caught Patience's eye, and she inspected the item.

"This *toile de jouy* silk-voile creation featuring whimsical pastoral scenes is stunning." She assessed the impressive craftsmanship about the dainty neckline accented with delicate white guipure lace. "I adore the Juliet sleeves. How I hope this fits me."

"Oh, it will, I promise." The modiste sat a small basket atop a side table and drew forth a pin cushion. "I used the same measurements Lady Rockingham provided for the previous gowns. If you will, step behind the screen and try on the dress so I can make any necessary adjustments to the hem."

"What previous gowns?" Patience walked into the improvised changing area and reached back to unbutton her frock. She doffed her frayed shift and pulled the *toile de jouy* over her head. "Do you reference the wardrobe Lady Rockingham purchased for the Little Season?"

"No, mademoiselle." The modiste chuckled. "I am talking about the lavish articles Lord Beaulieu commissioned for you. His Lordship garbs you like a queen. The burgundy was a true feat of artistry, but the emerald was the masterpiece in my collection for the Season, and I would have you know he outbid a viscount, two marquesses, and a duke to purchase the gem."

"I beg your pardon?" Praying for composure, but suspecting she had been duped, she strolled from behind the screen. The instant she peered at Arabella, Patience knew she had been fooled. "I was told those items belonged to the Marchioness of Rockingham."

"I think I hear Lord Rockingham calling." Arabella all but ran from the back parlor.

"Lord Beaulieu, what have you to say for yourself?" Patience folded her arms and tapped her foot in an impatient rhythm. "Well?"

"Madame Clothilde, would you be kind enough to give us the room?"

"*Oui, bien sûr*, Lord Beaulieu." The modiste scurried into the hall.

He gave Patience his full attention. "My dear Miss—"

"Don't you dare 'my dear Miss' me, sir." Patience squared her shoulders and lifted her chin. "I will know this instant what I am to you. Am I a joke? Am I a charity case? No more evasion, Lord Beaulieu. I will have the whole of it, or I will not marry you now or any other time. I shall pack what little belongings I own and depart London, and you will never see—"

He quieted her with a kiss.

No, not a kiss.

A soul-stirring, mind-numbing advance that obliterated her anger.

"You threaten me in earnest, and you should have care how you speak, when I have done nothing to merit such treatment," he whispered as he loomed toe-to-toe with her, but she refused to relent. "I am guilty of many things, but making sport of a lady who is more important to me than my life is not one of them. And know that you can run, but you cannot hide from me. There is no escape. There is no place you can go where I would not find you—and I would find you."

For several seconds, they stood there, at an impasse.

He bent over her, his head so close his breath teased her flesh, and for a moment she thought he might kiss her again. Prayed he would kiss her again.

"What are you saying?" she inquired, at last, as she processed his declaration.

"You are a smart woman, Patience." He licked his lips and studied her mouth. "You know precisely what I said, and I meant every word of it."

"But—why?" Suddenly giddy, she told herself not to leap to conclusions woven from whole cloth. Then again, Rawden left nothing to interpretation. Why did she still have reservations? What was he hiding from her? "My lord, it is difficult to believe in someone who does not believe in me."

"I have faith in you." He retreated, and she knew she was right. "I have always had faith in you."

"But not in yourself." He gave her his back, and she ached to hold him. To comfort him. "I know something is wrong. Will you not share your burden with me?"

"If I do, you will realize that I am a farce." He shook his head. "And you will scorn me."

"That will never happen." She walked to him and clutched his hand. He peered over his shoulder at her, and she spied the pain. The anguish he could not deny. "You struggle with guilt. You do not believe you deserved to survive the war that claimed so many lives. What I do not know or understand is why."

"You are very perceptive, Miss Wallace—"

"Patience."

"And I am Rawden." Now he rotated to face her, and he restored the mask he wore to conceal his suffering. "Or whatever love names you invent to summon me."

"Can you be serious?" She prepared a rapier retort and then forgot it. "What are love names?"

"I am being serious. And use your imagination, but my darling, my innocent angel, or my supreme seducer will do nicely." Given his shocking reply, she could only blink. He huffed a breath. "Is this your only impediment to our union?"

"Not precisely." She held her ground. "But it is the most pressing."

"Fine." Again, he moved into a position of intimidation, but she would not yield. "Marry me, and I will share everything with you."

"Have I your word, as a gentleman?" she asked with heightened anticipation. "You will withhold nothing if I consent to be your wife?"

"You have my word," he murmured as he caressed her cheek, "*if* you wed me."

"Then I promise to give your offer due consideration as we court." He appeared relived, until she added, "But I will not forget our terms, Lord Beaulieu. I will hold you to our bargain."

"SHE WANTS TO know what happened during the war." Rawden stood beside Rockingham and admired Patience, breathtaking in a gown of powder blue, as she danced with Greyson at the Howard's gala. "Indeed, she insists I tell her everything. What am I to do?"

"What can you do?" Rockingham shrugged and grinned at his bride, as she circled the floor with her father, the Earl of Ainsworth. "Besides, the truth will always out, and better she hear it from you than in the latest *on-dit*. And what do you fear? If she is to be your partner, she should know what troubles you."

"You know the whole of it. You know of my shame." Patience peered in Rawden's direction, and he winked. Her smile broadened, and his heart skipped a beat. "Were you in my position, would you share the disgraceful revelations with Lady Rockingham?"

"Without hesitation, but I take issue with your portrayal of your deeds." Rockingham nodded once. "Then again, in some ways, Arabella knew me better than I knew myself when we first met. During our courtship, she anticipated aspects of my character with uncanny accuracy. Never did she mock me or make sport of my pain. Rather, she helped me. I would wager Miss Wallace intends the same for you. She will offer support and comfort, if you let her."

"Were you so candid with Lady Rockingham?" Of course, Rawden knew well his friend initially resisted attempts at such forthrightness. "I seem to recall someone raising quite the fuss over a surprise appointment with Dr. Handley."

"And I was wrong, which I admit without reservation. By the by, you should give Dr. Handley a chance. He can help." Rockingham shifted his weight. "I do not mean to lecture, but I am trying to prevent you from making the same mistake with Miss Wallace." He came alert. "Lively, my friend. Our ladies draw near."

"I require a diversion," Rawden said in a low voice. He had done the pretty enough for the night, and he ached to be alone with Patience.

"Give me a few minutes, and you may make your exit through the terrace doors." Rockingham executed an exaggerated bow. "My dear Lady Rockingham, may I have the pleasure of this waltz?"

"My lord, you may have whatever you wish." Lady Rocking-ham curtseyed and inclined her head like a polished coquette. "I live to serve."

The blissfully married couple proceeded to enact a full-scale seduction perfectly orchestrated to the music, which captured the imagination of those present. Their connubial bond was the stuff of legend. It was the stuff of fairy tales promising a happily ever after that rarely succeeded in real life.

As the crush focused on the Marquess and Marchioness of Rockingham, Rawden clutched Patience's hand and led her toward the rear of the stifling ballroom. When they neared the open door, they were rudely bumped, and he briefly lost sight of her amid the throng. At last, she emerged, holding an envelope.

"Are you all right?" he asked as she rejoined him, and they stepped onto the flagged surface. "We took quite a jolt, but I did not see the perpetrator."

"It was a tad unsettling, because I was shoved from side to side, and then someone thrust a missive into my grasp." She glanced at the mysterious letter and frowned. "How odd. It is for you."

"That is strange." He gazed at his name scribbled in familiar writing on the parchment, and a shiver of dread coursed his spine. Even without unfolding the note, he knew the contents. Could recite the message from memory. That the sender had grown bold enough to deliver it via Patience, in a public venue, told Rawden he faced real danger. He had to marry her before she discovered the truth of his service and the resulting citation, else she would never wed him. What woman wanted a coward for a husband? "Let us take a stroll, as I am in need of fresh air."

"Of course." She rested her palm in the crook of his elbow. "Are you not going to open the correspondence? It could be important."

"It is nothing." The crunch of pebbles beneath his booted feet broke the silence as he steered her toward the tiny gazebo bordered by a crescent of mighty oaks, at the back of the rose garden. Dark and secluded, it was the perfect place for a lover's tryst, and he required a distraction else he might go mad. "This way."

A tall, thick hedgerow afforded ample cover from the silvery glow of moonlight on the clear night. At last, the diminutive structure appeared, and he lifted his lady up the two stairs. She moved to the center of the little summer house, and he stalked her. When she faced him, he pulled her into his arms.

"My lord, just what are you about?" She shoved at his chest. "I thought we were to take some air. You cannot mean to enact a rendezvous here, in the middle of the Howard's garden."

"Why not?" He relaxed his hold and breathed a sigh of relief that she did not completely pull away from him. He was not sure he could take her rejection just then. "But we do nothing wrong. I guarantee we are not the only couple sheltering in the shadows."

"That may be, but I have a reputation to protect, and my family name is not the best." Even in the faint light, he could neither evade nor ignore her unmistakable expression of disapproval. "While I have indulged your less than appropriate behaviors on previous occasions, those moments occurred when we enjoyed friendly territory. Here we risk discovery. Would you play fast and loose with my social standing?"

He was about to reply when voices signaled approaching interlopers.

"Shh." He pressed a finger to her lips. Then he whispered, "Follow me."

With her fingers wound in his, they ducked out the rear of the gazebo. Hunkered, they scrambled across a lawn and sheltered beneath the canopy of a large maple. As he suspected, a pair of partygoers sprinted into the gazebo.

"What do we do now?" Patience inquired in a low voice.

"We employ a decent measure of the trait for which you are named and wait." It occurred to him then he had his lady right where he wanted her. Alone, in the dark. It mattered not that they had no roof over their heads. They had the next best thing, a natural cover under which no one would notice two silhouettes. In silence, he drew her into his embrace. When she tensed, he rubbed the small of her back. "Do not be afraid. I only want to hold you."

Without a word, she moved closer. Then she shifted and wrapped her arms about his waist. Little by little, she relaxed until, at last, she rested her head to his chest. Delicious warmth seeped into his veins, spreading the length of his limbs and pervading every muscle. Desire flickered, the flame growing ever steady. Fully clothed and aroused, it was the most intensely erotic experience of his life.

A series of cherished vignettes played before him—the future he coveted. Patience aglow on their wedding day. Later, round with his heir. Fair-haired babes to rival Michelangelo's wingless angels. Family evenings spent in spirited discourse. Journeys to the Continent. Savoring sunsets with his wife, in the twilight of their years. And he wanted it all.

But an unknown villain threatened Rawden's plans, an ever-present reminder that he deserved none of it.

A lilting giggle snared his attention, and he just glimpsed Lord and Lady Rockingham stealing into a small enclosure that shielded a stone bench from view of the house. In the moonlight, the couple enacted a heated assignation that left Rawden tugging at his suddenly snug shirt collar. When he glanced at Patience and considered the scene through her eyes, he clenched his gut.

For a moment, she seemed transfixed by what she witnessed. Unrestrained passion. When Rockingham bent his head and thrust his face into his wife's decolletage, Patience's breath quickened, and with one hand she clutched her throat. Then she looked directly at him, dropped her gaze to his mouth, and again met his stare, and what he spied, the unbridled ardor, left him weak in the knees. And hungry.

"We should return to the ball." While he had no preference for such events, other than his ability to secure a companion for the night, his priorities had changed. Since he doubted his usually vaunted self-control in the face of his lady's inexpressible fervor, he required restraint of another sort. "Before anyone notices our absence."

She nodded, and they wound their way through the topiaries to a fountain. Just beyond the reflecting pool sat the west wing of the residence. As he anticipated, the doors to the back parlor were unlocked, and he pulled Patience into the dimly lit room. After securing the latch, he turned and tensed.

"How do you know the lay of the land so well?" The subtle tilt of her head, her rigid posture hinted at a temper. "I could scarcely see, but you knew precisely where to go. And how did you know we could reenter the house here?" He fought to muster a reply. Searched for an excuse to mollify her but came up woefully short. When he remained mute, she frowned. "This is not the first time you brought a woman here, is it?"

"No." Rawden could have lied, and he thought about it. But for him, with her, he opted for honesty. "In truth, there have been more than I care to admit."

"And I presume that once we are wed, I will be the lone recipient of such affection?" Now she set fists on hips. "Or do you intend to go on with such nefarious dealings? Am I to be humiliated? A figure of scorn for the *ton's* amusement?"

"Of course, not." He stomped to the hearth and gazed into the blaze. "My hope is you will hold my attention, exclusively."

"So, it is my duty to keep you entertained and satisfied." From the looks of it, his response had not improved his standing. "Else you will seek divertissement with another."

"I wouldn't say that." Yet, that was the way of things in most society marriages.

"But that's what you mean," she said with a sharp tongue that left him in no doubt of her disapproval.

"You are putting words in my mouth." He took a step in her direction.

"No, you put your boot in your mouth." She furrowed her brow and met him measure for measure. "I merely forced you to chew on the leather."

"My dear Patience, I would argue that I indulged in the behavior expected of a man, prior to our acquaintance." He leaned over her, bringing their noses mere inches apart. "But I submit I shall be too busy educating you in the intricacies of marital bliss to even consider taking another into my bed. And it should cheer you to know I have always believed an earl's private chamber is reserved for his countess. However, when I take a mistress, I am always discreet."

"I see." Crestfallen, she slumped forward, and he realized too late that he hurt her. "And what of me? Am I permitted to seek companionship, in kind?"

Knife to the heart with lethal precision.

"If that is your wish." The instant he delivered the statement he feared he might vomit. The second impression he got was he would never let that happen. "What say we form a pact."

"What do you propose?" He detected a hint of upset in her voice. "Because I am no longer sure we are on the same page when I was certain we were as one."

"Sweet darling, we could take an oath of our own making." Ideas formed in his brain in rapid succession. He had to do something—anything to avoid even a hint of infidelity on her part, because Rawden could not bear the thought of another man touching Patience. The answer, when it came to him, seemed so simple. And obvious. "I submit we agree, as a couple, to remain faithful to our vows and each other. Should there come a time when either of us is unhappy with the intimate aspect of our union, we pledge to discuss it in a preemptive attempt to alleviate the situation. Should we fail to devise a solution to the problem, then and only then would we be free to seek comfort from another. For this to work, we must commit to honesty above all else."

"That sounds reasonable, and I am especially intrigued by your emphasis on truthfulness. Indeed, I value candor more than you realize." She smiled, and the tension investing his spine eased. "Perhaps, now you will tell me what is in the letter? Is it from another woman?"

Once again, he danced in an abyss of misery of his own making.

"What—*no.*" Raking his fingers through his hair, he cleared his throat. "It is not that, I promise."

"Then you have no reason not to let me read the missive." When he failed to relent, she sighed. "If you have nothing to hide, then show me the correspondence. *Now.*"

They loomed at a precarious impasse, and he could find no way out of the predicament. If he refused her demand, she would believe him dishonest. If he acquiesced, she would hate him. With no other option, he drew the crisp piece of folded parchment from his coat pocket and presented it to her.

For a moment, she studied the nondescript seal. Then she

broke the wax and unfolded the letter. The room was silent save the mantel clock. Ticking monotonously toward his demise. She scrutinized the writing and ran a finger over the directive. At last, she peered at him.

"I do not understand." Patience wrinkled her adorable nose. "You were decorated for your actions at Quatre Bras, so what is the truth, and who wrote this note?"

"This is not the time to discuss the matter, and I already promised I would explain everything after we wed." Of course, that elementary declaration would never appease her, and he seized on a means of escape. "Suffice it to say, things are not so easily defined in war. As I have told you before, I committed deeds I am not necessarily proud of, to survive. Soon, I will share my experiences, in detail. But we should return to the ballroom, else we risk discovery."

"You are afraid." To his shock and amazement, she slipped her arms about his waist and hugged him. "You believe I will shun you if I know your sad tale, but you are wrong. My father is a general, so I know well the decisions that must be made in a hairsbreadth, during battle, and I would never presume to judge you. In fact, I promise I will never attempt to criticize your actions as a soldier." She released him and retreated a step. Taking his hand in hers, she led him to the door. "Now, let us rejoin the revelers. Soon, the dinner bell will ring, and I am famished."

CHAPTER SEVEN

T HE EXPRESSION OF unutterable vulnerability, the shadows dancing just beneath the surface, razor sharp in detail, plagued Patience's slumber after she returned to Rockingham House the previous night. In the dark, she tossed and turned, until she finally drifted into the land of anguished dreams. Still, Lord Beaulieu's boyish innocence, haunting and taunting in its arresting misery, pursued her. She recalled how he clung to her. How he trembled in her arms, as they hid in the Howard's back parlor, and how he hesitated before releasing her, so they could return to the ballroom.

At dinner, he composed himself, a gossamer mask comprised of forced overconfidence and smug pretension that fooled everyone but her, because an undercurrent of fear invested his every action had anyone chosen to see it. Something troubled him. A secret. A revelation he worked hard to conceal, yet the disclosure manifested in his troubled gaze every time he looked at her. She could not help but wonder what drove the guilt that gnawed at his soul, in a slow and painful torture?

What happened at Quatre Bras?

Pacing before the window in Lord Rockingham's study, she waited and considered her options with care. Somehow, she had to win Lord Beaulieu's confidence, in order to discover the identity of his tormentor. What did the unknown villain want from Beaulieu and to what purpose? Questions for which she had no answer. Hesitant to meddle, yet she had to unearth the truth. She knew, deep down, it was the only way she could support him as he recovered from the scars of war. She'd seen enough of Lord Rockingham's transformation with Arabella's assistance to know there existed a similar future for Rawden, if only he were brave enough to grasp the chance.

But that meant confronting the past.

"I beg your pardon." Lord Rockingham knocked on the door and furrowed his brow. "Am I interrupting something? Are you looking for Lady Rockingham?"

"My lord." She came alert and curtseyed. "Actually, I would speak with you, if I may."

"Of course." The handsome marquess crossed the room and sat in the leather high back chair behind his desk. "I am glad we have a moment alone, because I would have a word with you, as well, while my wife tends our son."

"Oh?" Patience perched in one of the matching Hepplewhite chairs and gave him her full attention. "Have I done something wrong?"

"Not at all." He averted his gaze and smiled. "Rather, I have a request of a delicate nature."

"Whatever I have, it is at your disposal, sir." She clasped her hands in her lap and stretched upright. "What can I do for you?"

"I would ask you not to share with Lady Rockingham your presence in the Howard's garden, last night." He blushed. "She is unaware we had witnesses to our amorous dalliance, and I would keep it that way. I do so adore her feisty spirit, and I would not see it stifled by embarrassment."

"My lord, I would never mention it, given I should not have permitted Lord Beaulieu to lead me astray, because we are not married, whereas you and Lady Rockingham had every right to be there. I promise, on my utmost discretion you can rely." She leaned forward. "The reason I am here is Lord Beaulieu."

"Indeed?" He arched a brow. "Now it is my turn to ask how I can be of assistance?"

"I am not sure where to begin." For a few minutes, she reflected on her initial concerns. She opened her mouth and then closed it. She pointed a finger and faltered. "I am at a loss."

"I believe the beginning is usually best." Kind and reassuring, Lord Rockingham rested his elbow atop the blotter. "Take your time and just talk to me, because I am your friend."

"Your Lordship, I know that, but it is another friendship that occupies my thoughts to the detriment of all else. I would like to know about Lord Beaulieu," she blurted. Then she checked her tone. "That is, what happened to him at Quatre Bras? I read the official account in *The Times*, but I am well aware the papers do not always tell the whole story. Lord Beaulieu intimates there is more to the battle than I know, and I am convinced his assertion is the cause of unfounded trepidation on his part. What does he believe he did wrong?"

"Well, that is an answer for Beaulieu." Lord Rockingham studied at her and then frowned. "Although I gather he has not been very forthcoming."

"Downright stubborn is more like it." She shifted her weight and clenched her fingers. "He refuses to discuss his military experience with me. However, at the Howard's, someone thrust a letter, addressed to Lord Beaulieu, into my grasp, as His Lordship ushered me through the crush. I did not see the sender, and His Lordship has been most secretive."

"Not again." Rockingham rolled his eyes.

"There have been other missives?" she asked, as a chill traipsed her spine.

"Aye." Rockingham rubbed his chin. "What did it say, or did you read it?"

"I did." She nodded. "After much cajoling and, dare I admit it, an ultimatum of sorts, Beaulieu relented. It bore but a single sentence."

"I know the truth of Quatre Bras," he replied without hesitation.

"*Yes.*" Stunned by Lord Rockingham's statement, she realized someone threatened Rawden, and last night was not the first time. "While Lord Beaulieu assures me it is nothing, I don't believe him. He is afraid, Lord Rockingham. He is consumed with guilt and shame for some unknown reason, and he will not confide in me. Can you enlighten me? Can you tell me who wishes ill on a man lauded a hero by the whole of England? Please, I beg you. I only want to help Lord Beaulieu."

"It is neither my place nor my story to tell." Lord Rockingham pounded his fist atop the desk and stood. "But I like you, Miss Wallace. I believe you will be the making of my friend, if you have the determination and fortitude, and that is why I support your cause. Still, I must know from you that you are committed to seeing him through to the end."

"Lord Rockingham, I will do whatever it takes to aid Lord Beaulieu, just as Lady Rockingham sustained you. Woe the person who menaces him." When he drew a leatherbound tome from a cabinet, she inclined her head. "I know that book. It belongs to Lady Rockingham."

"I should have known she shared it with you." He eased to the matching Hepplewhite chair beside her and flipped open the large volume. "This is Dr. Larrey's treatise on what he terms nostalgia, and it contains a wealth of information you will find useful if you are to succeed with Beaulieu."

"He suffers from the malady, too?" she inquired, as she perused a page with notes scribbled in the margins. "He endures the same symptoms?"

"I suspect we all struggle with our own demons after the war, some more than others." Lord Rockingham gave the book into her hands. "But I doubt any two soldiers share the same afflictions, as a result of their service. At least, that is the case according to Dr. Larrey. You might benefit from a meeting with Dr. Handley, because he is well-versed in Larrey's methodology."

"What of Beaulieu? Should I ask him to join me?" She wondered how well that request would be received, but she suspected she knew the answer. "Did Lady Rockingham invite you to her first appointment?"

"Uh—no." Lord Rockingham tugged at his cravat. "Arabella ambushed me, for lack of a better description, and I did not appreciate it—at first. However, I soon learned how useful Dr. Handley's suggestions, based on Larrey's recommendations for treatment, could improve my life and my ability to cope with the lingering effects of war."

"Then how should I broach the subject with Lord Beaulieu?" Patience located a section on guilt in relation to shame, which Beaulieu possessed in spades. "From my position, this seems daunting."

"Of that I have no doubt." Lord Rockingham chuckled. "But you are a smart woman, much like my bride, and I expect you will figure it out."

"Indeed, she is." Arabella strolled into the study. "And what will she figure out?"

"We were discussing Larrey, and I encouraged Miss Wallace to speak with Dr. Handley, concerning Beaulieu." Lord Rockingham slapped his thigh, and Lady Rockingham responded immediately. She stepped about his legs and sat in his lap. "I believe Beaulieu could only thrive with Dr. Handley's guidance, using Larrey's concepts."

"I couldn't agree more, but I would offer a word of caution." Arabella draped an arm about her husband's shoulders. "You can expect considerable resistance when you introduce the topic. Not because Beaulieu is familiar with Larrey but because military men have extremely hard heads, present company included."

"Now, I resent that, darling. Really, I do." Lord Rockingham pouted and Arabella nipped his nose. "In all seriousness, I would rather Miss Wallace be upfront and honest with Beaulieu about her motives, when it comes to Larrey. I do not think he will be so forgiving, otherwise."

"You are right." To Patience, Arabella said, "I hid the book from Anthony, and it was the wrong decision. He found it by accident, and he was none too pleased with me."

"That is because a measure of trust is necessary to accept assistance when confronting the ugliness of the past. Your deceit, however well intended, felt suspiciously like a betrayal. I could take duplicity from anyone but my bride." Lord Rockingham nuzzled Arabella, and she patted his cheek. "It was not easy for me. Indeed, it was downright hell, and I wager it will be more so for Beaulieu."

"Why?" Curious, Patience turned to a chapter on self-reproach. "Would he not want to get better?"

"It is not a matter of improving himself, and I speak from experience." Lord Rockingham compressed his lips. "While I know it is difficult to comprehend, the reality is Beaulieu does not believe he has a problem. He does not view his battle scars as an affliction in need of treatment or healing, and the first step must be his decision."

"You are correct in that I do not understand." Patience shook her head. "If Lord Beaulieu does not confront and address the wounds of the past, he will forever bleed."

"Which is why Beaulieu will need you to lead him down a curative path." Arabella cupped her husband's chin and held his stare. Unspoken words of unshakeable devotion passed between them, and Patience envied their steadfast bond. "And I can promise you a devil of a fight. He will resist your efforts. He may even turn away from you, yet you must persist in your goal."

"Eventually, he will discern the uncomfortable truth, and he will welcome your assistance." Lord Rockingham rubbed his nose to Arabella's. "And he will thank you for your intercession on his behalf."

The study grew unusually warm, and Patience closed the book and stood.

"Well, it appears I have quite a bit of reading to do, and I should not dawdle given I have no time to lose." She curtseyed. "My Lord and Lady Rockingham, I bid you a pleasant afternoon."

"Would you be so good as to secure the door behind you?" Lord Rockingham asked, as he gazed like a hungry predator at

Arabella. "And tell Merriweather we are not to be disturbed."

"Aye, Lord Rockingham." She did as he bade, and a feminine shriek echoed as she paused in the hall. Patience could not help but laugh as she strolled into the foyer, where she found the butler. "Merriweather, Lord and Lady Rockingham wish to be left alone."

"Understood." The manservant bowed. "Thank you, Miss Wallace."

Looming at the base of the grand staircase, she hugged the heavy tome to her chest and tapped her foot. Then she turned and set course in a different direction.

"Merriweather, may I trouble you for a spot of tea, in the back parlor?" She considered her next step in her quest to assist Lord Beaulieu. As Arabella championed Lord Rockingham, Patience resolved to support the man she decided, at some point, would be her husband. "Also, have you any stationary I might use?"

"There are writing materials in the escritoire by the window." Merriweather smiled. "And I shall see to it a fresh pot of tea and a plate of shortbread is delivered, at once, Miss Wallace."

"Thank you, Merriweather." She dipped her chin and strolled down the correct corridor, because she finally learned to navigate the massive residence.

In the cozy sitting room, she admired the décor of pale blue with soft gold accents, Arabella's signature colors. Indeed, much of the house boasted a woman's touch, and Patience pondered the fact that she might be expected to provide the same influence in Beaulieu's home.

The prospect seemed daunting from every angle she approached it.

It dawned on her then that she needed to enlist her childhood friend's assistance in learning the myriad duties expected of a chatelaine. Although Patience had been born and bred for the position of society wife, all the relevant training ended when her mother died. From memory, she recalled little of the obligations required of a noblewoman. Her studies necessitated additional coursework to prepare her for a future she had thought beyond her.

Returning her attention to the book, she trailed her fingers across the cover, which bore the title, *Soldier's Nostalgia and Other Battlefield Maladies* by Dominique Jean Larrey. Although she recalled numerous conversations with Arabella, regarding the material, their discussions revolved around Lord Rockingham's symptoms.

Beaulieu manifested his own trauma, along with an unidentified malefactor.

According to Larrey, nostalgia presented in three stages. First, the afflicted displayed heightened excitement and imagination. That description stopped her in her tracks. How was she supposed to distinguish whether or not the indications were due to an ailment or to Beaulieu's larger than life character, because she suspected he exhibited such traits prior to his military service?

The obvious answer far exceeded her basic knowledge of the man. Indeed, she needed the advice and direction of an expert.

A knock at the door intruded on her thoughts.

"Come," she called.

Merriweather set wide the oak panel, and Emily carried in a tray laden with a pot of tea and tempting treats, which she placed on the table.

"Will there be anything else, Miss Wallace?" the provincial lady's maid, always ready to lend a hand, inquired. "Shall I pour you a cup?"

"No, thank you, Emily." Patience moved the book from her lap and scooted forward. "I will serve myself."

Once again alone with her musings, she reflected on her goals. If she could not accurately assess Lord Beaulieu, how could support him? The answer was she could not. Indeed, she could do more harm than good. Her only solution was to seek guidance.

Patience glanced at the escritoire and jumped to her feet. She pulled back the matching chair and sat. After surveying the contents of a couple of drawers, she located blank parchment. From an inkwell, she drew a quill and wrote a salutation to the recipient.

Dear Dr. Handley...

IT WAS ANOTHER night, another ball, and another display of the bloated opulence that characterized the *ton*. Ambivalent after the flanking maneuver expertly executed by his unknown assailant at the Howard's ball, which situated Patience at the center of a dispute he could neither anticipate nor avoid, Beaulieu opted to journey to the Ellsworth's in his own rig. Still, he missed her presence and vowed to lure her into the garden, which he knew so well, and engage in an assignation designed to calm his frayed nerves.

She could do that for him.

Would do that for him.

At the main entrance to the grand residence on Park Lane, he lingered and waited for the Rockingham coach to appear. When it pulled to the curb, he peered down and brushed off his dark green coat. As always, he wanted to look his best for his lady.

One by one, Lord and Lady Rockingham descended the elegant equipage. At last, Patience emerged into the faint glow of the coach lamps, and Rawden stood stock-still at attention. The world around her faded into the background, as she stole center stage. Bedecked in *eau de nil* silk, which highlighted her glorious guinea gold locks, she rivaled Botticelli's singular subject in *The Birth of Venus*.

Then she spied him and smiled.

All he could do was stare.

Until Rockingham snapped his fingers in Rawden's face.

"I beg your pardon." Rawden scowled. "Have you naught better do to with yourself? Surely your wife has some need you can fulfill instead of pestering me."

"Perhaps, but I know that look, much like a flushed fox." Rockingham smirked. "Have spent many painful hours on the other side of that expression, and I would say you are in for a wild night."

"One can hope." Rawden pushed aside his friend to offer Patience his escort, before some ne'er-do-well beat him to the prize. "Good evening, Miss Wallace. May I have the honor of accompanying you into the ballroom?"

"Lord Beaulieu." She curtseyed, and what he would give to peel her out of that gown. "The honor is mine."

"Shall we join our friends?" When she nodded with enthusiasm, he chuckled. "I wager this will be an unforgettable fête, my dear."

"Oh, I hope so." She squeezed his arm as they strolled into the foyer. "I sat for more than an hour while Lady Rockingham's coiffeur styled my hair."

"He merely put a frame on a masterpiece, loveliest and cherished Patience." It dawned on him then, just how to win her hand. He had to lure her with irresistible temptations. He had to charm her. He had to entice and cajole. She was, after all, a woman. "Shall we wander to the back of the ballroom, where the *Triumph of Prudence* hangs?"

"Yes, please." They approached the front end of the receiving line, and while Lord Ellsworth greeted Patience, Lady Ellsworth turned aside, effectively cutting her guest. Too well-mannered to protest the slight, Patience pretended not to notice. "I am told the tapestry is one of the finest in existence."

"Indeed." He ushered her into the grand hall, nodding acknowledgements and seething as various members of society disregarded his lady. Could none of them see her worth? Did no one value her seraphic contentment, so pure in her delight? "It is said to have been part of the *Triumph of the Seven Virtues*, woven in the early fifteenth century."

"Do you know any more of its history?" She sidled closer and turned to meet his stare, and he wondered how anyone could ignore her. "I have heard it is somewhat a mystery."

"Indeed." How he adored her keen mind, so inquisitive. He would put her curious nature to good use, in an altogether different realm, once they were married. She presented endless delectable possibilities, and he would gladly spend a lifetime exercising her imagination. "Given it bears no weaver's mark, its origin is unknown, but some believe it comes from Brussels."

"How fascinating." She halted, and her mouth fell agape. "Oh, my lord, it is stunning."

"It is a wall hanging," he whispered in her ear. "You are stunning."

"Lord Beaulieu, I must protest." Patience pressed a hand to her oh-so-tempting bosom, but her accompanying giggle belied any offense taken. "Tell me truly, do women usually succumb to your bold proclamations? Are they so easily swayed?"

"Always." Now he guffawed. "But never more so than when I returned to England, after the war."

"Because you are a hero." When he sobered, she squeezed his fingers. "Please, do not worry. Regardless of your unknown tormentor, I support you."

"Miss Wallace, you make too much of nothing." He winked, hoping his customary bravado diverted her interest in his unidentified nemesis. "And no matter what you or anyone else claim, I will never consider myself a soldier worthy of such high praise. I did my duty and naught more."

"Well said, my lord." To his relief, she returned her focus to the artwork. "I presume that is Prudence, situated at center. But who holds the shield?"

"That is Zeus." He pointed for emphasis. "And the figure to the left is Titan Prometheus."

"Never have I seen such masterful craftsmanship." The first musical strains signaled the dance commenced, and she glanced over her shoulder. "Thank you for the lesson, Lord Beaulieu. I quite enjoyed it."

"Always a pleasure, Miss Wallace." He brushed the backs of her fingers to his mouth, and she blushed. "Shall we waltz, my dear?"

"Of course, my lord." She sketched a flirty curtsey.

Together, they navigated the crush. Then he slipped an arm about her waist and eased her into the rotation. Yes, he held her too close, but he didn't care. Patience spoke to him on a level no one else could reach. She had a way of soothing his frayed nerves and calming his inner demons. While he had yet to secure her hand in marriage, he vowed he would win her, if he had to make the rounds of every ballroom in London, and he set about to do just that.

As the evening progressed, he stood as sentry, guarding his lady. Although the wolves sniffed at her skirts, no one dared challenge Rawden. In no uncertain terms, he made it clear Patience had a suitor more than prepared to defend his claim.

"My friend, you should relax." Rockingham elbowed Rawden in the ribs. "And Arabella asked me to tell you to stop undressing Miss Wallace with your gaze."

"I do no such thing." He folded his arms and admired the subtle play of candlelight on Patience's soft, golden curls. When he glanced at Rockingham, his fellow wounded veteran arched a brow. "Well, I can't help it. Your lovely, nosy bride gowned my future wife in *eau de nil,* leaving nothing to the imagination, and I've surmised countless different ways I could take her out of that tempting frock. She looks like a Greek goddess, ripe for the picking. Do you blame me?"

"No." Rockingham chuckled. "But if you do not behave, I will have to deal with my wife, and I make it my business never to *deal* with my wife."

"Oh, all right. I will do my best, but I promise nothing." Rawden huffed a breath. "Indeed, I am convinced, and I will argue the point with anyone who gainsays me, that courtship is a vicious game concocted by marriage-minded mamas to drive men insane, such that we will promise anything when negotiating the betrothal contract. The wait is brutal. I am so aroused I could bounce guineas off my main mast."

"That is a thought I prefer not to envision." Rockingham winced. "But I understand. Still, you will try, for my sake?"

"Of course." He adjusted his black patch and glanced toward the heavens, starting when the dinner bell rang. "Excellent. Perhaps food will distract me."

"Not likely." Rockingham stuck his tongue in his cheek. "Believe me, I speak from experience. Prior to our nuptials, I took Arabella for ices at Gunter's, and was that ever a mistake. Never in my wildest dreams could I have foreseen the erotic adventures of consuming a simple confection, but suddenly all I could think of were naughty deeds one would hesitate to ask of a professional, much less a gently-reared virgin."

"Really?" Rawden followed Patience, as she strolled, arm-in-arm, with Lady Rockingham. In his mind, he pictured the particular sweet Rockingham referenced. The realization, when it came to him, brought gales of laughter. "Oh, I say, I never knew you had it in you."

"Brother, there is nothing so powerful, or intoxicating, as unspent passion." Rockingham slapped Rawden on the shoulder. "Especially when the desired is your future bride. Just keep your main mast leashed until you are properly wed. Then, with restraint and care, you can educate her in the finer aspects of marital intimacy."

"And how did that work for you, given you secured an heir?" Rawden asked in a low voice. "Can you honestly say you are satisfied?"

"To elaborate would be ungentlemanly." Rockingham paused and surveyed his marchioness. He winked, and she smiled. "Suffice it to say Arabella holds my interest, unequivocally, and I cannot fathom that ever changing."

With that, Rockingham claimed the seat next to Lady Rockingham, leaving Rawden to occupy the empty chair beside Patience. Ensconced in a dimly lit corner near a pair of open terrace doors, he draped his napkin in his lap and inhaled the fresh scent of roses and honeysuckle wafting from the gardens.

"Have I told you how lovely you look tonight?" He took Patience's hand in his and pressed his lips to the tender flesh on the underside of her wrist. He could eat her alive if given the chance. "That gown is inspiring."

Not for an instant would he consider telling her what she inspired, because his Jolly Roger was overly jolly and too ready to maraud.

"Lord Beaulieu, this is a treat." A certain importuning widow thrust her hip and almost knocked Patience to the floor. "It has been too long. Why have you not called on me?"

"Er—I beg your pardon." He tried but failed to dodge the previous dalliance. "Good evening, Lady Fauconberg."

"Now, now. When did we become so formal?" She raked her fingers through his hair, and he jerked free. "My, but I am parched. Be a dear and fetch me a glass of champagne, while I become acquainted with your charming little friend, General Wallace's unfortunate daughter."

To his horror, Patience pushed from the table and fled onto the terrace.

Without so much as a backward glance, he gave chase. In the cool night air, he halted and trained his ear for the slightest sound. A delicate pitter-patter of footfalls led him toward the maze. He rounded a large hedgerow and almost knocked down a couple involved in a heated tryst.

"Who goes there?"

"Apologies." To a hail of expletives, Rawden made a quick exit and ran beneath the arched entry to the network of paths. Again, he listened for any sign of Patience. The frantic pace of steps lured him toward a side egress, one he used to make a quick escape on a prior questionable foray. He burst forth onto a lawn. A soft, feminine sob drove him past the fountain to a narrow walkway. Sitting on a bench, partially shielded by a vine-covered arbor, he found Patience.

"Could you not leave me alone in my embarrassment?" She lifted her chin and sniffed. "Or do you take pleasure in my downfall?"

"You are mistaken, my dear." Slowly, he neared the small structure. "The shame is mine to own."

"How so?" She shrugged. "You are a man of means and title. As you've declared before, whatever you do, people must still bow to you."

"What I meant was prior to our acquaintance I conducted myself with no thought for propriety." She wiped a stray tear, and he cursed himself for making her cry. "I presumed that I alone bore the consequences of my actions. I never considered my—"

"Bride-to-be?" She shook her head. "What was I thinking? That an impoverished woman of no significance and no connections to recommend her could wed an earl and live happily ever after? This is no fairy tale. I am no princess, and you are no prince. I never should have considered a union with you."

"What are you saying?" He rested fists on hips. "Are you declining my offer of marriage? Do you reject my suit?"

She nodded, and his well-planned future came crashing down about him.

Rawden simply stood there, drowning, grasping for a lifeline. Something. Anything to save his cause because he could not begin to comprehend his future without Patience. Terror blossomed in the pit of his belly, and anger rode hard in its wake.

"So that is it? You run at the first sign of trouble?" He gnashed his teeth. "How mistaken I was about you. I thought you had courage. Yet, I see you, standing there with your nose pressed to the glass, always on the outside looking in, denying an irrefutable truth. You want to live in my world—you crave it. To know what I can do for you. What I can make you feel. You were made for passion and desire. You were made for me, and I can set you ablaze. I can teach you untold pleasures, but you yield the field in fear. I believed you were many things, but I never figured you for a coward. You may deceive yourself, but can you lie to me?

Admit it. You want me. Give me that much."

The resulting silence fell like a death knell between them.

He considered relenting, but everything in him raged against it.

He turned his vision to the sky and vowed hellfire and vengeance on—

"*Yes,*" she whispered.

In an instant, he came alert. For a moment, he thought he imagined her response. "What did you say?"

"Yes." She stood and faced him. "You are right. I'm tired of pretending I'm something I am not. That I am impervious to emotion. But I would surrender all my tomorrows to touch you, if only once."

"Then why deny me?" He took a single step in her direction. "Why forswear your genuine self?"

"Because I was raised to smile, even when my heart was torn in two, and to greet those who turned their noses to me. But I am done living according to some impossible standard, when I have known fear, hunger, and immeasurable loss." She advanced on him, and he held his ground. "And I do think of you when you are not with me. My lord, I dream of you. I wonder where you are and if you are happy or sad. I worry about you. And I would touch the flame, ever so briefly, else I should be consumed. You harken to my old self, the girl with her head in the clouds, and I should love to meet that girl again. Still, you need not marry me. I know what I am, and I will no longer run from my circumstances."

"I don't understand." He inclined his head. "Are you offering to be my mistress?"

"That or whatever you wish to call me." She lifted her chin, and he doubted her not for a second. "I accept my fate."

"Then you will be my countess." He kissed her.

And kept kissing her.

That first contact, achingly arresting, evaded his defenses, and he let go the reins. Moderation battled prurience, virtue waged war with vice, and the latter won. At some point, he drew her into his arms, and she speared her fingers through the hair at the nape of his neck. Soft and feminine, she opened to him, and he took what she offered, losing himself in a haze of raw lust. And irresistible hunger. He reached for her, and she reached for him, clinging to the lapels of his coat. Until a voice in his brain warned of restraint.

Somewhere in the deep recesses of his mind he reflected on honor and propriety, just as Patience suckled his tongue, and all rational thought abandoned him. He tightened his grip and brushed his lips to hers in a tantalizing sashay—when an exaggerated shriek brought him back to unbidden lucidity.

Three women loomed on the path.

Lady Ellsworth. Lady Seton. Lady Howard.

The collective of worst gossips in London.

"Lady Ellsworth." Stalling for time, he bowed his head, making no attempt to hide the fact that he'd been ravishing Patience in the garden. Still, he searched for an adequate explanation to spare his intended the taint of scandal. The answer, when it came to him, seemed so obvious. And deliciously devilish. Confidence surged in his veins. In his ears played the "Hallelujah Chorus" from Handel's *Messiah*, and his heartbeat pounded a frenetic accompaniment. "I wonder if I might trouble you for a favor."

To her credit, Patience remained silent.

"Well, I am not sure." Lady Ellsworth glanced at Patience and then back to Rawden. "What would you ask of me, Lord Beaulieu?"

"You see, Miss Wallace has just accepted my offer of marriage." Ah, the delicious triumph of that statement mingled with Patience's expression of ineffable shock, and he could have danced a merry jig in victory. "I wonder if you might do us the honor of announcing the first betrothal of the Season?"

CHAPTER EIGHT

DEW-KISSED GRASS GLITTERED like a carpet of diamonds beneath a clear azure sky, and a lone starling danced on the wind. Aglow in the bright morning sunlight, a small spider weaved a delicate web outside the window of her bedchamber, and Patience admired the intricate artistry. In a sense, she felt trapped in a gossamer snare, ironlike in its grip, of her own making, especially after last night's formal announcement of her engagement to Lord Beaulieu. No doubt, by now, the whole of London had heard of her impending nuptials, and everyone had an opinion. There was no going back.

For good or ill, she would be Lady Beaulieu.

"Are you going to hide in here all day?" Arabella asked, and Patience realized she could not forestall the inevitable. "While I know you would prefer to bury yourself beneath the bedclothes for the remains of the Season, and I cannot condemn your reasoning, you will have to deal with the *ton* at some point. Better sooner than later, as you only prolong your suffering."

"I suppose you are right." For a moment, she searched her mind, seizing on the minutest hint of a solution to her predicament. At a loss, Patience turned and faced her friend. "Still, I have no idea what to do next, and you know me. I never proceed without a well-coordinated plan."

"Well, that is not so difficult as you imagine. Let us focus on that which we can control. For instance, we must order your trousseau, one fit for a countess, so we have quite a bit of shopping to do." Arabella loomed in the entry that separated the cozy sitting room from the inner chamber. "By the by, I knocked, but I became concerned when you didn't answer. I brought you some weak tea and dry toast, which I set on the table. While I'm sure the shock of recent events has yet to wear thin, you must keep up your strength, especially for your wedding night. And how are you today?"

"Wondering how I got myself into this mess." Patience strolled into the sitting room and sat on the sofa. She lifted the pot and poured herself a cup of the steaming brew. Then she glanced at Arabella. "Did I dream it?"

"No." Arabella perched on the *chaise*. "But you looked as if you were caught in a nightmare when Lady Ellsworth marched you and Beaulieu to the front of the ballroom and disclosed your betrothal, as well as your intention of marrying in a month. Indeed, you were white as a sheet. Really, Patience, could you not have given me more time to prepare? A little warning would have been nice. Finding a dress will be an almost insurmountable challenge, though I wager we will have the pick of the modistes, given every seamstress in town would kill to bedeck you for what promises to be the wedding of the Season."

"You think I did this on purpose? How could I warn you of something I did not know about until it happened? That was Beaulieu's doing." Patience collapsed into a pillow and huffed a breath in frustration. Gowns were the least of her concerns. "Believe me, had I known what Beaulieu planned I should have protested. In the midst of the situation, why did I comply? Why didn't I protest?"

"Therein lies the question, given you are no prim miss to be led about by the nose. You have a voice and opinions which you can and do express with regularity." Arabella rested elbows to knees and frowned, and Patience pondered the same thing. Why had she not intervened when Beaulieu's scheme dawned on her? Why did she acquiesce? "And what were you doing in the garden?"

"The same thing I saw you and Lord Rockingham doing in the Howard's garden." Patience covered her eyes with her hands and groaned. She relived the tantalizing sensations as Beaulieu kissed her. The unmistakable hunger mixed with desperation. The way he touched her. How his firm lips felt against hers. And his tongue. His naughty tongue. "Oh, Arabella, it was beyond anything I have ever experienced. I could scarcely draw breath. Then we were rudely interrupted, and I was thrust from ecstasy to embarrassment in the blink of an eye. To say that I was shocked when Lady Ellsworth, Lady Seton, and Lady Howard found us is to put it mildly. But Beaulieu did all the talking, and I didn't quite get his meaning until it was too late."

"You saw me with Anthony at the Howard's?" When Patience nodded, Arabella shook her head. "Well, that is a surprise, but in our defense we are married. You could say our rendezvous was government sanctioned."

"Oh, dear." Patience flinched. "And now I've broken my promise to Lord Rockingham not to mention what I witnessed, after he assured me it would devastate you."

"Posh." Arabella smiled and waved dismissively. "That is all right. My thoughtful husband frets for my feminine sensibilities, when you and I know I am not so dainty. We will keep that our secret, because I would not disillusion him for anything in the world. But I hope you learned something, because a tour of the gardens can be quite titillating with the right partner, and I am a veritable Salome when it comes to seducing my man. Now then, tell me everything."

Despite her distress, Patience described the entire ordeal, sparing no detail. She explained the encounter with Lady Fauconberg, and the rude woman's dismissive tone. She related her retreat into the hedgerows. She recounted her conversation with Beaulieu, including her offer to act as his mistress. She did not give a kiss-by-kiss account of her tryst with the earl, but she did describe the moment of their discovery and the subsequent engagement proclamation. In response, Arabella exhibited a wide range of emotions, along with several gasps of audible astonishment.

"Upon my word, but you quite take my breath away." Arabella patted her brow. "It is no small wonder you looked on the verge of swooning. Why, you are still quite pale."

"Do you blame me?" Patience shuddered as she recalled the moment Lady Ellsworth signaled for the crowd's attention. "How would you react were you, without your permission, suddenly thrust into the limelight and affianced to a man who had yet to propose?"

"As I recollect, after the initial shock of my own impending nuptials wore off, I recognized Lord Rockingham was a good person in need of help." Arabella narrowed her stare. "And if I remember correctly, you were the first to recognize Anthony was my ideal candidate for a husband. Yet, you cannot see past Beaulieu's brash behavior to realize he is your perfect match."

"Do you really think so?" Patience hoped her friend was right, given she knew naught of connubial bliss, and her parents provided no example. "Because I need to believe in him, else my marriage, and thereby my future, is doomed."

"Do you seriously question his devotion and his motives, even now?" Arabella arched a brow when Patience indicated the affirmative. "My friend, you offered to act as the man's dove, sans a conventional agreement, which means he could have had you—all of you, without the nuptials and lifelong commitment. If that does not speak to his character, where you are concerned, then I know not what does. Whether or not you wish to admit it, and I can't believe I'm saying this, Beaulieu acted honorably. Only a fool would refuse him."

"This is true, and I am no fool." Patience reflected on the tumultuous events of the previous evening. Her decision came to her without hesitation. "Which is why I will marry him."

"Oh, thank heavens." Clutching a fist to her chest, Arabella exhaled. "I thought, for a moment, you might be stubborn and delay the unavoidable, when Beaulieu is the best choice for you."

"Pot meet kettle, because you were none too keen to wed Lord Rockingham, if memory serves." Patience burst into laughter. When Arabella surrendered to gales of mirth, Patience sighed in relief, because she needed a friend just then. "We are a fine pair, are we not?"

"Indeed." Arabella sniffed. "To our credit, we found ourselves equally estimable men, and I know Beaulieu will make a good husband. Much like Anthony, Beaulieu possesses a vulnerable side I suspect he reserves for only those he trusts, and he counts you among his closest confidants. Find a way to reach that part of him, and you cannot fail."

"I agree, and while I have reservations, I admit I care for Lord Beaulieu. I am not sure he would welcome that bit of information, so I will not divulge it, but I cannot help how I feel. Just as you were compelled to support Lord Rockingham, I believe Lord Beaulieu needs me. Why, I cannot say."

"What does it matter?" Arabella's optimism made everything seem so easy. "Have faith in your instincts. They have never steered you wrong. And read the books I gave you. They provide a wealth of information my mother neglected to share on the eve of my wedding. However, I must warn you, the deed is far more intimate than anyone can convey, in speech or in writing."

"Well, I have only had time to study the selections you marked, and they were rather startling on their own." In her mind, Patience envisioned the various descriptions and positions, body parts fraternizing, none of which made sense to her. At once, she shook herself. "Don't poke at me, but it does not seem possible."

"Do you mean—" Arabella made a crude hand gesture.

"*Yes.*" Patience fanned herself at the mere allusion to the act. "And does it hurt?"

"Hmm, a little the first time, and you will not be able to get out of bed the next day." Arabella wrinkled her nose and nodded. "But when you find your rhythm, so to speak, everything comes together beautifully, and you can relax and enjoy him. You never know, you may fancy it."

"*Relax?*" Patience shook her head. "That I cannot even begin to fathom. And what is there to fancy if I cannot get out of bed? Sounds terrifying."

"My dear Patience, that is the high point, because Beaulieu has made no secret his desire for you." Something in Arabella's expression gave Patience gooseflesh, and she shuddered. "I suspect neither of you will leave his bed for a sennight, if you are lucky."

"You think that lucky?" Patience swallowed hard and shifted her weight. "I am dumbfounded. So, you truly like what Lord Rockingham does to you?"

"You mean, what Lord Rockingham does *with* me." Arabella cast a smug smile. "Believe me, it takes two, and I quite crave my husband's affection. Indeed, while we were captives of that awful Dr. Shaw, Anthony bathed me, himself. And the usually harmless activity often led to deliciously carnal games well into the wee hours, but to explain more would be unladylike."

"I...I...I know not how to respond to that revelation." Patience envisioned Beaulieu, sleeves rolled up to his elbows, kneeling beside a tub and soaping her flesh. "And you have shared enough. Daresay I shall sleep nary a wink until I consummate my vows." A knock at the door brought Patience up short, and she pressed a finger to her lips. "Come."

"Beg your pardon, Lady Rockingham." Abigail sketched a rough curtsey. "Miss Wallace, Lord Beaulieu is just arrived and requests an audience."

As usual, Abigail sneered when she mentioned Beaulieu by name, and Patience bit back a snort of laughter.

"Speak of the devil," Arabella quipped as she stood and walked to the door. "Now then, you discuss your future with Beaulieu, and be sure to name your terms, so there are no misunderstandings. It is always best to start out as you mean to go on. In the meantime, I must send a missive to the modiste, because the future Countess of Beaulieu needs more dresses. And we must gather your trousseau. I hope you know I am gifting the linens and that lovely Rococo tureen you adore so much, so don't bother protesting."

"The devil is right," Abigail mumbled. Then she stated, in a sickeningly sweet tone, "Shall I show Miss Wallace to the drawing room?"

"No, thank you." In the corridor, Patience waited until Arabella rounded a corner before waving to the maid. "And what have you against Lord Beaulieu, when he has been the soul of charity?"

"I don't trust him." The abrasive servant scowled. "The man has secrets, and secrets are like a boil festering beneath the skin. The only way to heal the wound is to lance it. His Lordship must cut open his secret, and expose it, if he is to overcome it."

"That is quite enough, Abigail." Patience tugged the domestic's sleeve, even though she knew the maid spoke the truth. "I am going to marry Lord Beaulieu, and soon we will join his household. Remember, your behavior reflects on my family. Please, do not embarrass me. And what is wrong with secrets? Have I not hidden the truth of my situation from all but a few close friends?"

"But that is different." Averting her gaze, Abigail softened. "You were forced into circumstances beyond your control. How could anyone blame you for that?"

"And I could say the same of Lord Beaulieu, given he selflessly fought for our country." Patience arched a brow. "He is a war hero, and that distinction commands respect, which you will extend. Is that clear?"

"Aw, Miss Wallace." Abigail scowled. "It ain't nothing personal against Lord Beaulieu. He and I have an understanding, so to speak. I insult him, and he takes it."

In the face of such logic, Patience could only grin. "Be that as it may, do not aggravate him, for my sake."

"Yes, ma'am." Abigail saluted. "Shall I bring your tea to the drawing room?"

"No, thank you." Patience pressed her palm to her belly and navigated the seemingly endless hall. "It is entirely possible I could revisit whatever I consume, and I would rather not humiliate myself in front of my groom."

"I could tell him you have a cold." Abigail snorted, as they descended the grand staircase. "Or you were struck by a runaway carriage."

"Absolutely not, and he would never believe you." In the foyer, Patience peered at the double-door entry to the drawing room and rolled her shoulders. Arabella was right. Patience could run, but she could not hide. She stood by Beaulieu's side as Lady Ellsworth made the monumental announcement, and it could not be undone. Only the worst coward would renege.

And Patience Rosamund Wallace was no coward.

"Miss Wallace, are you sure you wish to marry Lord Beaulieu?" Abigail asked with a shaky voice. "We can still flee London. I have some money saved up, and it is yours if you want it."

"No, old friend, that is not the answer." Patience patted the maid on the back. "Thank you, for caring. Believe me when I say I know what I am doing."

Abigail nodded once and sniffed.

Patience gave her attention to the matter at hand. Steeling herself, she squared her shoulders and marched into the fray, fully prepared to meet her doom.

TWIDDLING HIS THUMBS in rhythm with the constant *tick tock* of the mantel clock, Rawden brooded near the window and gazed at passersby. He checked his appearance. Then he stomped to the sofa and sat near the end. He scooted to the edge of his seat. After shifting his weight, he stood and walked to the hearth. He folded and then unfolded his arms. With a huff, he tramped to a small wall mirror and smoothed a wayward lock of hair. Assessing his profile, he adjusted the patch that covered his wounded eye. Patting the tiny box in his coat pocket, he sighed and returned to perch on the sofa.

A single knock at the door warned him of Patience's arrival. The oak panel swung open, and she glided into the room. Gaining his feet, he stiffened his spine as if standing for inspection and simply stared at her, and she responded in kind. Painfully tense minutes passed. His well-rehearsed speech eluded him in his moment of triumph, if it was a moment of triumph because he remained undecided, and he lingered on the verge of panic. As a last-ditch effort to spare his pride, he resorted to what came naturally.

Riding a wave of determination, he strode straight to her and pulled her into his arms.

The first contact. The first touch of their lips sent a rush of heady desire surging in his veins, charging every nerve, and his loins erupted in flames. He suckled her delectable little tongue and groaned his appreciation when she speared her fingers through his hair.

That was what he needed. A reminder of the attraction. The passion he coveted for her. That fervor provided a foundation upon which to launch a successful union, given most relationships yielded naught but an indifferent wife, bothersome children, and irrefutable justification for taking a series of mistresses.

Patience offered the chance for something more.

Something he desperately wanted.

Soft and feminine, she melted against him, and he counted that a boon as he changed the angle of their kiss, intensifying the experience. It dawned on him then that she wanted him. An undeniable certitude he would use in his favor to gain the advantage in their marriage.

Then he cleared his mind and simply enjoyed her. The taste. The feel of her beneath his fingertips. The way she leaned into him. When he finally broke the tantalizing connection, much to his regret, he required a moment to gather himself.

"I was so sure I imagined it." Setting her at arm's length, he retreated a step. Rawden inhaled a calming breath and summoned chaste thoughts in an attempt to cool his blood. "But you are uncontrollably responsive."

"Is that a good thing?" She blinked. "Or have I done something wrong?"

"Trust me, you did everything right." And a little too encouraging. He planned to sit beside her on the sofa, while they discussed their betrothal, but he feared he might break something of importance given his uncharacteristically robust erection. He hadn't suffered that sort of cumbersome reaction since his days at Eton, when he discovered a new use for soap. "While I am beyond anxious to explore that aspect of our entanglement, for now, let us turn our attention to the matter at hand. Believe me, in my present state it is a much safer topic. We should discuss our impending nuptials and fix a date."

"I thought that had already been decided, given your announcement last night." Pretty as a picture in her morning gown of pale pink and her saffron curls piled loosely atop her crown, she furrowed her brow. "You told the *ton* we were to wed in a month."

"And that is exactly what I intend." He plopped next to her and winced. Glancing left and then right, he grabbed a pillow and hugged it to his lap. "Indeed, I have arranged to have the banns posted today, and I secured St. George's for the ceremony. May I suggest you engage Lady Rockingham's assistance in dispatching the invitations without delay, because I want the whole of London society in attendance when we take our vows."

"You prefer a large gathering?" She opened and then closed her tempting mouth, and he fought the urge to steal another kiss. "I presumed you would want a small, intimate affair, in light of my family ties."

"On the contrary." He clucked his tongue. "I want everyone who ever turned their nose up at you to bow in deference when you become my countess."

"You are incorrigible." She rolled her eyes, and he chuckled. "You leave me little time to find a gown or assemble my trousseau."

"You may come to me naked as the day you were born, and I should be content." Actually, he would be much more affected than that, but he kept that information to himself. "And whatever you require, we can purchase once you move into my residence."

"*Your* residence?" Based on her expression, he suspected that innocent misstep would cost him. "Am I to have no home?"

"Of course, I meant *our* residence." Bloody hell, how could he survive his marriage if he couldn't get through the betrothal without falling on his face? Then an idea occurred to him that just might save his arse. "By the by, what say we hire a decorator to renovate your apartment? Since it will be your private space, it should reflect your personal taste."

"Oh, could I—that is, if it does not cost too much?" Her demeanor changed in an instant, and her eyes sparkled with unfettered excitement. For her smile, alone, he would pay a fortune. "I promise, I shall be prudent in my choices."

"My dear, you may spend whatever you wish, as my only requirement is that you are happy." Her glow faded, and he braced. "Is something else wrong?"

"Not necessarily wrong." She shifted her weight and twiddled her thumbs. "But I have a question for which I must have an answer if we are to wed."

"What do you mean *if* we are to wed?" A chill shivered over him. "That has been determined. Do you renege?"

"No." She shook her head and averted her gaze. "My lord—"

"Rawden."

"Rawden." She sighed. "I would have you tell me the whole of what happened at Quatre Bras." To his dismay, she looked him straight in the eye. "I must know why someone threatens you and thereby threatens me. Also, I must know why you harbor so much guilt in the wake of the battle. What is it you believe you did or did not do?"

"We had an agreement." He pushed from the sofa and stomped to the window, where he paced. He needed to stall her. Needed to find a way to avoid answering her. "Have you no honor? Would you renegotiate now that our betrothal has been announced?"

"My lord, I renegotiate nothing." She stood and walked to him, placing herself directly in his path, and they loomed toe-to-toe. He mustered his most intense stare, and she folded her arms and lifted her chin. "You promised to share the details of your service if I accepted your offer of marriage. In case it escaped your notice, I accepted."

"I will tell you once we are wed." He mirrored her stance.

"That is not fair." She gritted her teeth. "You gave me your word, as a gentleman, and I would hold you to our bargain."

"What does it matter?" Rawden groaned and retreated to a safe space near the fireplace. Gazing into the blaze, he focused on the flames as they danced. Slowly, he journeyed through time. Back to the past. To the war.

Bodies littered the countryside. Cries of the wounded weighed heavy in the air. A rapid salvo of cannon fire reverberated, and thunderous hooves pounded the earth. Somewhere in the distance, the familiar *rat-a-tat-tat* of a drummer signaled a charge.

Patience neared and hugged him about the waist, and he flinched when she ripped him from the morbid reverie.

"I'm sorry." She rested her head to his chest. "Did I frighten you?"

"No." He lied. He ignored the rush of breath that left him gasping. He paid no heed to the perspiration that trickled down his temples. He disregarded his hammering heart. "I simply see no reason to dwell on the past when you are my future."

"Normally, I would agree, given my own personal history." When he wrapped his arms about her, she tensed. "But someone believes you guilty of an unknown offense, and I would not begin our marriage based on a foundation of lies. If I am to be your wife, I would know everything."

"What happens if the truth turns you against me?" It was a question Rawden had to ask. He had to know what he risked. "What if I reveal my shame, only to lose you?"

"That is not possible," quick as a wink she replied. "Now, shall we sit?"

"No." If he was to meet his doom, he would do so on his feet. "While I am not certain this is a good idea, I will relent. If you wish to know facts surrounding my charge at Quatre Bras, I will tell you, but I do so under protest."

"Acknowledged." She nodded curtly.

The long case clock in the foyer signaled the hour, and he searched for the right words. "I am not sure where to start."

"The beginning is best, or so I have been told." When Patience caressed his cheek, he turned his head and pressed his lips to her palm. "And know you have naught to fear. I am with you."

"All right." Rawden fought the lump in his throat, and he coughed. "It was late in the afternoon when my regiment, the Thirty-Second Foot, under Major General Kempt's command, arrived at the Charleroi-Brussels crossroads. The acrid stench of gunpowder weighed heavy in the air, and a sea of corpses blanketed the ground."

Cannon fire echoed in his ears, and he paused to compose himself. The cries of the wounded formed a macabre chorale of suffering. Somewhere in the deep recesses of his mind, *Le Marseillaise* played a taunting refrain, and he closed his one good eye.

"Remember, you are not alone, my lord." She led him to the sofa and drew him to the cushions. Perched at his side, she took his hands in hers. "Pray, continue."

"Ney sounded an attack, but the French advanced at a leisurely pace, which afforded us the opportunity to reinforce Wellington's grossly outnumbered troops." He rolled his shoulders and inhaled. "The allied position was perilous, and we took heavy fire when we entered the fray. That is when it happened."

Fighting cursed tears, Rawden bowed his head.

"I am here, my lord." Patience squeezed his fingers. "And I will never leave you."

"The Thirty-Second had a drummer, a lad of not more than twelve. His name, which I have not uttered since that fateful day, was Charlie Boyle." A vision took shape. A round face and bright blue eyes framed by a shock of guinea gold hair. "In an army filled with shameless braggarts, beaux spirits, and scramblers for notoriety, Charlie offered a purity of soul and welcomed calm, and I grew quite fond of him. Indeed, he was like a younger brother to me. With incomparable bravery, he did his duty, maintaining our steps or signaling commands without complaint. As always, he took the field with us, but on that awful day he never beat a single note. He took a round to the head before he ever got the chance."

"Oh, Rawden." Patience pulled him into her ready embrace, and he buried his nose in the curve of her neck. "I am so sorry."

In that moment, he let loose the misery that shackled his heart. He unleashed the grief holding him captive. Overcome with immeasurable pain, he clung to his lady and cried for the countless friends he lost. He wept for the unrealized dreams of a child who never had the opportunity to know a world without war. For the heart of the fanciful version of himself, enamored of the uniform and all of its prestige, long since sacrificed on the altar of freedom.

"Why do you apologize?" Pulling himself together, he withdrew from her and sat upright. He pulled a handkerchief from his pocket and wiped his face. Locked in his own hell on earth, which he well deserved, he stood and walked to the window. "You are not to blame. Rather, I am responsible, and I do not deserve to be here. I am a murderer."

"No," she responded with force.

"But I am, and I must accept it." Gazing at the sky, he sifted through various memories, the men he led to their deaths. "Over numerous battles, I had seen countless soldiers fall, but Charlie's demise I could neither contemplate nor accept. When it happened, I broke." Rawden bowed his head and whispered, "I broke."

"What do you mean," Patience inquired in a soft voice, as she positioned herself behind him. "How so?"

"I don't know." He swallowed hard, as he grasped at fragments, bits and pieces of the past that merged to form a mere glimpse of his personal tragedy. "That is to say, I am not sure how to describe it, but something inside me shattered. I scarcely recall what occurred next, but I am told I ran amok. That without hesitation, I charged the enemy without care for my safety, and my men followed in my footsteps. For good or ill, I led them to the slaughter. When I regained my wits, I left numerous casualties in my wake, and I had taken a bayonet to the eye. It was only then I learned that, with Wellington's division, we drove back the French and claimed victory. We held Quatre Bras. Two days later, with only five-hundred and three survivors, the Thirty-Second prevailed at Waterloo."

"Then it is true." Patience turned him to face her. "You are the hero of Quatre Bras."

"No." He wrenched free and bit the thick underside of his thumb. "Do you not see? Men are dead because of me. And I knew not what I was doing, because I lost control. I operated wholly on instinct, yet I was their captain. They relied upon me. How many lost their lives because of my folly? Because of my weakness? I am no hero to be lauded. Rather, I am flesh and blood—life-sized. I never was a hero. I am a charlatan, and I deserve to be known as such."

"Now that I will never allow." Again, his lady grabbed him by the shoulders, refusing to permit him a measure of retreat. "Why should anyone expect you to be anything other than what you are—human? You endured the worst of conditions, and you think you should be discredited because you found a way to cope with the horrors you confronted? Regardless of what you think, you are to be admired, not mocked. I will argue that point with the cowardly villain who threatens us, and I would trounce the dastardly rogue should I discover his identity. But until such time, know that I have never been prouder to be your fiancée than I am now, and I promise I will never leave you."

Her guileless defense, spoken without coercion, drove through the darkness and pulled him into the light.

"You are fierce, Miss Wallace." At last, Rawden relaxed. Wrapped in her support, he toyed with a loose tendril, and she neared. "So, you will marry me?"

"Without reservation, sir." With that, she kissed him.

CHAPTER NINE

T WIDDLING HER THUMBS, Patience second-guessed her actions and reconsidered her plan. In her mind, she dissected her last conversation with her future husband, and she knew she had to do something. The question was—what? In the sennight following her discussion with her beau, she wondered what could she do to reassure Lord Beaulieu that he merited a future, one that included happiness and love? While she made her choice, with Arabella's assistance, she could not escape the nagging suspicion that, despite her good intentions, in some form or fashion she betrayed Beaulieu by going behind his back. Then she comforted herself in the knowledge that, at some point, she would confess everything, and he would understand.

He had to understand.

As she sat in the plush Rockingham town carriage, she stared at the non-descript building on Albemarle Street, and the rig rolled to a stop at the curb. The understated residence constructed of red brick with Portland stone trim looked much like any other home, except for the professional placard near the front window. The liveried footman opened the door and extended a hand. For a scarce instant, she paused and drew up short. She still had time to reject Arabella's suggestion. But what then? Inhaling a deep breath, she decided to trudge forth, as if marching into battle, because she had to help Rawden.

With one of Dr. Larrey's books tucked in the crook of her

elbow, she strolled up the entrance stairs. The heavy bronze knocker cooled her heated palm, and she rapped on the oak panel. She took a step in retreat when a bespectacled gentleman answered her summons.

"Dr. Handley?" she asked with nervous agitation and almost swallowed her tongue.

"Ah, you must be Miss Wallace." Grey hair framed a friendly face, especially when he smiled. "Lady Rockingham tells me you are in need of my assistance. Will you come inside and share a pot of tea?"

"Yes, thank you." Patience nodded once and exhaled a shaky breath. In that moment, she prayed she was doing the right thing. After doffing her cloak, poke bonnet, and gloves, she hung her personal items on a hall tree. Then she noted the house appeared deserted. "Have I come at a bad time?"

"No." He ushered her into a well-appointed office. Two matching high-back chairs sat before a welcoming fireplace, with a warm blaze dancing in the hearth, and she eased to the cushions. "My wife is shopping, and the servants know I am not to be disturbed when I have callers. Permit me to wish you merry on your recent engagement."

"Oh, that. Indeed, it was quite a surprise. That is to say, Lord Beaulieu and I had not discussed the appropriate venue for the official declaration when Lady Ellsworth made the announcement." When he reached for a tea pot, which perched on a small table, along with a plate of scones, she held up her hand. In search of a distraction, she took the handle. "Pray, allow me to pour."

"Of course." To his credit, he said naught when she spilled the steaming brew. The delicate porcelain rattled against the saucer, given she trembled when she offered him a cup. "Am I to assume your visit has something to do with Lord Beaulieu?"

"You are direct, Dr. Handley." She clasped her fingers in her lap. "May I ask what is your expertise in dealing with wounded veterans?"

"In truth, I claim no such specialty, yet my medical opinions have been sought by numerous patients soliciting cures for maladies they can neither understand nor evade. Most seek only to cope, but there is no official remedy, because no two soldiers present the same symptoms. When they arrive at my threshold, they are often desperate and alone. I give them a friendly ear." He wrinkled his nose and frowned. "Our military excels at pomp and pageantry, dressing up mere mortals in resplendent regimentals and pinning medals on chests, but we have not done right by our brave boys when it comes to their complete health. We have no means of reintroducing them into society after they have witnessed the unspeakable horrors of war. Rather, we expect them to simply pick up where they left off, as if nothing happened. In that I am in full agreement with Dr. Larrey. I see you have been reading his work."

"Yes. It was a gift from Lady Rockingham." She caressed the leather-bound treatise, which she studied every night when she retired. "Larrey writes extensively on what he calls 'nostalgia' or 'irritable heart.' Must confess his conclusions fascinate me, in respect to Lord Beaulieu, because I see so much of him in Larrey's words. But before I continue, I must know that whatever we discuss will never leave this place. Lord Beaulieu has been hurt enough, and I would not add to his suffering."

"Of course, Miss Wallace. Know that you have my confidence, because I am nothing if not discreet." Dr. Handley shifted to face her. "Now then, what is it that troubles you? What behavior does Lord Beaulieu display that causes you to petition my advice?"

"Behavior?" She tapped her chin and reflected on her encounters with the irascible earl. Where could she start? "To be honest, it is not so much his deeds as it is his beliefs that concern me."

"How so?" he asked as he inclined his head. "Does he threaten to injure himself?"

"No." She waved dismissively. The mere notion struck her as ridiculous—until she pondered Rawden's conduct. Was she informed enough to judge his well-being? "Nothing like that.

Rather, it is his stated conviction that he does not belong here. That he does not deserve to live when so many others died."

With a heavy sigh she felt all the way to her toes, Patience related Rawden's account of the events of Quatre Bras. She detailed the death of the drummer boy, which precipitated Rawden's break with reality. How he claimed he lost consciousness and ran amok, which resulted in the spontaneous charge and numerous casualties. Deaths for which he assumed responsibility, however unfounded in her estimation.

"So, what you are telling me is Lord Beaulieu did his duty." Dr. Handley adjusted his spectacles on his nose and narrowed his stare. "Yet he insists he should not have survived."

"Indeed." From her reticule, she pulled an envelope she stole from Lord Rockingham's desk. Beaulieu left behind the most recent correspondence in hopes Lord Rockingham might discover the sender. "But even worse, some unknown villain torments Lord Beaulieu with menacing letters claiming to know the truth of Quatre Bras and promising to expose Beaulieu as a fraud."

"Well, this is a sad and unexpected development." Dr. Handley unfolded the missive and examined the message. "I can only imagine Lord Beaulieu's distress, given this directive reinforces his assumptions. In fact, I wager the situation compounds Lord Beaulieu's agony."

"I believe you are correct." Patience pictured her fiancé's expression when he shared his experiences. How he wept. The way he shuddered in her arms, and she ached to hold him. To assure him that he was safe, and she would never let anyone harm him. "Beaulieu speaks of little else. It consumes him. Likewise, I am determined to find the scoundrel who dares imperil my man." She checked her composure. "I—I mean, Lord Beaulieu."

"That is quite all right, Miss Wallace." Dr. Handley chuckled. "If it will put you at ease, know that you exhibit the healthy solicitude one would expect of a bride-to-be. What can you tell me of Lord Beaulieu's personal habits? Does he eat? Does he sleep? Does he take any unnecessary risks with his person that would lead you to suspect Lord Beaulieu is a danger to himself?"

"Of course not." Then she thought about Dr. Handley's question. There was something that troubled her. "Well, not directly."

"Can you explain?" Dr. Handley asked in a low voice. "Take your time."

"I am not sure." Patience sifted through the memories of her most recent exchanges with Beaulieu. "If I recall, Larrey defines the *maladie du pays* in three stages. First, there is heightened excitement and imagination. In regards to Beaulieu, that might be normal behavior. Second, the patient endures fever and gastrointestinal discomfort. I know not of any direct implications in that respect, because Beaulieu has always displayed a robust appetite in my company. Third, the subject presents frustration and depression. There again, I would argue much about his demeanor supports Larrey's conclusion, yet I am not sure such conduct is merely part of Beaulieu's character. What can I do about it? How can I tell the difference?"

"My recommendation is to encourage Lord Beaulieu to talk about his experiences. If possible, urge him to explore his feelings." Dr. Handley raised a finger. "But do not pressure him to do more than he wishes. And listen to him. Do not offer advice or solutions to his predicaments, and recognize that you cannot solve what ails him. The key is to support him, while he works through his difficulties. Even then, you must accept that Lord Beaulieu may never fully recover. Rather, the goal is that he learns to cope. To manage his fears. To realize that he has earned the right to live and be happy, even as he bears the scars of war."

"And love," she blurted with abandon. Patience averted her stare and smoothed her skirt. "Forgive me, Dr. Handley. I forgot myself."

"Miss Wallace, there is nothing to forgive." He smiled. "Everyone deserves to be loved, most especially our war heroes. And, I would submit, they need it more than most. Make no mistake, Lord Beaulieu is a hero."

"Thank you, for that." Now she fought tears and fumbled for a handkerchief. "I couldn't agree more. If only Lord Beaulieu could see that."

"But you must know that may never come to pass." Dr. Handley scratched his chin. "Lord Beaulieu struggles with consuming grief and guilt. While he may always feel a measure of culpability for the events that transpired at Quatre Bras, he can restore his self-confidence. He can learn to love himself, again."

"All right." Patience rested Larrey's book squarely in her lap. "What do I do? What is my plan for approaching Lord Beaulieu?"

"Well, it is not that simple, because no two veterans respond to the same methods." He scratched his temple. "I suggest a series of efforts. A sort of trial and error to see what works. Prompt Lord Beaulieu gently with queries regarding his military service, but be cautious not to judge his words, else it is almost certain he will close himself off from you. Note his reaction to your interest. In fact, you might chronicle his conduct, and let him dictate your path. You must develop your own remedies, so to speak, because there are no proscribed routines. Thus, you will have to devise solutions that succeed with Lord Beaulieu."

"In much the same way Lord Rockingham has improved under Lady Rockingham's care." Patience recalled Lord Rockingham's demeanor, so tremulous the night of his engagement dinner, when Arabella had to console him in her father's study. Visibly shaken and pale, the anxious marquess barely made it through the meal, and twice he dropped his fork. With Arabella's support and encouragement, Lord Rockingham seemed a changed person. "I should inquire after her course of action."

"That is for you to decide, but I am not at liberty to comment on my other patients or their treatment. However, if Lady Rockingham is amenable, I would consider her an excellent resource." Dr. Handley pulled a watch from his pocket and checked the time. "Good heavens, it is later than I thought. My wife should return soon."

"Then let me away, Dr. Handley." Patience peered at the

mantle clock and started. "Oh, dear. I am behind schedule. I was supposed to meet a decorator at Lord Beaulieu's almost a half an hour ago."

"Permit me to collect your cloak and gloves." Dr. Handley offered his escort, and they strolled down the hall and into the small but well-appointed foyer. As he held her items, he said, "Whatever happens with Lord Beaulieu, do not lose hope, Miss Wallace. Stay the course, and I believe you will reap the benefits of your efforts, but do not expect Lord Beaulieu to make it easy for you."

"I wager he will make it almost impossible." In truth, hers seemed a daunting prospect, and she doubted Rawden would cooperate, because it was not in his nature. And, sooner than later, she would have to tell him of her objective, because she could not lie to him forever, regardless of her aim. "But it will be worth it, in the end, if Lord Beaulieu can find even the smallest measure of happiness."

"That is why we do what we do." Dr. Handley patted her arm, as they descended the entrance stairs. Then he handed her into the waiting carriage. "Remember, you are not alone, and I am here to provide counsel and a shoulder on which to lean. Have a pleasant day, Miss Wallace."

"Thank you, Dr. Handley. And the same to you." She dipped her chin, and the footman secured the door. Reclining in the squabs, she reflected on her interactions with her groom-to-be and shook her head.

While Patience doubted not her ability to engage Rawden in conversation, she was not so confident in her capacity for choosing the topic. Lord Beaulieu preferred to focus on her, or specifically what he wanted to do with his tongue and her body, starting at her ear and working his way to her toes. Even in the confines of the carriage, her cheeks burned. In an instant, she came alert.

Seduction reigned supreme as his favorite subject. No matter how hard she tried to divert him, he always found a way to bring their discourse back to the art of enticement. Or he reverted to kissing her. Was that a means of coping or avoidance? Could she use his predilections to direct him accordingly? She would have to ask Arabella at the first opportunity.

After a brief ride, Patience arrived at Lord Beaulieu's town residence. To her surprise, he loomed on the front stoop. Breathtakingly beautiful in his dark green hacking jacket sans cravat, he spoke to a stable hand. When he spied the Rockingham rig, he waved and ran to meet her. The carriage had not stopped when he opened the door.

"Where have you been?" he inquired as he drew her from the cabin. "Mr. Holland is waiting, and I just returned from Rockingham House in search of you but was told you were out."

"I'm so sorry." Grasping for a suitable excuse, she skipped up the entrance steps with Rawden in tow. Then she seized on a plausible explanation. "I ventured to Bond Street to order new stationery, and it took longer than anticipated. After all, the future Countess of Beaulieu cannot correspond as Miss Patience Wallace."

In the foyer, she doffed her outerwear.

"I put Mr. Holland in the drawing room. Lucky for you, he has been busy preparing various drawings and material samples for your inspection." Rawden took her hand in his and pressed his lips to her bare knuckles. "Perhaps, you can dine with me, afterward?"

Something in his demeanor suggested food was not his only offering. For Patience, the invitation presented the opportunity to launch her private campaign to help him.

"My lord, it would be my honor."

IN THE BACK parlor of his town residence, Rawden scrutinized the place settings on the small table he requested for an intimate dinner with Patience. On the nearby trolley, he lifted the lid from a covered dish and inhaled a tempting aroma. In the oval wall mirror, he checked his appearance, straightening his cravat and flicking a speck from the sleeve of his burgundy coat. Then he raked his fingers through his hair.

The butler knocked on the door, which stood ajar. "Beg your pardon, my lord, but Mr. Holland is just departed. Shall I bring in Miss Wallace?"

"Of course. Show her in, at once." He stretched tall and smoothed his lapels. "Also, have the stablemaster maintain my coach at the ready, to convey Miss Wallace to Rockingham House. And then you are dismissed, because we will serve ourselves."

"Very good, my lord." Mills dipped his chin.

Inhaling a deep breath, Rawden rolled his shoulders. Again, he glanced at the Sèvres china, the polished silver, and the family cut glass crystal. He wanted everything to be perfect for his first intimate meal with Patience. And, while he would never admit it, he needed her company.

Ever since he shared the details of his shame, he found it difficult to sleep. He struggled to go about his day or perform normal functions. He seemed locked in an endless nightmare, despite the fact that he was awake and *compos mentis*. No matter what he tried, he could not escape his past, so he clung to the future. And his future was Patience.

"My lord, are you all right?" He blinked and flinched. When he turned, he discovered the object of his affection studying him, and she smiled. It was then she noticed the little table. "Oh, how charming. Did you do this for me?"

"Of course." Suddenly nervous, he shuffled his feet. "I rarely ever use the back parlor, but I thought it perfect for a quiet evening, just the two of us. And I sent word to Rockingham House that you would be joining me."

"You are so thoughtful." For a moment, she simply stared at him. Then she did something he never would have foreseen. She walked straight to him and slipped her arms about his waist. Perched on her toes, she kissed him. A mere whisper of a touch, it should have inspired naught. But for him, with her, it was all he could do to maintain control. "Thank you, my lord. In the event I forget to tell you later, I had a wonderful time tonight."

"My dear, at the risk of frightening you, I must warn you not to be too accommodating until we are wed." It took every bit of strength he possessed to withdraw from her warm embrace. "I prefer to preserve your honor, not debauch it, given you are to be my countess."

"And were I otherwise unattached?" She inclined her head. "What then, my lord?"

"How many times have I asked you to call me Rawden?" He grasped at something—anything to distract him from her mouth, which inspired all manner of questionable behavior. Then again, he always found confidence in seduction. In that arena, he excelled, and passion never failed to help him recapture a measure of his old self, so he retraced his steps. "Or, I could savor your lips as a most luscious hors d'oeuvre."

On normal occasions, his lady could be relied upon to react with shock and reproach, and how he relished his ability to ruffle her delectable feathers. Indeed, she often retreated a safe distance, well beyond his reach, and he always pursued her. To his unmitigated astonishment, she held her ground.

"If it pleases you." She smiled and lifted her chin. "As you are so fond of reminding me, we are to be married. Where is the harm?"

"The harm in what?" Discomposed. Stunned by her uncharacteristically bold demeanor, he stumbled backward. "Just what are you about, Miss Wallace?"

"Why so formal?" Frowning, she stalked him, and he sheltered behind a fortuitously placed sofa. "And we've kissed before. Why not now?"

"We are not married." As if that ever made a difference with him, but at the moment he was desperate. "As you said, it is not proper."

"Yet, we are for the altar." Patience rounded the overstuffed chair and gained ground. "Besides, we are not children. You are a man, and I am a woman, lawfully betrothed."

"Trust me, that is the most dangerous combination known to humanity." He tugged at his cravat and stepped to the rear, in a paltry attempt to evade her approach. "And yours is a rake's appeal, my dear."

"Is that so bad?" she asked with a mischievous grin. "We are to wed in three weeks. And we have shared numerous kisses, if memory serves. All at your insistence, my lord."

"Uh—would y-you care to d-dine, my dear?" He cursed when his voice cracked. While Rawden was more than comfortable enacting a tryst with his bride-to-be, he knew not how to handle or even respond to any sort of ravishment initiated by her. He executed a brilliant flanking maneuver and held her chair. "The food is getting cold, and I am famished."

"Shall I serve us?" To his relief, she sat and inspected the fare, and he positioned himself opposite her. Then she bounced and proclaimed in a high-pitched voice, "Turbot with lobster sauce? Why, that is my favorite, and I haven't had it in ages."

"And for dessert, we have Eccles cakes filled with black currants." He arched a brow when she cast a questioning expression. "I inquired after your partialities, and Lady Rockingham was kind enough to enlighten me."

"Rawden," she remarked in a breathy tone. When she reached across the table, he took her hand in his, and she squeezed his fingers. "Now I will claim that kiss in grateful appreciation of your thoughtfulness, my lord."

"After we eat, else I may faint." He draped his napkin in his lap and summoned dispassionate thoughts. In his mind, he hummed "God Save the King." When that failed him, he harkened images of old Willie Doyle, Rawden's batman, and his gout-plagued big toe, and that produced serviceable results. He reached for his tankard of ale.

"You do not drink wine, my lord?" Patience inquired in her soft, lilting voice. The woman could charm candy from a babe. "Is it not to your liking?"

"It is interesting." He toyed with the pewter handle of his antique stein, as she filled their plates. "Before the war, I preferred wine, along with brandy. But my men always chose brown ale. Even in the regimental mess, ale flowed more often than wine. After a while, I simply accustomed myself to it. Now, I cannot do without it."

"What is a regimental mess, if I may inquire?" She passed him his meal and picked up her fork. "I read the daily account of the war in *The Times*, but it often described little beyond casualty reports and various campaign outcomes. What was life like in camp? That is, if you wish to talk about it."

"Of course." He eased back in his chair and relaxed his shoulders. "Although the officers whose society I kept had diverse backgrounds, and our reasons for joining the army were just as numerous, we shared a common belief that we served a greater good. And not just for King and Country. Rather, we believed we fought for the whole of the world. For freedom from Napoleon's tyranny."

"How noble, my lord." When he gave her a stern look, Patience bit her bottom lip. "Rawden."

"That is better." Between bites of delectable morsels, he explained the myriad intricacies of the military. "A regimental mess is considered the heart of camp, and it is never arranged the same in more than one place."

"Indeed?" She leaned forward and propped an elbow on the table, resting her chin in her palm. "Why the change? I should think it easier to replicate the structure at different locations."

"Ah, but therein lies the rub. Given no two geographical places are exactly the same, the mess must alter to meet the immediate needs of the officers." Rawden cut a boiled potato in half and shoved a large portion into his mouth. "The surroundings dictate the organization. You see, at the Pyrenees, we quartered in multiple small villages. Thus, there were several tiny versions of the mess. In Orthez, we pitched our tents in a large field, so we shared a single mess."

"I understand." She inclined her head, and he admired the swanlike curve of her neck. "So, what occurs in the mess? Is it just a shelter in which to take sustenance, or are there other activities?"

"Well, as I said, the regimental mess is the heart of the camp." He pushed a healthy bite of turbot across his plate. "It is a refuge, of sorts. It is a safe haven where officers come together to discuss their day. Their charges. Upcoming battles. It is an indispensable locale wherein we can speak freely, without fear of retribution. It is in the mess where we foster the camaraderie and familial affection that enable us to lead our men. It is where we mourn our casualties and assess our replacements."

"Replacements?" Patience inquired with a quizzical expression.

"That is how we refer to incoming soldiers whenever the regiment has sustained heavy losses." It always struck him as rather impersonal and detached how the army simply restored their numbers with fresh bodies, without any real acknowledgement of the fallen, while the broken were sent home to little if any fanfare. His men were not just faces to him. They were his friends. They were his brothers in arms. They were people with individual histories that should have been marked and remembered with something better than a cold piece of granite engraved with naught more than the name of their regiment. "They merely fill a vacancy."

"I am so sorry, Rawden." When his lady covered his hand with her own, he realized she had moved her chair to rest beside his. "I cannot begin to fathom the burden you carry, but the responsibility is not yours alone to bear. I would share your pain, if you allow it."

"Why should you?" he asked with more scorn than he intended. "That is to say, what concern is it of yours? They were nothing to you."

"You couldn't be more wrong." She wove her fingers in his. "They are important to you, so they are important to me. As your countess, it is my duty to provide support in all forms."

"Ah, I am your duty." That was the splash of cold water he needed to shake him from his morbid reverie. "For a moment I thought—"

"What?" She scooted closer. "What did you think?"

"You really wish to know?" Of course, he had no intention of telling her the truth. That she disappointed him. When she shook her head in the affirmative, he asked, "Even if it is not flattering?"

"Especially if it is not flattering." She refused to surrender his hand when he tried to pull away. "My—Rawden, I want to know you. I want to know everything about you, given we are to be married. Beyond that, you are quite simply the most fascinating man of my acquaintance."

"You must have very limited acquaintances." He snickered.

"On the contrary. My father is a general, and when he was in residence, we regularly entertained officers." Patience thrust her chin, in the adorable affectation that belied her calm demeanor. "You are much like an onion, in that you possess many layers, and I would know every part of you, if you permit it."

"Because you consider it your duty," he replied with sarcasm.

"No." She shook her head and narrowed her stare. She seemed so sincere he almost believed her. Almost. "It is my duty to support you in your enterprises. All of them. There is no requirement that I share your interests or become an active participant. That is entirely my doing. As I said, I want to know you. Does that surprise you?"

For a moment, he reflected on her question. He studied her green eyes full of promises he desperately wanted to believe. Given her unabashed candor, he did not suspect her. How he longed to kiss her. To claim a measure of the fire that burned bright within her. If he could capture even a bit of her spirit, he just might reclaim something of himself. "Honestly, no."

"Good," she responded in a prim manner, which brought a smile to his face. "Because I should be sorely vexed if you doubt me."

"My dear, I am many things, but I am not daft. I would never be foolish enough to doubt you." He chuckled, and she blushed. "Perhaps it is time to change the subject. As I mentioned earlier, I had Cook prepare Eccles cakes with black currents. May I tempt you?"

"Yes, please." She stretched upright in her chair. When she reached for a round, flaky pastry, he gently pushed her aside.

"Allow me," Rawden said in his most seductive voice.

After collecting the treat, he pulled off a decent bite and held it to her lips. Holding his gaze, Patience leaned forward and accepted the *bonne bouche*. The slightest touch of her tongue to his flesh left him covered in gooseflesh, and he shuddered. Trifle by delicious trifle, he fed his future wife. In the seemingly pedestrian act, he found purpose. He discovered a portion—perchance the best part of himself unsullied by the horrors of war. That fragment of himself he would give to her, because he owed her that much. He had naught else to give her.

"Oh, my goodness." She turned aside her head and pressed a palm to her belly. "I cannot eat another crumb else I fear I shall burst."

"Then it is time I take you home." After tossing his napkin on the table, he rose to his feet. "Shall we?"

"I suppose." Patience stood and accepted his proffered escort. "You are quite the host, Rawden."

"Only to those I deem worthy of my efforts." In the foyer, he collected her bonnet, cloak, and gloves, which she quickly donned. "And you, my charming fiancée, are most definitely worthy of my efforts."

"Am I?" She batted her eyelashes as he handed her across the threshold. "Then may I ask a favor?"

"You may ask me anything." He lifted her into his waiting coach. Again, she surprised him when she made no protest as he eased beside her in the squabs. On normal occasions she never failed to admonish him. "Are you comfortable?"

"Yes, thank you." She sidled close when he draped a blanket over her lap. "I was wondering, if your schedule permits, whether or not we could continue our private dinners?"

"Enjoyed yourself, did you?" To his amazement, Patience merely rested her head against him and sighed. "My dear, I should be delighted to entertain you on a regular basis."

"Wonderful," she replied in a whisper.

In silence they journeyed the short distance to Rockingham House, but Rawden's mind was anything but quiet. He could not get over the change in his heretofore-proper fiancée. Given her behavior that evening, he was sincerely looking forward to his wedding night. Had a betrothal mattered that much to her? Had he known, he should have made his offer sooner and spared himself untold torment.

The coach pulled to the curb and rolled to a halt. The footmen leaped into action, and Rawden descended to the pavement and turned to collect his lady. Hand in hand, they strolled to the main entrance of the elegant residence. At the top of the stairs, she perched on tiptoes and kissed him. It was neither the most refined nor the most seductive, but it moved him beyond words.

Indeed, hers was the sweetest kiss he had ever received.

Then he assumed control of their oh-so-enthralling exchange, angling his head and deepening the connection. Too soon, he released her, else he might never surrender her. Patience turned—and walked straight into the closed door.

Immediately, she gave vent to a series of curses that would make a common sailor proud and cupped her nose, and he couldn't help but collapse in laughter.

"Are you wounded, my dear Patience?" he inquired softly, biting the insides of his mouth.

"Only my pride." In the lamplight, he framed her face to check for any sign of injury, and she avoided his stare, as he fought to control his amusement. He gave her a gentle peck on her offended appendage and swallowed accompanying mirth. "Could you pretend you didn't see that?"

"I suppose, but I don't want to, because I find you inexpressibly adorable." Rawden grasped the heavy brass knocker and gave it a sound pounding. Then he bent and stole another kiss. "While I have been known to move women, I've never sent one crashing into a stationary object. This is a first."

The butler soon appeared, and Patience stepped into the house. She paused and peered over her shoulder. "Thank you, again, for a lovely evening, Rawden. I wish you a pleasant night."

"And the same to you." He sketched a bow.

Stunned by the burn of a blush in his cheeks, he stood at attention until she disappeared from sight, and then he strutted back to his rig. *Oh, yes.* Their marriage would be a singular success.

CHAPTER TEN

T HEIR MARRIAGE WOULD be an unutterable failure.
If Patience could not manage to keep her wits after a single little kiss, how could she help Rawden overcome the pain of his military service? As if on cue, her face went up in flames, and she huffed a breath in frustration. Standing in the middle of a boutique with questionable origins, she shopped for her trousseau with Arabella.

"*Patience?*" Arabella gave Patience a minor shake. "Are you all right? I called you three times, and you never responded." She arched a brow. "Upon my word, but you are flushed. Are you unwell? Shall I summon the carriage?"

"No." Patience pressed a palm to her heated cheek. "And it is not what you think. I suffer the lingering effects of what I thought was naught but a pedestrian expression of affection for Lord Beaulieu. Even now, the memory gives me shivers."

Arabella gasped. She glanced left and then right. Then she drew Patience to a small bench perched in a quiet corner of the tiny shop. Together, they plopped atop the cushion. Arabella turned to Patience.

"Tell me everything." Arabella bounced with unconcealed excitement and then asked, in rapid fire succession, "Did he caress you? Did you kiss? Did he curl your toes?"

"Yes." Patience nodded and closed her eyes. "And he curled *everything.*"

"Ooh, how exciting." Arabella grinned her cat-savoring-cream grin. "Congratulations, my friend. I couldn't be happier for you."

"Happy? You think me happy?" Patience groaned as she relived the tender recollection of last night. "I am not happy, I am disgusted. We shared a kiss. A simple kiss, and I walked into your front door like an addlepated schoolgirl. My nose still smarts."

For a moment, Arabella just sat there. Then she burst into laughter, and Patience covered her face with her hands.

"Now, now." Arabella snorted but quickly composed herself. "I am sure Lord Beaulieu found you quite charming, and your reaction did much to soothe his male pride."

"*His* pride?" Patience choked on the words. "What of mine? I humiliated myself before my future husband."

"You did no such thing." Again, Arabella surrendered to unrestrained mirth. From her reticule she collected a handkerchief and daubed the corners of her eyes. "I wager Beaulieu found your actions rather flattering. Trust me, men, especially husbands, need to be desired. If he had any doubts as to the constancy of your affection, I should say you dispelled them in dramatic fashion."

"You do not think me a clumsy nincompoop?" Patience inquired in a soft tone. "You do not think he regrets offering for me, because I wanted to die? I ran upstairs whereupon I collapsed and sat on the top step for how long I am not sure. When I finally made it to my bedchamber, I hardly slept a wink."

"Dearest friend, you make too much of what happened." Arabella waved to a grey-haired woman. "Trust me, Beaulieu viewed your behavior as a testament to his rakish skills. I guarantee he is pleased. Now then, allow me to introduce you to an indispensable ally in the marital bed."

"Ah, Lady Rockingham." The stodgy character made no attempt to disguise her scrutiny of Patience. "And you have brought with you a new customer, *oui?*"

"Indeed." Arabella nodded. "Madame Chiasson, I present Miss Patience Wallace, soon to be the Countess of Beaulieu."

"Oh, Miss Wallace, you do us a very great honor. I read of your engagement in the paper, and you are the talk of London." Madame Chiasson curtseyed and signaled for Patience and Arabella to follow her. Over her shoulder, she said, "So you are here to purchase something special for the occasion, *n'est-ce pas?*"

"*Oui,* Madame." Arabella caught Patience by the elbow. "And I am in need of a new distraction for Lord Rockingham. By the by, he adored the rich blue ensemble you created for me."

"I am not surprised, and we talked about black the last time." Madame Chiasson held up a scrap of lace. "What about this?"

"Marvelous." While Patience tried to wrap her brain around what she witnessed, Arabella examined the sheer material. "Have you a matching garter? And have you anything in red?"

"Of course, and let me see what is available in the sewing room." Madame Chiasson walked to a side door. "And for Miss Wallace, I think I have something to complement her eyes."

"Arabella, where have you brought me?" Alone with her friend, Patience yielded to panic and wrenched Arabella's arm. "And to what purpose?"

"Relax." Arabella assessed the delicate garment that functioned as more an afterthought than serviceable clothing. "Is this not stunning?"

"I am not sure." Entirely out of sorts, and pulse racing wildly, Patience blinked. "What *is* it?"

"What do you think?" Arabella smiled. "It is a gift for my husband. Anthony testifies before the Wakefield Commission tomorrow, and I would ensure he sleeps tonight. This should suit my needs."

"How so?" Patience draped the diaphanous garment across her palm and gulped. "Do you mean you intend for him to wear this? For Lord Rockingham, that is?"

"Of course, not," Arabella stated with an expression of unimpeachable confidence. "I shall don it for his pleasure. Thereafter, I will seduce him. I will exercise and exhaust my husband thoroughly, and then he will rest. Ah, such is the sacrifice a dutiful wife must make on behalf of her spouse."

"Arabella, you quite take my breath away." Patience clutched her throat. "Do I dare inquire after the details?"

"I should think so, given you are to marry Beaulieu." Arabella clucked her tongue. "Even before I wed Anthony, I heard tales of Beaulieu's exploits in the provocative arena. I should prefer you approach your wedding night with a proper education. Besides, women should discuss such topics. Lord knows that particular aspect of connubial expectations is entirely ignored in our studies. Did you finish reading the books I gave you?"

"Well, I completed the one by Cleland." Patience shuddered as she contemplated the licentious tome. "But I simply could not continue with Aretino. Really, I never imagined such things possible. And you are not going to pretend you got those works from the Temple of the Muses."

"Certainly not." Arabella humphed. "I did what any woman of sound judgement and resourcefulness would do. I borrowed them from Anthony's private library."

"With his permission?" At the prospect, Patience suspected she might swoon. "He knows of your...hobby?"

"Do I look like a harebrained ninny?" Arabella scoffed. "My dear friend, I am rather more than seven, and you underestimate my capability as a temptress. I simply took them when he was unaware, and I shall return them in much the same fashion, once we have completed your salacious tutelage."

"But, will he not be angry if he discovers your questionable behavior?" Patience stepped close and whispered, "Is Lord Rockingham privy to your interests?"

"I should say so." Holding the titillating item to her bosom, Arabella studied her reflection in a long mirror. "It was Anthony who first loaned the Aretino to me. Later, I took the Cleland one evening while he was at White's. In the ensuing months, we improvised many of the intricate techniques to mutual satisfaction, and there is nothing wrong with that."

"It is just not something I ever considered acceptable for a well-bred lady." Patience worried her bottom lip. "But I want to please Beaulieu. I refuse to become a typical society wife, adopting an air of indifference and looking aside while my husband spends his nights with his latest mistress."

"You know, Anthony explained it best." Arabella pressed a finger to her chin and inclined her head. "He said that if I could teach him to gratify me, I would fulfill him. And I have endeavored to do so ever since. What I realized is that, for all their professed bravado, men are quite fragile when it comes to seduction. They require encouragement and praise to perform what comes naturally. In the bedroom, they want us to believe they are cavalier, when they are really sensitive creatures prone to insecurity."

"What a curious statement." As Patience pondered the tantalizing assertion and its myriad consequences, Madame Chiasson returned.

"Apologies for the wait." Madame Chiasson set a stack of garments on a table and pulled a particular item from the pile. Holding what appeared to be a gossamer robe, she said, "This is the latest design from Paris. It would be perfect for Mademoiselle Wallace on her wedding night."

"Indeed, it is lovely." Patience studied her reflection, turning from side to side. "Is there a matching night rail?"

"No." Madame Chiasson frowned and wagged a finger. "No, no. Mademoiselle, we do not cover ourselves on our wedding night. It is a special occasion, and we must focus Lord Beaulieu's attention on your considerable charms, and trust that nature will do the rest."

"Daresay, it will." Arabella smirked. "But you really should try it on so Madame Chiasson can fit it to you."

"How could it not?" Patience ignored her hammering heartbeat. "There is not much to it."

"Lady Rockingham is correct." Madame Chiasson led Patience to a small corner and drew a curtain. "Now, take off your clothes, and I will record your measurements."

Patience tugged at her simple dress of sprigged muslin and enacted a strange dance before wrenching free. Then she doffed her chemise. Standing nude but for her garters, hose, and slippers, she cleared her throat and draped the transparent garment over her shoulders. She inhaled a deep breath and summoned courage.

"All right." With a sweep of her hand, she pulled back the curtain halfway. "How do I look?"

"It is too long." Madame Chiasson knelt and grasped a fistful of the fabric. "I must hem the gown."

"And the shoulders are too broad." Arabella narrowed her stare and tapped her cheek. "Perhaps a touch of lace at the opening would be nice. Something to call attention to her physical attributes."

"As always, Lady Rockingham's taste is excellent." Madame Chiasson sat on her ankles and furrowed her brow. Then she stood and noted various measurements. "But I think silver embroidery may be better, in specific places, to attract the male gaze to certain aspects of Mademoiselle Wallace's figure. After all, we must use every weapon at our disposal to bring your husband to his knees."

"What a marvelous idea." Arabella glanced at Patience and nodded with enthusiasm. "But nothing else. I believe the gown will suffice, and it is doubtful she will wear it very long."

"If that is meant to inspire confidence, you failed miserably." Patience wanted to flee. To run away and never look back. Not because she didn't want Beaulieu. Rather, she feared she was unprepared to fulfill the duties of his wife.

Regardless of her education, she realized there was still so much she didn't know about married life and least of all the lingering effects of war. That she could not ignore. However, when she considered her groom's torment.

His palpable anguish. She resolved to persevere, but everything inside her rebelled.

"Oh, Arabella, I am afraid. I am terrified I will disappoint him. What if I fail? What if all I do is for naught, and Rawden remains locked in a prison of his own making? What then?"

"Shh." Arabella clutched Patience's hands. "Remember, you are not alone. You have me, and you have Dr. Handley. Together, we will find a way forward for you and Beaulieu. Now, get dressed, because we are due at home."

"Of course." That was a request Patience was more than happy to honor. After quickly pulling on and securing her gown, and allowing Arabella to tie her laces, Patience fixed her poke bonnet and gathered her cloak and gloves. "All right. I am ready to depart for Rockingham House."

"Let us away." Arabella collected her parcels. Then she said to Madame Chiasson, "You may send the rest of our order when the items are completed. And I would commission something in burgundy, perhaps, with seed pearls."

"*Oui*, Lady Rockingham." Madame Chiasson curtseyed. "It is always an honor."

"Thank you, Madame Chiasson," Arabella replied with an air of nonchalance.

"It was lovely to meet you." Patience dipped her chin. "If it is not too much trouble, I should like an ensemble in pale blue embroidered with old gold or an Alençon lace overlay."

"But, of course, it is no trouble at all, and the lace would look best." Madame Chiasson smiled. "Your other purchases will be delivered by the end of the week, Mademoiselle Wallace."

Together, Patience and Arabella returned to the Rockingham coach. No sooner had Patience eased to the squabs than the coachman set a course for Grosvenor Square, at Arabella's insistence.

"What is the hurry?" Patience struggled to pull herself upright. "Is there a matter of utmost importance I missed?"

"Anthony should be home, and I don't want to leave him alone with his thoughts, because he often imagines the most horrible things." Arabella peered out the window and frowned. "I will not sit idly while he suffers. If I could spare him tomorrow, I would. Since he cannot avoid testifying before the Wakefield

Commission, and he would help those veterans still imprisoned in asylums, abandoned by the very country for which they bravely fought, I would occupy my husband. I would focus his attention on me that I might ease his agony."

Patience noted the rigid set of her friend's jaw. The stress that invested her shoulders as she stretched upright and gave her attention to the passing landscape. Arabella loved Lord Rockingham. Patience knew that the night of their engagement dinner. Had seen the way her usually independent chum doted on the reluctant marquess. How she rushed to his aid when he sought her company.

The coach slowed to a halt before Rockingham House, and Arabella opened the door and disembarked before the footmen were in place to assist her. Patience followed in Arabella's footsteps and entered the home as the butler appeared in the foyer.

"Good afternoon, Your Ladyship." Merriweather bowed and appeared a tad put out that Arabella had already doffed her outerwear. "I apologize I was not here to greet you upon your return."

"Posh." Arabella waved dismissively. "Is Lord Rockingham in residence?"

"Yes, my lady." The butler nodded. "He is only just arrived and takes a brandy with Lord Beaulieu in the study."

"Then I shall join him." Arabella grabbed Patience by the wrist. "Come. Let us welcome our men."

Patience fought to keep pace, as Arabella all but ran down the hall. Without knocking, she grabbed the knob and thrust open the heavy oak panel.

"Hello, my cherished lord." Arabella rounded the large desk and stepped about Lord Rockingham's knees. He eased back in his chair just as she plopped into his lap. "Did you miss me?"

"Always, when we are apart." Lord Rockingham smiled. "Have you been shopping?"

"Yes." Arabella cast her husband a side glance, and Patience shuffled her feet beneath the weight of Beaulieu's stare. "We added to Miss Wallace's trousseau."

"And broke my bank account in the process." Lord Rockingham chuckled. "Have we any money left?"

"Plenty, darling." Arabella bit her bottom lip. "Although I spent a frightful amount at *Le Petit Oiseau.*"

The atmosphere in the room changed in that moment. Lord Rockingham blinked and sputtered. Then he downed his brandy and stood, lifting Arabella from his lap.

"Beaulieu, I believe we are done here, and my marchioness requires my company, unreservedly." Lord Rockingham led Arabella to the door. "I will see you in the morning."

As soon as the couple exited the study, Arabella shrieked, and Lord Rockingham chuckled.

With a devilishly rakish expression, Rawden gave Patience his full attention. "And what, if anything, did Miss Wallace procure from *Le Petit Oiseau?*"

"You know the merchant?" she replied, feigning casual indifference.

"Oh, yes." He leaped from his chair and cornered her against a wall. She found herself set upon by over six feet of aroused male. "Tell me, what did you purchase?"

"A lovely garment for our wedding night." She gasped when he thrust his face into the crook of her neck. Arabella, God bless her, had been right. The mere hint of seduction altered Rawden's personality in Patience's favor, and she realized, without doubt, she could help him. She would use every weapon at her disposal to heal or at least soothe his invisible wounds. Licking her lips, she sighed. "And a few other items."

"Madame Chiasson has my eternal gratitude," he stated between tender nibbles of her flesh. At one time, she would have rebuffed his advances. Instead, she wrapped her arms about his waist in implicit consent. "Any particular color?"

"I am not telling." She giggled when he caught her ear lobe between his teeth. "It is a surprise, and I refuse to spoil it."

"How exceedingly cruel, my dear." Before she could respond, he kissed her. In play, he suckled her tongue and then lifted his head. "Have dinner with me. You know there is no way Lord and Lady Rockingham will emerge from their quarters prior to sunrise, tomorrow. Dine with me—not from any sense of duty as my fiancée but because you want to be with me."

All her doubts seemed to fade in an instant, given his earnest request. "Lord Beaulieu, it would be my pleasure."

ON AN UNFORGIVING wooden bench Rawden shifted his weight, as he perched beside Patience. Behind him, Warrington, Lord Michael, and Greyson gathered. Sitting at a table, and surrounded by Lady Rockingham and a solicitor, Lord Rockingham provided testimony, in chilling and graphic detail, before the Wakefield Commission.

Tasked by the Parliamentary Committee on Madhouses, Edward Wakefield, a prominent statistician, investigated and revealed numerous abuses in the asylums charged with managing those deemed incapable of caring for themselves. For the wealthy, like the Duke of Swanborough, Lord Rockingham's father, involuntary commitment of his only surviving son evidenced a lucrative business exploited by medical professionals peddling a variety of cures for the right price. With each successive description of the hell Rockingham endured in Little Bethlem, Rawden grew tense.

"I was beaten. I was starved. I was forced to persist in my own waste. I was stripped of my clothes and restrained. I endured what is referred to as cold baths, in which I was left naked and submerged to my neck in a frigid pond overnight. It is by sheer luck and force of will that I s-survived." Rockingham's voiced cracked, and he cleared his throat. "Dr. Shaw treated me like an animal, not a man. He did so while assuring my family that I was being properly tended. In truth, I was being tortured to the point of near death. I was robbed of my dignity and my humanity and almost my life."

Struggling to remain calm, when the overpowering urge to run grew ever more enticing, Rawden drew a handkerchief from his coat pocket and daubed his brow. His ears rang, and his heart hammered in his chest. When Patience clutched his hand, he flinched. He peered at her, and she scooted closer. He bent his head.

"It is all right, Rawden," she whispered. "I am here, and I will never let anyone hurt you."

"But I was not injured by Rockingham's confinement," he responded in a low voice.

"Were you not?" With her thumb, she caressed his heated palm, and he relaxed his shoulders. "Has not any wounded warrior cause for concern, given what happened to Lord Rockingham? That a man of his stature and rank could be deprived of liberty and brutalized should worry every veteran who served."

Patience couldn't have known it, because she knew not of his internal unrest, of the lingering battle that waged war within him, but she hit upon the source of his discomfit. Ever since that night in Weybridge, when Rockingham sacrificed himself to save his wife and unborn heir, Rawden endured horrifying dreams. Unspeakable nightmares. In his tormented visions, he imagined himself strapped to the strange contraption upon which he found his friend. Almost unrecognizable. Half-drowned by a dastardly villain.

While Rockingham appeared to have moved beyond the incident, Rawden remained trapped somewhere between the past and the present. Forever locked in an invisible prison comprised of the persistent effects of war and so-called civilized society's attempts to heal wounded soldiers. As if any such cure existed.

What the Wakefield Commission revealed, to catastrophic results, as evinced by the former patients Rawden helped liberate from Little Bethlem, was a systemic failure in the treatment of injured veterans either too physically weak or lacking the mental ability to defend themselves against unscrupulous, self-proclaimed experts promising miracles and hawking worthless medicaments for money.

"Lord Beaulieu. Lord Beaulieu, are you all right?" a gentleman asked. When Rawden indicated the affirmative and stood, the organizer replied, "We will accommodate you now, if you will come forth and be heard."

"Of course." Rawden shook himself alert. He eased into the aisle, with Patience in his wake. He hadn't asked for her support, but to her credit she was there nonetheless. Lord Rockingham, pale and visibly shaken, with Lady Rockingham firmly anchored at his side, peered at Rawden, and he nodded once. Then Rawden assumed his place at the main table.

In that moment, Wakefield flipped through some papers. "Lord Beaulieu, I have in my possession your prepared testimony, describing the conditions you personally witnessed and vouchsafed. Can you provide insight as to the situation you found when you first arrived at Little Bethlem?"

"Aye, sir." Rawden lifted his chest. Again, Patience took his hand in hers, and he composed himself. "I journeyed with the Earl of Greyson and the Duke of Swanborough to Little Bethlem from London. Upon arrival, we were denied entry. Swanborough insisted he be granted an audience with Dr. Shaw. When we made it clear we would not leave without seeing Shaw, we were at last admitted. Two guards escorted us down a side hall, whereupon we noted sounds of an unholy nature emanating from a particular room. Greyson and I forced open the door, and it was then we discovered Shaw torturing what we came to realize was Lord Rockingham."

"Yes, I see." Wakefield adjusted his spectacles. "You related a cruel form of treatment that employs water, I believe."

"Indeed." An image of Rockingham, wrenching helplessly against his restraints, flashed before Rawden, and he gasped for breath. Briefly, he closed his eye.

"I am with you, my lord," Patience murmured. "There is no danger here."

"Pray, continue, Lord Beaulieu." Wakefield arched a brow. "Or, if it is too difficult, you may be dismissed."

"No." Rawden stared at Patience, and she squeezed his hand. Then he gave his attention to the panel. "We found Lord Rockingham strapped to a table. He was bound from his neck to his ankles. There was an unusual hinged panel, which yielded at one end to render Lord Rockingham reclined at an unnatural, extreme angle. A cloth had been draped over Rockingham's face. Shaw poured water on Rockingham's head. To be honest, I was surprised Rockingham persisted. Damn brutal business."

"I had hoped I somehow misinterpreted your written account of the events." Wakefield inclined his head. "Can you elaborate on your findings in regard to the men who shared Lord Rockingham's chamber?"

"I can." Rawden swallowed and glanced over his shoulder at the three veterans who also suffered in Little Bethlem. They returned to London to support their comrade in arms. "Charles Lumley, of the Fifty-Second Light Infantry, Henry Whetham, of the Thirty-Second Foot, and Thomas Pulteney, of the Twelfth Light Dragoons, were located in dismal quarters. The bed linens were filthy, and the putrid stench of human waste lingers in my senses to this day. To my inexpressible regret, it is a sight I shall carry to my grave. These were our war heroes, yet they were treated worse than my hounds."

"It is most unfortunate, Lord Beaulieu." Wakefield frowned. "We have not done right by our wounded warriors, and this investigation will provide ample proof of the continued need for asylum reform. On a personal note, I wish to thank you for your service to King and Country. If you have anything further to add to your testimony, you may do so at this time, or you may be excused."

"I have nothing more to say." When Rawden made to stand,

his knees buckled, and Patience wrapped an arm about his waist. Stiffening his backbone, he lifted his chin. In the aisle, he passed the Duke of Swanborough, and Rawden refused to acknowledge the nobleman. Instead, he sought the empty seat beside Lord Rockingham.

Ghostly pale, Rockingham clung to his wife, and he shook visibly. When his father spoke, Rockingham suddenly lurched upright. Without so much as a backward glance, he fled with Lady Rockingham. In no mood to listen to Swanborough bleat, which always selfishly centered on himself, Rawden followed his friend, with Patience in tow.

Outside, he tugged and then untied his cravat. After unhooking his collar, he took large gulps of air, yet he feared he might suffocate. The world seemed to spin, and he clutched Patience to keep his feet. Leaning against the building, Rockingham fared much worse. Bent over, he wretched violently. When Rockingham faltered, Lady Rockingham waved to Rawden, and he responded.

"We have you, brother." Rawden wrapped an arm about his lifelong friend's shoulders. On the other side, Greyson mimicked Rawden's movements. "We will never let you fall."

"I cannot stay here." Rockingham dropped back his head and then grimaced. Without warning, he convulsed and dry heaved. "Please, I beg you, get me out of here. *Get me out of here.*"

"*Oy.*" Rawden signaled the coachman. Ignoring the footmen, Rawden yanked open the door of the Rockingham town coach and lifted his friend to the bench. Lady Rockingham climbed aboard, followed by Greyson. Then Rawden secured the latch. "Drive on, and make haste. We will be right behind you."

"We will meet you at Rockingham House," said Lord Michael. "I will see to the others, as well."

"Thank you." Rawden dipped his chin and turned to Patience. "Let us away, my dear."

That was what he needed. A diversion. Something to take his mind off his own misery. He could compose himself then. He could adopt his carefree façade and dally with his lady, temporarily forgetting his past and the bastard that hunted him.

As usual, he plopped beside her, and he awaited her protest with heady anticipation. Of course, he would ignore her admonishments. He would not heed her pleas for propriety, because he needed her. It was that simple.

His was not a physical requirement.

Rather, his was an emotional compulsion.

As soon as the rig lurched forward, Rawden drew down the shades and pulled Patience into his lap. Again, he expected all manner of reproach. Instead, she relaxed in his arms. Resting her head to his shoulder, she sighed, and he caressed her cheek.

"You don't mind?" he inquired. Without doubt, she knew what she referenced.

"No," she replied without hesitation, much to his surprise.

"Why not?" He couldn't resist posing the question when she had been so determined to observe the proprieties.

"Because you need me."

"How can you be so certain?"

"I know you."

"You only think you know me." Her unerring assessment troubled him. "You will learn otherwise when we are married."

"All right." Patience turned toward him, pressing her tempting bosom to his chest.

"That is it?" he inquired hoarsely. "No argument?"

"Why should I argue when you've already had a stressful morning?" She wove her fingers in his hair and drew him to her. They shared the briefest kiss, but it was enough to set him alight.

"Do not pity me." A beautiful woman offered herself to him on a proverbial platter, and that was his first thought? What was wrong with him?

"My prickly husband-to-be, I have never met a person less in need of pity, unless you wish to enlighten me." He noted the flirty lilt of her tone.

"I am not prickly." Thus, he claimed despite the fact that he bristled at her reply. "Men are never prickly. We are overconfident."

To her good sense, she did not contradict him. The carriage came to a halt, and anxious to end the conversation Rawden eased her from his lap. After descending from the carriage, he turned and handed down his lady. Together, they strode into Rockingham House.

In the foyer, the butler indicated the others gathered in the drawing room. The Mad Matchmakers assumed their usual positions. Upon entering the elegantly decorated chamber that now reflected a woman's touch, Thomas Pulteney, one of the soldiers who survived Little Bethlem with Rockingham, stood and approached Rawden.

"Lord Beaulieu, on behalf of the men, I wish to thank you for seeing to our care after our rescue." Pulteney extended a hand, which Rawden accepted. "It is doubtful we would have recovered had you not taken us into your home and summoned a physician. We are in your debt, my lord."

"Nonsense. I did what any veteran would do to help another." He glimpsed Patience, who stood beside him with her mouth agape. "And it is Rawden. So, how goes it in the Peak District."

"Very well, Cap'n." Pulteney grinned and swept a lock of red hair from his forehead. "As planned, I married my Martha two months ago, and we opened a bakery in Bakewell. We are quite content and much in your debt, given we could not have managed without your investment, which we still intend to repay at the first opportunity."

"That is not necessary, because it was a gift." Rawden shifted his weight beneath Patience's unwavering stare. "And I was happy to help."

"But you did more than that, sir." Charles Lumley, an infantryman who lost both his legs to a mortar blast at Waterloo, smiled from his chair. "You enabled us to start anew. Like Thomas, I reconciled with my family and my ladylove. Rose and I wed in a small ceremony, last January. We were sorry you could not attend."

"Alas, the weather did not cooperate, and I could not make the journey." Rawden glanced at Patience, and her smile gave him collywobbles. "I understand you formed a partnership with Whetham."

"Indeed, we did, Cap'n." Henry Whetham, who sacrificed a leg at Quatre Bras, nodded with unveiled enthusiasm. "We combined the funds you provided and formed a partnership, transporting goods from America. We purchased three ships, and we should reimburse you within the year. But that is not our only good news. I am to marry Charles's younger sister in October."

"Now that is cause for celebration," said Lord Rockingham, as he strolled into the room, on his wife's arm. His gaunt appearance improved slightly since they departed the hearing, but Rawden knew his friend still suffered in silence. "Shall we move this party to the dining room for a light repast?"

"Hear, hear." Greyson ushered Warrington and the other Mad Matchmakers down the hall.

As Rawden made to follow the group, Patience halted him.

"You helped those men?" She lingered dangerously close, and his body reacted accordingly. He could not get her to the altar fast enough. "You housed and cared for them? Then you provided the funds needed to enable them to begin anew?"

"Aye." He tried not to notice the subtle honeysuckle scent she favored.

"In the study." She turned on a heel. "*Now.*"

CHAPTER ELEVEN

FINGERS FUMBLED IN a tangle of clothing. A rush of male breaths mingled with muffled feminine sighs. Passion sparked and quickly raged out of control. Patience raked Rawden's hair, as he tugged at the bodice of her gown and then loosened her chemise, baring her for his perusal. She should have shied away from him, yet she grew emboldened by his praise. When he bent his head and set his lips to her sensitive flesh, she bit the underside of her thumb to stifle her cries of pleasure. In a teasing yet delicious torment, he grazed his teeth to her—

"Patience, are you listening to me?" Arabella asked with unveiled exasperation and clapped twice. "Where are you, and what are you thinking?"

"Er—nothing." Patience pressed her palm to her heated cheek, as the memory of her tryst in the Rockingham study captured her senses. Rawden had been fervent yet inexpressibly gentle, which disarmed her, and she realized she would have given him anything he wanted had he requested more of her. But in the midst of their heated rendezvous, he suddenly brought everything to a halt, much to her frustration and disappointment. There were times when the man could be too noble for her pride. "So, you wanted to continue my questionable lessons."

"I will, in a moment." Arabella narrowed her stare, and Patience squirmed, because she knew what loomed but not how to avoid the interrogation. "I want to know what happened between you and Lord Beaulieu, after you arrived for the impromptu reception that followed the meeting with the Wakefield Commission. Or did you think your extended absence went unnoticed? Even Anthony inquired after you."

"It was nothing." Occupying a table near the front window in a crowded Gunter's, Patience shrugged and toyed with the *neige de pistachio*, her favorite flavor. How was she supposed to help her future husband if he refused to be seduced? "Rawden, that is, Lord Beaulieu was upset, and I merely offered comfort."

"In what form?" Arabella arched a brow and compressed her lips. "And I know you too well, my dear. You are distracted, and I am privy to the manner of distraction Beaulieu employs where you are concerned, because the man is nothing if not consistent." Then she frowned. "Pray, I should like to get you to the altar sans scandal. Once you are the Countess of Beaulieu, you may surrender your maidenhood and anything else you like to your husband, and I will applaud you. Please, tell me you indulged in nothing more than a few illicit kisses and caresses."

"Of course." Well, that wasn't entirely true, but Patience would die before she admitted it. Some things were just too personal to air in public, even to a lifelong friend, especially when she could not understand her man's reaction. Why did her groom cease his play? Did he not desire her? No. That was not the case. Beaulieu desired her. She knew it as sure as she knew her name, yet something stayed him. "But Lord Beaulieu can be rather persuasive."

"I gather as much, but you need only persist for two more days, and then you may give free rein to your most ardent fantasies." Arabella shifted in her chair and lifted the bulbous confection to her mouth. "Now then, to prepare you for the momentous occasion, let us return to wifely tutelage. As I explained last night, you must take great care not to deploy your teeth. Made that mistake once, and poor Anthony had to summon Dr. Handley, in the middle of the night. Between us, we struggled to invent a plausible story to account for the curious injury, and it was quite embarrassing."

"I can imagine. What was the explanation?" Patience inquired, as she delayed what she anticipated would be an exercise in humiliation, because she simply could not fathom what Arabella proposed. "And do you believe Dr. Handley suspected the truth?"

"Well, Anthony claimed he rode too long in breeches that were too tight." Arabella giggled. "To be honest, I am not certain Dr. Handley believed my blushing husband. Thereafter, Anthony endeavored to school me in the proper method, which turned into its own game with delightful results."

"That I cannot comprehend, because Lord Rockingham always seems so dignified and reserved." Blinking, Patience studied the sweet protuberance and did her best to conjure the prospects, with Rawden as the primary recipient. "Are you certain this is done, because I have never heard of such a thing?"

"All the time, although no one admits to it, but you will not let that stop you. And why would you have heard of it? You have never been married. However, no one knows what goes on between two married people other than the two married people. And had you read the Aretino, as I suggested, you would know such behavior is as normal as breathing, which you should do before you faint, because you grow pale. Now, pick up your ice and follow me." Arabella demonstrated, and Patience feared she might swoon. "Pay attention. First, make judicious use of your tongue, from the base to the tip."

"What if someone notices?" Hesitant, Patience surveyed their surroundings, but no one paid them any notice, and hunkered in her chair. "I would be mortified if someone discovered our intent."

"Nonsense. Anyone would assume we merely enjoyed our treats with enthusiasm." Arabella wrapped her lips about the full girth of the dessert and reversed her maneuvers. "Be careful not to choke yourself, because that is not flattering. Also, according to Anthony, you cannot use your tongue too much, but never tell him I shared that tidbit."

Against her better judgment, Patience did as her friend bade. The delicious fare did much to ease her nerves, and she gave herself to the task. Still, she could not apprehend doing to Rawden what Arabella suggested, and she dreaded discovery. To her right, a couple of ladies laughed. Behind Arabella, a gentleman and what appeared to be his young son dug into a dish of chocolate ice cream. None seemed the wiser to the licentious representation occurring at the next table.

"By the by, Anthony told me Beaulieu received another threatening letter." Arabella took a healthy bite from her ice cream. "Apparently, there are no identifying marks. But he suspects Beaulieu's assailant is a soldier, possibly someone who fought beside him at Quatre Bras."

"Anthony said as much?" Patience centered her thoughts. "Because Beaulieu has shared naught about the situation. Indeed, every time I inquire after the possible villain, he remains stubbornly silent."

"Well, Anthony can be a bit more forthcoming in the throes of...passionate exhaustion." Arabella grinned. "Take note. A husband is far more pliable in a state of sated bliss. They are so thankful they will do whatever you ask. That is usually when I ask him for money."

"You are shameless." For a pregnant pause, Patience held her breath. Then she burst into laughter. "Are men really that easy?"

"You would be amazed." Arabella rolled her eyes. After glancing from side to side, she scooted closer to the table and leaned forward. "If you ever betray my confidence, I will...I will...well, I will do something horrible. In any event, whenever Anthony suffers most, I deploy this technique. Even in the grip of a nightmare, it never fails to calm him. Yet, in his study, on a quiet afternoon, it often has the opposite effect, and I reap the rewards of my labors. Marriage is an ongoing compromise. If you are smart, look for ways to please your man, and he will please you."

"What if Beaulieu is not like Lord Rockingham?" Patience

asked in a low voice. "What if he requires alternate measures?"

"Read the Aretino. It is a treasure trove of knowledge in the sensual arts." Arabella averted her stare. "Withhold nothing from Beaulieu, and he will withhold nothing from you. At least, that has been the way of it in my union. Anthony has had every part of me, and I mean *every* part of me. In the beginning, I feared I might disappoint him. I spent most of my life studying science and discourses on women's liberation. None of that prepared me to be a wife, and I had to find my way, merging the two sides of my character. I cannot be entirely what society expects, but neither can I ignore social conventions to the extent that I shame Anthony. As I said, it is a compromise."

"But you appear to have mastered the role and the compromise." Patience reached across the table and grasped Arabella's hand. "If I succeed half so well as you, I shall be quite content. Perhaps, now you can tell me about the letter. Did it contain the same tired threat?"

Just then, the throng surged, and several customers jostled Patience. She fell from her seat and landed on the floor. A couple of gentlemen helped her upright, and she returned to her chair.

"Are you all right? There is an estimable crush today." Arabella collected Patience's reticule. To the gallant men, she said, "Thank you, for your assistance. I fear my friend might have been trampled if not for your kindness."

"Think nothing of it," the younger of the two replied and then bowed. "Lord Oliver Stapleton, at your service. This is Erasmus Ludlow. We served in the Fifth Cavalry Brigade."

"What a coincidence." Arabella pressed a hand to her chest. "My husband is a major in the Fifth Cavalry. Perhaps you know him? Lord Rockingham. I am Lady Rockingham, and this is Miss Patience Wallace, soon to be Lady Beaulieu."

"Oh, I say. Know him well, Lady Rockingham." The scamp, who may have been in his mid-twenties, grinned. "Know Lord Beaulieu, too. Devil of a soldier."

"If you are wise, you should rethink your attachment to

Beaulieu." Ludlow scowled at Patience, and she shivered. "He does not possess the fortitude to uphold a lifelong commitment."

"How dare you insult Lord Beaulieu." Patience gained her feet in the blink of an eye. "He is the most thoughtful, generous man of my acquaintance, and I will not let you disparage his good name."

"I beg your pardon if I have given offense, but I speak the truth, and you should know it." Ludlow bowed. "I shall await Lord Oliver outside."

"Of all the nerve." Irate, Patience plopped into her chair. She steadfastly refused to consider what Ludlow said about her fiancé. "That man is rude, and he knows nothing of Lord Beaulieu."

"I do apologize, Miss Wallace, and you must forgive him." Flushed beetroot red, Lord Oliver swallowed hard. "Ludlow lost his younger brother at Quatre Bras. He served under Lord Beaulieu, and I fear my friend, however unfairly, blames Lord Beaulieu for Adam's death."

"That is unreasonable." Arabella frowned. "Not to mention ridiculous. How can any one person be held accountable for the unpredictable nature of war?"

"I understand, Lady Rockingham." Lord Oliver studied his boots, which he shuffled just then. "Lost one of my older brothers at Waterloo, yet I would never criticize Wellington, given his leadership won the battle and the campaign."

"I am very sorry for your loss, Lord Oliver." Patience peered at him and smiled. "Daresay your family is proud of you."

"Thank you, Miss Wallace." He clasped his hands behind his back and rocked on his heels. "Well, I should rejoin Ludlow before he gets into trouble, which he is wont to do these days. Please, give my regards to Lord Rockingham and Lord Beaulieu."

"We will do so." Arabella dipped her chin, and then he bowed. After he disappeared into the throng, she glanced at Patience. "That was a rather odd encounter."

"Yes, it was, and I am not sure what to make of it." Patience reflected on the conversation and Ludlow's demeanor. Then, her eyes lit upon an envelope protruding from her reticule. Curious, she tugged at the parchment and studied the missive. When she read the directive, she caught her breath. "Arabella, look. It is addressed to Lord Beaulieu, and it has no identifiable marks in reference to the sender. It must be another threat."

"Open it, and let us see for ourselves." Arabella scooted closer. "Hurry."

"But this is Lord Beaulieu's personal correspondence." Patience bit her bottom lip and considered Arabella's request. Could she keep something of such importance from her future husband? Or should she apprise him of her questionable conduct? "Shall I begin my marriage on a foundation of deceit? Oh, I know not what to do."

"Then let me have it." Arabella swiped the enveloped from Patience's grasp. "If I break the seal, then you can truthfully claim innocence in the matter."

"My friend, we both know that is not the case." Patience pondered her predicament, which afforded no easy answers. "For good or ill, I am here, and if you reveal the contents of the letter, I will most assuredly read the details therein. How does that acquit me?"

"Must you fret over the minute particulars?" Arabella carefully separated the wax from the parchment and unfolded the note. She scanned the missive, and Patience could have screamed were they not in public. "Well, whoever our villain is, he certainly lacks in originality." She passed the letter to Patience. "Have a look for yourself."

"Let me see." Patience digested the ominous warning and gritted her teeth. "The impudence. Of all the petty, mean-spirited, outlandish bilge. I swear, when I find out who is attacking Rawden, I shall scratch his eyes out. I shall—I shall—" It was then she noticed Arabella's smile. "Whatever you are thinking, don't say it."

"But I will, and you know it." Arabella laughed. "Because you can always rely on me for absolute candor. However, I must profess even I didn't fully appreciate the depth of your attachment to Beaulieu until now. I mean, I was aware you cared for him, else you would never in your right mind consider marrying him, but you are in *love.*"

"I am not."

"And you deny it. Your protest as much as confirms it."

"My but you are diverting, my friend." Patience sought distraction in the original purpose of their visit. "Shall we continue your titillating tutelage?"

"Now you change the subject. This is delicious." With unabashed excitement, Arabella bounced in her chair. "How long have you known of your devotion? When did you discover the depth of your constancy? And have you made your declaration?"

"Please, stop." Patience groaned. Overcome by the ferocity of her feelings for her groom-to-be, she wanted to shout her commitment to the world. One thing kept her silent. "No, I have not told Rawden, because I am not sure he would welcome the revelation. While I have long suspected my sensibilities tended toward the stuff of poets, especially after the assistance he provided you during Lord Rockingham's confinement, it was only when I learned of his support of the soldiers he rescued from Little Bethlem that I knew without doubt. I am in love with Lord Beaulieu, and I couldn't be more terrified."

"I believe I understand." Arabella nodded and wiped a stray tear. "When Anthony and I made our declarations, we were fleeing Dr. Shaw, and then we were parted. During our forced separation, I struggled with pain so persistent I feared I might yield. Love is a rather peculiar emotion. It can make you feel invincible in one moment and in the next leave you collapsed on the floor in a broken, vulnerable heap. I will say this, only you can decide when the time is right to make your stand. Trust your instincts, and you cannot go wrong. Now, let us commence our game."

"BEAULIEU. BEAULIEU. *BEAULIEU*." Rockingham pounded his fist on his blotter, and Rawden started. "Stop woolgathering and pay attention."

"Er—what?" Blinking, Rawden shook his head to dispel the mental fog, sat upright in his chair, and composed himself. "What did I miss?"

"I was writing a list of possible suspects in your nasty affair, so this involves you. I should think you might want to be present, given we gather for you." Rockingham sighed and dropped his pen on the desk. "But you are clearly somewhere else, my friend. Tell us what troubles you beyond the obvious."

Rawden peered at the Mad Matchmakers.

"Well, I have a rather unique problem." He shifted his weight. The four wounded veterans were more than just his friends. They were his brothers. He and Rockingham had been inseparable since the cradle. He could tell them anything, and they would listen and offer support without judgement. "I am wondering what might cause a previously reserved young lady of character to suddenly transform into a brazen seductress? An enchantress to rival Circe."

"Are we speaking in the abstract?" queried Warrington, as he leaned forward and rested elbows to knees. "Or has Miss Wallace revealed a new, enticing, and oh-so-welcome side to her?"

"And just what do you mean by 'brazen seductress?'" Lord Michael asked with a sly smile. "Do tell. Has Miss Wallace coveted your longsword?"

"Has she raised your battle flag?" Greyson waggled his brows. "Did you take a turn among the cabbages?"

"Stop it, else I will box your ears." Rawden folded his arms. "And did I mention any names? I'm just curious to know what might inspire such intrepid behavior in a usually prim and proper woman."

"Well, it depends." Rockingham lowered his chin and grinned. "Are we discussing a few intemperate kisses or a full-scale debauching?"

"Oh, there were more than a few kisses." Rawden crossed and uncrossed his legs as his body reacted to sweet memories. "Wait a minute. Forget I said that."

"Not a chance," Rockingham replied. "And we cannot counsel you unless we are fully apprised of the situation."

"All right." Rawden shrank in his seat and summoned delectable visions. Was there anything so erotic as his respectable Miss Wallace ravishing him? With haste, he added, "There may have been some illicit caresses, too."

"Illicit caresses? Do share, old friend." Greyson snickered and stretched his booted feet. "Did she stroke your main mast?"

"Did she grant you unfettered access to her wickedly tempting bosom?" Lord Michael chuckled. "And while we're on the topic, I would ask my brothers to find me a mate similarly endowed, given fortune has smiled twice in our endeavors."

"Did she lift her heels for you?" Warrington clucked his tongue. "Did you claim her bride's prize prior to taking the vows?"

"Blister it, she gave me no warning of her new attitude until she unhooked my breeches and—" Rawden cleared his throat and caught himself. "Never mind. It was a harmless supposition."

"That is some supposition," Lord Michael quipped. "So, there is a fiery streak beneath all that delicate lace and feminine deportment?"

"Did she suckle your Jolly Roger?" Greyson asked.

"Did she fire your cannon?" Warrington smirked.

"That is quite enough," Rawden replied a little too forcefully and glanced at Rockingham for assistance. "You could intervene on my behalf, you know."

"Don't rip at me." Rockingham shrugged. "You started it, and you are doing rather well on your own."

"And we are only too happy to finish it," chimed Lord Michael. "So, give over."

"Gentlemen, do not disparage my future countess, because she did naught more than I allowed, and I may have encouraged her." Rawden reflected on Patience's adorable if untutored attempts at seduction. His ears still echoed with her muffled cries of pleasure when he suckled her breasts for the first time. Her soft gasp when she touched his most proud protuberance during her fledgling enticement. Telltale warmth flooded his cheeks. "However, she has always kept me in check, so I merely ponder what could motivate a creature of heretofore-devout decorum to abandon every conceivable rule of etiquette and charge me like a salacious seraph."

"You *may* have encouraged her?" Rockingham inquired with a healthy dose of skepticism. "Given your expertise, and her naïveté, I find it difficult to believe she initiated the exchange, unless…just a moment."

From a drawer, Rockingham retrieved a key. He stood and walked to a cabinet, which he unlocked. After flipping through various books, he turned and tried but failed to suppress a grin.

"What is it?" Rawden straightened his spine. "What do you know?"

"I believe I have discovered the source of Miss Wallace's newfound courage." Rockingham shook his head and chortled. "If my suspicions are correct, it appears my enterprising marchioness loaned to her lifelong friend a couple of books from my private collection."

The Mad Matchmakers silenced.

"What *sort* of books?" Rawden inquired in earnest. "Or do I want to know?"

"Well, it is not as bad as you might presume," Rockingham replied with a blush. "The Cleland and the Aretino."

Shocked beyond words, Rawden simply sat there, senses reeling.

In the process of sipping his brandy, Greyson broke into a violent coughing fit.

THE ACCIDENTAL GROOM

"Bloody hell." Lord Michael opened and closed his mouth. "Do you mean to tell us you exposed Lady Rockingham to such...dare I call it *literature*?"

"Is that even legal?" inquired Warrington.

"No, it most certainly is not," replied Lord Michael.

"Men, Arabella and I are married. We are husband and wife, so our intimate endeavors are consensual and our affair." Averting his gaze, Rockingham scratched his cheek and then laughed. Rawden suspected his friend left something unsaid. "And it isn't as if you are ignorant of her inquisitive nature. She has a curious mind that I overlook and underestimate at my own peril. Early in the first months of our marriage, when she expressed a sincere desire to satisfy me, I merely supplemented her education as best I knew how, given I had never been a husband, and there are no instructions on how to be a dutiful spouse. However, I introduced her to the Cleland, knowing full well she would help herself to the Aretino, because she could not resist it."

"That is some education." With a handkerchief, Warrington daubed his brow. "Although Beaulieu might take issue with the illicit enlightenment of his future wife."

"Surely, you jest." Beaulieu snorted and considered the possibilities. Did his gently-reared virgin embark on a study of a sensual sort? The prospect exercised his imagination to new heights. "Indeed, I am in Rockingham's debt, and I cannot wait to discover the results of Patience's prurient pedagogy, at least, beyond what I already know. While I am buoyed by the revelation, I would prefer she not do anything too obliging until after we are wed. Believe me, it was all I could do to withstand her charming assault without embarrassing myself, although she moved me." To Rockingham, Beaulieu said, "By the by, you might want to replace your blotter."

"Bloody hell, Beaulieu. In my study?" Rockingham frowned and swept the item from his desk. "Well, that was an unforgiveable breach of hospitality, and you could have told me sooner. I may have to repay you, in kind."

"Be my guest." Rawden winked. "Perhaps, I shall have Patience watch you. It would be rather exciting to witness a seduction through her eyes."

"Now you go too far." Rockingham narrowed his gaze. "Arabella's personal habits are for my pleasure, alone."

"You are no fun," Rawden teased.

"All right." Rockingham slapped his thigh. "Ready to permit me to observe you with Miss Wallace? What of the other Mad Matchmakers? Care for an audience?"

"*Never.*" Rawden bared his teeth and then relaxed. "I get your meaning."

"Gentlemen, while I am as ever amused by your banter, I recall there was a purpose to our meeting." Warrington reclined in his high back chair. "Have we exhausted the limits of Beaulieu's prospective villains, or shall we return our discussion to his predicament?"

"There is naught more to say on the matter until the blackguard escalates his attack." Rockingham rubbed his chin. "As to the mysterious rogue's motives, we can only engage in conjecture. What say we adjourn for today, because I promised Arabella I would fetch her from Gunter's."

"Is Patience with her?" Rawden asked. In light of the afternoon's conversation, he ached to see her. When Rockingham nodded, Rawden said, "Care for some company?"

"Of course." Rockingham cast a knowing glance. "But I would have your discretion in regard to my bride's reading preferences. While she did not ask my permission to borrow my property, I would not stifle her inquisitive spirit. And I have no doubt Arabella's intentions were good."

Together, the Mad Matchmakers stood and filed into the hall.

"My friends, what is going to happen when my unknown tormentor reveals the truth of Quatre Bras?" Rawden donned his coat and gloves. "What will you do when my shame is revealed?"

"What do you mean?" Greyson asked with a deep-set scowl.

"What is to become of me?" Rawden couldn't resist inquiring. "I expect you will go on as you always have, given your luck." Lord Michael chucked Rawden's shoulder. "You have always been blessed with the uncanny ability to escape hair raising predicaments with nary a scratch."

"One thing that is not in doubt is our relationship." Rockingham opened the door. "We will stand with you, come what may. Now, let us collect our ladies."

Beneath the portico, the Rockingham rig sat. After Rawden dispatched his coach, he bade farewell to the other Mad Matchmakers and then joined his friend. As he settled himself, he peered at Rockingham.

"All right. Tell me what you neglected to say in your study." When Rockingham remained silent, Rawden arched a brow. "And don't even try to deny you omitted something."

"How well you know me, brother." Rockingham stared out the window as they drove into Grosvenor Square. "It has to do with the circumstances surrounding my wife's interest in the sensual arts. As usual, Arabella had a purpose."

"And that was—"

"To provide comfort in the wee hours." Rockingham sighed. "When I am suffering."

"Still seeing the visions?" Rawden queried in a soft voice. He mentioned nothing about his own private torment.

"And nightmares." Rockingham raked his fingers through his hair. "I hate disturbing her, but there are times when only Arabella can reach me. And she, alone, knows how to soothe my inner demons, be it through whispered reassurance or other means. She admitted that is what motivated her dubious quest for knowledge of a bawdy sort. Her love and captivating conduct never fail to divert me."

"I thought you were improving." Rawden leaned against the inside of the coach. "What of your visits with Dr. Handley?"

"I would say my sessions with Dr. Handley have resulted in my much-improved state of mind." Rockingham adjusted the empty sleeve pinned to his lapel. "But Dr. Handley told me, upfront, that there is no cure for my symptoms. I will never be fully healed. However, you should not let that stop you from making an appointment with him."

"To what do you refer?" Rawden fidgeted, given his friend skirted close to the truth. "I have nothing that requires his attention."

"That you confess to, but I submit you are just better at concealing your pain." Rockingham cast a lopsided grin. "Since we share our affliction, in slightly different respects, I see your distress. You may fool the others, but you cannot hide from me."

"If what you claim is true, it would appear I cannot mislead Patience, either." Rawden recalled their heated tryst in Rockingham's study. How she surrendered with little effort on his part. In hindsight, it was her salacious campaign, not his. "Now I suspect she employed the same tactics as your lady, with similar justification, and I am not sure how I feel about that."

"What does it matter?" Rockingham inquired as the rig pulled to the curb. "Her motives are pure."

After stepping to the pavement, Rawden strolled to the entrance and set wide the door to Gunter's. Together, they weaved through the crush of patrons, and he nodded acknowledgements to various members of society. At last, he spied his lady occupying a seat at a table near the front window, and he drew up short and caught his breath. A shiver of awareness traipsed his frame.

Slowly, Lady Rockingham swirled her tongue along the bulbous tip of her confection, and Patience followed suit. Then both took their respective sweets into their mouths, while bobbing their heads in repetitive motion, ever so gently. At first glance, Patience and Lady Rockingham appeared to be doing naught more than savoring their odd-shaped ices. To the more discriminating eye, leaning in an altogether lewder direction, their movements bordered on scandalous.

"Bloody hell." Rawden stayed his friend with an upraised hand and nodded toward the titillating twosome. "Rockingham, are they doing what I think they are doing?"

"Upon my word." Rockingham blinked, and then he smiled. "So it seems. Just wait until I get my wife home."

"Then Lady Rockingham favors you—"

"Not another word."

"I *am* impressed."

"Shut up."

"How are we going to get through this?"

"Keep your coat buttoned, and have care how you sit." Rockingham grasped a fistful of Rawden's lapel and said through gritted teeth, "Whatever you do, do not embarrass my bride, else I *will* hurt you."

"Are you serious?" Rawden fought not to laugh. "I am eternally in your debt, because I never would have dreamed of broaching such a service with Patience. At least, not yet."

"Then I rely on your discretion." Rockingham strode forth with Rawden following in his wake. As they neared their women, Rockingham stated loudly, "Darling, how are you?"

"Hello, my lord?" Lady Rockingham beamed at her husband.

On the other hand, Patience coughed violently. When she peered at Rawden, she flushed beetroot red, and he counted her expression of shock a priceless boon he would carry into the hereafter.

"Good afternoon, my dear." He took her ice from her and bit off a healthy portion. "Mmm, delicious." Then he leaned over and whispered, "But I prefer your rosy lips."

Once again, Patience hacked, and he wondered if it were possible for a woman to blush from top to toe. She lowered her head and then lifted her chin and met his gaze. He spied shame mixed with welling tears, and he took her hand in his.

"Hello, my lord." She looked left and then right. "I didn't expect to see you here."

"Forgo an opportunity to enjoy my fiancée's company?" He narrowed his stare. "Never."

"But we are to marry in two days." She shifted in her seat.

"Then you will never be rid of me."

It dawned on him then. The courage it took for his prim and proper Miss Wallace to participate in the education Lady Rockingham imparted. Patience had to abandon every natural instinct ingrained in her personality. And what motivated her? Without doubt, he knew the answer. Patience did it because she cared for him.

Rawden bent and pressed a not-so-chaste kiss to her knuckles and said, "And even then, a lifetime will never be enough."

CHAPTER TWELVE

THE SUN SHONE bright in a clear azure sky, as Patience donned her mother's gown in preparation to marry Rawden. Originally fashioned of white silk brocade trimmed in old gold, in the Georgian sackback tradition, the heavy skirt overlays had been removed and replaced with a more contemporary, svelte silhouette of pale blue organza with a matching silk liner. The bodice had been redesigned in a conventional empire style, and an extended train, festooned with seed pearls, had been added. Gazing at her reflection in the long mirror, she turned from side to side.

"Oh, Miss Wallace." Teary-eyed, Abigail pressed a handkerchief to her nose and sniffed. "You are a vision. Mrs. Wallace, God rest her soul, would be so proud."

"Thank you, dear friend." Patience adjusted the diamond tiara, a surprise gift from Rawden, atop her head and smiled. Plagued by second thoughts, because she knew Rawden didn't love her, she would find a way to reach him. Somehow, she would win his heart. A knock at the door interrupted her scrutiny. "Come."

"Apologies for the intrusion, ladies." The Earl of Ainsworth, Arabella's father, peered into the room and grinned. Given the curious disappearance of Patience's only surviving family member, a predicament that cast a pall over her special day, Lord Ainsworth graciously offered to walk her down the aisle. "It is time to depart for the church, else we will be late, and the groom does not strike me as a forbearing sort."

"Then let us away, because Lord Beaulieu most certainly is the last person I would ever describe as forbearing." Patience collected her bouquet of white and pale pink roses, another gift from Rawden, and rushed forth to meet her fate. In the hall, she accepted the earl's escort, and they steered toward the grand staircase. "My lord, pray, do not let me trip and fall on my face."

"My dear Patience, I would never let that happen." He chuckled and patted her hand, as they crossed the foyer. "My only regret is that General Wallace is not in attendance, but I am honored to act in his stead, given your longstanding acquaintance with our family. Indeed, you are a daughter to me, as well as a sister to Arabella, and I would defend you like one of my own."

"Thank you, my lord." Beneath the portico, he provided unshakeable support as she climbed into the Ainsworth coach. Ensconced amid the squabs, she settled her skirt and arranged the heavy train. When the rig lurched forward, she glanced out the window.

Again, she reflected on the difficulties that loomed on the horizon. The myriad duties she contemplated as Lady Beaulieu. Responsibilities for which she had been born and bred, yet her skills lacked given her dire straits. Financial ruin had a way of changing priorities. Now, she had to resume the life of a society lady of means, with a husband haunted by the horrors of war. And then there was the unknown tormentor threatening Rawden.

The journey from Grosvenor Square to Hanover Square proved too short, and she pressed a palm to her nervous belly as the equipage slowed to a halt. A footman opened the door, and another situated a small stool. Lord Ainsworth descended and turned to hand her to the pavement. For a moment, she hesitated.

"It will be all right, Patience. I suspect everyone reappraises their decisions when the time grows near." The earl furrowed his brow, compressed his lips, and leaned close to impart in a whisper, "Even Arabella had to be coaxed to surrender the security of her bedchamber on her wedding day. She took hold of the back of a chair and refused to yield until I summoned her mother."

"She never told me that." Patience paused in the shadows of the six-columned entrance of St. George's. Well-wishers gathered for the event, and she waved a greeting at several children, as she traversed the short distance to the church. "She seemed so peaceful when she took her vows."

"Looks can be deceiving, because she was terrified, so you are in excellent company." Lord Ainsworth pressed a chaste kiss to her forehead and then arranged her veil. He assumed his place at her side, and she uttered a silent prayer. Attendants opened the double doors, and inside the crowd stood at attention. The "Air for the G string" from Johann Sebastian Bach's *Orchestral Suite No.3 in D major* played, and she swallowed hard. Just before she took her first step, the earl said, "Lady Ainsworth and I are very proud of you. You will make a fine Countess of Beaulieu, my dear, and you do credit to your ancestors."

"Thank you, Lord Ainsworth." She squeezed his arm, when everyone focused on her. As she surveyed the crowd, she recognized many faces, including some who previously cut her in public. "Please, know that I am grateful for your support."

And so Patience began the most significant walk of her life.

At the other end of the aisle that cut through the box pews, which were filled to capacity with the crème of London society, Rawden waited. Smiling, and so handsome it hurt to gaze upon him, he cut a fine figure in his military dress uniform of crimson trimmed in gold.

When she neared, he extended a hand. Lord Ainsworth gave her into Rawden's care, and together they approached the altar, where Mr. Robert Hodgson, the rector at St. George's, stood.

Rawden leaned close to say, "Nice dress."

Patience stifled a snort of laughter.

"Dearly beloved family, friends, and distinguished guests, we have come together in the presence of God to witness and bless the joining together of this man and this woman in Holy Matrimony." Mr. Hodgson held high the Book of Common Prayer as he read. "Therefore, marriage is not to be entered into unadvisedly or lightly, but reverently, deliberately, and in accordance with the purposes for which it was instituted by God."

"Love the slippers, too," Rawden whispered. "But I believe I shall prefer your feet bare."

"Behave." She quietly shushed him as the ceremony progressed. "You are not going to make me laugh in the midst of our nuptials."

"Not even married, and you're already bossing me?" He arched a brow. "Now that will never do."

"Into this holy union Lord Rawden Philip Carmichael Durrant, the Earl of Beaulieu, and Patience Rosamund Wallace now come to be joined." Reverend Hodgson cleared his throat. "If any of you can show just cause why they may not lawfully be married, speak now or else forever hold your peace."

The church was as silent as a tomb, and Patience exhaled in relief. She didn't realize she had been holding her breath until that moment. Only the previous night, she woke from a dream in which several of Rawden's past conquests, and of that there were many, objected to and stopped the wedding.

"Are you sure about this, my dear?" Rawden inquired in a soft tone. "There is still time, if you wish to flee."

"Do you renege, my lord?" She almost choked on the words. "Do you regret your choice?"

"Not on your life," he replied without hesitation. "But you are soon to be mine, for all eternity. Once you give yourself to me, I will never let you go."

"I would offer you the same warning." She gave her attention to Reverend Hodgson.

"Patience Rosamund, will you have Rawden Philip Carmichael to be your husband; to live together in the covenant of marriage?" The rector adjusted his glasses. "Will you love him, comfort him, honor and keep him, in sickness and in health; and, forsaking all others, be faithful to him as long as you both shall live?"

"I will." Steeling her spine, she nodded the affirmative and took her vows, which well-nigh brought her to tears.

"You are mine, Patience. You have been from the moment I first saw you at the Rockingham's engagement dinner. You just didn't know it." Following Reverend Hodgson's prompt, Rawden took her hand in his. "This is but a formality, my darling girl." Twining his fingers in hers, he pledged, "From this day forward you shall not walk alone. My heart will be your shelter, and my arms will be your home."

It was his last covenant that eased her worried mind. She would pin her hopes on his oath, she would meet every challenge he posed, and she suspected he would take her measure at every opportunity. Still, she clung to the staunch belief that he possessed the capacity to love her. She would keep the faith.

Reverend Hodgson addressed the attendees. "Will all of you witnessing these promises do all in your power to uphold these two persons in their marriage?"

"We will," the audience responded in unison.

"Grant that married persons who have witnessed these vows may find their lives strengthened and their loyalties confirmed." Doffing his spectacles, Reverend Hodgson closed his book. "And now I pronounce you husband and wife. Lord Beaulieu, at your insistence, you may kiss your bride."

"With pleasure." Rawden turned to face her. After lifting her veil, he pulled her into his ready embrace.

Patience wasn't sure what she expected, especially since such physical displays were not the norm, but when her new husband set his lips to hers, her knees buckled. In a few minutes, he turned an elementary gesture to seal their union into a fiery exchange that sent her pulse racing and her ears ringing. And more than a few chuckles echoed in the church. Unabashedly, he rotated her to the crowd, and her cheeks burned and her heart pounded.

To much applause, they sprinted down the aisle, beneath the ornate organ, installed in the west entrance nave in seventeen-twenty-five. Outside, soldiers from his regiment formed a Guard of Honor, saluting them with a makeshift archway composed of their ceremonial military sabers. At the curb, the Beaulieu coach, emblazoned with the earl's coat of arms, sat. Liveried footmen leaped to provide assistance, and with her train draped over her arm, she climbed into the opulent rig.

Based on previous experience, she knew Rawden would not permit her to sit across from him, so she eased to the opposite end of the bench to make space for him. When he scrambled beside her, he narrowed his stare.

"Now that we are married, you allow me privileges?" Before she could respond, he yanked her into his lap. "Tell me, my oh-so-luscious bride, what else am I licensed to indulge in, given our new status?"

"Rawden—"

"Perhaps, this?" He bent his head and nipped at her neck. "Or this?"

He claimed another soul-stirring kiss, altering his angle, deepening the contact. In her slippers, she curled her toes. She couldn't help it. Couldn't resist the temptation he posed. Just when she found her pace, he broke the connection, and she gasped for breath.

"That was not fair." Patience collapsed against him. "Couldn't you have given me some warning?"

"Where is the fun in that?" Rawden murmured seductively. "Given our acquaintance thus far, you should prepare yourself to receive my unfettered affection with regularity. Indeed, I intend to be a most attentive husband. Morning, noon, and night."

"Somehow, I think I knew that." She gulped, in light of his suddenly wolfish expression. "I only ask you to remember that I am a novice in such matters, while you are a past master. I hope I do not disappoint you."

"That is not possible, *Lady Beaulieu.*" The husky emphasis he placed on her new title gave her delicious shivers, which did not escape him. Her husband bent his head and whispered in her ear, "You like that, Lady Beaulieu?"

"Yes." She shifted and wrapped her arms about him, and he sighed. The coach drew to a halt before Four Cavendish Square, her new home, and with reluctance she eased from his lap. "I suppose we should prepare ourselves to receive our guests."

"And we will." Rawden jumped from the rig and turned to lift her to the pavement.

Or so she thought.

Rather than free her, he carried her to the entrance steps, where the household staff lined up to greet the new lady of the manor. She expected her husband to release her, but he maintained his hold and her awkward position.

"Lord and Lady Beaulieu." With unimpaired aplomb Mills bowed, as if the sight of his employer toting a woman were an everyday occurrence. "On behalf of the staff, I congratulate you on the occasion of your wedding and extend a warm welcome to Lady Beaulieu."

"Thank you, Mills." Rawden continued into the residence without permitting her the opportunity to respond to the butler, and didn't stop until they gained the privacy of the drawing room. "Alone, at last, Lady Beaulieu."

He shifted, and she slid down the front of him, but he kept a firm grip about her waist. For the second time, her husband claimed an affecting kiss. Until someone cleared their throat.

Rawden flinched and peered over her shoulder, and Patience followed suit. Beneath her fingertips, he flinched and asked, "What in bloody hell are *you* doing here?"

"We had news of your nuptials." An elegantly dressed, grey-haired woman smiled and rose from the sofa, where a gentleman remained sitting in silence. "I am certain our invitation must have been misdirected, given our travels."

"There was no misdirection, because I pointedly neglected to include you in the guest list." Rawden stiffened, and Patience rotated to face the couple, who inspired numerous questions in light of his ungracious reaction. "Now, if you will excuse us, my bride and I are anticipating our guests at any moment. Perhaps, you can arrange to visit another time."

"You would deny us the chance to celebrate your union?" The gentleman, his face mottled with unspent anger, stood. "You would throw us out of your home like common rabble?"

"Yes," Rawden replied in a soft voice that did nothing to dispel his ire. "I will not have you ruining my wife's special day."

"My dear, we would do no such thing." The lady glanced at Patience. "And this must be Lady Beaulieu. What a pretty thing you are. But I know little of your connections. Will you tell me of your family?"

"Don't answer that." Rawden pulled Patience to rest against him. "She does not require compliments from you to know the obvious. And you are not welcome here. Please, leave."

The unknown man narrowed his stare. "Now, see here—"

"No, *you* see here." Rawden shifted his weight. "My wife's connections are none of your affair. I chose her because she meets my desires, and yours must perforce yield to mine in regard to my marriage. We neither want nor need your approval."

"My lord, perhaps I can have Mills add two place settings." Patience struggled to relax, in light of Rawden's aggressive demeanor. "If you would make the introductions, I would accommodate our visitors."

"Absolutely not, because they are not staying." With that, Rawden stormed from the room.

"Well, then." Shocked, Patience summoned the singular trait for which she was named and clasped her hands. "I beg your pardon, but Lord Beaulieu is not himself. But I am Lady Beaulieu, and I welcome you to our celebration."

"How very kind of you." The gentleman bowed. "I am Harold, Marquess of Hertford, and this is Lady Hertford. We are Lord Beaulieu's parents."

"ARE YOU EVER going to say anything?" Patience inquired, as she sat beside Rawden at the center of the feast in honor of their nuptials. "Perhaps, you might tell me why you greeted your mother and father with such hostility."

"Why did you include them in our celebration?" Rawden peered at his parents and gritted his teeth. Just looking at them angered him, and he clenched his fists. "I thought I made my preferences known. In future, I shall take more care to inform you of my wishes, which I expect to be honored, given I am master of this house."

"I'm sorry if their presence bothers you, but you haven't explained why you regard your family with such disdain." She toyed with a fried oyster on her plate, and he regretted his harsh attitude. "While my intention was not to cause you unrest or disobey you, I cannot in good conscience cut my in-laws, especially when they outrank me. Polite decorum requires I treat them with the deference due their position."

"Believe me, they are owed nothing," he replied acerbically. "But I must assume some of the blame myself, because I should have shown them to the door from the first."

"*Rawden.*" Patience glanced from left to right and then met his stare. "Pray, tell me what is wrong. I would not begin our marriage with discord."

"Suffice it to say, when I needed them most, they abandoned me." He recalled the painful past and shuddered. At the rear of the ball room, where he hosted their wedding feast, Rawden noted his friends making a grand entrance, waving his saber, and he stood. "I can only assume my sister informed them of our wedding, the little traitor. I will have words with her, but now it appears it is time for us to cut the cake."

"All right." He held her chair, and she rose with admirable grace and elegance, while he felt like a lost boy. "But I will have the whole of it, sir. In that I will not relent."

"Indeed?" He placed his palm at the small of her back and led her to the table that held the mountainous confection of six layers. In a whisper, he stated, "I hope you bring the same force of spirit to our bedchamber, later."

To his delight, gooseflesh covered her arms, and he chuckled.

Together, they navigated the crush of revelers and gathered with the Mad Matchmakers. Although he portrayed a confident and calm groom, inside he roiled with unspent passion and a hunger he could scarcely contain. He required a diversion. Something to replace his troubled thoughts, as he slowly drowned in anger.

"Lord Beaulieu, your weapon." Rockingham presented the polished ceremonial saber decorated with a large white bow at the hilt.

The throng broke into cheers as, perched behind his bride, Rawden wrapped his arms about Patience and clutched the heavy sword. She rested her hands to his, and they sliced the bottom layer, to raucous hoots and hollers. Then, while their guests savored dessert, Rawden escorted his lady to each table to offer their personal thanks to all in attendance. When he turned and discovered his family, he stiffened his spine. Grasping for a semblance of composure, he tried to form a suitable greeting, but words failed him.

"Lord and Lady Hertford, Lord Beaulieu and I are so honored you could be with us today." Patience inclined her head and glanced at his sister. "And you must be Lady Stamford."

"Please, call me Hannah." Rawden's younger sibling smiled. "I know we're going to be the best of friends."

"We are so happy to make your acquaintance." His mother peered at him, and he averted his stare. "We would love to host a private dinner, at the first opportunity, that we might welcome you into the family."

"She requires no such invitation, because she is my choice, not yours." Rawden slipped an arm about Patience's waist and pulled her closer to his side. "And I will not allow you to hurt her."

"That is quite enough." His father scowled.

"You're bloody well right that is enough." Rawden tightened his hold on his wife. "You are not wanted here. I didn't invite you, because all you do is cause grief. You had your chance to support me, and instead you betrayed me when I needed you most. If you think I will allow you to treat Patience with the same cruelty and indifference, you are wrong."

"My son, I freely admit I made mistakes, and I wish to atone, if only you would permit me to make amends." His father splayed his hands. "How many times must I say I'm sorry before you forgive me?"

"I'm not sure." Tense from top to toe, Rawden inhaled a deep breath. Inside, he was spinning out of control. "When I reach that point, I will let you know. Until then, we are done here." To his mother and his sister, he said, "Ladies, so good of you to honor me with your company. For now, I bid you farewell."

Without waiting for a reply, Rawden ushered Patience into the hall.

"That was inexcusable, and on our wedding day." Patience sighed. "Are you ever going to confide in me?"

"I will." He steered her to the grand staircase. "But not now. At this moment, we have more important business to settle."

"Business?" She glanced at him and blinked. "I don't understand."

"It is time to seal our vows, my dear." And his senses aligned with one specific objective. At last, he would satisfy the unchecked lust for his lady, and then he would lose interest, because women ceased to entice him once he had them. All he needed was a taste, and the madness—the obsession would end. Then he would find peace. "If I have my way, and I always have my way, I will be at you until dawn."

Upstairs, they strolled through the gallery and turned right. At the end of the hall, she attempted to free herself, but he refused to relent.

"My lord, I will summon Abigail and prepare myself." Her cheeks blushed a charming pink. "Shall I come to you, or do you come to me? How is it done?"

"In the future, you will come to me." He drew her to the double doors that led to his sitting room. "But today, I consider it a treat to undress you, so we have no need of valets or maids, my dear."

"Oh." Despite her attempts to appear calm, she bit her bottom lip. Was it his imagination, or did she drag her heels? "Is that customary?"

"I wouldn't know, given I have never been married." He snickered and gave her a gentle push into his lair. "But we won't let that stop us, will we?"

"No, I don't suppose we will." She came to a sudden halt in his outer chamber. Again, he nudged her until she stopped in his bedroom. At the foot of his large four-poster, she clasped her hands in front of her. "I never entered your private apartment during the renovation of my suite. It is far more imposing than I anticipated."

"Imposing? What a curious description." From atop the tallboy, Rawden collected a crystal balloon and filled it with brandy. Then he pulled a chair closer to afford him a clear view of his bride and sat to enjoy his entertainment. "Now then, take down your hair for me."

"I beg your pardon?" She jumped to attention and faced him. She opened her mouth and closed it. She appeared to mull her response before she replied, "Oh, I see."

For a moment, he wondered if she would refuse his request. When she tugged the first pin from her coif, he relaxed. One by one, thick curls cascaded over her shoulders. Long had he pondered the length of her blonde locks of silken spun gold, and he would finally learn the answer to the mystery that held him spellbound.

"There." Freed of restriction, she deposited a small pile of pins on a side table and ran her fingers through her glorious tresses, the length of which fell to her waist. "If you wish, I can collect my brush from my room."

"No." He took another long draft of brandy and smiled. She manifested every dream he'd ever conjured. "I would like you to remove your gown. If you give me your back, I will untie your laces."

It was then Rawden reflected on what manner of woman he married. Over and over, in the months leading up to his nuptials, he mulled his wife's reaction to the more erotic aspect of his personality. He wanted a partner willing to explore all that was possible in the realm of pleasure. To that end, she needed an adventurous spirit. Would she abide his bawdy behavior or rebuke him?

A battle raged within her, as written in the everchanging emotions that flitted across her delicate but sublime features. She delayed. She fidgeted. Just when he thought he would have to repeat his entreaty, she relented and presented herself. After setting aside his glass, he reached and tugged until he achieved his goal.

"Shall I take off my slippers?" she asked without turning to look at him.

"Just the dress." She was nervous, and he smiled because she did not fight him, so he added, "For now."

When she flinched, he compressed his lips.

After easing the garment over one shoulder, she repeated the movement and slid the heavy garment to her hips. It was then he tugged on his sash and loosened the yard-length swath of crimson silk. He stood and shrugged from his coat, as he kicked off his shoes. With speed and ease, he shed his serpent and lion's mask clasped belt and unfastened the buttons of his uniform dress coat. His shirt of fine lawn followed, just as Patience stepped from her grown, which rested in a pool of silk on the floor. Wearing naught but his trousers, he approached her.

Struggling to maintain control, he circled her, taking in every superb aspect of her body. To his surprise and disappointment, she kept her head bowed and her arms crossed over her enticing bosom. Frustrated, he tipped her chin and brought her gaze to his.

It was as if he had been punched in the gut.

The fear—the raw terror—set him on his heels.

"Patience." He trailed a finger along the elegant curve of her cheek and tried to compose some sort of sentiment to comfort her, but before he could speak, she suddenly thrust herself at him. With her arms wrapped tightly about his waist, he could hardly draw breath. "Uh, darling. Are you all right?"

"No," was her only reply.

"Are you unwell?" Confused, Rawden rubbed the small of her back. "My dear, you're shivering. Are you cold?"

"No."

He waited for additional commentary, but Patience proved less than forthcoming.

"Then what is wrong?" For several minutes, he simply held her, soaking up her warmth. Her signature scent of honeysuckle mingled with feminine musk, and all he wanted to do was soothe her fears. "Please, talk to me."

He should've reconsidered his request, because she did exactly as he asked.

"This is never going to work." She shifted, staring at him with tear-filled eyes, and blurted in rapid succession, "I don't care what Arabella says, I see nothing reassuring in the idea that I will be unable to get out of your bed tomorrow. If the pain is not so bad, why will I be incapacitated? Will I bleed that much? Is that normal? And I understand she has no quarrel with Lord Rockingham's size, but I cannot fathom anything that large fitting inside me. At least, not *there*. You should have seen the length of that banana, it was—"

"*No*." Horrified, Rawden flinched and shook her gently. "No, no. My lady wife, I can tolerate a great many things on this momentous occasion, but that is far more than I ever want to know about Rockingham's Jolly Roger."

"But I'm *scared*," she said with palpable desperation.

"And that is a perfectly understandable, if irrational, reaction to something you have never experienced." He pressed a chaste peck to her nose.

Yet, her overt dread coupled with her violent trembling touched something within him. Drew forth uncharacteristic compassion. His well thought plans, driven by his impulses, yielded to something foreign and elusive. Despite his intent to charge her fertile fields with the force of fifty men, he could not do it. Suddenly, he wished he had listened when Rockingham imparted sage advice on the treacherous task of claiming a virgin. Then he recalled a particular bit of wisdom. Keep it simple.

"Perhaps, we should begin with something harmless." For the first time in the midst of a seduction, Rawden abandoned his selfish objectives and concentrated on his partner's needs. It was an utterly foreign encounter. "Touch me."

"You think that harmless?" she replied with unveiled skepticism, and he masked his amusement.

"Just try. I won't hurt you." With care, he gripped her wrist and brought her palm to his bare chest. "There. Is that so bad?"

"Well, no." Tentatively, she splayed her fingers. "Your skin is so warm."

"Is it?" Somehow, he mastered control of himself as she explored him. "I hadn't noticed. Feeling better?"

"Yes." She nodded.

"Excellent." He rested his hands to her hips. "Now, kiss me."

To her credit, Patience did as he bade. Again, he fought every instinct within him and followed her lead. It was a simple, yet arresting, overture to the consummation, but he poured years of finesse into the elementary contact. He nipped at her pliant flesh, brushing his mouth along the rise of her cheek and trailing a series of feathery caresses along the curve of her throat.

And then he released her.

She retreated from him and said nothing. Not a word. She

met his stare, and he admired her lovely bosom, which rose and fell as she breathed heavily. He flexed his fingers, as everything inside him screamed to advance, but he had no idea where to go from there without scaring her.

Until she flung herself at him.

Unprepared for her charming, if unschooled, approach, Rawden held Patience as he stumbled and somehow managed to keep them upright. She bit his bottom lip and yanked his hair, distracting him when the backs of his knees connected with the footboard of his bed. Knocked off center, they teetered. Together, they tumbled onto the mattress.

Wasting no time, he pulled her toward the pillows and stripped her of her chemise, slippers, and garters. When she reached for the blankets, he brushed aside her hand.

"Never cover yourself in my company." He shifted, unhooked, and doffed his trousers. "You are the most beautiful woman I have ever seen. Indeed, when I first spied you, in the drawing room the evening of Rockingham's engagement dinner, I thought you sent from heaven to save me."

"Rawden," she uttered his name in a whisper and lifted her arms in an achingly sweet summons he could not deny.

"Try and relax. That's all you need do."

He gave her his weight, nudging her legs apart so her body could receive him. Perfectly positioned, he paused, because he didn't want to hurt her, but he knew not how to avoid it other than to prepare her. In a swift move, he claimed her mouth as he thrust. Beneath him, Patience tensed, digging her nails into his shoulders. He held still and kissed her, teetering on the edge of insanity as he waited for her to respond. To accept him. To adjust to his invasion. Every natural inclination told him to plunder the softness of her intimate embrace, yet he persevered. Only when she mingled her tongue with his did he move his hips.

Again and again, he plunged into her silky honeyed depths, losing himself in her sweetness, taking all that she offered, and then he stole more. She met him with charming little gasps, breathtakingly dulcet tones, each with a unique pitch voiced in time with his rhythm, which drove him into a frenzy. He wasn't aware of when he lost control—only that he lost it.

While she was the virgin, he felt untouched until then. Exposed. He'd never taken an innocent, had avoided them like the plague, but there was something about making love to his wife that made the experience fresh and new even for a man with numerous conquests in his personal history. The knowledge that no man had ever rested between her thighs aroused him to the point of madness, and his nerves fired with intoxicating desire. Every muscle suffused with luscious heat. He simply could not get enough of her.

"Lift your heels for me, love." To his infinite gratitude, she complied, with no complaints.

No dramatics. Just a carefree wantonness that far exceeded his expectations. It was to his amazement and embarrassment that release beckoned so soon. It was a direct shot to his pride. Applying himself in earnest, Rawden rode Patience hard and fast to the brink, and together they leaped headlong into the magical abyss of a mind-numbing completion that left him weak and trembling.

CHAPTER THIRTEEN

A SUDDEN BURST of sunlight startled Patience from a deep
slumber. Rubbing her eyes, she moaned and rolled onto her
side, too exhausted to form a rebuke, even as every muscle cried
in pain. Whispers penetrated the lingering fog of sleep, of which
she had much too little, and she stretched her legs. Could she not
have a moment of peace? Glancing about her, she noted her
surroundings and panicked. Nothing looked familiar. Then she
came alert and recalled the wedding ceremony that forever tied
her to Beaulieu. The reception and the quarrel with his parents.
She had work to do there, but it would have to wait.

She yawned and shifted to her back.

Staring at the rich burgundy canopy, she wiggled her toes as
she relived various images from a memorable night. The door
opened, and she lifted her head.

"Oh, you're awake." Arabella smiled, dispelling some of the
embarrassment that plagued Patience. Then again, Arabella was
happily married, so she understood what occurred there. She
neared the foot of the bed and retrieved Patience's robe. "Abigail
ordered a bath, and I am to assist you. A long, hot soak will do
much to revive you before Beaulieu returns, and on that you can
rely, so we had better hurry. Why, Anthony didn't even permit
me to break my fast before he came at me again, so we dare not
waste time. Do you need help?"

"I'm not sure." Patience sat upright, winced, and slumped

forward. Soreness beset her from top to toe. "Upon my word, but I ache in places I did not know I could ache. Is this normal?"

"It is the first time, but your body will soon become accustomed to marital duties, not that I consider it a chore." Arabella approached and draped the silk garment about Patience's shoulders. Of course, the sheer material did nothing to conceal her nudity. "Just lean on me. Trust me, you will feel much improved after a substantial meal."

"Indeed, because I am starved, though I know not why." Vignettes of passion, of unimaginable sensuality, flashed before her, and she gasped when she recalled the intimacies she relished in Rawden's steady embrace. Patience walked behind the screen, where she dropped the garment and eased into the steaming water. "I usually prefer only tea and toast in the morning."

"Ah, but this is not a usual morning, is it?" Arabella pinned Patience's hair in a topknot. "So, how was it? Although, I am not asking for a detailed account of Beaulieu's naughty habits. In general, did I provide adequate preparation?"

"Well, yes and no." Patience reflected on the consummation. The gentle caresses. The tender kisses. The whispered praise. The overpowering emotions she had never experienced. Had never thought possible. "While I had reservations, I was not taken unaware, but I am convinced Rawden is not human. The man has a boundless supply of energy. He goes on and on and on. By the by, where is my husband?"

"*Oooh*, that good? I am delighted to hear it." Arabella giggled and then yawned, suggesting she passed a similar night with her spouse. "Somehow, I suspected as much, and Beaulieu is riding in the park, with Anthony. Yes, I know it is unfair, given they seem to require no recovery, while we spend the better part of our day napping. I arranged for Abigail to send for me as soon as he departed, because I knew you would need support. While I had Emily's assistance when it was my turn, what I really wanted was my closest friend. Then and there, I vowed I would be here for you when it was your time. It is personal, is it not?"

"That is putting it mildly, and I thank you, dear friend. As usual, you are right, and you have always been so thoughtful. I appreciate it." Patience sighed as she recalled the inexpressibly sweet-tempered side of her earl. A sympathetic characteristic of which she thought him incapable. There was far more to her man than she ever thought possible. "Now I understand what you meant about not getting out of bed. I am positively spent. Rawden kept me quite occupied for most of the wee hours and into the morning."

"Then you shall retire as soon as the linens are changed, because you must steel yourself for another night of amorous games." Arabella unfolded and held up a towel when Patience stood. "And I will bring you a tray, because you must keep up your strength. I wager Lord Beaulieu will be rather attentive upon his return. If memory serves, Anthony couldn't keep his hands off me for a fortnight. Of course, he remains inordinately obliging, in that respect."

"Obliging?" Patience arched a brow.

"Dedicated?" Arabella compressed her lips and then burst into laughter. "Upon my word, but the male sex is rather reliable when it comes to amorous games."

"Well, I cannot claim to be surprised, given Rawden made it clear he intends to keep me thus occupied for the foreseeable future," said Patience, as she shrugged into one of the sheer robes she purchased specifically for Rawden's pleasure. After belting the diaphanous garment, she returned to the huge four-poster and eased beneath the sheets. "Must admit you were correct in your supposition, because he presented an altogether different personality in our most intimate moments, although I cannot go into specifics."

"Never would I expect you to divulge such privileged information." After tucking the blanket securely about Patience, Arabella retrieved a tray laden with covered dishes and a teapot, which she set in Patience's lap, before perching on the edge of the mattress. "Just as I have never revealed Anthony's softer side, which I gather you now understand. What your husband shares with you is for you, and you alone."

"Indeed." Patience sipped the jasmine brew, her favorite, which Rawden so thoughtfully anticipated. Then she took a healthy bite of scrambled eggs, as she pondered the sensitivity with which Rawden approached the consummation of their vows. It did not escape her that he restrained himself in deference to her fear. "Still, I was wrong about him. Prior to our nuptials, I believed he considered no one but himself. I thought him selfish, especially when he tormented me without mercy. But there is so much more to him, Arabella, and I find him hard to resist."

A knock at the door had Arabella peering over her shoulder, and she said, "Come."

"Ladies, Lord Beaulieu has returned, and he will be here shortly." Abigail rushed forth. "If Lady Rockingham will accompany me, I will take her through my lady's chamber, that His Lordship will not know of her presence."

"Of course." Arabella stood and smiled. "Is there anything else you require while we're here? Or would you like me to remove the tray?"

"No." Still ravenous, Patience studied the kippers and toast. "I will ring when I am done. And I thank you, again, for your friendship. I don't know what I would do without you."

"Always, my dear." Arabella nodded once. "Now then, I shall away before I am discovered."

"If you will follow me, my lady." Abigail led Arabella into the tiny corridor that connected Patience's chamber to Rawden's.

No sooner had her supporters departed than her husband strolled into the bedroom, whistling a flirty little ditty. With a pronounced strut, he approached and thrust out a hand, in which he held a single long-stem rose.

"For my lady wife." Then he favored her with an adorable pout. "Is that a night rail you wear? Did I or did I not forbid night rails in my apartment?"

"What?" Was it possible to resist the boyish charm her husband revealed only to her? She peered down and shook her head. "No, my lord. It is a robe, which I purchased for you only, a fact I hope you appreciate."

"Well, that depends." He lifted and set aside the tray. Then he drew back the covers. Sparks flared in his gaze, and slowly he smiled. "Now this is an unexpected surprise."

"You are pleased?" She held her breath as he caressed her breasts and then ran his palm over her belly. "Because I want to please you."

"Believe me, you do." Rawden trailed a finger along the curve of her jaw. Cupping her chin, he leaned forward and kissed her. "Shall I forgo my usual visit to my club and devote my attentions to you, instead?" When he tugged at his cravat, he licked his lips. "I am quite content to commit my interests to you, unreservedly, for the remains of the day and well into the night."

His expression, so pure, told her to refuse him would be devastating. Much like the patch that concealed his injured eye, he wore his pain as a very real, very visible reminder of the invisible scars he bore as a result of the war.

"My lord, I should prefer nothing more than your company." His immediate look of relief spoke to her on some otherworldly level she couldn't quite discern. At that moment, her stomach growled, and she laughed. "First, I require sustenance, given you exercised your countess thoroughly. I fear if you do not let me eat, I shall faint."

"Never let it be said that I starved my bride." To her surprise, he returned the tray to her lap and collected the fork. Then he proceeded to feed her delicious morsels interspersed with equally delectable kisses. It was, without doubt, one of the sweetest, most memorable experiences of her life.

When the last bite had been consumed, Rawden removed the dishes and quickly shed his remaining clothes. Naked and aroused, he joined her between the linens, but she stayed him with a palm to his chest.

"My lord, I have a favor to ask." Well, more an indulgence of epic proportions.

"My lady, your every wish is my command." She gathered he would soon regret that declaration. If only he would consent.

"Last night, you explored every part of me. Indeed, you left nothing untouched." That was an understatement, because he surpassed her dreams. Given the books Arabella lent Patience, her imaginings stretched the limits of decency, and she believed herself ready for everything Rawden might attempt—or so she assumed, however incorrectly. Her resourceful husband showed her otherwise. She inhaled a shaky breath as she prepared to advance on him, because she surrendered the consummation to his control, against all her hard-won preparation and tutelage. "It is in that spirit I make my request. Will you permit me the same courtesy?"

"I don't understand." He furrowed his brow, and she surmised he knew exactly what she meant. "What have I withheld?"

"I want you to remove your patch." She swallowed hard and quickly uttered, "I want to know everything about you. After all, I am your wife."

"You think me ignorant of that fact?" he inquired in a high-pitched voice, which belied his calm façade. Then his demeanor changed, and she confronted the familiar, confident Beaulieu. The battle-hardened soldier who had witnessed countless horrors. "My dear, I am only too agreeable to demonstrate my knowledge of your new position in my world. On that you can rely, but what you ask is—"

"Reasonable."

"I beg to differ."

"Why?" Patience implored.

"Because what you ask is too personal," Rawden replied in an abrupt tone.

"How can you say that, when you had your head between my thighs at one point this morning?" Had she really just uttered what she uttered? His rapid blinking confirmed he not only heard but also comprehended her bold statement. "Did I deny you? Did

I conceal any aspect of myself from you?"

"No." His charming sulk almost waylaid her, because all she wanted to do was hold him. She would have to remember that tactic, else he would easily bend her to his will in their marriage.

"Then why refuse me?" She had to stand for her man, and she had to do so from the start. He had to know she planted herself firmly in his camp.

"Because the injury is repulsive." There it was, the manifestation of shame, just as Larrey predicted in his book. Shame and guilt functioned as her enemies, and she would prevail if it killed her. And it might.

"And that is why you keep it hidden?" She brushed his cheek with her thumb and quietly asked, "You believe you will frighten people?"

"Aye." He nodded once.

"But you could never be repulsive to me." The self-loathing presented a formidable foe, one she had to defeat. With a finger, she traced the generous outline of his lips. "Please, Rawden."

"Would you embarrass me?" Ah, the wounded fledgling returned to weaken her resolve, and how he called to her.

"Never." With infinite care, and half-expecting him to fight her, Patience pushed aside and removed the patch, which she tossed to the floor. He kept his head bowed and his gaze averted, his unease apparent.

A jagged scar cut from just below his brow to beneath his eye, with spidery red and purple lines marking his skin. The lid hung limp and misshapen. Lifting her chin, Patience pressed her lips to his gnarled and twisted flesh, and he jumped. Sitting stalwart, Rawden hindered her efforts, but she persevered. She framed his face in her hands and drew him closer. Again and again, she placed tender kisses along his injury to convey her unqualified acceptance and devotion, something she realized he desperately needed.

Little by little, he yielded.

"Are you not afraid?" His breath quickened, and he flexed and shifted against her. When he seduced her, he engaged his entire body. "Or would you prefer I leave?"

"I beg your pardon?" She wrapped her arms about his broad shoulders and anchored him. "My lord husband, were you to abandon me now, I would raise a fine protest."

"Would you?" He ran his tongue along the curve of her neck, and she shivered. "You like that. So, what would you do to entice me to stay?"

"Hmm." The question hung in the air, and she studied him. Again, his vulnerable side charged the fore, and the pessimism beckoned. He anticipated boundaries. And for him, boundaries represented rejection. That was why he worked so hard to scandalize her. To force her to rebuff him, thereby fulling his prophecy. He considered himself unworthy of happiness, and he presumed she shared his opinion. But how could she dispel his outrageous stance? The answer, when it came to her, seemed so obvious. "Anything."

"I beg your pardon?" he inquired; his surprise evident. "Are you sure about that?"

"I am," she answered, without hesitation, understanding full well what that meant. Although, given her relative lack of expertise, she knew not precisely what she offered, and she suspected she would pay for her ignorance.

He kissed her then, teasing her with playful flicks of his tongue to hers. And then he angled his head and deepened the expression, as he pressed his hips to hers. A slow but aggressive display of desire intended to shock her. But she refused to be shocked.

To her amazement, he removed the robe with remarkable expedience and pushed her into the pillows. With his knees, he nudged her legs wide to receive him.

"Shall I test the constancy of your commitment, Lady Beaulieu?" Arms locked, he loomed above her, waiting. Indeed, it was a test.

Patience smiled and pulled him to her. "Lord Beaulieu, you

may do whatever you wish."

SUNLIGHT GLITTERED LIKE a field of diamonds on dew-kissed grass in the park. Birds chirped a cheerful sing-song. Leaves rustled in the breeze, as formidable oaks gently swayed in the wind. Overhead, nary a cloud marked the seemingly endless blue sky. Rawden leaned back his head and closed his eye, as his stallion whinnied.

Soft, feminine sighs played a sultry symphony in his ears. Limbs of velvet wrapped about him, forming an unshakeable, intimate embrace. Cries of pleasure beckoned, and he ached to answer the call as he shifted in the saddle and smiled.

"Surprised to see you up and about so early, Beaulieu. I had thought you would not show a leg for at least a month." Reining in, Rockingham cast a lazy grin when Rawden reluctantly emerged from his provocative reverie. "It is good to be a husband, is it not?"

"Oh, shut up." Rawden exhaled a breath in frustration when Rockingham laughed. "Must you be so obnoxious?"

"Admit it, you are quite taken with your wife." Rockingham waggled his brows. The insufferable arse. "And who would blame you? If I were not so in love with Arabella, I might have pursued Lady Beaulieu before the war."

"The devil you say." Rawden clamped his mouth shut too late, when he realized his friend deliberately baited him, as was his way. Then again, he rarely kept secrets from Rockingham. He rolled his shoulders and relaxed. "In truth, Patience is magnificent, and I am rather fond of her, but that is all."

"Praise, indeed." Rockingham cast a side glance. "I will have to inform Arabella her private lessons proved successful, and her erstwhile pupil pleased you."

"You may tell your lovely, nosy countess to cease all instruction, immediately." Rawden reflected on a particularly embarrassing mishap that occurred that morning. "No more trips to Gunter's and seductive savoring of ices."

"Oh?" Rockingham snorted. "Your countess is intrepid. Let me guess. You suffered premature cannon fire in your crotch."

"*Enough.*" To his chagrin, Rawden recalled how he lost control, culminating in a most disconcerting accident that required the expeditious washing of his wife's face and hair, and cursed when his cheeks burned. "Bloody hell, it was humiliating. Haven't suffered such an adolescent exhibition of male virility since I was in short coats, but how was I to prepare for the shock? We are but a sennight into our marriage, and Patience was a virgin when I first took her."

"I sympathize." Rockingham scratched the back of his head. "And I suppose I am partly responsible, because Arabella, no doubt, imparted such knowledge. But, in her defense, she means well. She was dreadfully unschooled when we consummated our vows, but she took to marital duty with her characteristic enthusiasm for life, and I wouldn't have her any other way."

"That is surprising, given she has a mother. I would have thought Lady Ainsworth explained the particulars." Rawden shrugged. "On the other hand, Patience had only your wife to educate her."

"And I'm certain Arabella did her best to fill the void." Rockingham clucked his tongue. "You will recall she lent your lady the Aretino."

"Oh, I recall." Rawden revisited the moment Patience locked her lips about his main mast. He had no warning, and he hadn't fathomed requesting such service of his high-born debutante. At least, not yet. "Forgive my indelicacy, but I require your counsel, and I depend on your discretion. My winsome countess has employed various positions I would hesitate to ask of a seasoned doxy."

"One would think you should be grateful, and you may rely on me." Rockingham stretched upright. "Why do you sound muddled? What troubles you, my friend?"

"Well, I was wondering." Rawden considered his words. He refused to insult Patience. "How long did it take for you to become accustomed to Lady Rockingham?"

"*Accustomed?*" Rockingham asked with unveiled astonishment.

"Indeed." Rawden's mount shuffled its weight, and he drew closer to his friend. Glancing from side to side, he asked in a low voice, "At what point did you gain your fill?"

"Gain my *fill?*" Rockingham blinked.

"Yes, you addlepated lackwit." Rawden groaned. "When did your desire wane?"

For a moment, Rockingham simply sat there and stared. He opened and closed his mouth. At last, he said, "If it ever happens, I will let you know."

"I beg your pardon?" Incredulous, Rawden ignored the unease traipsing a merry jig down his spine. Something told him he had seriously miscalculated. "Do you mean to tell me you still covet the same passion for Lady Rockingham as you did prior to your nuptials?"

"No." Rockingham averted his stare and the hint of a smile played on his lips. "If anything, since our marriage I crave Arabella with too great a hunger for restraint, and she encourages me. My desire for her has not dimmed. Rather, my appetite for her has burgeoned beyond my control. Thus, I indulge her naughty games to my irrepressible benefit. Should I die abed in the throes of seduction, I shall be all the better for it, for her embrace is my heaven on earth."

"But—how is that possible?" Rawden shuddered at the implications. The only thing that provided a modicum of comfort in his marriage bed was the idea that, at some point, he would be able to manage his baser appetites. His bride certainly offered no assistance in that respect. Whatever he asked of her, she yielded much to his obstreperous gratification. "You have her every moment of every day. She is yours to command. She is a familiar presence between your sheets, much like enduring the same meal for dinner, every night. How have you not grown weary?"

"What a curious question." Rockingham rubbed his chin. "One that I believe you can answer for yourself. So, let me inquire after you. Now that you've had a taste of your own unrivaled paradise. Now that you've claimed your bride's prize, and you alone have enjoyed her gifts, a singular fact to which I suspect you are neither unaware nor inured, are you bored with your chosen mate? Can you comprehend seeking the company of another merry widow, with their easy friendships, tired embraces, and expensive demands? If your reply is the affirmative, can you envision one of our contemporaries taking your place and thus occupying your countess?"

"Like bloody hell." It was too late when Rawden noted the vehemence in his response. The mere suggestion was enough to move him to violence. Of course, when he mulled his friend's position, he had to admit Rockingham was right. While he desired Patience before marrying her, the emotions he experienced in the aftermath of the consummation grew inexorably, like a bonfire raging without restraint. He had left her side no more than half an hour ago, yet he still yearned for the heat of her supple body. Without doubt, he would return to her at the first opportunity. He simply could not manage or explain what he felt. "It is not as if I haven't had other women. But I was so sure I would tire of her."

"If it is any consolation, I confronted the same situation." Rockingham snickered. "There we were, imprisoned by a dastardly villain, facing unknown dangers, and all I could think about was when I could have Arabella again. There were days in our captivity when we never left our bed. Love will do that to you, I suppose."

"I said nothing about love," Rawden quickly corrected his fellow wounded soldier. "Indeed, I am incapable of such commitment, and I am unworthy of Patience's heart. It is doubtful she will ever make a declaration, and I refuse to entertain such nonsense."

"Still fighting the inevitable." Rockingham shook his head. "I wager you will learn otherwise, sooner than later. I only hope that, in your stubborn dismissal of the inescapable, you do not hurt your lady. You would have to live with that on your conscience. By any chance, have you ever made Lady Beaulieu cry?"

"No." Rawden cleared his throat. "At least, not to my knowledge."

"Heed my advice." Rockingham wagged a finger. "Never provide any provocation for tears. Trust me, nothing reduces a man to a useless puddle of flesh and bones faster than a weeping woman, especially when you care for her—and do not try to convince me you care not for Lady Beaulieu, because I lack an arm, not a brain."

"And how would you know, given your professed devotion for Lady Rockingham?"

"On two occasions, one of which you witnessed."

"Ah, yes." Rawden revisited that dreadful night in Weybridge, when Rockingham sacrificed himself to save his wife. "Given the circumstances, with your father's blackguards on your tail, you could not possibly blame yourself. The situation was untenable, and you had no choice. So, what was the other unfortunate instance?"

"You really think that matters?" Rockingham vented a self-deprecating snort. "Brother, I caution you, because I would rather face the fate of Prometheus, forever chained to a rock and suffering the eagle's daily liver feast, than countenance Arabella's lament. And I refer to the night I woke to the gut-wrenching sounds of my wife's mournful pleas, as she wrestled with nightmares during my recovery, following my liberation from Little Bethlem."

"How is that your fault?" Rawden inquired in disbelief. "Rockingham, you take too much on yourself. I was there, and you were in deuced bad shape."

"Says the man who carries the weight of the world on his shoulders." Rockingham frowned and averted his gaze. A veil of melancholy passed over his face. "During my convalescence, I separated myself from Arabella. I could not bear for her to see me in that condition, and I thought to spare her unnecessary misery. What I did not anticipate was how my behavior would hurt her. She may not have been confined to an asylum, but she was wounded by the whole miserable affair. Then, when we were reunited, my deeds gave the appearance that I spurned her. My actions caused her further pain—pain she did not deserve, and she struggles to this day with the memory of it."

"Commiserations." Rawden wondered if that was why the Rockinghams lived so intrenched in each other's pockets, however unfashionable. To some degree, he understood the obsession. He hated being separated from Patience, even for a few hours. "Still, you are blameless. And I'm positive Lady Rockingham does not hold you accountable. Despite her sex, she is an uncommonly intelligent creature, similar to my wife."

"But you did not summon me to praise my marchioness. So, what did you want to discuss?" Rockingham eased the reins of his Andalusian. "I gather you received another objectionable missive from your mysterious adversary?"

"Aye." From his coat pocket, Rawden produced the telltale unfranked parchment, which Rockingham accepted and perused. "It was delivered last night. As with previous communications, the messenger was approached on the pavement, after making a delivery, by a hooded figure. He was given ten pounds and my address. He had no knowledge of the sender. However, this note is more ominous in its purpose."

"A demand for payment to maintain a secret that is no secret. Well, I could have predicted this." Rockingham furrowed his brow and shot a glance at Rawden. "*Five hundred pounds?*"

"That was my reaction." Except Rawden did not agree with his friend. He feared the threat and the ensuing fallout should the unknown villain reveal the truth of Quatre Bras and his shame.

While he cared not for his place in society or possible censure, he couldn't lose Patience, and that scared him more than anything the enemy could devise. "It is an outrageous sum but one I can easily afford."

"Don't tell me you're considering paying the blackguard." With a hand pressed to his chest, Rockingham appeared aghast. "You know that if you give money now, it will never end. Like the Sword of Damocles, there will be endless requests and ultimatums. You will never escape your pursuer, and by extension neither will Lady Beaulieu. You realize you are not the only target? She is in danger, too."

"You think me unaware of the perilous circumstances? My only hope is to set a trap and attempt to catch the rogue." And thereby protect Patience. From every angle Rawden assessed the situation, his new bride manifested his lone weakness. She was the only thing without which he could not live. Couldn't even contemplate his world without her in it. "If I were truly smart, I never would have married her."

"You cannot be serious," replied Rockingham, his tone invested with shock. "Do you expect me to believe you regret your union?"

"She is a vulnerability I cannot sustain."

"Because you care for her."

"I never said that."

"You didn't have to, given it is written all over your face every time you look at her." Rockingham tucked the note in his pocket and drew rein. "Do you genuinely not know the *ton* was rife with speculation regarding your relationship long before you offered for her? Your attachment had become accepted as fact months prior to the announcement of your engagement. Did everyone know but you?"

"That's impossible, because I always intended to make her my mistress." Rawden regretted the words the minute he uttered them, and he sulked. He knew it. And he hated himself for it. "How could they know what I didn't know until I proposed?"

"Now, even that is beneath you, brother." Rockingham shook his head and frowned. "Do not insult your wife, or I shall be forced to defend her honor. She is too fine a lady."

"That I do know. Certainly, too fine for me." In silence, Rawden vowed to make amends. If only he had the courage to make a bold, outward gesture. "I could commit a thousand good deeds and never deserve her. I must've been mad to claim her."

"I would try to enlighten you, but I don't think you're ready to hear the truth." Rockingham grinned and turned his mount. "You will tell me when you've figured it out for yourself. In the meantime, I will gather the Mad Matchmakers and strategize the questionable remittance that we might end your torment and remove an impediment to your future happiness."

"You do that." His friend's expression did not inspire confidence. "We can meet at White's, this evening."

"I will see you there." Rockingham waved farewell.

For a long while, Rawden sat in the park, staring at nothing.

Since returning from the war, he had expended considerable effort erecting barriers between himself and those closest to him. Given his shame, trust, not to mention intimacy, was a luxury he could ill afford. So he withdrew from society and shunned his family, maneuvering in the shadows of life. Hiding in the dark. Never granting entry into his private pain. Yet, Patience evaded his defenses, reaching through the misery to touch him. He knew there was something about her the minute he first glimpsed her across a crowded drawing room at Ainsworth's dinner party.

She called to him on some mystical level he had never experienced but suspected had always been there. Some elusive realm he purposely avoided, preferring to remain safely tucked in the margins. It was a place he could share with no one but her. Something inside him recognized that, and he could not resist her. Like a moth to a flame. That was why he had to have her. Because she represented all that was good and light in the world. And in him. She, alone, held the best parts of himself, and he would fight to the death to keep her.

CHAPTER FOURTEEN

I T WAS EARLY in the day when Patience assessed her appearance in the long mirror. She turned left and then right, scrutinizing her crisp ensemble of sea blue wool and her coif of curls piled atop her head. After tugging on her gloves, she smoothed a few wayward tendrils and emerged from her private apartment. In the hall, the first thing she noticed was the crystal vase filled with fresh mixed blooms sitting on a side table. It was the most outward expression of her presence on what previously had been known as a bachelor residence.

In the three weeks since she married Rawden, she undertook her role as Lady Beaulieu with relative ease, preferring to learn the inner workings of the residence before making any changes. Once she assumed her place as chatelaine, she met with Mrs. Price, the housekeeper, and Mills, the butler, to inquire after their duties and possible areas for improvement, placing emphasis on their input. Soon thereafter, she hired an underbutler, an additional hall boy, and two kitchen maids.

As for the grand house, she enlisted Mr. Holland's critical gaze to assist in minor renovations. Plans included commandeering half the back parlor to function as her study, of a sort. There would be new wall coverings and updated paint colors, as well as pillows and lap blankets. The home cried out for a woman's touch, and she was happy to oblige.

Descending the main staircase, she trailed her palm along the polished surface of the oak balustrade and was pleased to discover nary a hint of dust on her kidskin glove when she reached the bottom step. In the foyer, the marble floor boasted a high gloss. Intent on escaping without notice, she tiptoed to the hall tree and reached for her cloak.

"And where are you off to on this fine day?" Rawden inquired in an inquisitive tone, and she recoiled. Still garbed in his silk robe, with matching trousers, he assessed her appearance with his usual interest, as he collected her cloak and draped the wool garment about her shoulders. "How charming you look, which is rather disappointing, because I had hoped to exercise you well into the afternoon."

"I have errands I've neglected far too long, but I will r-return in time for d-dinner." She shivered and giggled as he trailed a series of butterfly kisses along the curve of her neck. "I expected you to venture to your club, to engage in gentlemanly activities with your friends."

"I prefer ungentlemanly activities with my countess," he murmured against her flesh. "So do not tarry, my lady. Besides, I have a few surprises in store for you."

"I promise, I will come home before you have a chance to miss me." She patted his cheek.

"But I miss you already." To her dismay, Rawden opened the door and frowned. "Where is the coach?"

"I had thought to take a stroll, given the weather is perfect." The truth was she didn't want anyone to know her destination. The last thing she needed was the earl's coat of arms emblazoned on the rig and drawing attention to her presence amid the London gossipmongers. "You know my fondness for walking."

"My dear, if you wish to promenade, I shall be only too happy to accommodate you during the fashionable hour, but it is unacceptable for a woman in your position to be traipsing about like a beggar in the streets." Her husband glanced over his shoulder. "*Mills*, Lady Beaulieu is departing."

The butler approached from the side hall and bowed once.

"Of course, my lord. I will send word to the mews, at once."

"Until then, let us wait in the privacy of the drawing room." Before Patience could protest, Rawden ushered her into the quiet chamber and shut the doors. In the relative silence, the steady *ticktock* of the mantel clock filled her ears.

And then he pounced.

Beset by more than six feet of aroused male, she backed into a wall and made a pitiful attempt to fend off his assault. The man seemed to sprout hands, given he caressed her everywhere, while licking and nibbling playfully at her lips. She wrapped her arms about his neck even as she feigned protest. Thus they dallied, as he tried to undress her, and she fought to remain clothed.

"My lord, you are insatiable." Laughter bubbled in her throat. "Rawden, please, you must control yourself."

"Why?" He redirected his play to her ear, grazing the crest with his teeth, and her breath caught. "We're married, and this is what married people do."

"That does not absolve us from our responsibilities," she replied pertly, and he chuckled. "If I delay much longer, I will be late for my luncheon with Lady Rockingham. Now, I believe I hear the horses, so I will bid you good day."

"Just a moment." Her husband cupped her chin and stared into her eyes. Then he bent his head and bestowed upon her an achingly sweet kiss. "Think about me while you are gone, lady mine."

"Why don't you mark the hours until I return?" she asked as he swept her into the foyer. "Although I never see you consulting a timepiece."

"That is because I don't carry one," he stated matter-of-factly.

"Whyever not?" Patience peered at her reflection in the wall mirror and adjusted her lace-trimmed poke bonnet.

"I don't trust them." Standing as her escort, Rawden opened the door and led her across the threshold and down the entrance steps. "One hand is longer than the other."

She could not help but laugh in the face of such ridiculous

logic. Ignoring the footman, her husband steadied her as she climbed into the coach. Once the latch was secured, she eased into the squabs and blew a kiss to her charming spouse. Resting her hands in her lap, she glanced at the passing scenery and tried to calm herself. A nice walk would have been preferable to the ride, given the questionable nature of her undertaking. What troubled her was deceiving Rawden.

Since she met the irascible earl, she had always been honest with him. Today, that changed, and once she departed his company, nothing would ever be the same between them.

The brief journey to South Audley brought her to her own personal Rubicon.

The rig rolled to a halt, and liveried footmen leaped into place. Patience descended to the pavement and told herself she was doing the right thing. If she said it enough, she just might believe it. But nothing could resolve her inner torment in relation to misleading Rawden. She would make her confession at the earliest opportunity, when she had reasonable certainty that he would respond rationally. And then a lone thought occurred to her.

Rawden?

Rational?

At the door, she lifted the heavy knocker and pounded twice. A very precise butler set wide the oak panel.

"Good day." He bowed.

"Hello." From her reticule she retrieved her card and handed it to the manservant. "Lady Beaulieu to see Lord and Lady Hertford. They are expecting me."

"Of course, Lady Beaulieu." He retreated a step and extended an arm. "They await you in the drawing room."

After doffing her cloak, bonnet, and gloves, Patience followed the domestic to a resplendent chamber bedecked in soft white with old gold accents. Lord and Lady Hertford stood as she entered.

Lady Hertford smiled. "Lady Beaulieu—"

"Please, you must call me Patience." She slid to the chair Lord Hertford held for her. "After all, we are family."

"How very kind of you." Lord Hertford walked to the window but made no offer, in kind, and she wondered if she pushed too hard. "We cannot in adequate terms express our gratitude for your acceptance of our invitation. We would have included our son, but we suspected he would refuse and prohibit you from speaking with us, and someone must make the first overture."

"I understand, completely." Indeed, Patience knew without doubt that would have been Rawden's counter. "In defying Lord Beaulieu, I hope you can appreciate the delicacy of my position. Am I to presume you wish to explain the situation regarding your conflict with my husband?"

"Yes." Lady Hertford nodded. "May I pour you a cup of tea?"

"Thank you." Patience settled herself. "Perhaps you might describe the circumstances, because I would dearly love to rectify the matter, but I know not where to begin. Or you could share details of Rawden's youth. I've often wondered what he was like as a boy."

"The man resembles little of the lad," Lady Hertford replied with a wistful glance. "And he worshipped his father. That is what makes our predicament so distressing. We were close to our son, before the war changed everything."

"How so?" Patience asked and scooted to the edge of her seat. "What happened?"

"Lord Beaulieu is my heir. He is my only son, thus the marquessate is his to inherit." Lord Hertford peered at the sky and frowned. "As a boy, he followed me everywhere, always asking for virtuous tasks. At Eton, he applied himself with dedication and discipline, often earning top marks in his class. He continued his commitment at university, and never was any father so proud. Never once did he give us cause for complaint. And then he threw it all away to purchase a commission in the Army, in defiance of my directive. When he returned home, a permanent wound left him disfigured. Rather than continue his noble pursuits, he wasted his days drinking to excess and chasing widows."

"As usual, Lord Hertford abridges the circumstances to the minutest point, which really isn't helpful." Lady Hertford leaned back on the sofa and furrowed her brow. "My dear, from an early age, Rawden was terribly shy, but he was also very sensitive. He cried when he found a dead butterfly. He nursed an injured duck in his room. It was quite startling to discover the poor creature floating in Rawden's tub. And he spent many afternoons carrying wayward turtles to the pond on our estate in Hertfordshire."

"I remember that." Lord Hertford chuckled. "He called himself a turtle rescuer. But his real passion was collecting toy soldiers. Fancied himself a general, and we had a costume made especially for him, on his eighth birthday, complete with epaulets."

It was then Patience realized that was the youthful affectation she glimpsed in her temperamental earl on rare occasions. She could just imagine Rawden, fresh-faced and idealistic, embarking on a military career. Recalling the brutal account he shared with her, she wanted to cry for him. For the youthful Lord Beaulieu filled with promise and dreams of saving butterflies, ducks, and turtles.

"Forgive me, Lord Hertford, but what happened when my husband purchased a commission?" She set the now empty tea cup on a table. "You indicated earlier that you did not support his choice."

The marquess clasped and unclasped his hands. He opened and closed his mouth. He paced for a moment and then stopped. Then he wiped his forehead.

"Tell her, Norman," said Lady Hertford.

"I am ashamed to admit I lost my head over the revelation after I expressly forbade him from joining the effort. I demanded he surrender the commission on pain of disinheritance, which he promptly refused. To my inexpressible shame, we did not go to the docks on the day he sailed for the Continent. He departed our shores assuming we scorned him." Lord Hertford slumped his shoulders and quietly stated, "In the heat of the moment, I said and did so many things I regret. In my defense, it is not every day one finds out his beloved son is off to war."

"I see." Patience reflected on numerous exchanges with Rawden. Prior to their wedding, she could not reconcile the generous benefactor who paid her servants no small sum in back wages and purchased food to fill her belly with the arrogant nobleman who behaved in an indelicate manner whenever he manipulated her into a private audience. Given what she learned from his parents, everything made sense.

While the military could train Rawden to take up arms against the enemy, no amount of drilling and preparation could teach him how to stop being human. It was that vulnerable aspect of his personality that both preserved and destroyed him. Leaving the man torn between multiple realities, fighting for control of the tormented soul that remained.

The fanciful turtle rescuer and the battle-hardened soldier represented two sides of the same coin.

Somehow, she had to find a way to help him live with his past and his present, else he had no future.

"Patience." Lady Hertford inclined her head. "Are you unwell?"

"No." She was in shock, and she pressed a hand to her temple. "I'm merely pondering how to approach my husband."

"May I ask, if it is not too personal, how did you meet?" inquired Lord Hertford.

"At Lord and Lady Rockingham's engagement dinner," Patience explained. "Lady Rockingham and I have been close friends from the cradle, so I was invited to the celebration."

"And your father is General Wallace?" Lord Hertford tapped a finger to his chin. "He was a devil of a soldier in his prime. A pity about your mother. Theirs was a love match."

"Yes." Patience shifted as her cheeks burned. Given her father's fall from grace, she feared Rawden's parents might have objected to the union. "He was never the same after Mama died. Did you know her?"

"A broken heart can do that to anyone, and I was vaguely acquainted with Mrs. Wallace." Lady Hertford lifted a plate filled with tea cakes. "Would you care for a sweet?"

"No, thank you." Patience was too nervous to eat anything. "I must depart soon else I may be discovered."

"What will you do about our son?" Lord Hertford neared and perched on the sofa beside Lady Hertford. "Can you help us? I give you my word, I want naught more than to restore harmony between our two houses."

"I will do my best, given I share your aim, but it will not be easy." Patience recalled the vehemence with which Rawden responded to his parents. "Lord Beaulieu experienced unimaginable horrors in battle. From what you describe of his childhood, he is much altered. Despite doing his duty, and an official commendation, he covets deep and abiding shame. And there are those who would exploit and hurt him. I would elaborate, but it is not my story to tell."

"We understand." Lady Hertford rested her hand over Lord Hertford's. "We know only what was printed in the papers, but we suspect there is more to the events at Quatre Bras than was published for public consumption. But he has confided in you?"

"He has, and I would never betray him." Patience stood and strolled to the hearth. "But I am determined to make him happy. He has fought and suffered for our country, and in return he surrendered an eye and so much more. I will do whatever is necessary, for however long it takes, to ease his pain that he may enjoy his hard-won life."

Lady Hertford grasped Lord Hertford's arm and then whispered something to him. When the marquess nodded, Patience contemplated what she did wrong. In truth, she cared not for anyone's good opinion save Rawden's. He, alone, commanded her loyalty, and she would defend him even against his parents.

At last, Lady Hertford said, "You love him."

Patience gripped the mantel as her heartbeat hammered in her ears. Gooseflesh covered her arms, and tears welled in her eyes. She could try to deny it, but she wanted to proclaim the truth to someone—anyone. She had yet to rally the courage to declare herself to Rawden, because she suspected he wasn't ready to hear it.

Unwavering, she replied, "I do. I love my turtle rescuer very much."

THE SUN ROSE high in the sky when Rawden emerged from his quarters, freshly bathed, shaved, and dressed. He would have preferred to spend the afternoon making love to his wife, but she had not returned from her errands. Then again, were Patience in residence, he could not surprise her, and he dearly loved surprising her. As he descended the stairs, Abigail met him halfway.

"Lord Beaulieu, it's here." The old crow smiled. "The delivery men are bringing it up the back stairs."

"Excellent." He reversed course and made for his wife's apartment, just as a few workers carried in the new vanity he commissioned.

The bespoke transitional dressing table, made in the tradition of Jean-Georges Schlichtig, boasted rosewood, rosewood veneer, stained wood, and geometric decorations of braces and cubes in *trompe-l'oeil* frames. It was not the cherished possession Patience inherited from her grandmother, which his bride sold to feed her household. Despite his search, he could not locate the original heirloom. With Abigail's assistance and a detailed description, Rawden purchased an expensive replica.

"Place it here, against the wall." Abigail directed the workers. "Oh, look at it. My lady will be so happy, my lord."

"That is certainly my hope, given I paid a beastly sum for it."

When he noted tears in Abigail's eyes, he remarked, "How unusual. I thought only humans could cry."

"You know, my lord, I could say something rude, except two wrongs do not make a right." She cast a smug expression. Engaging in fiery banter with the crusty domestic ranked as one of his favorite pastimes. "Take your parents, for example."

"Aw, you sound reasonable. It must be time for my medication." Rawden stuck his tongue in his cheek and awaited her rejoinder. How he enjoyed arguing with Patience's lady's maid. When Abigail made no comment, to his disappointment, he gave his attention to the matching chair. "A thought crossed my mind."

"It must have been a long and lonely journey," the domestic quipped, as she transferred a silver-backed hairbrush and a comb to the top drawer. "Of course, I do not presume you are dense. You simply have bad luck when thinking."

"I suppose I could verbally tangle with you." Rawden collected a variety of hair accouterments and placed them in the vanity. "But I never engage in mental combat with the ill-equipped. And you've employed that insult before."

"Oh, I like that." Abigail cackled with laughter and slapped her palms together. "You're learning, Lord Fussy Breeches. And I'm not insulting you. I'm describing you."

"You know, I'm unutterably jealous of all the people that haven't made your acquaintance. Now then, what else can I procure for Lady Beaulieu's delectation?" In his mind, he composed a list. "I want Patience to have everything she lost as a result of her father's downfall, and nothing is too little or too great. I would have her want for naught."

"Well, let me see." Abigail scratched her chin and narrowed her stare. "You've already bought her more dresses than she's owned in her lifetime, although you seem to believe night rails unnecessary. You have fresh hothouse roses placed in her apartment on a daily basis. She has more jewelry than she can wear at any given time. You stock her favorite jasmine tea. But there is something. Five years ago, she sold her horse, a beautiful Arabian mare, to settle several of General Wallace's debts, after a bill collector hassled her in the park. Lady Beaulieu cried for a sennight, and I wager she still grieves the loss."

"It's been five years?" Rawden doubted he could secure the same mount, but he could contact his man at Tattersalls. "I had better speak with the dressmaker about a new riding habit. Would she prefer a particular color?"

"Emerald green, my lord." Abigail arranged a perfume bottle and a bracelet inasmuch as Patience had left them on the old vanity that morning. "Lord Beaulieu, if I may, why do you buy all these things for Lady Beaulieu? Her ladyship married you because you were her choice, although I always believed her a woman of sound judgement and sense. She has never been one given to avarice. Rather, she's always been a good-natured and generous in spirit."

"I understand, and would that your question were easy to answer." Yet, Rawden knew exactly what motivated him. What kept him awake at night. Why he would move heaven and earth to make Patience happy. He couldn't utter the words. Couldn't even think them. But the reason was engraved on his heart, and it terrified him. "Suffice it to say I suspect I know not even half the hardship she endured in the last few years, since her mother died. It is my intent to ensure she never lacks for anything again."

"My lord, I could almost like you, if I didn't find you so odious." Abigail cackled. "Now absent yourself so I can tidy Lady Beaulieu's room."

Rawden saluted and marched into the hall. On a table, a large crystal vase boasted a collection of hothouse blooms. Since his wedding, fresh flowers all but littered the house. In every room and corridor furnishings had been subtly altered. Porcelain trinkets, in every conceivable shape, evidenced the presence of a woman in residence. Fringe-edged pillows and new drapes appeared as if from nowhere, and he adored every frilly bit of it.

It meant he was no longer alone.

In his study, he strolled straight to his desk and sat in the leather high back chair. He glanced at the daybed Patience had situated against the side wall and grinned. At first, he protested what he considered the invasion of his domain. Then his blushing bride proceeded to demonstrate her purpose, and the skills obtained via the Aretino, in an afternoon of wanton pleasure such as he had never known, the memory of which he would carry to his grave.

After dipping a nib into the inkwell, he composed a letter to his man at Tattersalls, requesting recommendations to secure a new horse, preferably a sweet-tempered Arabian. On a clean sheet of parchment, he scribbled instructions to the dressmaker, offering an obscene bonus for a garment completed in a sennight. Just as he sealed and franked the second missive, someone pounded on the door.

Anticipating his wife's return, it never occurred to him that she wouldn't knock. In a handful of strides, he entered the foyer with baited breath, longing to show his bride the vanity. He could only guess at how she would express her appreciation of his efforts.

"I'll get it, Mills." When he set wide the heavy oak panel, he blinked. "Lady Rockingham. What are you doing here?"

"I had thought to join Lady Beaulieu for tea." Lady Rockingham crossed the threshold while tugging off her gloves. "She inquired after my opinion on a change of color in the back parlor. Is she available?"

"Lady Beaulieu is out, I'm afraid." A sneaking suspicion gnawed at his senses, but he refused to entertain any hint of impropriety on Patience's part. "However, I was given the impression you were to luncheon with her."

"Oh." A strange look flitted over Lady Rockingham's face. While she comported herself brilliantly, her calm demeanor was not enough to fool him. Even though, at the moment, he desperately wanted to be fooled. "Oh, yes. Now I remember. How silly of me to forget. I should away before I am late."

"Indeed?" Folding his arms, he arched a brow. "Do tell, where were you supposed to meet?"

"Where were we supposed to meet?" Lady Rockingham asked, wide-eyed.

"Yes." Undeniable realization dawned, and inside him something died. "Where were you to eat?"

"Where were we to eat?" She swallowed hard as she wrung her fingers. "I'll give you three guesses."

"You know, Lord Rockingham was right." Rawden shifted his weight. "You are a terrible liar."

She shuffled her feet, and her cheeks flushed bright red. "Uh, there must be some mistake."

"And Lady Beaulieu made it." Furious, he gritted his teeth. "But I will be sure to tell her you called."

"Please, Lord Beaulieu. You mustn't punish Lady Beaulieu for my blunder." Pale, she retreated to the front step. "I'm sure there is a reasonable explanation. I can be awfully harebrained—just ask Anthony. You should not hold my foibles against Lady Beaulieu."

"I gather you are departing?" he stated acerbically. "So soon?"

"I must be going." She waved as she ran for her coach with nary a backward glance.

Rawden slammed shut the door and paced like a jungle cat. Struggling to draw breath, he tugged at his cravat and stripped the linen from his neck. As he staggered down the corridor toward his study, he clung to the wall. Dizzy, his ears ringing, he stumbled into the room and inhaled the faint aroma of cigar smoke. From a small table near the window, he collected a crystal balloon and a decanter filled with brandy. Before the hearth, he fell into one of the matching overstuffed chairs and poured himself a healthy drink.

Staring into the flames, he counted off the minutes, focusing on the lulling *tick tock* of the longcase clock in the hall. His pulse slowed. On the armrest, he drummed a constant rhythm and marked the passage of time in a sun ray's path across the Aubusson rug. He reached for something, an emotion to manifest an outlet for the nameless torment holding him prisoner. Instead, he felt nothing. So, he sat there.

Waiting.

He knew not the hour when familiar sounds emanated from the foyer. Despite the uncontrollable desire to go to his countess, he held his place, because she would come to him.

And then there would be a reckoning.

As if on cue, Patience appeared in front of him, as if posing for inspection. He hadn't even realized she had walked into the study.

"My lord, how are you this fine evening?" Pretty as a picture, she could have passed for Galatea, the beautiful sea nymph of Greek mythology. "Did you have a pleasant day?"

"I would call it enlightening, my dear." He remained still, even as he seethed with unspent ire. He planned to toy with her but found himself asking, "How was your luncheon with Lady Rockingham?"

"Speaking of lunch, I am famished." With nervous laughter, she pressed a palm to her belly, and he had her. "Shall I change for dinner?"

"In a moment." He lifted his chin as he gripped the chair. "I asked you a question, and I will have your answer *now*."

Tension weighed heavy as she met his stare.

For a while, she simply stood there.

Then she broke the silence and to his surprise quietly said, "You know that I did not luncheon with Lady Rockingham."

It was a statement.

"She arrived this afternoon, looking for you." Slowly, he stood. "So, where were you?"

"Please, I can explain." With a shaky hand, she tucked a stray tendril behind her ear. "I met with your parents—"

"My *parents*? For the love of all creation, why?" Somehow, her admission made the situation much more grievous. "And how could you lie to me? How could you betray me so completely as to go behind my back?"

"Because I wanted to know why you quarreled with Lord and Lady Hertford, and you refused to talk to me about it." She splayed her palms. "Rawden, do you think me blind? Do you honestly believe I cannot see how you suffer? You must know that what hurts you hurts me. If I could be of assistance, given you seem intent on running from your problems, I had to try. If I could ease your pain, there is nothing I would not do for you."

"You make yourself sound so noble," he remarked in a scathing tone. He wanted to wound her as she wounded him. He wanted her to ache as he ached. "But you intentionally deceived me."

"Yes, and I'm sorry." She bowed her head. "If I had it to do over again, I would not alter my tack, because I finally comprehend why you will not receive them. But you must know they regret their actions. They wish to make amends."

"I don't care what they want." He assessed her trembling form and sighed. "And right now, your immediate concern should be what it will take for me to forgive you. Of all the failures I have experienced, you are the greatest disappointment of my life. As of this moment, I cannot abide the sight of you. Go to your room. I will have a tray sent up to you, else I fear I shall revisit my dinner if I am forced to endure your company."

With a sob, Patience hiked her skirts and ran from the study.

At once, Rawden fought contrition.

How could he expect perfection of Patience when she was human? She was everything good and pure in his world, and yet she was not infallible. And how could he issue a command in much the same fashion as had her father?

Clutching his crystal balloon, he drained the contents in a single gulp and hurled the glass into the hearth. He dragged his sleeve across his mouth and sprinted into the hall. He ascended the steps two at a time and dashed to Patience's chamber. Without ceremony, he flung open the door and stormed past her sitting room into the inner apartment, where he found her admiring the vanity.

"You did this for me?" she asked in a shaky voice. When she turned to him, he cursed himself as he spied her tear-spangled lashes. All the anger he ardently embraced vanished.

"It is not the original," he explained in a soft tone. Some nameless affliction plagued him, a heavy sensation filled his chest, and he resisted every instinct to flee. But he felt like he was drowning. "Abigail provided a description, and I commissioned a new piece for you. I wanted to surprise you."

"And I ruined it." She sniffed and pressed a palm to her forehead.

"No." He neared and reached for her, but just as fast he withdrew. "Patience, I want to understand you. I want to know why you lied to me. You knew what I was before you married me, just as I thought I understood you. Of all things to take from someone, to steal a leap of faith is an egregious offense. What motivated you to destroy my trust?"

"Oh, Rawden, do you truly not know? Are you so blind to what the world must surely see?" She faced him fully, and the agony that marred her delicate features nearly broke him. "I love you. I am *in* love with you."

Dumbfounded, he could not move.

Stunned, he could not speak.

Struggling in vain, he sought a response, but nothing came to mind. He lingered there dazed and silent, searching for the words to comfort her, but he could not ignore her declaration. Never did he fathom anyone could love him. Not a man shamed in the heat of battle.

Yet his wife made her pledge not once but twice.

Patience covered her face with her hands, and in a state of unutterable confusion, mortified by his inability to communicate his feelings, he slowly walked to the small corridor that joined their rooms, closing the little door behind him. It was then his bride cried aloud, and he pressed a clenched fist to his teeth. Her mournful sobs echoed in his ears, and he closed his eye. He wanted to go to her. To console and reassure her. But he was afraid. Of what, he couldn't comprehend.

Instead, Rawden leaned his back to the oak panel and slid to the floor. Pulling his bent legs close, he rested his forehead to his knees and wept.

CHAPTER FIFTEEN

T HE FOLLOWING MORNING, Patience stepped from the Beaulieu coach and crossed beneath the portico of the palatial Grosvenor residence. For a moment, she checked her appearance and inhaled a calming breath. Before she could knock on the door, Arabella appeared and rushed forth.

"Lady Beaulieu, it is so good to see you." She smiled. "I've been watching for you since I received your note. Heavens, but it sounded grievous. Let me take your cloak and gloves. How are you?"

Had she asked any other question, Patience might have been able to maintain her composure. But after the events of the previous night, she desperately needed a friend. When she burst into tears, Arabella grabbed Patience and hugged her tight.

"Everything...is...awful," Patience said between sobs. "Rawden hates me."

"Oh, dear." Arabella gently shrugged free and took Patience by the wrist. "To the back parlor—*now*."

Dutifully, Patience followed in her friend's wake. Once they were safely closeted in the cozy room, she plopped in an unladylike manner on the sofa and covered her face with her hands.

"I made a horrible mess of things." After fumbling in her reticule, she located a handkerchief and blew her nose. "Rawden will never trust me again."

"That cannot be. I refuse to believe that." Arabella lifted a teapot from a tray and filled two cups. "I had Cook prepare refreshments. Can I offer you a cake or a shortbread?"

"No, thank you." Patience wiped her brow and sniffed. "I feel as if I swallowed a lead shot, and I fear I would revisit anything I consumed."

"This is all my fault." Arabella bowed her head. "I never should have arrived on your doorstep unannounced, assuming you would be there. Had I known you made other plans I would have stayed away. Can you ever forgive my dreadful breach of etiquette?"

"My friend, you are blameless, and there is nothing to excuse." Patience dried her eyes and mulled the situation. She had hoped to make a stand for her man. Instead, she alienated him. "I got into this mess on my own. Although I thought you were meeting with your mother. I mistakenly believed my actions would go undetected."

"Until I showed up and ruined everything." Arabella frowned. "And my schedule changed after Mama decided to join the Duchess of Swanborough for lunch. When Lord Beaulieu confronted me, despite my confusion I knew I committed an egregious violation of social decorum, which I swear will never happen again. Indeed, he did not in any way conceal his displeasure. I knew he was furious, though I knew not why. I had my driver take a tour of Bond Street, in search of you, because I would have warned you, but it was for naught."

"That is because I was not shopping." Patience hugged a throw pillow and rued her actions, however well-intended. From every angle she dwelled on her spectacular misstep, she could deduce no solution. "I paid call on Rawden's parents."

"How intriguing. Must confess I am not well acquainted with Lord and Lady Hertford." Arabella averted her stare and tapped a finger to her chin. "Anthony mentioned there was some discord in that relationship, but I never assumed it could cause friction between you and Lord Beaulieu. Is it something you can share?"

"I don't see why not, since he made no attempt to disguise his reaction from you." Still, Patience chose her words carefully as she explained how Lord and Lady Hertford objected to Rawden's military commission and service, as well as the fact that they did not make their farewells when he set sail. "But I think the worst part of the entire affair is that Lord Hertford threatened to disinherit Rawden."

"You can't be serious." When Patience nodded, Arabella gasped. "How awful but, perhaps, not too surprising. Anthony told me His Grace was furious that he and John took up arms. Had both brothers been killed, the dukedom would have gone unclaimed upon His Grace's death. His Grace wanted Anthony to remain in England, to ensure one of the heirs survived, but my husband refused to yield. I suspect there were a great many fathers who protested, and I daresay numerous ultimatums were employed to no avail."

"May I ask, has Lord Rockingham forgiven His Grace?" In that moment, Patience recalled how fragile Lord Rockingham looked after Rawden rescued the marquess from Little Bethlem, a notorious private asylum for the mentally ill, after the Duke of Swanborough had his son imprisoned. It was during that crisis that Patience became acquainted with Rawden, given he seemed forever intent on tormenting her. While she protested his bawdy behavior, as would any well-bred woman of character, secretly he fascinated her. He lived in the margins of polite society, dancing along the fringe of what was and was not acceptable, without care for anyone's good opinion. His sense of freedom appealed to her. "Have they reconciled?"

"I'm not sure how to answer that." Arabella compressed her lips. "Anthony tries. He truly tries to do the right thing, because he is the best of men, and that is why I love him. But I must admit I find it difficult, if not impossible, to make allowances for, much less forgive His Grace. And yes, I know it is not the charitable attitude, but I cannot muster a shred of absolution for Swanborough. Whenever I am in his company, I must resist the overwhelming urge to hit him in the face."

"Do the nightmares still plague you?" Patience inquired in a soft voice.

"Yes." Arabella stared at her hands neatly clasped in her lap. "I don't understand why I cannot stop them, when the incident has long since ended, yet I routinely wake Anthony with my unrest. If I regret anything it is that I often disturb him, and I am certain he holds himself responsible for my distress despite my protests to the contrary."

"I'm so sorry." Taking into account what Lord and Lady Rockingham endured, Patience thought her predicament paled by comparison. What right did she have to quibble over a disagreement, when Lord Rockingham was almost killed? "Is there anything I can do to be of assistance?"

"You have done enough." Arabella smiled. "Indeed, I owe you a debt I can never repay. So instead, I must inquire after the support I might provide you."

"I'm not sure my situation can be resolved." Patience recalled the heated exchange from the previous evening and shuddered. "Rawden banished me to my room. He said he could not abide to look at me."

Then she doubled over and wept.

"Please, don't cry." Arabella came to sit beside Patience and enfolded her in a comforting embrace. "It will be all right, I promise. I'm sure he didn't mean it."

"But he did." Then again, Patience second-guessed herself. Early that morning, in the pre-dawn hours, she woke to find Rawden curled protectively about her. In her bed. Later, when she roused for the day, she noted a fire blazing in the hearth, and he was gone. Hurriedly, she dressed in hopes of breaking her fast with her husband. But by the time she reached the dining room, he had departed the residence, much to her disappointment. "Or did he? Arabella, I am at sea."

"Did something else occur?" Arabella asked over the rim of her teacup.

"Yes." Patience pondered how much to share. Of course, Arabella was like a sister, and she would never reveal what Patience divulged. "Rawden slept with me last night. In my chamber."

"Did you—"

"No."

"Are you sure?"

"Yes."

"Would you even know?"

"I believe so."

"How?"

"I was still wearing my night rail."

"Ah, I see." Arabella nodded and giggled. "That is the best indicator of husbandly games. However, I would argue his presence in your apartment suggests he was not so angry as you thought. If I were you—" Someone knocked on the door, and she peered over her shoulder. "Come."

"Hello, love." Anthony strolled into the back parlor, with Rawden bringing up the rear, came to an abrupt halt, and bowed. "My apologies, darling. I didn't realize you had company. Good afternoon, Lady Beaulieu."

"Lord Rockingham." She dipped her chin and quickly glanced in the opposite direction, refusing to look at Rawden.

"Well, this is a serendipitous occasion, because—oh, I say. Blast your miserable hide, Beaulieu. You didn't have to kick me." Lord Rockingham cleared his throat. "My lady wife, if you would grant me a private audience in the hall, I would...I should...bloody hell, I am going to kiss you silly."

"Anthony."

"What?" He snickered. "We are all friends here, and I wager they know exactly what we're going to do, so why claim otherwise?"

"How can I argue with such logic?" Arabella tittered and glanced at Patience. "Excuse me, while I bestow my womanly favors on my affection-starved husband."

Alone with Rawden, Patience picked at the lace hem of her sleeve. The small chamber grew silent as a tomb, and the mood seemed just as morose. Conscious of Rawden's movement, she turned on the sofa and gave him her back. To her consternation, the cushion sank as he sat beside her.

"I don't suppose you want anything to do with me, given my shameful behavior last night," he stated in a whisper.

"Considering what you said, I would have thought the reverse true," she replied with a sniffle.

"I acted badly, and I owe you an apology." Given his lordly personality, that admission had to have hurt him, so she accepted the olive branch.

"On the contrary, I should not have deceived you." To her inexpressible shame, she wrestled with the urge to bawl like a newborn babe. "The blame is mine."

"Patience, please, look at me." He shifted and cupped her chin. "I cannot bear your indifference."

"*My* indifference?" She met his stare, and he frowned. His expression, the lost little boy in turmoil, gutted her. "You dismissed me out of hand. Yes, I know what I did was wrong, because you own my allegiance by marriage, but you rejected me when my motives were honorable."

The resulting pain was too much. To her unutterable humiliation, she buried her face in her hands and collapsed in a spate of tears.

"No." He patted her head. "No, no. Don't do that."

At his admonishment, she only wept harder.

"I didn't mean it. I was upset." He pulled her close and held her tight, cupping her cheek so that she rested against his chest. He toyed with her fleshy ear lobe and rocked her gently. "I didn't think. I simply reacted in haste and anger, without care for your feelings. I should have known better. Bloody hell, I do know better. Please, Patience, I beg you, stop crying. If you do, I will give you a surprise."

"I've already had it. Several times, in fact." She choked on a sob. "Ever since we married."

"I wasn't referring to that, although I like the way you think, and I'm always happy to oblige you." He ran his thumb along her bottom lip and smiled. "So let us not entirely abandon the idea. Perhaps, a delay, because I have something I wish to share with you?"

"What is it?" She accepted the handkerchief he offered and wiped her face. "Or do I dare ask?"

"Come with me." Standing, he took her by the hand. "I vow there will be no more tears shed today, Lady Beaulieu."

At the door, he paused and turned to her. Framing her jaw, he bestowed upon her the sweetest kiss, astonishingly intimate given its brevity. Inhaling a shivery breath, she responded in kind. Slowly. Tentatively, he deepened the exchange, teasing her with playful flicks of his tongue. Then he lifted his head and stroked her cheek.

"Rockingham was right. I would rather be gutted with a dull pen knife and have my entrails ripped out with a rusty fishing hook than make you cry." He rubbed his nose to hers. "I'm truly sorry, Patience."

"Such lovely sentiment." She relaxed her shoulders. "And I'm sorry, too. I never should have lied to you. On my honor as your wife, it won't happen again."

"Then let us put the entire awful affair behind us and start anew." In that moment, he drew her into the hall. "Because I dearly want to make you happy." In the foyer, Rawden shouted, "Rockingham, we're leaving."

At the end of a side corridor, the door to the study opened, and Arabella emerged, with Lord Rockingham in tow. Patience stifled a snort of laughter, when she noted her friend's mussed hair and disheveled appearance. But when Lord Rockingham, equally rumpled and missing his cravat, coat, and waistcoat, gazed wide-eyed and tugged at the back of Arabella's skirts, Patience giggled.

"I beg your pardon, but we are departing." Patience tucked a tendril behind Arabella's ear. "I hope we didn't interrupt anything of significance."

"Oh, it was nothing we can't continue, posthaste." Arabella yelped when her husband swatted her on the bottom in play.

"Well I like that." Lord Rockingham pouted. "What do you mean it was nothing? Perhaps I should dine at my club. A little absence might make your heart grow fonder."

"You do, and you can sleep on the daybed in your study," Arabella replied pertly.

"That is a fate worse than death." Anthony peered at Patience and Rawden and quickly added, "Not that I would know."

"Of course, not." Rawden threw open the door and called over his shoulder, "Have my driver return the coach to the mews. I will take Lady Beaulieu home in my new rig."

"New rig?" Patience asked in wonderment. At the curb, she spotted a glorious curricle drawn by a perfectly matched pair of bays. Gooseflesh covered her arms, and she shivered with excitement. "Oh, my lord, they're beautiful."

"Care for a ride?" he asked as he lifted her to the box seat. "And to clarify, I am not referring to our usual afternoon exercise."

"Rawden."

"Haa." He waggled his brows and leaped beside her. Taking up the reins, he leaned close and whispered, "Ah, I love it when you blush. What it does to me. And what I want to do to you."

Before she could reply, he stole a quick kiss. Then they set off, flying across Grosvenor Square. With a peal of delight, Patience clung to Rawden as he took a sharp left onto Duke Street at full speed. Shuffling his grip, he draped an arm around her so that he hugged her, in a scandalous public display of affection as he drove the team through Mayfair. She found his joy infectious, and she forgot the pain of yesterday and gave herself to the here and now.

When they came to Oxford Street, he slowed only a tad, and they perilously negotiated a right turn. Then he eased his grip on the reins, and the pair soared. A small vendor cart pulled in front of them, and Patience covered her eyes and shrieked. Taking a quick peek, she discovered Rawden navigated around the obstacle with skill and ease, although the other driver waved a fist in the air.

"Are you enjoying yourself?" he asked as they veered onto Holles Street, which took them to Cavendish Square and home.

She glanced at her husband, and her breath caught.

His guinea gold hair rustled in the breeze, and his cheeks flushed a charming pink. Unguarded, his expression evidenced unfettered euphoria and infinite vigor. Strong yet vulnerable, he persisted in a state of turmoil, as both the turtle rescuer and the hardened soldier, an irresistible combination, battled for control of him. Somehow, he had to learn to reconcile the two aspects of his personality.

"Very much." She longed to hold him. To soothe his sharp edges and reassure him. "And you?"

"Always, when I am with you." He winked and steered toward the house they shared.

The admission, spoken without artifice or coercion, touched her without actually touching her, and she understood Arabella's fierce defense of Lord Rockingham. In that stark instance of clarity, everything made sense. She realized that, no matter what he said or did, he owned her heart. She loved the youthful dreamer and the skilled warrior. The playful sprite and the arrogant seducer. And whether or not Rawden realized it, he was in desperate need of a protector.

Come what may, she would fight anyone who tried to hurt him. Regardless of the cost, Patience would be his champion.

CLOSING HIS ONE good eye, Rawden bent over Patience and lightly bit the flesh at the nape of her neck as he caressed her breasts through her gown. His ears rang, his heart hammered in his chest, and beneath his feet the world shifted, such that his knees buckled. White hot lightning shot straight to his groin, and he gnashed his teeth against a groan. Soul-stirring completion stole over him like a warm blanket on a cold night, and he surrendered to mind-numbing ecstasy. Slowly, he drifted to the mortal plane. Drunk with newly spent passion, and weighted with sated bliss, he gasped for breath as he held his wife.

"When you told me you secured a private box for the theatre, and you intended to fulfill a lifelong fantasy, I assumed it had something to do with the David Garrick play or the lead actor." His arresting bride clung to the back of a chair, and he admired her peach-shaped bottom, so tempting in its perfection. "Never did I imagine the evening's entertainment involved wanton seduction in a public place."

"We aim to please," he whispered as he withdrew his flesh from her body. After righting his clothes, he steadied her while she stood and settled her skirts. Then Rawden offered his handkerchief, which she accepted. "And didn't I tell you? You are my evening's entertainment, which has only just begun, and you did not disappoint. But wait till I get you home."

"Praise, indeed." Perched on tiptoes, Patience planted a wet kiss on his lips and favored him with a brilliant smile, which never failed to move him. "I look forward to your encore. Now, if you will excuse me, I will attend my personal needs and return before Lord and Lady Rockingham arrive."

"Hurry back." He winked and she blushed.

For a few minutes after she departed, he loomed in a daze of lust mixed with some nameless impression he could not recognize and grinned like an idiot.

In the days following her breathtaking declaration, he worked hard to anticipate and fulfill her every desire. He endeavored to keep her happy, given he could not bear to lose her. Since he could not reciprocate, because war injuries rendered him incapable of such sentiment, he would have to find other ways to show affection.

Because he could not live without Patience.

As Rawden drew back the heavy velvet drapes that shielded his box, he tried to ignore the emotions swirling inside him, wreaking havoc on his senses. He did not identify or explore the feelings, because he feared what he might discover. It was easier to assume that whatever took hold of him would not last long. Then he could focus on his greatest concern.

Keeping his wife's love.

But that posed a new, seemingly insurmountable problem.

Namely, how could he covet Patience's heart without yielding his own?

Would she understand if he explained he had no heart? How that part of him died on the battlefield with so many hopes and dreams? That he remained locked in an invisible prison from which there was no escape? However much he tried, he could not share that aspect of himself with her, or anyone, so he would conceal his affliction. He would suffer in silence, as he showered her with expensive presents and lavished upon her physical intimacy, and pray that was enough to satisfy her.

"Ah, here we are—oh, Beaulieu." Lord Rockingham, hugging his wife from behind, in what appeared a very compromising position, blinked and started. He released Lady Rockingham. "What are you doing here so early?"

"Er—Patience has never been to the Theatre Royal, and I thought to give her a tour before the crush arrives." Rawden raked his fingers through his hair. To Lady Rockingham he said, "My bride was momentarily indisposed. Perhaps, you might provide assistance?"

"Of course. I'm sure she's somewhere in the box-lobby." Lady Rockingham patted her husband's cheek. "Don't brood, darling. I will be right back."

Alone with his friend, Rawden noted too late that the cushioned seats remained askew. Haphazardly, he lifted the telltale chair and brought it to its original orientation. He glanced from left to right, searching for anything amiss.

"Bloody hell, have I taught you nothing?" Rockingham rolled his eyes and drew a handkerchief from his coat pocket. Then he approached Rawden and daubed his brow. "You are flushed beetroot red like a virgin on her wedding night, and tuck in your shirt."

"I beg your pardon?" Rawden peered down and discovered his disheveled state. "I may have dressed in a hurry. Patience was excited to get here."

"Blaming your innocent wife?" Rockingham adjusted Rawden's cravat and snorted. "A rake of your caliber should always know how to turn himself out in trim, especially following a tryst. I have seen more convincing expressions in a toddler caught with its fingers in the cherry compote."

"How did you know?" Rawden frowned. "What gave us away?"

"Why do you think I'm here at this hour?" Rockingham neared the chairs and scowled. "Which one did you use?"

"In the middle," Rawden said with a nod. "I will sit there."

"I gather the waters have calmed between you and Lady Beaulieu?" At Rawden's glare, Rockingham explained, "My wife tells me everything, but you know that."

"Hell and the Reaper, am I to have no privacy in my marriage?" Rawden paced and then plopped in his seat.

"No." Rockingham crossed his legs and grinned. "But you know that, too."

"Can you not do something?" Rawden shook his head. "Demand that she ceases encouraging my countess."

"I would sooner ask Arabella to stop breathing." Rockingham slapped his thigh. "Besides, your pathetic attempts to avoid the inevitable are rather entertaining."

"Go to the devil." Rawden immediately regretted his outburst, because it indicated an utter lack of control.

"I may soon enough." Rockingham lifted a shoulder in a half-shrug. "But permit me to impart sage advice before you completely bungle your relationship, although I must commend you on your dedication to catastrophe."

"Why do I get the feeling I don't want to hear what you have to say?" Rawden folded his arms. "And I am certainly in no mood for a lecture."

"Not a lecture—a suggestion. Or deliverance, in your case," said Rockingham quietly. "Tell her you love her. Trust me, you can give her a castle filled with priceless trinkets, a fortune in jewels, a title, and unlimited power, but nothing can rival your declaration. The longer you fight it, the worse it will be for you."

"Is that how you felt about Lady Rockingham?" Rawden recalled the night his friend sacrificed himself to save his bride and his unborn child. "If memory serves, you delayed and admitted as much."

"Indeed, and I am trying to spare you from making the same mistake." Rockingham sighed and averted his gaze. Sadness flitted over his face and was just as quickly masked. "Yes, I thought I could evade the inexorable truth. I believed, however incorrectly, that I was protecting myself. Instead, I denied myself the most important commitment a man can make in his life. Later, almost too late, I made my declaration in a moment of haste, under duress, when I had no opportunity to celebrate the occasion with my lady, because I waited. Had Shaw succeeded in his scheme, Arabella would have never known what she meant to me. While I know you are afraid, because I once stood in your shoes, you must remember that fear is but a passing discomfort. Regret lasts an eternity. We none of us know what tomorrow will bring, and you may never get your chance. Make haste, Beaulieu. Make haste."

An usher walked into the box and bowed. Rockingham quieted and stretched upright.

"Lord Beaulieu." On a silver salver, the usher bore an envelope with chillingly familiar markings. "A message for you."

"Thank you." With dread, Rawden opened the missive and digested the contents. "Well, we have payment instructions."

"Are you serious?" Rockingham took the letter and read it.

He stiffened his spine. "They must be joking. You are to deposit the sum of five hundred pounds into a haversack to be left in an alleyway in Cheapside? You must know that if you pay, it will never end. The bastard will always ask for more."

"Indeed." Rawden rubbed his chin. "That does not concern me, as the money is a trifle. What troubles me is the threat to Patience. That is a new and most unwelcome development."

"You don't think your villain is stupid enough to harm a woman of rank?" Rockingham narrowed his stare. "That would be suicide."

"At this point, I can't assume anything." Rawden resolved to hire additional footmen to protect his countess. And he would limit her exposure. She wouldn't like it, but he had no choice. He would not risk her safety. "We must gather the Matchmakers, posthaste."

"I will send word, at once." Rockingham peered into the gallery. "This will be a crush, tonight. Are you sure you want to stay?"

"I can't imagine the blackguard would attack us in a public venue." Rawden glanced toward the door to his box, just as Lord Ormonde leaned against the frame. But it was the woman Ormonde escorted that had Rawden cursing under his breath as he stood. "Ormonde. Lady Fauconberg. Good evening."

"Rockingham. Beaulieu, old man, it is wonderful to see you." The Marquess of Ormonde, a devil of a cavalryman wounded by shrapnel at Waterloo, which left him with a noticeable limp, smiled and extended a hand. "It has been a long time. When Lady Fauconberg told me you were attending tonight's play, I had to see you. By the by, felicitations on your wedding. I'm sorry I missed it, but I was in America."

"Thank you." To Rawden's horror, Patience and Lady Rockingham chose that moment to return to the box. Immediately, he reached for his wife and made a point of ignoring his short-lived mistress. "Darling, permit me to introduce a longstanding acquaintance, the Marquess of Ormonde, and you remember

Lady Fauconberg."

"Indeed, it is a pleasure, Lord Ormonde." With grace, Patience curtseyed. Then she gave her attention to Lady Fauconberg and lifted her chin. Red-faced, Lady Fauconberg dipped in deference.

"What a charming little thing you are, Lady Beaulieu. And beautiful, although I expected nothing less." Ormonde, ever the charmer, caught her hand and pressed his lips to her gloved knuckles, and Rawden fought the urge to punch Ormonde in the face. The uncharacteristic reaction caught him off guard, because he never suffered bouts of jealousy for any woman, but he wanted Patience to himself. "You must tell me, how on earth did Beaulieu convince you to marry him, of all people? How did he snare you? Come now, don't be coy. I must know his secret."

"Perhaps I pursued Lord Beaulieu, Lord Ormonde," Patience replied in a flirty tone. "How do you know I did not catch him?"

"Oh, I say." Ormonde burst into laughter. "It would appear the notoriously fickle Lord Beaulieu finally met his match. I wager more than one debutante swooned when you announced your engagement. There must have been broken hearts across London."

"Enough, Ormonde." Lady Fauconberg sneered. "Let us leave the adorable couple and locate our box."

"Of course." Ormonde cast a pained expression. "We should meet at the intermission and have a brandy."

"I look forward to it." Rawden saluted and then drew Patience to their seats. "I'm sorry, darling. I had no idea Lady Fauconberg would be here, tonight. Would you prefer to go home?"

"And let that wretched woman spoil your thoughtful surprise?" Patience humphed. "Absolutely not."

Still, there was visible tension in her expression, and she held herself upright and unflinching. Rawden clasped her hand in his and traced circles in her palm. She licked her lips and met his stare, and in her clear blue depths, which he could read like a book, he spied her question before she asked it.

"She means nothing to me, Patience. And believe me, the same could be said of her in relation to me. I was no more than a conquest, a prize, where she was concerned." With care, he brushed his finger along the curve of her cheek. "I dallied with Lady Fauconberg in much the same careless fashion as the other women I considered a temporary distraction. A salve to ease the pain of the past."

"I suppose it is never easy to confront a husband's former dove." Patience opened her mouth and paused as if to ponder her response. "It may sound strange, but I am envious of all the ladies who've known you. Perhaps, because I want you for myself."

"My dear, you shouldn't be concerned, because from them I sought only the brief oblivion of release." With his thumb, he swept the gentle curve of her neck and lightly teased the triangle-shaped indentation at the base of her throat. How could he explain what he couldn't put into words? "With you, it is different."

"How so?" Innocence personified, she posed her question with no ill intent, which was why he owed her honesty.

"Patience, is it not obvious?" When she blinked and furrowed her forehead, as if lost in confusion, he reminded himself she lacked any real experience with men prior to their nuptials. "Because I am invested. Because I care for you."

Had he known the five pedestrian words would garner such a reaction from his wife, he would have uttered them much sooner. Aglow with unfettered joy, and bouncing with uncontrolled excitement, she blessed him with an effervescent smile, the memory of which he would savor on his deathbed. In her green eyes, telltale sparks ignited, and she shifted, pressing her thighs together. His loins went up in flames.

"My lord, would you think me ungrateful if I said I would like to go home, after all?" She leaned near and whispered, "I want to be alone with you. Indeed, I would not share you with anyone. Not even our friends. Please, Rawden?"

"Of course. I am, as ever, at your service." He stood and drew her to his side. To Lord and Lady Rockingham, he said, "I beg your pardon, but we've decided to retire for the night. Enjoy the play."

"I bid you a pleasant evening," Rockingham replied with a grin and murmured something to his marchioness.

Rather than take the bait, Rawden steered Patience into the hall. In the box-lobby, they shuffled through the crowd and made their way to the stairs. On the ground floor, he found her a safe place near the front entrance to avoid being trampled.

"I will collect our coats from the cloakroom and return for you." He pressed a chaste kiss to her temple. Later, in the privacy of their private chamber, he would indulge his desires, unchecked. "Wait here."

"My lord." She stayed him with a squeeze of his arm. "You dropped something."

In her grasp she held the note. To his horror, she surveyed the directive. She recoiled and met his stare. Without hesitation, she opened the offensive message and scanned the contents, her eyes darting from left to right.

"Patience, you must not worry," he said in a soft voice. "Please, don't be alarmed. I will let no one harm you."

"You think I fret for myself? You are my concern. How dare they threaten you." There in the lobby, in full view of society, she wrapped her arms about his waist and hugged him tight. Resting her head to his chest, she sighed when he rubbed the length of her back. Then she peered at him with tear-spangled lashes. "I don't care what happens to me, but I will allow no one to hurt you. Rawden, I *love* you."

It startled and humbled him, how easily those words rolled off her tongue. And he coveted her declaration as a priceless treasure he wished he could reciprocate, but he would not lie to his wife. There were other ways to express devotion, and he would employ them all, with ruthless abandon, to bind her to him.

"Let us depart." He stepped aside. "I can send a footman to fetch our coats."

"No, don't be silly." Patience wiped her eyes. "I'm not a child to be coddled. You go, and I will remain here."

"All right." He frowned at the long rows of patrons. "I will be back soon."

As he navigated the crush, he nodded acknowledgements to various members of society. To his surprise, the queue moved quickly and Fate smiled upon him when Lord Michael waved for Rawden to join him.

"Are you leaving?" Lord Michael asked. When Rawden indicated the affirmative, Lord Michael said, "But the box is yours."

"I received another letter." Rawden shifted his weight and inwardly cursed the unknown villain. "It was delivered here."

"Which means you are being watched." Lord Michael's gaze flared. "Bloody hell."

"Precisely." Rawden checked on Patience and discovered her in the company of Lady Ellsworth and Lady Howard. "I am taking my countess home, because I will not risk her safety unnecessarily."

After retrieving their coats, Rawden bade Lord Michael farewell and turned toward his bride. To his bewilderment, he walked straight into Lady Fauconberg.

"Lord Beaulieu, don't tell me you are leaving before the play begins?" She sidled close, and he retreated. "Where is that charming little creature you married? Did I frighten her? Is she afraid of the competition?"

"Lady Beaulieu has courage and unmatched intelligence, along with beauty and kindness. At your best you could never rival my wife, Eleanor." Rawden tried to evade her, but she moved directly in front of him. "You are not in her league. If you will excuse me, Patience needs me."

"What is this?" Lady Fauconberg blinked. Then she assessed him with a head-to-toe glance. "Good lord. Just when I thought I'd seen everything, Lord Beaulieu, Hero of Quatre Bras and breaker of hearts, is in love."

"Don't be ridiculous, Eleanor." Again, he attempted to elude her, but she persisted. "What do you want from me?"

"You don't know, do you?" Now she laughed, which only aggravated him. "You really have no idea. Oh, this is delicious. I'm not sure whether to pity or congratulate you."

"You're not making sense, and I have no time to indulge you." He drew up short when Lady Fauconberg touched his arm. "It's over, Eleanor. It's been over for a while, and I suspect you know that. Whatever obligation you may or may not believe you hold for me, I release you."

"Of course, you do, dear man." She leaned forward and pressed a friendly kiss to his cheek. "I'm happy for you, Rawden. And I wish you merry. Truly, I do. Now, you had better claim your countess before Ormonde steals her, because he prowls perilously close to his target."

In that moment, Rawden gave his full attention to Patience. As Lady Fauconberg intimated, Lord Ormonde assumed a familiar stance, one to which Rawden took exception. Until Patience wagged a finger in Ormonde's face, and the marquess arched his brows, appearing to find her amusing before bowing and quitting the field, and Rawden relaxed.

It was then Patience looked in his direction. When she met his stare, he struggled with a foreign reaction. His cheeks burned. His head spun. His ears rang. His pulse quickened. It was as though the floor collapsed beneath his feet, and he tumbled, headlong, into an abyss. Yet, he did not struggle. Did not fight it. They stood at least twelve feet apart, but she touched him. Provoked tenderness. Possessiveness. Was it possible? Had Rawden fallen in love with his wife?

CHAPTER SIXTEEN

T HE SUN SAT below the yardarm, as her husband was fond of saying, when Rawden and Patience gathered in the foyer to receive the Mad Matchmakers for what was her first dinner party as Lady Beaulieu. For hours, she labored over the menu, at last deciding on a course of brown onion soup, followed by roasted pork ribs, with salamongundy, blanched asparagus, and Bath buns with black butter. For dessert, she selected a tart lemon cream and Shrewsbury cakes.

"Stop fidgeting." Rawden tapped the tip of her nose. "You look beautiful in that shade of blue, although I prefer you naked and blushing. Besides, they're family, and family never stands on formality."

"My lord, you are trying to distract me, when I want everything to be perfect." She turned left and then right, scrutinizing her coif in the wall mirror. "We always convene at the Rockingham's, and Arabella anticipates everything. She knows everyone's preferences, and I am a novice."

"My dear Lady Beaulieu, you worry for naught." Rawden pulled her into his arms and brushed her neck with his lips before meeting her stare, and she shivered. "Shall I tell you my plans for tonight, once our guests take their leave?"

"Has it to do with that odd looking piece of furniture the footmen carried to your chambers this morning?" Patience recalled the strange contraption, which resembled something between a bench or a backless chair, except it featured a peculiar set of footrests on the cushioned bottom and a shocking pair of what appeared to be stirrups on the upper tier, along with what were presumably handrails. She had never seen anything like it, and she cast a narrow gaze. "What do you intend, my lord?"

"Well, it occurred to me that I have done my very best to debauch you since we wed, yet you remain innocent as a dove despite my efforts. So, I decided to deploy countermeasures, given you present a challenge such as I have never known, and I commissioned an item of my own original design that might help me in my quest to ravish you." With a devilish expression, he bent and whispered naughty deeds, shocking exercises that stretched the limits of her imagination, in her ear, and she gasped. Then he grazed his teeth along the curve of her jaw. "Think about that while we host our friends, my oh-so-delectable countess. Tonight, once our guests depart, you are mine."

"Indeed?" She flinched, and he rubbed his palms along her upper arms. "What if it is a late night? The Matchmakers tend to enjoy their cigars and brandy, and I asked Mrs. Price to ensure the cabinet in your study was fully stocked with your libation of choice for the occasion."

"Worry not, my dear countess." He claimed another kiss just as the first guest knocked. "I will always make time for you. Now, let us greet our friends."

Patience smoothed the front of her gown and stood up straight as Mills opened the door. "Lord and Lady Rockingham," the butler announced.

After doffing her outerwear, Arabella smiled and extended her arms. "So wonderful of you to host tonight's games."

"Thank you, for sharing all the little quirks and proclivities," Patience whispered. "I had no idea Lord Warrington abhors potatoes."

"And Lord Greyson believes tomatoes are evil because they are red and slimy." Arabella rolled her eyes and shook her head. "I thought he would faint dead away when I accidently served him the offensive fruit in a salad. And don't forget, Lord Michael prefers ale to wine."

"As does Rawden," Patience remarked. "Something about joining the men in their pursuits when in camp."

"Lord Warrington, Lord Greyson, and Lord Michael Donithorn." Mills bowed. The manservant walked to Patience. "My lady, dinner has been served buffet-style, with each course progressing from left to right, in the family dining room, per your instructions."

"Thank you, Mills." Patience lightly clapped twice. "Good evening, everyone. I hope you brought your appetite, because Cook has prepared a lovely feast. Since this is an informal gathering of close relations, I decided to follow Lady Rockingham's direction and commence the meal from the first. Shall we?"

"Hear, hear." Using his walking stick to check his surroundings, Lord Warrington rubbed his belly. "I'm so hungry, I could eat my toenails."

"How appetizing." Lord Greyson grimaced. "I hope that is not on the menu."

Rawden escorted Patience, as they navigated the hallway toward the back of the house. Beneath a striking ceiling mural depicting the Egyptian Battle of Kadesh and the soft light from a Baroque period ormolu chandelier by Andre-Charles Boulle, a particularly stunning fixture, she strolled to the sideboard and collected a gilt-edged bowl.

"Everything looks delicious." Arabella ladled a decent portion of soup and strolled to her seat, where Lord Rockingham held her chair. "I see you requested my favorite dessert."

"How could I cater to the men and ignore my best friend?" After assuming her place beside Rawden, instead of the other end of the table, because she suspected he would protest otherwise, Patience draped her napkin in her lap. "And we ladies have to stick together, especially when we are surrounded by a motley group of surly soldiers."

"I take exception to that characterization, my dear." Rawden narrowed his stare. "Complicated degenerates is a much more apropos description."

"Oh, you are all that and a tin of biscuits, my lord." Patience smiled when he winked. "So, since we are present and accounted for, shall we discuss the recent letter and the requested payment? How do you intend to make the settlement?"

"Please, let us delay until after dinner." Lord Greyson frowned. "Nothing spoils an appetite like talk of extortion."

"Indeed." Lord Michael grinned and plopped into his chair. "One never plans revenge and possible murder at the table. It ruins the mood."

"We beg your pardon." Arabella leaned over to cut the meat into bite-sized pieces on Lord Rockingham's plate. "As we would never wish to offend your delicate male sensibilities."

"Rockingham, will you do something about your wife?" asked Lord Michael.

"Of course." Lord Rockingham bent and kissed her cheek. "That's my girl."

"That's not what he meant," replied Warrington.

"Sister, I was just thinking." Patience tapped a finger to her chin. "Perhaps it is time we identify and approach prospective mates for the remaining Matchmakers, Lord Warrington, in particular."

"I will be quiet now." Warrington emptied his wine glass in a single gulp.

The evening continued in relative silence, with occasional banter seemingly devised to inflict embarrassment and laughter. A contest to deliver the greatest insult. Inside quips effectively excluding the ladies. She knew better than to complain. There were still adjustments to be made, despite the established presence of two wives.

Once the meal concluded, the Matchmakers convened in Rawden's study, to partake of cigars and brandy, as Patience anticipated. Like dutiful spouses, she and Arabella retired to the back parlor.

"It is entirely unfair, not to mention the height of rudeness, that we are relegated to the gallery while they devise their strategy on the main stage," Arabella said with a huff as she perched at the other end of the sofa. "They believe they are protecting us, when in reality they leave us in a vulnerable position and open to attack. You'd think they would know that."

"My dear friend, they are men." Patience recalled Rawden's expression of longing, the brief smoldering gaze, as they parted in the corridor. She reflected on the activities he devised once their company departed. "Daresay their actions are rooted in concern for our safety, however misguided."

"That's ridiculous." Arabella stood and reached for Patience's hand and drew her close, arm-in-arm. "I, for one, will not be ignored. We're going in there and assert our authority, because we're angry."

"We are?" Patience asked as she stumbled on the rug.

"Yes." Arabella marched down the hall but faltered before the open door.

The Matchmakers had positioned their chairs in a circle near the hearth. As Arabella made to enter the room, Lord Rockingham said, "It is a shame the villain chose to include Lady Beaulieu in the most recent correspondence."

"It is a tactical maneuver." Lord Michael rubbed his cheek and to Rawden stated, "The bastard can wound you by striking at your bride."

"I wish I had never wed her." Rawden stretched his booted feet, oblivious to the injury he just inflicted on Patience, and she squeezed Arabella's fingers. In agony, she resisted her friend's efforts to retrace their steps. "She would be in no danger had I stayed my original course."

"Which was—what?" Lord Greyson propped an elbow on an armrest and settled his chin in his palm. "I thought you wanted to marry her."

"I intended to sponsor her," Rawden explained with unimpaired aplomb. Another direct hit that almost brought her to her knees, and she leaned against the door frame for support. Again, Arabella tried to retreat, but Patience resisted. Pain tore at her gut, and her legs buckled. "I never planned to propose."

"So, you claim you are what, an accidental groom?" Lord Warrington shook his head and snickered. "Pull my other leg."

"I for one—" Lord Rockingham spotted Patience and Arabella just then, and he cleared his throat and motioned with a flick of his wrist. "Er, ladies. How good of you to join us."

"*Patience.*" Rawden stood and met her stare, surprise evident in his expression for a mere hairsbreadth. For a while, he said nothing, and the study grew eerily silent. She waited for a sign of contrition; some insistence she'd heard wrong. Instead, he appeared numb. As if he remained unaffected. Indifferent. Relieved she finally learned the truth. "Will you come in and sit with us?" he asked in a calm voice.

Overwhelming anguish almost suffocated her. She tried to move, but it was all she could do to breathe. Inhale. Exhale. Her thoughts scrambled. Her ears rang, like the bells in a Wren steeple. Her gut wrenched. In the remote recesses of her brain, she screamed.

"Perhaps, we should be going." Lord Greyson checked his pocket watch and turned to assist Lord Warrington. "It is quite late, and we have devised a plan that should see us through to victory and end this entire miserable affair."

Never had the Matchmakers moved so fast. Like a troop movement by Wellington's command. She might have laughed had her husband not so thoroughly devastated her. Shaking herself, she mustered the strength to function as hostess, concealing her shattered state.

"Permit me to summon Mills." Patience closed her eyes for a moment, when Arabella tugged her elbow. "I'm all right, Lady Rockingham."

"Know that I am here for you," Arabella whispered as they walked into the foyer. "I will be available tomorrow, if you have need of me."

"Thank you, for attending my first dinner party." Patience could not meet her friend's stare, else she feared she would collapse. "I know how busy you are, so I appreciate your support."

"I understand." Arabella pulled Patience into a steady embrace. "I shall stand at the ready, if you have need of me. Send a note, if you cannot journey to Grosvenor Square, and I will be here, I promise."

"Safe journey." When Arabella refused to let go, Patience gently pushed free. To the Matchmakers she said, "Gentlemen, so kind of you to honor us tonight with your presence."

The wounded soldiers bowed in concert and extended what could best be described as awkward acknowledgments. Only Lord Rockingham approached her.

"Lady Beaulieu, on behalf of my friends, allow me to offer my deepest gratitude for daring to host our meeting. I suspect it was a rather intimidating prospect for a new bride, yet you handled it admirably and with distinction." Then Lord Rockingham leaned forward and in a low voice stated, "Take heart, Lady Beaulieu. Love does not come easy for men."

Unsure how to reply, she simply nodded once.

In the tomb-like atmosphere of the main entry, Mills ushered the Matchmakers and Arabella to their rigs, while Patience stood as sentry. Calling on her upbringing, she waved farewell with a smile on her face, while inside she died a little more with each subsequent breath. As Rawden dismissed the butler for the night, she calmly walked to the stairs.

"Patience, may I speak with you in my study?" Rawden inquired.

"Not now, my lord." She gave him her back and navigated the first few steps. She needed to cry. To howl in pain. And she required no witness to her agony. "I am quite tired."

"Then I will be brief." When she continued to the landing, he pursued her. "You can run away, but we are going to settle this matter before we go to bed."

"*We* are not going to bed." She hiked her skirts and sprinted down the hall, as the tears trailed her cheeks. As her husband chased her, she rounded a corner and lost her footing, and her slippers skidded on the polished floor. Wildly flapping her arms, she regained her balance. Seconds later, she dashed into her private apartment and slammed shut the door. Just as she turned the key in the lock, Rawden rattled the knob and pounded on the oak panel.

"Patience, you are fooling yourself if you think you can avoid me." He hammered so violently she retreated to the opposite side of her sitting room and slid to the thick rug, with her legs tucked beneath her, suspecting he might bring the house down about her. With ear-piercing admonishments, he assailed her, but she hurt too much to care. Leaning against the *chaise*, she doubled over and wept in horrible, ugly sobs.

When Rawden grabbed her from behind, she screamed.

"Let me go," she shouted repeatedly, as she realized he gained entry via the tiny corridor that connected her apartment to his.

"Not until we talk." Ignoring her protests, he lifted her from the floor and carried her to an overstuffed chair near the hearth in her bedroom. After settling her sideways in his lap, he said, "I owe you an apology, and I will make amends."

"How d-do you intend to do that, when you h-humiliated me so completely in front of our friends?" To her utter mortification, she heaved and choked in her misery. "You don't want me. You *never* w-wanted me—"

"That's not true."

"I heard you." She inhaled between discomposing hiccups, so overwhelmed by emotion she could scarcely form a coherent thought. "You stated your aims clearly, leaving no room for misunderstanding. You told your friends you never intended to wed me. That you wished to sponsor me. Did I not offer to be your mistress?"

"Aye."

"Then why did you propose?" She glanced at him and whimpered. "I would have given you what you wanted, of my own free will and spared us both the pretense of a union."

"It is not a fate to which I would condemn you, because you are too good for that life." Gently, he cupped her cheek and pressed her head to his chest. "You needed a husband. A protector to watch over you and keep you safe."

"I never asked you to marry me."

"And I couldn't live with myself if I did otherwise."

It was a stunning admission.

Discomfiting silence weighed heavy between them broken only by the low but constant keening she could not cease. For how long they sat there she neither knew nor cared. Burdened by heartbreak so acute, she shivered in his grasp as he whispered words of contrition.

"I'm sorry, Patience." He raked his fingers through her hair, loosening several pins and a comb. "You deserved better, but I was too selfish to surrender you to someone else."

"You make no sense." Suddenly exhausted by the overwhelming tide of emotion, she rubbed her eyes and yawned.

"What I'm trying to explain is I lied." Rawden shifted and tipped her chin, bringing her gaze to his. "Poor little love. You are worn out, and who could blame you?"

"I don't understand you." She sighed when he kissed her forehead. Somnolently, she said, "You could have had anyone."

"Because I would have no one but you," Patience thought she heard him say, as she fell asleep in his arms.

The hour grew late, and nightfall blanketed the city. In the distance lightning flashed, signaling an approaching storm. The normally bustling footpaths in one of the seedier parts of London were bereft of a single soul. His coach turned onto Ironmonger

Lane from Cheapside and slowed. About midway down the block, the rig came to a halt beside the opening to an alleyway. Making no attempt to disguise his activity, because he wanted the mysterious blackguard to see him, Rawden collected the haversack filled with pound notes.

After thrusting open the door, he leaped to the pavement. Glancing left and then right, he scanned the vicinity for any sign of the villain and walked toward a large stack of wooden casks as directed in the note. His pulse beat a rapid salvo in his chest, and his ears pealed. Around the back of the pile, he crouched and pushed the pouch against the wall. Standing, he dusted his hands and peered toward the other end of the alley, where a couple of destitute figures slumped against a pile of pallets mixed with various rubbish.

To the ordinary observer, the unfortunate vagabonds appeared to be two poor Londoners without a home. In reality, it was Lord Greyson and Lord Warrington, dressed in dirty togs borrowed from Greyson's stablemaster. When the unknown extortionist tried to fetch his ill-gotten gain, Greyson would pounce.

Of course, the disheveled duo was not alone.

High atop the roof, Lord Michael perched in order to shout the alarm at the first hint of trouble. In the house across the street, Lord Rockingham sat by the window, watching the main road. Now, all Rawden had to do was wait.

And he hated waiting.

For a man accustomed to getting what he wanted—when he wanted, waiting always struck him as a useless endeavor better suited to the less fortunate. It was a socially enforced behavior designed to make those with little or nothing at all feel good about whatever scraps society deigned to throw their way.

He should not have to wait.

Because he was Beaulieu.

The coach rounded the corner of King Street, and Rawden turned the hinge and let himself out before his rig stopped. As soon as he cleared the road, his driver flicked the reins and departed the area, as planned. Quickly, he sprinted to the alley that led to the back sides of the row houses. In the dark, he located the well-worn gated rear entrance to Three Ironmonger Lane.

Moving with the stealth and ease of a skilled soldier, he navigated the tiny yard and knocked on the back door. Moments later, the old widow, Mrs. Barney, who resided therein appeared and opened the heavy oak panel.

"Milord, welcome to my humble home. Please, come inside and take your ease." She struggled to curtsey and groaned as she straightened. "Lord Rockingham is in the parlor."

"Thank you." He reached into his coat pocket and withdrew a small bag of gold coins, which he surrendered to Mrs. Barney. "For your trouble, Ma'am."

"It was quite a surprise and an honor to be afforded an opportunity to help a nobleman such as yourself, given my modest accommodations." She smiled, a gesture that revealed a few missing teeth. "I'm glad to be of service."

"Again, I am in your debt, Mrs. Barney." He handed her a card. "If you ever have need of me, know that you have my unfailing support."

"You are most kind, milord." She dipped her chin. "I will be in the upstairs parlor if you require assistance."

Rawden strolled the narrow hallway, the veil of saffron from a single candle lighting the way. The walls bore signs of wear, with peeling paint and cracked plaster, and the floor groaned beneath his weight. He passed an ancient longcase clock, its gears creaking with age. Toward the front of the house, he found Rockingham crouched before a window in a dimly illuminated room.

"Anything?" Rawden inquired.

"No movement." Rockingham drew the curtain and turned to face Rawden. "How are you holding up?"

"I'm fine." Rawden blew out the taper and set it on a side

table. "I just want to end this horrid ordeal."

"That's understandable." Rockingham paused, as if deciding what next to say. Then he scratched the back of his head. "How is Lady Beaulieu, or am I permitted to ask that question?"

"Would that it were easy to answer." Rawden sighed and peered out the window. To his chagrin, the pavement remained deserted. "But I suspect you already know, given my wife's longstanding friendship with yours. Did Patience not confide in Arabella?"

"It would appear not, because Arabella is concerned and mentioned as much to me." Rockingham narrowed his stare and quieted. He frowned. "I thought I saw something, but it was just a stray cat. In any case, Lady Beaulieu has not sought Arabella's counsel, and my marchioness is quite worried."

"As am I." When he retired after his disastrous admission in his study, he found he could not tolerate his empty bed. Patience sought refuge in her own chamber, not that he could blame her, and he still felt the force of her tears. For half the night, he sat with her in his lap, while she alternated between bouts of violent weeping and fitful dozing. Once she collapsed in his arms, he carried her to her four-poster, undressed her, and tucked her beneath the blankets. As would a gentleman, he removed to his own accommodation.

After an hour spent tossing and turning, Rawden realized he could not sleep without her by his side. So, in the middle of the night, he relocated to her apartment where he'd finally found peace. But she woke him repeatedly, crying out and kicking with her feet, as if she fought some invisible demon. To his surprise, she calmed at his touch, drawing from him a tenderness he did not know he possessed until that moment, and it pleased him to know she found comfort in his embrace. She still slumbered when he left her that morning. "We barely spoke today, other than when she wished me luck with tonight's endeavor."

"Has it occurred to you to apologize, or does that terminology not exist in your vocabulary?" Rockingham arched a brow, and

Rawden braced for a verbal lashing. "Lady Beaulieu is a fine woman, and you had no cause to humiliate her like that. However, I would submit you only embarrassed yourself, because we are not blind. Whether or not you admit it, you are in love with your countess. The sooner you accept it the better for all involved."

"You're angry with me." Rawden rested his shoulder against the wall. For as long as he remembered, he had always been able to count Rockingham in his corner. "If it's any consolation, Patience is furious with me. Have I lost your friendship, too?"

"You could never lose my friendship, but I am disappointed in you, and I hope that means something." Rockingham silenced and narrowed his stare. Rawden glanced toward the alleyway but spied nothing. "Your actions upset Arabella, and that I cannot ignore. She weeps for her childhood chum and rains an impressive streak of curses on your head. You needn't worry, however, because I found a useful diversion to redirect all that emotion. Like my wife, I'm concerned for my roommate from Eton and university. How could you be so careless with your words when we both know you did not speak the truth?"

"But I did." Rawden stared at the empty footpaths and swore under his breath. "Patience would be safe if she were not my wife. The only reason the villain threatens her is because of me. If something happens to her, if the bastard, whoever he is, harms one hair on her head...God help me, I won't be held responsible for my actions. I will move heaven and earth to find the blackguard, and bring him to justice. There is no place he can hide that I cannot reach."

"Spoken like a man in love."

"Go to the devil."

Rockingham laughed and shook his head. "You realize the longer you delay the worse it will be for you? And you risk losing your lady, in the process. However you approach the situation, you hurt your wife."

"You think me ignorant of that fact?" Indeed, Rawden had

considered his predicament, again and again. He had thought of nothing else, even though he should have been focused on the unknown attacker taunting him with menacing ultimatums. "On another note, how did you secure this location? Were you acquainted with Mrs. Barney prior to this evening?"

"I had my man make inquiries. Mrs. Barney is Lord Fosberry's retired housekeeper." Rockingham settled the worn drape and plopped into a nearby chair. "After Fosberry lost his fortune trading in worthless mineral rights, he released his staff with nary a pension. Only a small parting gift. When I approached her, she was quite motivated to help us."

"No wonder she was so grateful." Rawden reflected on the elderly woman with the amiable countenance. "Given what I paid her, she should be able to survive in comfort for the remains of her days." He glanced at Rockingham. "Why don't you rest. I'll take the watch and wake you if anything happens."

"Are you sure?" Rockingham situated a pillow behind his head.

"Aye." Rawden gave his attention to the street, hoping—praying for an end to his nightmare. Only then would he be free to explore his feelings for Patience. First, he had to win her forgiveness.

Quiet fell on the modest chamber. Time ticked past, as marked by the constant rhythm of the clock in the hall, and Rawden tried to keep his mind on the matter at hand. But regardless of his attempts to center himself, as he would on the precipice of battle, all thoughts led back to Patience.

No matter how he tried to reassure himself that he would get her back, that she would pardon his inexcusable offenses. That she would look beyond his weaknesses and see the man who desperately needed her.

That she would love him again.

He feared the opposite.

He would give his life to hear her declaration one more time. To have her expressed affirmation fill his ears even as he ceased to exist on this earth, if it were the last thing he heard before passing into the hereafter. But he didn't know he coveted Patience's heart until he broke it.

It had to be the ultimate cruelty to lose something so precious before he discovered the extent of its worth. Something for which he always expected he would have to beg, borrow, or steal to attain. But he hadn't had to seek his treasure. Hadn't had to fight for it. It had been freely spoken. Offered without expectations in return. Under no obligation to reciprocate. He never expected her devotion. Never believed it possible. Now, he was obsessed with it—and her. So he stood there in the dark, awaiting the mysterious rogue who imperiled all Rawden held dear.

He didn't know how long he compiled solutions and strategies in his brain, but the faint golden streaks cutting across the indigo sky brought him alert. To his chagrin, no one had gone near the small fortune tucked behind the wooden casks. He'd remained on guard all night, and only a bloody cat appeared in the lane.

Reaching over to his friend, he shook his shoulder. "Rockingham, wake up."

"Huh?" Sniffling and snorting, Rockingham lurched upright. "What is it? Did the blackguard take the money?"

"No." Rawden raked his hair and considered the implications. "The bastard never appeared. I'm beginning to wonder if this isn't some sort of game to torture me."

"To what purpose?" Rockingham yawned and stretched his arm, before standing to rub the small of his back. "If avarice is not the incentive, what is the end goal?"

"I don't know, but one way or another, I'm going to find out." Rawden chucked his friend's chin. "Come, let us go home to our wives."

After bidding farewell to Mrs. Barney, Rawden and the Matchmakers flagged a hired hack that didn't fit all five soldiers into the carriage, so Rawden rode up top, beside the driver. The bracing morning air did much to ease his spirits. One by one, they deposited the wounded warriors at their doorsteps until only he remained.

Given the early hour, it was calm and hushed when he entered his residence in Cavendish Square. Not even the servants had stirred to light the fires in the hearths. In the foyer, he doffed his coat, hat, and gloves. Exhausted, he clung to the rail as he ascended the stairs.

In his chamber, he stopped when he noted the empty bed. Once again, Patience had declined to share his quarters, despite his stated preference on their wedding night. Something had to be done about that. She had to know that she was wanted, but he was too tired to press the point.

At his washstand, he yanked off his eye patch and doused his face in cold water. Behind an oriental screen, he stripped his clothes and shrugged into a black silk robe. Barefooted, he strolled to the center of his room and heaved a breath.

He was traversing the little corridor that joined their apartments before he realized he'd moved. A ray of sunlight peeked through a break in the heavy velvet drapes, and he crossed to the smaller four-poster. With a dip of his shoulder, he let his flimsy garment fall to the cushioned rug.

Naked and aroused, a development he did his best to ignore, he slid between the sheets and scooted toward Patience, as she slept on her side. Gently, so as not to disturb her, he eased his arm beneath her pillow and hugged her from behind, tucking his knees to the backs of her legs. Pressing his nose to her golden hair, he inhaled her subtle flowery scent and sighed.

It was then she stirred.

"My lord, is all well?" she asked dazedly. "Did you catch him?"

"No." Rawden kissed the sensitive spot at the side of her neck, and she turned to him.

And he turned to her.

For some reason he could not fathom, yet anticipating her refusal, he leaned forward and pressed his lips to hers. Immediately, she responded, grasping the hair at his nape and suckling his tongue. It had been too long since he tasted her, and her reaction did much to soothe his frayed nerves. Levering over her, he pushed her into the mattress, and she lifted her ankles to cradle him.

In a small part of his brain still functioning, he told himself to prepare for her rejection. That in humiliating her, he could and should expect retribution. Instead, Patience thrust her hips into his, in unmistakable invitation. She wanted him. She missed him, too. In that moment, Rawden could have wept.

Seconds later, her night rail hit the floor.

CHAPTER SEVENTEEN

I T WAS LATE in the morning, almost noon actually, when Patience, dressed and coiffed as best she could manage on her own, tiptoed across the floor of her private chamber. For a moment, she stood at the footboard of her bed and stared at Rawden as he slept. Relaxed in slumber, he seemed harmless in repose. An unearthly creature. A fallen angel with hair of spun gold, an eye of the purest ocean blue, and lush lashes she could contemplate for days. Oh, how looks could be deceiving. When she retired, she assumed he had no desire to share an accommodation, given his stated objection to their marriage. But she woke to discover him protectively folded about her, in the two nights following her disastrous dinner party.

With a finger, she traced her lips, remembering how he made love to her with such tenderness, in the wee hours. The praise and reassurance, which she longed to believe, he whispered as he took her. The murmured expressions of regret and remorse, forcefully ardent, that reached beyond her misery to touch her very soul. The way he held her after they found release, and she pretended he belonged only to her. She wanted to stay like that forever, but daybreak and reality intruded on their refuge, and she had to face the truth.

While Rawden held her heart, she would never claim his.

Quietly, she scurried into her sitting room and continued into the hall. Halfway down the stairs, she met Abigail.

"My lady, I was just coming to wake you." Abigail scrutinized Patience's hair and frowned. "Why didn't you ring for me? Shall we return to your chamber, so I may turn you out properly?"

"No, there's no time." In haste, Patience descended to the main floor and strolled into the foyer, where she tugged on one kidskin glove and another and accidentally split the side seam. "Oh, bother. It appears I must add an additional errand to my list of chores for today."

"Are you late for an appointment, my lady?" Abigail inquired, as she draped Patience's cloak about her shoulders. "Is everything all right?"

"I'm lunching with Lady Rockingham." Checking her reflection in the wall mirror, Patience pretended not to notice her swollen face, irrefutable proof of too many spent tears. "Why do you ask?"

"You have not seemed yourself." Abigail, the housekeeper turned faithful lady's maid, inclined her head and frowned. "Lady Beaulieu, has something happened? Have you heard from General Wallace?"

"No, and I don't expect to hear from him." Patience tugged the bellpull. "It is my understanding Lord Beaulieu blocked the sale of the Bedford Square property, as it was part of my mother's jointure and passed to me upon her death. Given my father's temperament, and his penchant for brandy, I suspect it could be years before I see him again—if I ever see him again."

"Good morning, my lady." Mills bowed and pointedly ignored Abigail. "How can I be of service?"

"By vacating the premises," Abigail replied acerbically.

Patience compressed her lips to conceal her amusement. It was common knowledge in the household that the two domestics grated on each other like truth and a member of Parliament. "Mills, would you have my carriage brought around, and ask the stable hand to be quick about it? I fear I may be late for an engagement with Lady Rockingham."

"Or you could hitch yourself," Abigail said in a clipped tone.

"A neddy can pull as well as a horse."

"So speaks the nag." Mills flinched and peered at Patience. "Apologies, my lady. I will send word to the mews, at once."

"Thank you, Mills." Patience cast an expression of reproach at Abigail, as the butler departed. "I wish you wouldn't antagonize Mills. What did he ever do to you?"

"He was born." Abigail folded her arms. "The man thinks he knows everything. He dared question how I perform my duties, when I have been in service since I was but a girl of five and ten."

"And Mills is an experienced and valued member of Lord Beaulieu's staff." The last thing Patience needed was added strife under her roof. "As a butler, his education and knowledge are without equal."

"Well then," Abigail said with a sickeningly sweet smile, "I am so pleased he doesn't let all that experience and knowledge get in the way of his ignorance."

"*Abigail.*" Patience pressed her fingertips to her temples and closed her eyes. "Please, for my sake, try to make peace with Mills. I have enough to deal with, without mediating between you and the butler. You know better, and you will not disappoint me."

"I'm sorry, my lady." Abigail reached out and rested a palm to Patience's forearm. The longstanding friendship transcended rank and beckoned a confidence Patience feared would break her in her current state. "Are you certain there is nothing wrong?"

"I'm fine, old friend." After patting Abigail's cheek, Patience composed herself, donning the mask she wore in public, the false face she endured as she suffered the insults and gossip of those who derided her prior to her wedding. Now, they welcomed her with their pretty façades that didn't fool her for a minute. She withdrew and crossed the threshold, as the carriage pulled to the curb. "Please, tell Lord Beaulieu I will return in time for dinner."

A liveried footman handed her into the rig, and she settled her skirts. Patience sat up straight and lifted her chin as the graceful equipage lurched forward and entered the lane of traffic.

She gazed at the footpaths and smiled as fashionable Londoners paused to note the passing coat of arms emblazoned on the door.

The drive from Cavendish Square to Grosvenor Square, which included a dash down Oxford Street, took mere minutes, and Patience soon pounded the heavy brass knocker at the home of Lord and Lady Rockingham. As usual, Arabella answered. Without a word, she grasped Patience by the wrist and yanked her into the foyer.

"I'm so glad you're here," Arabella said over her shoulder, as she all but dragged Patience to the back parlor. "I could scarcely sleep a wink just thinking of your visit, such that I may have exhausted poor Anthony in trying to divert myself."

"Daresay he was happy to accommodate you." Again, Patience thought of Rawden and the passion they shared last night. The underlying edge of desperation in his demeanor. But his attentions were driven by normal male urges, physical lust, and naught more. Never a sincere emotional attachment, and that distinction crushed her.

"Indeed, he was, and I do love him for it." Arabella drew Patience to the damask-covered sofa. "Now, you must tell me everything. How are you?"

"Fine, really." She lied. "I've come to a realization in regard to my marriage."

"All right." Arabella looked exceedingly skeptical. "Pray, continue."

"Not everyone is meant for the kind of devotion you share with Lord Rockingham." As Patience uttered the words, something inside her died. It was hope. "Lord Beaulieu is a complicated man. Our union is a conventional sort, whereas yours is the stuff of fairy tales, and I don't regret it, really, I don't. I will never live the dream, but I am content with my station and resolved to make the best of it."

"No, please, don't say that." Arabella scooted close and clasped Patience's hand. "I know what Beaulieu said—I heard him with my own ears. Believe me, what he needs is a good punch in the nose, to shake loose his brain, because he cares for you."

"You've been reading too many novels again," Patience said softly. She had no such luxury. "But I can no longer deceive myself. To continue down this path is to invite my own demise, because I simply cannot bear it. I played the game, and I lost. For good or ill, I must learn to content myself with what remains."

"That is it?" Arabella clutched her throat. "One complication, and you are ready to quit the field?"

"*One* complication?" Patience gave vent to a self-mocking snort of laughter. "Be honest. Lord Beaulieu's indifference is but the most recent of our myriad of problems, not the least of which is his obsession with the war. I am quite out of my depth. It was wrong of me to presume I might be able to help heal him, when I can scarcely help myself. But that ends today. Now."

"Patience, you and I have known each other from the cradle, and I have never lied to you. We have laughed. We have cried. We have mourned together. When my husband was taken from me, you stood by my side." Arabella's eyes glittered with unshed tears. "You are my sister, as surely as I am yours. Hear me well. You were meant for so much more. You were meant to be loved."

"A delightful sentiment, often sold in bedtime stories to gullible children, and I share all but the last. There are those lucky few like you destined for the extraordinary, while still others must accept mediocrity." Patience swallowed a sob of misery. "It is reasonable to assume, given my life thus far, that I am fated for the latter. But there are compensations. I am Lady Beaulieu. I suppose that is something." From a low table, she collected a napkin and draped it in her lap. "Shall we enjoy this wonderful lunch you've served?"

"Of course," Arabella whispered, and she prepared a plate with small egg salad sandwiches and a tea cake.

The meal passed in relative silence. It was the first such occasion between them, and Patience wondered if she'd just lost something else she coveted. Her friendship with Arabella.

Whereas Patience had always shared her true self with her lifelong chum, she donned her mask, her false smile, praying someday her face might grow to accommodate it.

"Would you care for some company while you run your errands?" Arabella inquired. "I have no plans for the afternoon, and I would be happy to accompany you."

"You intended to spend the day with your son, and I will not deprive you of such a charming charge." Patience wiped the corners of her mouth. There was a time she would have leaped at the offer. "When I complete my shopping, I will go home directly."

"As you wish." Crestfallen, Arabella stood and took Patience by the arm. With an air of solemnity, Arabella escorted Patience to the door. After collecting her cloak and gloves, she turned to depart, but Arabella caught Patience in a tight hug. "I'm here. I'll always be here. No matter what happens, I will be here for you."

"Thank you." Almost choking on her pain, Patience kissed her friend's cheek and spun on a heel. Without a backward glance, she stepped into her rig. To the driver, she shouted, "Le Petit Oiseau."

No, it wasn't proper etiquette for a lady to bark destinations at her staff, but at that moment she didn't give a fig. She was tired and wrestling with emotions she could barely contain. If she offended some unfortunate observer, so be it.

After quick stops to retrieve two new night rails, if she could call the transparent scraps of material that, she continued to the hosiery, where she purchased several pairs of stockings and garters decorated with tiny rosettes. Then she asked the driver to take her to Bedford Square.

At her old home, a once dignified residence in the estimable neighborhood, she rued the peeling paint, broken window, and dangling address placard. In her mind, she envisioned the house in its prime, when her mother planted flowers in large earthenware pots at either side of the door. She could try and fool herself into thinking she was content then, but the truth was a dark pall seemed to hover over her family for as long as she could remember. There had been little if any happiness there.

Wallowing in self-pity, and hating herself for it, Patience shook herself alert and pounded on the roof of the coach. The driver turned onto Tottenham Court Road and then Oxford Street. Soon, she arrived at Cavendish Square, where she accepted the footman's assistance as she disembarked.

On the entrance stairs, she tugged on her gloves, noted the tear, and halted. "Oh, bother. I forgot one final errand."

The driver flicked the reins and steered the equipage toward the mews. Patience peered at the sky and calculated she had plenty of daylight remaining to walk to Bond Street and back. Inhaling deeply, she rolled her shoulders and found her stride. As she crossed to Henrietta, she realized she missed her daily exercise, the lengthy jaunts brought about by necessity and poverty.

Picking up her pace, she decided to travel the less populated and narrow Old Cavendish to Oxford Street. Somewhere, in one of the homes a babe cried. Bits and pieces of rubbish danced on a gentle breeze. As she navigated the road, which had no pavement, she noted a weathered hackney slowly rolling toward her. Yielding, she hugged a brick wall. As the rig neared, two large persons dressed in dark attire and wearing masks jumped from the moving carriage.

Patience froze. When they approached her, she shrieked and turned to run, but one of the blackguards grabbed her about the waist. She tried to scream, but the other villain stuffed a rag into her mouth. Kicking and struggling, she aimed for shins, and her attackers cursed. Together, they dragged her into the rig and thrust her to the floor.

Someone whistled, and the team picked up speed.

From behind, a canvas bag was pulled over her head, and her hands were bound. Panicked and fighting to catch her breath, her mind raced. Had Rawden's unknown tormentor resorted to kidnapping to claim his money? Somehow, she had to break free.

With fierce determination, she pumped her legs, landing occasional blows, as evidenced by grunts and bellows. When she tried to perch on her knees, she was knocked down, and without warning a clap of pain exploded behind her ear.

She thought of her husband. What her demise would do to him. Then she reminded herself that Rawden did not love her. Perhaps, he would not suffer.

And then her world collapsed into a whirling vortex of darkness.

LATE IN THE afternoon, Rawden strolled into White's and waved a greeting to the Matchmakers, who occupied a table in a quiet corner. Given the hour, the gentlemen's club was filled to capacity, and he sidled between the crush of bodies to join his friends. As usual, he was swarmed by well-wishing idiots.

"Ah, if it isn't the hero of Quatre Bras," declared one fool, as he slapped Rawden on the back. "Permit me to buy you a drink, Lord Beaulieu."

"But it is my turn," another sop replied.

"Thank you, but that is not necessary." Rawden leashed his temper, restraining the urge to lash out at them, because they knew no better. And his situation was not of their making. "Perhaps, another time."

As he crossed the room, he noticed Lord Oliver Stapleton standing with Erasmus Ludlow and immediately came on guard, recalling Ludlow harassed Patience at Gunter's. He still suspected Ludlow sent the threats, in light of Ludlow's professed disdain. Part of him wanted to challenge Ludlow and have done with the entire sordid affair, but Rawden held himself in check.

"We saved you a chair." Rockingham pushed a glass toward Rawden. "And we ordered you a brandy."

"You are too kind." Rotating his wrist, Rawden swirled the

amber liquid but did not taste it. "Any news?"

"I was about to ask you that question." Warrington propped an elbow on an armrest and leaned to the side. "Have you had a letter?"

"No." Rawden shook his head and reminded himself Warrington could not see him. "That is, I have heard nothing since the original extortion note, although I expected something, but I am not sure what. More threats. Another demand for payment. Some manner of escalation."

"How is Lady Beaulieu—*ouch*." Rubbing his shin, Greyson glanced at the collective of pained expressions and compressed his lips. "Are we not supposed to ask that?"

"I thought we discussed it amongst ourselves and decided that some topics are a bit too dangerous to dare." Lord Michael glanced heavenward. "You are treading in shark-infested waters, brother."

"No, he's not." For some reason Rawden couldn't identify, he found considerable comfort in talking about Patience. In thinking about her. Even when she was not with him, he carried part of her entrenched into his very person. "Thank you, for inquiring after my wife. She is in fine fettle."

As Rockingham tactfully changed the subject, Rawden gazed at a ray of sunlight slanting through a window and revisited the pre-dawn moments he shared with his bride. The intoxicating grip of her arms as she clung to him, wrapping him in her warm embrace. How she hugged him with her velvety thighs. Her soft little exhalations in perfect rhythm with his thrusts.

He tried to convince himself there was nothing unusual in their lovemaking. He'd done the deed with plenty of other women and took his pleasure. His countess possessed the same general anatomy, so there was nothing physically unique in their interludes.

Except it *was* different.

Whether or not he admitted it, the truth was no one had ever moved him the way his wife moved him. While Patience had no experience on their wedding night, she took him to the heights of heretofore unimaginable, soul-stirring bliss. With her, he achieved passion beyond anything he had ever found with a skilled Ace of Spades. Somehow, without his cooperation or consent, when he rested between her legs the elemental connection of their bodies scored a direct hit to his emotional center, and he was powerless to guard against her.

He tried to maintain a safe distance. To remain detached and aloof. But for him, with her, he simply could not defend himself. Perhaps it was because she accepted what he gave her. Issued no ultimatums. She made everything so easy. Was that why he withheld naught from her?

And then there was the inexplicable, all-consuming, provocative hunger.

In the past, he often grew tired of his companions after one or two trysts. Seduction lost its fire after he caught his prey, and he set his sights on new game. With Patience, there seemed to be no end to his desire for her. He simply could not have her enough, even when they occupied their bed, his flesh still held deeply in hers. He always wanted her again. And his yearning grew with each successive joining. Whether or not she knew it, she owned him in and out of their private apartment. With or without her presence, he ached to be inside her. To protect her. To keep her safe from harm. If he had his way, she would never leave his bed.

God help him if she ever discovered the power she wielded over him.

It was a humbling position in which to find himself, but he didn't give a tinker's damn.

"Beaulieu, my good man, how are you?" a slightly jug-bitten Lord Chatham queried as he slapped Rawden on the shoulder, sloshing the brandy he held in his grip and spilling some of the liquid on the floor. "Give us a story. Regale us with a tale of your heroism at Quatre Bras. Tell us why you fought with such distinction, when you could have taken a position at the rear, with the other officers."

"Hear, hear," came a multitude of shouts from the crowd.

Suddenly, Rawden found himself the center of attention.

Rockingham stood. "Now, see here—"

"It's all right." Rawden waved his friend to be seated. He stared at the throng, and something inside him snapped. It was past due to break free of the invisible chains holding him captive. To escape his self-made prison. For Patience as much as himself. Heaving a sigh, in a single gulp he drained his glass, set it on the low table, and rose from his chair. "You ask why I fought, and that is an interesting question."

For a moment, he pondered his response.

"I wish I could rely on the obvious answer, for King and Country. But that would be a lie. Although that was my motivation when I was young and naïve, prior to my deployment, but my reasons changed as the war progressed, and I confronted reality." Rawden inclined his head and looked at his friends. "At first, I purchased my commission out of a misguided sense of duty and honor and, I suppose, an idealistic notion of what it meant to don the regimentals."

"Beaulieu, you don't have to do this," Greyson said in a low voice.

"Yes, I do." Rawden smiled. "If only for the ones who never came home. For those we left behind." To Lord Chatham, he said, "War is exciting when you have no firsthand knowledge of it. But it becomes altogether uglier the more you kill. You find yourself surrendering your dignity and your humanity to justify your actions. To take a life. It is a foul occupation wrought of violence and death that destroys your soul inasmuch as it does the one you dispatch to the hereafter."

All activity in the club ceased, and incoming members joined the rapt audience.

"You tell yourself you are only following orders. That you are not responsible for your conduct, yet you suffer the consequences, regardless. You call them the enemy, whatever makes it easier to vilify them, but their faces haunt you as you try to gather the fragments of your existence and survive in some fashion, as if you can put back the pieces and return to normal, whatever that means. And then there are your fellow soldiers." Rawden swallowed hard. "I refused to remain with the officers, because I would not ask of my men what I was not willing to undertake in my own capacity."

In that moment, Erasmus Ludlow neared, with Lord Oliver at his side. Ludlow met Rawden's stare and nodded once, as if to encourage him to continue.

"I led the Thirty-Second into the fray because those poor bastards were conscripts forced from their homes and their families into a conflict not of their making. Yet they answered the call, donning their uniforms and taking up their infantry rifles. They showed unimaginable courage in desperate circumstances, often outnumbered and in miserable conditions, in exchange for pitiful wages and inedible food I wouldn't serve to my hounds. But they never complained."

Gunfire echoed in his ears, and *Le Marseillaise* played softly, as if from a distance. Bowing his head, Rawden closed his eyes against the bitter memory. Inhaling a shaky breath, he lifted his chin and gazed at the well-dressed fops, with their gleaming boots and tailored clothing so far removed from the battlefields of Europe.

Word by word, he recounted the events surrounding his much-heralded charge, including his loss of control, at Quatre Bras, sparing no detail, however embarrassing. He wanted it all out in the open. No more secrets. No more lies. He thought he would dread the public disclosure of his actions. Instead, he savored a sense of relief. He felt free.

"I'm sorry to disappoint you, Lord Chatham." Just then, Rawden spied his father, an expression of sympathy etched in his patrician features, weaving to the fore. "But war is not about victory, medals, braided epaulets, tales of valorous exploits, or parades. Ultimately, it is about loss. Unfathomable loss. Of humanity. Of honor. Of innocence. The destruction of childhood dreams of glory, especially those of an impressionable lad with a penchant for arranging battles with tin soldiers and saving turtles."

With glittering eyes, his father pulled a handkerchief from his coat pocket and wiped his nose.

"In the end, I fought not for my country, or any other noble ideal, but for Charlie Boyle." Rawden gazed at Erasmus Ludlow. "For Adam Ludlow. For Francis Sedgwick. For so many souls gone and all but forgotten. Buried in mass graves on foreign land, because they were not important enough to bring home. Their names were never printed in *The Times*. They were infantrymen, the lowest of the low, but they were warriors nonetheless. They were my friends. My brothers-in-arms. I will carry them with me until I breathe my last." To Chatham, Rawden said, "I am no hero, sir. But I had the privilege of fighting alongside many such estimable soldiers deserving of that distinction."

An eerie stillness blanketed the club.

Rawden braced for recriminations. For accusations of fraud.

Instead, Lord Chatham stretched tall and proclaimed with reverence, "Well done, Lord Beaulieu."

Someone in the middle of the horde shouted, "Three cheers for Lord Beaulieu, the hero of Quatre Bras."

"*Hip hip hurrah!*" the pampered aristocrats bellowed the annoying refrain in unison.

Stunned and confused by their reaction, Rawden stumbled backward, as the floor seemed to pitch and roll beneath his feet, and his knees buckled. Immediately, he found himself supported by the Matchmakers, and his father approached.

"I've got you, my son," his father stated as he hugged Rawden. "I've got you, my precious boy. I won't let you fall."

"There's a private room available." Rockingham directed the group as the club members celebrated Rawden like a conquering general. "Let us remove to a more peaceful environment."

Dazed, Rawden leaned on his father and Greyson, with Erasmus Ludlow and Lord Oliver bringing up the rear. Ensconced in an overstuffed leather chair, Rawden took the glass of brandy Rockingham offered and brought it to his lips. He trembled so violently he had to use both hands. He looked up and discovered Ludlow studying him.

"Well, out with it." Rawden inclined his head, recalling his suspicions regarding Ludlow and the mysterious threats. "Now that my secret is laid bare, what have you to say for yourself?"

"I don't take your meaning, Cap'n." Ludlow always addressed Rawden by his military rank, instead of his title, because Rawden never relied on his social standing to lead the Thirty-Second Foot.

"You never liked me, Ludlow." Rawden scowled. "You never showed me even the smallest measure of respect, and you tried to warn my wife away from me. Tell me the truth. Are you behind the letters?"

"You're wrong, Cap'n. I said what I said because of your reputation with women. Your behavior sullied the uniform. But I suspect I owe you an apology after that speech." Ludlow scratched his cheek. "And what letters, sir?"

"You mean you don't know?" When Ludlow indicated the negative, Rawden's spirits sank.

"Someone has been sending Beaulieu ominous messages, the last a demand for extortion monies," Rockingham explained.

"Bloody hell, why didn't you tell me?" his father asked. "I would have helped you."

"Forgive me, but it was not a subject I wanted bandied about like the weather." Rawden frowned.

"Who would do such a thing?" Lord Oliver queried.

"The worst sort of blackguard," Lord Michael replied.

"But that is all over now, because you spiked the unknown villain's guns," remarked Warrington.

"Daresay, that will give Lady Beaulieu peace of mind." Greyson perched on an armrest.

At once, Rawden's thoughts turned to Patience. The person he most wanted to see. Yet, he detected her unfailing support. She was with him. Loving him. Somehow, she managed to imprint her stalwart influence on his very being, and he gained strength from her, even in her absence. He was not alone.

And then a stark realization struck him between the eyes, and he gasped for air. An incontrovertible truth dawned, shining a light on the dark recesses of his soul, and comforting warmth settled in his chest. The gentle but unshakeable influence had been there all along had he chosen to acknowledge it.

"Feeling better?" Rockingham squatted and rested a palm to Rawden's shoulder.

"I love Patience," Rawden blurted, heedless of those present. "I *love* her."

With a smile that broadened to a grin, Rockingham softly responded, "I know."

"Good God, he's delirious," exclaimed Warrington.

"Quick, someone fetch a doctor," Greyson asserted.

"And a bottle of brandy," Lord Michael added.

"Make it two," Warrington continued. "I need my own after this."

"How?" Rawden asked Rockingham, ignoring the quips at his expense. The world seemed to spin out of control, and he dug his fingernails into the upholstery. "How could you possibly know what I didn't understand until now?"

"Lady Rockingham." Rockingham chuckled. "I covet the same attachment for her, and I know the signs."

"Ah." Rawden stood and swayed, and several hands reached out to catch him. "I need to go home. I must speak to my wife."

"I will send for his rig if the rest of you will get him to the entrance in one piece." Greyson paused at the threshold. "And for heaven's sake no more maudlin declarations in White's. Is nothing sacred anymore?"

After navigating the crowded club, Rawden gained the solitude of his carriage and reclined in the squabs for the journey from St. James's to Cavendish Square. The temporary seclusion provided him the opportunity to compose a plan. A strategy for expressing himself in a way that would garner mutual affection and not hilarity or worse, rejection.

Never before had he offered his heart to anyone, and the prospect terrified him.

He contrived appeals.

He formulated his tone.

He strategized a seduction to consummate their new, shared commitment.

Everything came together, and his confidence swelled.

When his gig drew to a halt before his house, he had trouble moving from his seat. As he descended to the pavement, the front door opened, and Mills waved frantically.

"What is it?" Rawden skipped up the steps and strolled into the foyer. "What's wrong?"

"My lord, it's Lady Beaulieu." The normally staid butler wiped perspiration from his brow. "She returned to the residence this afternoon. The driver and footmen stated they deposited Lady Beaulieu at the entry, but Her Ladyship is not here."

"What do you mean, 'she is not here?'" Ignoring the gnawing sensation in his gut, Rawden paused and peered at the landing, just as Abigail descended to the first floor. "Where is Lady Beaulieu?"

"My lord, Her Ladyship never returned from her errands." The lady's maid shuffled her feet and wrung her fingers. "Please, my lord. I know something horrible has happened. I feel it in my bones. Lady Beaulieu would never leave without telling where she was going, and she promised to be back for dinner."

"My lord, there is another matter of importance." Mills held an envelope for Rawden's inspection. "This correspondence arrived almost three hours ago."

Rawden snatched the letter from the butler and scrutinized the directive. While the lack of franking was the same, the handwriting was decidedly different from the threatening notes. He broke the seal and read the contents.

A chill settled in the pit of his belly, followed quickly by white hot rage, and he stiffened his spine.

"Mills, have word sent to White's. I need Lord Rockingham, Lord Greyson, Lord Warrington, and Lord Michael here, immediately." Rawden strode toward the grand staircase. Over his shoulder, he said, "Tell them to dress for battle."

CHAPTER EIGHTEEN

FRIGHTENED AND CHILLED to her marrow, Patience held her bound wrists to her chest and shivered. Sitting on what felt like a wooden bench of some sort, she tried to pry her fingers beneath the tether at her neck. Footsteps drew near, and she stiffened. Through the thick canvas bag that covered her head, she could discern nothing but sound and scent, and that afforded no comfort. Exhausted and starved, she directed her thoughts to more pleasant memories, clinging to a volatile past that imparted more unrest than succor.

But what she tried to ignore—what she steadfastly endeavored not to contemplate was Rawden's reaction to her disappearance. Still, thoughts of him swamped her. Would he search for her? Would he care? Or would he consider himself fortunate to be rid of her? That she knew not the answer only compounded her terror.

"Good evening, Lady Beaulieu," came a murmur smooth as honey on a hot scone. "I must apologize for my men. I had no idea they would treat you so haphazardly, when my intent was not to injure you. Your presence is required to secure payment of a rather large debt."

Suddenly, the fastening at her throat eased, the bag was gently tugged, and she squinted in the light. A well-dressed stranger loomed before her. With hair black as a crow's feather, and inky eyes to match, he cut an imposing figure. Almost as tall as her husband, yet lacking aristocratic refinement, he oozed strength and virility mixed with indisputable confidence. Broad shouldered and rather handsome, his chiseled features emitted a palpable air of danger. His open appraisal of her person gave her gooseflesh, and she dreaded her fate. When he drew a knife, she could not stifle a sob of horror, and she flinched. To her amazement, he bent and cut the gag, which he removed with care.

Ceiling high stacks of pallets, crates, and barrels filled what she guessed was a warehouse, given the pungent odor of rotting produce, but where was she?

"What debt? Who are you?" she asked in a shaky voice. "And why am I here?"

"I think that, perhaps, your question is better answered by him." He motioned behind her, and she peered over her shoulder.

"Patience, I am so sorry." The familiar face and the expression of contrition, genuinely enunciated, wrenched her heart.

"Papa." Unable to stand given the shock, she shuffled sideways. Then she noted his hands were similarly lashed together. "What on earth are you doing here? What is happening? Are you in some sort of quandary?"

"My dear, I fear I've made a grave miscalculation, and I hope, someday, you will forgive me." Dirty and unshaven, her father appeared frail and unwell in his rumpled clothes. "I never meant to involve you in my affairs, but I had no choice."

"I don't understand." Confused, she glanced at the imposing figure who leaned against a post in a relaxed stance. "I beg your pardon, but I would know my captor, sir. Pray, what is your name?"

"Lucas Thorne, my lady." He bowed with the incomparable finesse she would not have anticipated for a man of his size.

"What is your association with General Wallace, Mr. Thorne?" she asked in a prim manner.

"He owes me money." Mr. Thorne did nothing to disguise his interest in her, and Patience slumped her shoulders and fought a blush of discomfit. "Quite a lot, I'm afraid."

"Papa, is this true?" When her father averted his stare, her heart sank, and she realized they were in trouble. "Mr. Thorne, in what amount is General Wallace in arrears?"

"His marker totals four hundred pounds, my lady." She almost swooned given the sum. Again, Mr. Thorne surveyed her with boldness that gave her gooseflesh. "Of course, there are many ways to dispatch the obligation, and you are an exceptionally pretty bit o' muslin. I would consider some sort of agreement with you, if you're willing to work off his commitment with me."

"I beg your pardon?" She blinked, and amid the disorientation of her circumstances a shocking realization dawned. "You will keep your distance, sir. I am a married woman."

"But you said naught about being a *happily* married woman." Mr. Thorne grinned, which did nothing to soften his harsh appearance. "Believe me, I could make it worth your while, and you wouldn't be the first noblewoman to warm my bed."

"How dare you speak to me thus." She gathered herself with the regal hauteur one would expect of a countess. "If you would only set me free, I would secure the funds to settle the general's account, in full."

Just then, three unsavory characters ran into the warehouse.

"Thorne, he's here, and he brought company." A surly creature took a position at her left, while the other two henchmen joined Mr. Thorne. "And he's wearing regimentals."

To Patience's eternal shame, Rawden, along with the Matchmakers, Lord Hertford, Lord Oliver Stapleton, and Erasmus Ludlow proceeded from between the piles of wooden containers. For an instant, Rawden studied the floor, as if in contemplation. As he lifted his chin, the battle-hardened soldier emerged. The merciless warrior who fought Napoleon's army and survived the brutality of war.

The taut hold of his jaw. The lines of stress etched at the corner of his eye, coupled with the black patch, all merged to convey an intensity she'd never seen in him. When she met her husband's stare, the force of his anger shook her to her core. It was then she apprehended that she had never confronted that aspect of his personality. He had spared her that part of him—until then.

"Rawden," she uttered his name in a half-whispered plea.

"It's all right, sweetheart." He raised a palm as if to calm her, but all she heard was the endearment. "I'm here."

"Lord Beaulieu, this is an honor." Thorne sketched a salute. "Lucas Thorne, at your service. I am known by your kind as the Game Maker. I arrange private parties for the rich and powerful in society, but I do not recall you frequenting my hazard tables."

"That is because I do not gamble, and I know who you are, but I don't give a damn about what you do beyond your reason for taking my wife captive." Rawden inclined his head and narrowed his eye. "Why is Lady Beaulieu's cheek swollen, and who struck Her Ladyship?"

"I apologize, my lord." Thorne shrugged. "It would seem my men were a little too enthusiastic in their endeavors. I meant her no harm."

"Then why did you seize her?" Rawden asked in a razor-edged tone.

"General Wallace, I believe that is your prompt, based on your promises to me." Thorne braced his legs and folded his arms. "This was your scheme, not mine. Tell them what you devised."

"I...that is to say...my original plan would have succeeded had you not interfered," Papa said to Mr. Thorne. A sick feeling came over Patience as her father stated to Rawden, "If only I had been free to retrieve the money. But Thorne grew tired and impatient. He snatched me off the street as I made my way to the alley off Ironmonger Lane. Had I remained at large, I could've paid the marker with none the wiser."

"Yes." Thorne snickered. "And the payment is in the post, and I will still respect you in the morning. You've slipped through my fingers one too many times, Wallace. Tonight, we end your bungling enterprises."

"Wait a minute." Rawden blinked. He glanced at Patience and then at her father. "*You* sent the threatening letters?"

"It was the only way to secure the funds I needed." Papa's entitlement left her reeling, as she struggled with the knowledge that her father tortured Rawden. Slowly, she descended into hell. "My pension is not enough to support me in the style to which I am accustomed."

"What of the bride's price you collected from Lord Beaulieu?" Patience inquired as nausea swirled in her belly. How would Rawden ever forgive her? "You charged him four hundred pounds to marry me."

"My dear, I had a run of bad luck." Her father frowned, and she struggled with the urge to slap him. "I had hoped to double my money, but instead I lost all that and more. It could happen to anyone. But now that Lord Beaulieu is here, and I knew he would answer the summons in light of your presence, His Lordship will deal with Thorne."

"That's quite a stretch, General. But why torment me?" Poor Rawden looked so wounded, and she desperately longed to comfort him, but she doubted he would ever want anything to do with her, given her father's detestable behavior. "I received your first missive before I ever offered for Lady Beaulieu."

"You must be joking." Papa had the temerity to gloat, as if he outsmarted everyone. "Your affinity for my daughter's company was common knowledge among the *ton*, but I never expected you to marry her." At his callous admission, she gasped. "After I read your response to Wellington's report on Quatre Bras, I comprehended your position. The stark vulnerability entrenched in every sentence communicated a clear message and an opportunity for the shrewd. I saw an advantage, and I exploited it. I should be commended for my ingenuity."

Rawden remained eerily still, and Patience ached to go to him. To console him. But she was unsure of her reception.

"How fascinating." Fixed on Rawden, Thorne rubbed his chin

and laughed. "My lord, why would you shackle yourself to a woman when you might savor her wares as your mistress?"

Without hesitation, Rawden peered at Patience and said, "Because I love her."

Tears welled, and she staggered to her feet and mouthed, *I love you.* For as long as she lived, she would never forget that moment. But what if he didn't mean it? What if he were merely moved by the circumstances? To her immense relief, Rawden extended a hand and flicked his fingers. She stepped in his direction but started when one of Thorne's subordinates moved to block her.

A high-pitched hiss pierced the quiet, and a glimmer of steel flashed before her.

"Oy, I'm bleeding." The villain clutched his chest. A thin red line appeared from his neck to his waist, just visible in a clean slit in his clothes. "He cut me. The bastard cut me."

"The wound is superficial. A warning. Advance on my wife again, and I will split you from navel to nose." Rawden brandished his saber and bared his teeth. Again, he beckoned her. "Come here, darling. It's all right. No one will hurt you."

Quickly, she ran to him. He caught her in an embrace so fervent they rotated a half-turn, and he lifted her feet from the ground. Despite the contentious audience, he bent and plundered her mouth in a smoldering kiss. Slowly, he eased his hold, letting her slide down the front of him, but he kept her tucked in the crook of his shoulder. Using his sword, he severed and removed the rope from her wrists and brought her chaffed flesh to his lips.

"Thank you, for rescuing me." She cupped his cheek.

"Always." He winked, and the tension gripping her eased a tad, and then returned his attention to Mr. Thorne. "I would surrender General Wallace to you to do what you will, but I suppose Lady Beaulieu would have a problem with that. So, how do we resolve our dispute?"

"All I want is my money." Thorne thrust his hands in his coat pockets. "I have no quarrel with you."

"Ah, but I have a quarrel with you, Thorne." Rawden wrapped his arm about her waist and tightened his grip. "Come anywhere near Lady Beaulieu again, even by accident, and you will not live to apologize."

Behind Thorne, two of his minions appeared far too interested in Rawden for her liking. One pointed, and the other nodded in agreement. Then the shorter of the two approached Thorne and said something to him.

"Are you threatening me, my lord?" Thorne asked with a hint of amusement.

"I never threaten, Thorne." Rawden smiled. "I promise. And I always keep my promises."

"My men claim to know you." Thorne arched a brow. "They say you served in the Thirty-Second. The hero of Quatre Bras you are called, which I've heard, but they know you as Captain Durrant—not as Lord Beaulieu."

"In combat, I preferred to conceal my social status, especially with my conscripts, to foster a spirit of camaraderie." Rawden nodded once. "And it was a point of pride, given I earned the military rank, while I gained the title by luck of birth."

"Well said, my lord." Thorne scratched his cheek.

"I told you it was him." The underling cast an expression of fear. "He killed seventy-five enemy soldiers."

"I heard it was a hundred," the other lackey said.

Patience noted the quirk at the corners of Rawden's mouth.

"Lord Beaulieu, I am not at odds with you." Thorne splayed his palms. "I only involved Lady Beaulieu at General Wallace's request. My interest is in payment of what I am owed. Four hundred pounds, no more or less."

"Rockingham." Rawden turned to his friend and collected a leather haversack, which Patience recognized from the failed extortion remittance. As he passed the money to Mr. Thorne, Rawden said, "I presume the sum of five hundred pounds will suffice to ensure you never extend credit to General Wallace or grant him entry to one of your...events again?"

"If that is your wish." Thorne tossed the sack to a henchman and chuckled. "Although General Wallace has been my most devoted customer."

"I'm afraid that relationship must end, because it could be hazardous to your health. Indeed, it could be the death of you." At last, Rawden sheathed his saber. "And now, we will take our leave."

"I like you, Beaulieu." Thorne grinned, but it did nothing to dispel his sinister stature. "If you ever have need of my services, you need but ask."

Rawden said nothing. Merely settled a hand at the small of her back and turned her toward the stacks of pallets and crates. Outside, a cool breeze rolled in from the Thames, filling the air with the scent of brine and kelp, and she discovered she had been held at a warehouse at a wharf near the London docks.

Multiple rigs sat on the road, and Rawden led her to their coach.

"Lady Beaulieu, on behalf of the Matchmakers, I am grateful for your safe return." Lord Rockingham glanced at Rawden and said, "Lord Hertford is taking custody of General Wallace. He's going to have Wallace removed to the country."

"That's very kind of Lord Hertford, but I would not impinge on his g-generosity." Patience shrank as Rawden turned and lifted her into their plush vehicle. "My lord, my father is my responsibility, and I intend to exact recompense for his misdeeds. He has wronged you, and I cannot let that go."

"Sweetheart, I want you to stay here. I'm going to speak to my father and make arrangements for General Wallace." When she tried to protest, he pressed a finger to her lips. "Wait here." To Rockingham, Rawden said, "Guard my countess."

"Aye, Cap'n." Rockingham saluted and gave his attention to Patience. "Have you a message for Lady Rockingham? She was scared out of her wits when I shared the contents of Thorne's letter to Beaulieu."

"I'm so sorry." Patience scooted back into the leather-covered squabs. "Please, tell Lady Rockingham I am well and will visit at the first opportunity."

"Lady Rockingham will be glad to hear it." Rockingham retreated when Rawden returned. "Are we all done here?"

"Yes." Rawden and Rockingham locked forearms. "Thank you, old friend."

"I will convey the other Matchmakers home, and Lord Hertford is transporting Ludlow and Lord Oliver, along with General Wallace." Rockingham chucked Rawden's chin. "You require privacy."

In silence, Rawden climbed beside Patience and pounded the ceiling. As the coach lurched forward, he pulled her into his lap, and she rested her head to his shoulder. For a while, they simply sat there, clinging to each other, communicating in a language that transcended verbal conversation.

Finally, when she could bear no more, she asked, "Can you ever forgive me?"

"Forgive you?" With a handful of her hair, he tugged gently and gazed into her eyes. "For what? You are blameless."

"But my father—"

"Is responsible for his actions." Cradling her close, he rested his cheek to the top of her head. "Now rest, my little angel."

"We need to talk," Patience persisted, because there was so much she wanted to say.

"In the morning." Rawden quieted her with a heartrendingly tender kiss. "Darling, today has been exhausting for both of us, although I would argue you definitely endured the worst of it. You've been assaulted and kidnapped, so you win the prize. What we need is a hot bath, a decent meal, and a warm bed. Everything else can wait until dawn."

Reluctant to argue with him, she relaxed and sighed, but still something troubled her. "Rawden?"

"Yes, my heart?"

"Will you tell me again?"

"I love you."

THE SOFT SCRATCH of the nib on parchment penetrated the quiet of Rawden's bedchamber, as he sat at his writing desk and composed instructions regarding General Wallace's care. He would have Wallace removed to his family's ancestral estate in Surrey, where he would receive proper attention and avoid future entanglements with nefarious characters like Lucas Thorne. For a moment, he paused and lifted his head, staring at the motionless form of his wife, as she remained tucked between the sheets and sleeping after what could be described as a trying day.

A soft *chink* interrupted his thoughts, and he glanced over his shoulder. Standing, he tightened the belt on his robe and walked into his sitting room, pulling the double doors shut behind him so as not to wake Patience. He was surprised to discover Abigail rolling a trolley laden with covered dishes.

"Good morning, my lord." The lady's maid curtseyed. "I brought some of Lady Beaulieu's favorite marmalade, along with the breakfast you ordered."

"Thank you." He noticed the footmen carrying in a small table and two chairs, and he shook his head. "We need only one seat. You may return the other to the back parlor."

"Are you planning to stand, my lord?" Abigail inquired with a furrowed brow.

"Don't worry about what I'm planning." Rawden inspected the fare and poured a cup of jasmine tea, Patience's favorite, with a touch of cream, just as she liked it. "That will be all, Abigail."

"My lord." The crotchety lady's maid stared at him and frowned. "I wanted to thank you for saving Lady Beaulieu. I've known her since she was born, and she couldn't be dearer to me if she were my own blood."

"I understand, Abigail." He detected a note of hesitancy in her manner as she lingered. "Is there something else?"

"Aye, my lord." Abigail added more cream and stirred the

drink. "Just a shade darker than buckskin is how Lady Beaulieu takes her morning ritual. And put a small piece of shortbread, for dunking, on the saucer."

"I will remember." In silence, Rawden promised to spoil his wife with the start of every day.

With that, the lady's maid nodded and exited the sitting room.

Behind him, a soft rustle brought him alert, and he turned as Patience strolled from the inner chamber, her hair of spun gold draped about her shoulders, reminiscent of Poussin's *Venus*. Shielding her eyes from the bright glare of sunlight spilling through the large sash windows, and dressed in one of his black silk robes, which dragged the floor, she approached him and wound her arms about his waist.

"Lady Beaulieu." Cradling her head against his chest, he pressed his lips to her temple. "How did you sleep?"

"Much better, after you relented and let me have my way with you." She sighed, and he chuckled as he recalled her adorable attempt at seduction, in the wee hours. "I should always wake you when the lark sings. Never have you been so...receptive. My lord, what's to become of my father?"

"Darling, as much as I enjoy making love to you, you needed rest after yesterday. For you, kidnapping and assault is not a regular occurrence." After handing her the cup, he led her to the lone chair and sat. Then he gently drew her into his lap. "But I am more than happy to atone for any perceived neglect for as long as you wish. As for General Wallace, I'm sending him to the country, where he can recover from his bad habits and stay out of trouble. At the very least, I would have him avoid further endangering you, which I would not forgive. Indeed, I may not let you out of my sight for at least a sennight. Perhaps, a fortnight...or never."

She traced the outline of his lips, and he nipped at her finger-tips. "Rawden, I know you only wish to protect me, but you cannot keep me under lock and key forever."

"But I can keep you beneath me." He nibbled playfully at the crest of her ear. "A prospect I find rather delightful."

"As your countess, I have many obligations," she stated pertly, despite the fact that she wore naught but his robe.

"The first of which is to satisfy your earl." Tipping her chin, he ran his tongue along the curve of her neck. "All else must perforce yield to my desires."

"What of my numerous responsibilities? Lady Beaulieu has a multitude of commitments." She set the cup and saucer on the table and wrapped her arms about his neck. Her expression declared she teased him. "You put me in a difficult position, my lord."

"Well, we will try several positions and see which one you prefer." Rawden bent and stole a kiss. "Ah, you're blushing. You know what that does to me."

"Yes." She rubbed her nose to his and whispered, "It makes you want to debauch me."

"My dear, I always want to debauch you." He squeezed her bottom, hitching her higher, and he knew the precise moment she noted his arousal. "But I'm thinking we can pretend we are at Gunter's, and you can ravish me for a change."

"I never should have started that." She flushed beetroot red.

"But you did, and you are so accomplished, especially when you employ your naughty little tongue." He lifted and set aside a silver cover. With a fork, he stabbed a portion of scrambled eggs and fed his bride. "I'd wager you committed to memory the Aretino from cover to cover."

Patience choked and spluttered.

"Are you all right, sweetheart?" He patted her back and adopted an innocent stance, if that was possible. "Was it something I said?"

Her eyes watered, and she took a long draft of tea. When she faced him, she appeared so small and fragile he couldn't resist tightening his hold.

"You know about the Aretino?" She blinked. He would have

compared her eyes to saucers, but in that instant, they more closely resembled dinner plates. When he nodded and winked, she emitted something akin to a smothered shriek. "Who told you?"

"Rockingham." Rawden broke off a piece of rasher and thrust it into her mouth. "And I am most interested in exploring the extent of your salacious education, in light of what I know of that particular literature. But what I most want to understand is why you undertook such an endeavor, given your virtuous disposition. Must confess, it's a compelling combination and an added benefit of our union that I never anticipated. You are a woman of surprises, Lady Beaulieu."

"It was Arabella's—that is, it was Lady Rockingham's idea." Patience bowed her head. "It is no secret that you were popular with the merry widows, and I feared I might disappoint you, when I so wanted to please you. I will not share you."

"Darling, you do please me, apparently more than you know, but I will correct your assumption and leave you in no doubt as to the constancy of my affection. And you will never have to share. Given your misapprehension, for which I feel responsible, I will spend a lifetime righting the wrong I've done you." Grasping her wrist, Rawden kissed the sensitive underside and pressed her palm to his heart. "What I must make clear, before another moment passes, is the reason I married you."

In the solitude of their private apartment, he stared at her. He waited for some sign of comprehension. She had to have an inkling. A hunch. A vague notion of how he felt. Of his unequivocal commitment. After a while, she shrugged sheepishly, and a ripple of unease coupled with regret rocked his frame. Had he been standing he would have crumpled to the floor. She had no idea what she meant to him.

Framing her face in his hands, he said, "Patience, I married you because I love you."

She burst into tears.

"No." He showered her with kisses. "No, my heart. Please,

don't cry."

"I never thought you would offer your declaration, even though I desperately wanted it." Collapsing against him, she sobbed uncontrollably, and he whispered words of adoration and devotion intended to reassure her. To comfort her. "I supposed your admission last night, after the exacting events involving my father, might have fostered an emotional reaction driven by anxiety, as opposed to any real resoluteness."

"Do you believe me so fickle?" he inquired with a touch of amusement. He lifted her chin and met her tear-spangled stare. "Sweetheart, I would destroy an army, singlehandedly, for you. I would search the world over, surpass any limits to find you. I would brave countless obstacles to reach you. There is no enemy too great, no impediment too colossal that would keep me from you." With his tongue, he wiped away the salty streaks from her cheeks. "I would conquer kingdoms, if only to lay the spoils at your feet and win your declaration, in kind."

"And if I want only y-you?" she asked with a hiccup.

Her simple yet arresting truth utterly disarmed him.

"That goes without saying." He wrapped her in an unyielding embrace, and she twisted, pressing herself to him. Pushing even closer. "I'm yours, Patience. I've always been yours. On the battlefield. In the trenches. Through every bloody engagement, I waged war in the seemingly never-ending quest for an ideal. For a fantasy that dangled like a carrot before me. For an illusion so real it buoyed me during the most compelling evils life could throw at me. For an extraordinary hope that sustained me, although I didn't become conscious of it until yesterday. And that dream was you. From the top of your blonde head to your cute little toes that curl when I take you. Even before we met, I loved the promise of you."

"Rawden." Patience pressed her forehead to his, as she speared her fingers in his hair. "I do love you."

"And I you." He chuckled. "You know, I finally comprehend why Lord and Lady Rockingham live in each other's pockets. The mere hint of parting from you inspires an almost violent rebuke in me that I may forever nestle in your skirts—quite happily I might add."

"Does it shock you that I would let you?" She nuzzled him, and his senses roused. "That I would encourage you?"

"What happened to my prim and proper debutante?" he inquired in a seductive tone.

"You happened, my lord." To his delight, she wiggled her hips in an unmistakable invitation. "Shall we retire to our bed?"

"In a moment." He toyed with a thick tendril hanging just behind her ear. "First, I want to tell you about my experience at White's."

Rawden always suspected it would be difficult to wrestle with his past deeds, and he anticipated derision and rejection once his actions were revealed. To say that he was surprised by the reception at the gentlemen's club was putting it mildly. Even as he recounted what occurred, he found it difficult to accept that he was still hailed a hero.

"How I wish I could have been there for you." Patience gave him a squeeze. "And I am not in any way amazed by the response. Whether or not you want to reconcile yourself to it, you are a man of great courage, and you deserve all the adulation and praise." She paused and furrowed her brow. "My lord, I was wondering, just how many of the enemy did you dispatch at Quatre Bras? Was it seventy-five or a hundred, as Thorne's henchmen suggested?"

"Twelve," he replied in a quiet voice. "Only twelve on that day."

"That is a far cry from a hundred." She appeared startled. "Why did you not correct them?"

"Because, my dear, there are times when it is better to be known as the biggest, baddest soldier in the British Army." Rawden claimed her mouth in another impossibly tender kiss and savored the unique taste of her, sweet jasmine tea and cream. "Now, I have a favor to ask."

"Anything, my lord." The softness in her charming countenance suggested an altogether decadent offering. "Today and forever, I am yours to command."

"I like the sound of that, and I will hold you to it." He drew imaginary circles on her silk-covered hip. "But I would secure your consent in another matter, entirely. I want to make an appointment with Dr. Handley, but I require your presence. I cannot do it without you."

"My lord, nothing would make me happier, and of course, if you wish, I will attend a session." She hesitated. "Still, I wonder if you might prefer privacy, given the situation. I would not push you, and neither would I be offended if you chose to exclude me. Indeed, the only reason I have refrained from any attempt to influence you is because it must be your choice."

"I love you for that, and I'm ready." It was then he realized he'd been holding his breath. "I've been ready. I want to charge the future, with you at my side. I want to build a life with you. I want to create a family with you. I want to grow old with you and sit by a warm hearth, reminiscing of the wonderful moments we've shared."

"We will have all that and more," Patience murmured and slipped from his lap. Clasping his hand, she gave a gentle tug and he stood. Favoring him with a flirty backward glance, she pulled him to their chamber. With a diverting wriggle, she shrugged free of his robe and released him, so the garment dropped to the floor. "Come, my oh-so-enterprising lord. Our comfortable bed awaits, and it's past due to begin our good work. It will take our concerted efforts to produce children, but I believe you are up to the task. Ah, such are the trials and tribulations of Lady Beaulieu."

EPILOGUE

London
October, 1817

A BRISK AUTUMN wind rolled in from the Thames, the scent of roasted chestnuts wafted from the street carts, and brittle leaves rustled in the trees, showering the earth in a colorful mosaic of bright yellow, vivid orange, and rich browns and burgundies. Given the approaching Little Season, Patience embarked on a day of shopping with Arabella, to order new gowns and a few lacy confections for Rawden's delectation. With a smile and a light heart, she descended from her carriage and braced against a strong gust that threatened to topple her on the pavement. Quickly, she navigated the entrance stairs and rushed into the warm foyer.

Behind her, a small complement of footmen hauled stacks of boxes to be conveyed to her suite.

"Good afternoon, Lady Beaulieu." Mills bowed and took her cloak, bonnet, and gloves. "Everything is prepared, as you requested, for tonight's dinner, my lady."

"Excellent. It must be perfect, given Lady Rockingham's surprise." She smoothed a stray lock of hair from her face. "Is Lord Beaulieu in residence?"

"Yes, my lady." In an unusual occurrence, the butler appeared somewhat disconcerted. "His Lordship is in the study, and he asked to be informed of your return."

"Thank you. Tell His Lordship I'm going to change before our guests arrive." Hurriedly, Patience hiked her skirts and ran to the second floor, sprinting down the hallway to her private apartment. The recent acquisition of a particular gown filled her with a sense of mischief, as she prepared to dangle herself before Rawden like a proverbial carrot.

As she traversed the gallery, she saluted her husband's ancestors, an ocean of Beaulieus past. Humming a fanciful little ditty, she bounced along the corridor, turned a corner, and frolicked to the double-door entrance to her sitting room. It was a calming space bathed in soft neutrals and emerald green, her signature color, with dark mahogany trim. The inner chamber continued the scheme. She lifted her head as she gained the solitude of her most private place—and came to an abrupt halt.

"What on earth?" she exclaimed.

Tentatively, she advanced, wondering for a moment if she'd somehow wound up in one of the many guest quarters. She gazed at the wide expanse of plush rugs and rotated a full circle. Then Patience retraced her steps. No, she was most certainly in the right apartment. As she approached the bell pull, Rawden emerged from the narrow passage that connected their respective accommodations.

"Darling, I have been waiting for you with baited breath." With a smoldering expression he stalked her, as if he noticed nothing amiss. "How was your outing with Lady Rockingham?"

"It was lovely, as usual." She glanced left and then right and splayed her arms. "My lord, what have you done with my four-poster?"

"Ah, I love it when you use that *governessy* tone," he replied in a sultry murmur, as he pulled her into his tight embrace and thrust his face against the curve of her neck. "And I had it removed."

"I can see that." She gasped, as he scored the edge of her jaw with his teeth and thrust his hips against hers. "But—why?"

"Because it occurred to me that you required a gentle reminder of our agreement." When she quirked her brows in question, he brushed his lips to hers. "You are to sleep in my bed, but you seem to forget that whenever you are vexed with me, and I will not tolerate it." He pouted, and she fought to maintain her stern countenance. "I cannot rest without you by my side, so now you have no other alternative."

"You call that a *gentle* reminder?" She snorted. "And to think, I planned to reward you with a new purchase from *Le Petit Oiseau*, while you were pilfering my belongings."

"Black, blue, green," he said with a lusty growl, "or red?"

"British Army red, with gold accents."

He groaned as if she'd struck him. "Lace or some sort of sheer confection?"

Patience leaned close and murmured, "Both."

Suddenly, she found herself beset by fourteen stone of aroused male, as Rawden pushed her against a wall and licked and suckled her mouth. Weak-kneed, she speared her fingers in the thick hair at his nape and moaned as he caressed her breast. Always an enterprising sort, her husband made quick work of her bodice and commenced his ravishment, and all semblance of protest died in her throat.

"My lady, Mills told me—have mercy." Dazed by passion, Patience peered over Rawden's shoulder as Abigail shielded her eyes. "Apologies, Your Lordships. I was to dress Lady Beaulieu for dinner, and the hour is pressing, but I can come back."

"That is not necessary—"

"We will ring when we are ready for you."

"It's all right, Abigail." Patience loosened his grip. "I will not be late for my own gathering. Will you be so good as to retrieve the gown I asked you to air?"

"Yes, my lady." With her gaze averted, Abigail rushed into the small room that held Patience's wardrobe.

With a frown, Rawden retreated a hairsbreadth and met her stare. "Are you denying me, Lady Beaulieu?"

"Not at all." She giggled as he relented.

How Patience adored the playful version of her errant earl, the brave soldier who'd embarked on an even more dangerous mission, to make peace with his turbulent past. Regular visits with Dr. Handley had brought about a slow and subtle change in her husband. In the last couple of months, the boyish turtle rescuer emerged, more and more, with the tormented warrior fading into the background, ever present but not so persistent. While there remained numerous challenges, they resolved to face them together.

"Only delaying the inevitable, after an evening of friendship and strategizing to bring another Matchmaker to the altar. If you cooperate, when we retire, we can pretend it's Christmas, and you can unwrap me."

"Oh, I savor the special occasions when you let me stand in for your lady's maid." Rawden showered her cheeks with kisses, and she giggled.

"Perhaps, if you are very good, we can put the Aretino to use." On her tiptoes, she whispered particularly naughty exercises in his ear, and he tensed. "Will that please you, my lord?"

"Holy Mother." He shuffled his feet and grimaced. "I may be hard until next year. How am I supposed to go downstairs with a fully loaded cannon in my breeches? If I don't break something of importance, I may scandalize our guests. And I still must beget an heir."

"Oh, just summon unenthusiastic thoughts, keep your coat buttoned, and you will be fine." She walked to her vanity and kicked off her slippers. "Given your efforts and your hard work with Dr. Handley, and your much-professed desire to improve, I expected naught but honorable intentions from my devoted husband."

"Bloody hell, I'm no eunuch." Rawden stomped to the door that led to his chamber. "And the dishonorable intentions are so much more fun."

With Abigail's assistance, Patience rearranged her coif, leaving a single thick curl dangling at her throat. She donned the remarkable chemise-like item in British Army red, made of crêpe-de-chine with tantalizingly placed transparent chiffon inserts at her bosom and trimmed in lace and gold braiding, secured by sweet little silk ties. To complete the alluring ensemble, she purchased matching garters and hosiery intended to drive Rawden mad with desire.

To conceal her provocative attire, she chose a deceptively simple gown of silk charmeuse in cream. The only decorative aspect was a reinforced band heavily embroidered with roses and intertwining leaves along the skirt hemline. The shockingly lowcut bodice allowed a titillating glimpse of the ruffled edge of the undergarment. To the casual observer, the flounce appeared part of the dress.

Only Patience and Rawden knew otherwise.

"My lady, His Lordship will be beside himself when he sees you." Abigail stood back and admired her handiwork.

If Patience were lucky, he would be beneath her, atop her, behind her...

"Thank you, old friend." After one last check in the long mirror, she marched into the hall.

As she loomed at the top of the grand staircase, Rawden greeted Lord and Lady Rockingham in the foyer. Patience admired his guinea-gold hair and polished gentlemen's attire. Her fallen angel rising from the ashes. As if sensing her presence, he glanced straight at her and smiled the lazy smile that declared she was in for a wild night.

Struggling to control her excitement, she descended to the first floor and approached the group. Rawden immediately draped an arm about her waist and pulled her to his side.

"Good evening, Lady Beaulieu." He nuzzled her in front of their friends, and she realized she was in for a wicked ride. Then his gaze settled on her bosom. "How delicious you look this evening."

"Thank you, my lord." She bubbled with nervous laughter. "Lord and Lady Rockingham, it is wonderful to see you. We're in the family dining room, if you wish to gather there."

"Shall we, darling?" Lord Rockingham offered his escort.

"As long as we are not too early." Arabella furrowed her brow but appeared to relax when Patience nodded.

"Everything is prepared, and you are punctual, as always." Patience couldn't help but grin as her lifelong friend dragged her man down the hall. A tiny box holding a pair of knitted white baby booties had been placed at Lord Rockingham's setting.

"Am I missing something?" Rawden asked.

"Yes." She tugged him into the drawing room. "You will learn soon enough, but Lady Rockingham is increasing, and she wants to tell Lord Rockingham, in private, before sharing the news."

"Ah." Of course, he mentioned nothing of their diligent efforts at conception. Instead, he bent his head and skimmed his nose along her décolletage. "Am I to take it this tempting red ruffle is but a peek at what lies beneath?"

"You are correct." Patience retreated against the back of the sofa, and Rawden placed his hands at either side of her. "I bought it for you, and you alone."

"A lovely gesture, but I wager it looks better on you." And then he covered her mouth with his in a searing kiss she felt in her toes.

"Bloody hell, not again," Lord Greyson groused.

Rawden and Patience parted as if they were two naughty children caught with their hands in the cherry compote.

"What is it?" Warrington inquired. "What's happened."

"Oh, nothing out of the ordinary." Greyson rolled his eyes. "Just Beaulieu ravishing his wife again."

"For the love of all creation, have you two not had enough?" Warrington shook his head. "You've been married for months."

"Yet it seems like yesterday." Rawden drew Patience into the foyer. "And stop complaining, else I will find you both brides."

"I'm not complaining." Greyson elbowed Warrington. "Are you complaining?"

"Will you shut up?" Warrington struck the floor with his cane. "Where are the others? I'm starved."

"Lord and Lady Rockingham are in the family dining room." Patience bit the sides of her mouth to keep from laughing. "Perhaps we should await Lord Michael there."

With Warrington and Greyson bickering about the evils of matrimony, Rawden and Patience stole flirty caresses as they walked to the back of the residence. When they entered the comfortable space, they found Lady Rockingham perched in Lord Rockingham's lap, wrapped around him and sharing a startlingly intimate kiss.

"Not you, too. Is there no escaping this madness?" questioned Greyson with a scowl. "And will someone explain to me what unwritten rule states that a wife can no longer occupy her own chair?"

"What now?" Warrington barked.

"It's Lord and Lady Rockingham, *in flagrante delicto*." Greyson averted his stare.

"What are you, a virgin?" Lord Rockingham claimed another kiss from his marchioness and grinned. "Besides, we're celebrating the momentous news that we are soon to add another lord or lady to our family, and this arrangement suits us."

"Hear, hear." Rawden pounded a fist to the table. When Patience tried to take her place at the other end, he caught her by the wrist and drew her with him into his seat. "There now. Isn't this nice and cozy?"

For a moment, she considered objecting to the shocking display, but she reminded herself that their rather odd extended family possessed its own eccentricities. Each individual personality manifested singular peculiarities. A little latitude would hurt no one, except Greyson and Warrington. Even then, the two most stubborn Matchmakers found common ground in the search for love when it came to their fellow soldiers.

As a servant offered glasses of champagne, in observance of Arabella's wonderful news, Patience snuggled into Rawden's arms.

"Do you wish it was us?" he whispered. Despite their efforts, they had yet to conceive a child.

"It will be, when the time is right." Beneath the table, she squeezed his fingers and mentioned nothing about the fact that her monthly courses were late. *Very* late. She would say nothing without confirmation. To the group, she said, "Now then, should we compose a list of prospective candidates for Lord Michael? Have you any ideas—"

Just then, the man of the hour burst into the dining room. His hair was unruly, and his attire appeared disheveled and covered in road dust. As if he'd just come to London from a long journey. He went straight to the sideboard, and she presumed he intended to pour himself a brandy. Instead, he drank directly from the decanter.

Breathing heavily, Lord Michael assessed the group. He opened his mouth and then closed it. He paced before the windows.

"Glad you could join us." Rawden gazed at Patience and then Lord Michael. "Are you unwell, brother?"

"I may have met my bride." Lord Michael took another healthy gulp of the amber liquor.

"He is most definitely unwell." With a pained expression, Greyson stared toward the heavens. "Someone fetch a doctor."

"No, I'm fine." Lord Michael half-fell into his chair and tugged off his cravat. "But I tell you I found her. At least, I think I found the one for me...sort of."

"Lord Michael, perhaps you should start at the beginning," Patience said quietly. Never had she seen the normally staid gentleman so discomposed.

Resting his elbows atop the table, he cradled his head. When he lifted his chin, he swallowed hard. "It happened at Lady Monmouth's house party..."

About the Author

A proud Latina, *USA Today* bestselling, Amazon All-Star author Barbara Devlin was born a storyteller, but it was a weeklong vacation to Bethany Beach, Delaware that forever changed her life. The little house her parents rented had a collection of books by Kathleen Woodiwiss, which exposed Barbara to the world of romance, and *Shanna* remains a personal favorite.

Barbara writes heartfelt historical romances that feature not so perfect heroes who may know how to seduce a woman but know nothing of marriage. And she prefers feisty but smart heroines who sometimes save the hero before they find their happily ever after.

Barbara is a disabled-in-the-line-of-duty retired police officer. She earned an MA in English and continued a course of study for a Doctorate in Literature and Rhetoric. She happily considered herself an exceedingly eccentric English professor, until success in Indie publishing lured her into writing, full-time, featuring her fictional knighthood, the Brethren of the Coast.

Connect with Barbara Devlin at BarbaraDevlin.com, where you can sign up for her newsletter, The Knightly News.

Barbara Devlin Website: barbaradevlin.com
Facebook: BarbaraDevlinAuthor
Twitter: @barbara_devlin
BookBub: bookbub.com/authors/barbara-devlin
Goodreads:
goodreads.com/author/show/6462331.Barbara_Devlin
Pinterest: bdevlinauthor
Instagram: barbara.devlin